# SPARTACUS JONES
# AND THE
# FILM NOIR COWBOY

# Also by Adam Adrian Crown

Eclipse of the Heart
Trade Winds

# SPARTACUS JONES AND THE FILM NOIR COWBOY

ADAM ADRIAN CROWN

Knight-errant Press

Spartacus Jones and the Film Noir Cowboy

Copyright 2020 by Adam Adrian Crown

Published by Knight-errant Press

1045 Coddington Road Ithaca NY  14850

Cover design by Richard Turylo

This is a work of fiction. Names, characters, businesses, places, events, and incidents are either the product of the author's imagination or used in a fictitious manner. Any resemblance to actual persons, living or dead, or actual events, is purely coincidental.

ISBN-13: 978-0997445961

For Kelsey

*Darlin' you know that I love you true*
*And I'll do anything that you asked me to*
*Confess all my sins like you want me to*
*But there's one thing that I've got to say to you*
*I'm not like everybody else...*

– The Kinks, 1964

# PART ONE:
## Spartacus Jones

PART ONE

*I wanna be yours pretty baby*
*Yours and yours alone*
*I'm here to tell ya honey*
*That I'm bad to the bone*
"Bad to the Bone"
George Thorogood and the Destroyers

# Prelude:
# The Champagne and Egg Roll Blues

Life is just full of fucking surprises.

Most of those surprises I could do without.

Every once in a great while you get one that's golden. An act of grace. A gift from the Spirits. Incredible luck. Whatever you want to believe in.

Sometimes, it's one of those mixed-blessing surprises. Like a dogshit sandwich on really, really, good organic whole grain bread, fresh out of the bakery oven.

But whether sweet, rotten, or half-assed, those surprises all have the left hook–right uppercut effect. Because you don't see them coming, you're not prepared, and they rock you all the way down to your sweat socks, knock the mouth guard right off your teeth, to leave you staggering on rubbery legs, hoping to make it back to your corner where you can just sit for a minute and let your crew try to put Humpty back together again.

Marlo was a surprise.

A golden surprise.

She hit me so hard, she untied my shoelaces.

She was intelligent, sensitive, with a .44 magnum ethical compass and the balls to follow it no matter what. She was passionate. She was,

1

to my eye, beautiful. She was a sexual green beret. She liked horses, and, more importantly, horses liked her.

And she kind of loved me.

It was a gift.

A golden gift.

An undeserved golden gift.

The kind that almost made you believe in an all-loving, all-forgiving God who was also a lousy decision-maker.

So, naturally, I had to fuck it up.

Now, I ask you, what would you do in that situation?

Wouldn't you thank your lucky stars, count your blessings, say a quick "Hail Mary," take the money and run?

Sure, you would.

That's what I would do.

That's what I *thought* I would do.

That's sure as hell what I *should* do.

But that's not what I did.

And now, I was kicking myself. I didn't know if I'd ever see Marlo again, and I had prepared myself for the possibility — the probability — that I wouldn't.

See, I'd given her something to read. Half memoir, half True Confession, half-assed attempt at being noble. I wanted to be with her and I was with her, but, no, that wasn't enough for me. I wanted her to be with me, *really* with me, and to be *really* with me, she had to know me, all of me, including my scars and my warts, and not just my boyish charm and my pretty nose.

So I'd told her things.

Private things.

Secret things.

Dark and bloody things.

Twisted, decadent things. Dangerous thoughts and forbidden dreams. I should have known better. I was looking a free horse in the mouth and that's a good way to get bitten. It's also a good way to take a hard fall, if she decided to squeal. Not that I thought she was a rat. But I've been burned before. Where I come from we have a saying: "Fool me once, shame on you; fool me twice and they find your body in the trunk of your car." Fortunately, I'd at least had the good sense to fuzzy up a few critical details that would be necessary to unfuzzy if you wanted to interest a prosecutor. Just in case.

If Marlo read my gagnum opus, and if she had a lick of sense, she'd steer clear of any further involvement with me.

I swear, somebody must have dropped me on my head when I was a baby.

When she showed up at my door, I figured either she hadn't read my grim tome, hadn't understood it, or she didn't have a lick of sense.

She came by a little after feeding time. I had just come in from the pasture, kicked off my boots, and slipped some classic Wes Montgomery onto the turntable. We were Bumpin' on Sunset, when she knocked, in perfect rhythm with the tune.

"I come bearing gifts," she said.

"You *are* the gift," I told her. That got me a soft kiss on the mouth.

She tasted of garlic.

I love garlic.

She came bearing two huge brown paper shopping bags. The kind with handles. One of them contained an assortment of cartons from Chin-Lee's restaurant, best Chinese take-out in the wild, uncivilized, hinterlands east of the Windy City and west of the Big Rotten Apple. I could smell the spicy chicken with cashews from ten feet away, and the aroma made my mouth water.

Or maybe it was Marlo's scent that made my mouth water.

"Quite a feast," I said.

"I think I remembered all your favorites."

She had.

She knew she had. She always does.

I arranged the savory-smelling cartons on my kitchen table, which is also my dining table. Found the chopsticks in the bottom of the bag along with little packets of duck sauce. Didn't bother with plates. She liked eating right out of the carton. For her, it was like camping out. For me, it meant no dishes to wash, and I hate washing dishes. Bad memories.

From the other shopping bag, Marlo produced a couple of bottles of Asti Cinzano, smooth as mother's milk and a lot better for you.

3

"What is this, my birthday?" I said.
She smiled.

"So I read that thing you gave me," she said, expertly popping a champagne cork. She said it casually, as if she were asking me to pass the steamed dumplings.

I tore my wooden chopsticks from their paper envelope, fumble-fucked the hand-off and dropped them on the floor, but then scooped them up swiftly and slickly like I'd planned the move. That's me: the Marques Haynes of cheap chopsticks.

"You read it," I said. As if there was something else she was supposed to do with it.

"Yes, I read it," she said again. Laughed a little. Nervous laughter? A good thing or? Hard to tell.

"Any thoughts on it?" I asked, like "You want fries with that?" Never ask a question if you don't really want to know the answer.

She took a swig of sparkling vino right from the bottle, shifting into full fuck-it-all mode in keeping the spirit of the occasion.

"I have some questions. If you don't mind."

"I don't mind at all," I said, spearing one of the dumplings in the tin pan and dipping it in salty sauce. "You're not wearing a wire are you?"

"Would you like to search me?"

"Absolutely."

A search ensued. I delved into every inch of her, inside and out, using my very best probes. It took quite a while to satisfy myself that she was, in fact, not wearing a wire.

By the time we got around to her questions, the sun was hitting the snooze alarm in hopes of stealing fifteen more minutes of rack time, and all that remained of the Chinese feast was one cold and lonely egg roll, like one tin soldier who'd forgotten to ride away. We gave it the Solomon treatment.

"Is it true?" she said, munching on her half.

"Is *what* true?"

"The *thing*," she said, giving Captain Obvious a playfully admonishing smack on the arm.

"What do *you* think?"

"I don't know. That's why I'm asking."

"But what do you *think*?"

"Some of it is definitely true. Just from what I know of you, I'm sure of that. Some parts could be true. There are some parts I hope are true, but they might not be. Other parts, I hope aren't true at all, but I'm afraid they might be."

"What if it's all true?" I casually poked around in the clutter. I could have sworn there was another envelope of duck sauce hiding out in that bag.

"Is it?"

"Only my hairdresser knows for sure."

"Wait, what?"

"Skip it."

"You're being evasive," she said, drawing closer, posing the question to my cheek, and then licking the perspiration from my throat.

"I'm doing my best."

"C'mon, is it true?" She arched one eyebrow brow in that Marlo way I find much too irresistible.

"Maybe it's only a story," I said. "My Great American Novel. My Don Quixote. A tall tale like Paul Bunyon. Felonious Flynn and his Big Blues Axe."

"Tell me."

"Axe me no questions, I'll tell you no lies."

"Come on." She prodded my chest with a finger. "Is it true?"

"What if it is? Would it change anything?

"I don't know," she said. "It would explain a lot, for sure. There are parts of it that scare me, but…"

"But what?"

"Sometimes I like being scared."

"You're sick and twisted," I said. "I like that in a woman."

We polished off the remains of the sweet and bubbly. Champagne and egg rolls. Nothing like it. Try it sometime.

"I have another question," she said, raising her hand as if she were a shy little girl in class, asking permission to ask. The gesture conjured up a memory of the gawky ten year old ugly duckling she had been when I first met her, lo these many years ago. She was that no longer. Nor was she shy. Nor did she ever have to ask my permission to ask a question; if she had, I'd have lost all respect for her. But I played along.

"Yes," I said, pointing to her over the others' heads. "Question? Young lady there in the back?"

"Thank you, Mr. President. Lois Lane, Daily Planet. Is there more to the story? I feel like there's more to the story."

"There's always more to the story," I said. "Can you be more specific?"

"Hmm. I don't know," she said. "I'm not clear on how you — on how the hero got here from there. Oh, and whatever happened with that girl he met in Mexico?"

"Long story," I said.

"Also, a little curious about the one he's involved with now, the one he's writing all this for? She sounds fascinating. Tell me more about you and her." She punctuated the leading question with that devilishly arched eyebrow.

"Are you sure you want to know?"

"You know what they say," she shrugged innocently, "in for a penis, in for a pound."

I guess somebody must have dropped *her* on her head, too.

*Young girl, get out of my mind*
*My love for you is way out of line*
"Young Girl"
Gary Puckett and the Union Gap


# CHAPTER ONE:
# MARLO AND ME


I don't have a "type," when it comes to women, unless strong and smart is a type. If I did have a type, I think Marlo might be the exemplar. Her given name was Marilyn, but she had nothing in common with her voluptuous blonde namesake. Unlike her namesake, Marlo was petite and hard as a quarter-mile sprint up Bald Hill. She had long, straight hair so dark brown it looked black, and large, almond-shaped eyes that were even blacker than black, that shined like polished obsidian and cut as sharply. Combined with full, pouting lips, aquiline nose and bronze skin, she looked to be kin to an Aztec queen. Her breasts were no bigger than small oranges, her belly was chiseled into well-regulated sections, and her succulent cunt was framed by a rich forest of coarse curls, a narrow hedgerow of which extended up in a fine line to her belly button. Dark, muscular, flat chested and hirsute.

Some would say a little androgynous.

Some would say a LOT.

Some would say I must secretly be gay because I like such "masculine" women.

Some can go fuck themselves.

It was a Sunday, and I was worshipping at my favorite church, Our Lady of Eternal Tumescence. Marlo had flown into town on a rare visit, and I had spent Saturday night doing my best to make her consider visiting more often.

Saturday she'd been guest soloist with the symphony and I'd had the pleasure of watching her play the cello. To say she "plays" the cello is an understatement on the order of "the fantail of the Titanic got a little wet." There are no words adequate to describe the phenomenon. One moment she's waltzing with an old love regretting their last fight, the next she's a witch riding that thing to the sabbat's delight. Her fingers dart masterfully over the neck with complete abandon, her cheeks flushed, her eyes half-closed, perched on the edge of orgasm forever. Watching her is almost as enjoyable as listening to her. Best porn ever.

We'd had a playful morning. Like me, she's an early riser — it's nearly impossible for me to sleep past dawn — so we enjoyed a little run as the birds were tuning up. We followed up with a few rounds on the bag, and then sparred a couple. Caught me with a sweet left hook. I love a woman who knows how to throw a decent punch, and Marlo can throw one that'll knock a man twice her size right on his ass.

I should know. I'm the one who taught her how to throw it.

We showered together, which took rather a long time. Got soap in her eyes. And a few other places. Afterward, I made us a boxer's payday repast of steak and eggs-over-easy. Fried up some leftover potatoes with onions. Coffee. Black as Texas tar and almost as thick. No cream or sugar for her. Takes it like a man. Like me.

I liked watching her eat, too. Nothing dainty about it. Shoveled her food in like a lumberjack, made little moans and such to demonstrate how delicious the food tasted. I like a woman with extraordinary appetites.

I suppose, in some part of my heart, I loved her and always had. But I'd never tell her that. I'm older than she is. And I don't mean by a few years. I'm talking a few decades here. She's the alpha and I'm the omega. She's just stepped into the ring. Me, I'm going into the championship rounds. Hell, I've got a jump rope older than she is. We share a passion for music, a love of hard physical work, and of wanton, uninhibited sex. What more do you want? Why go all cuddly and cute, and gum up the whole works with "love?" She'll eventually find someone of appropriate breeding stock and pair up with him. Kids, family, dog, white picket fence. Fade to black. That's as it should be.

In the meantime, we'll share what we share as long as it feels right to share it, and when it no longer does, we'll move on. Love, in this case, would be a burden for her, not a gift. Loving her is a gift to me, a gift I've done nothing to deserve. I'll keep it to myself. No need to tear off the wrapping paper or open the box. I know what's inside. That's enough. That way, I protect her. And I guess I protect me, too.

Sometimes you zig when you might zag, or you're five minutes too early or five minutes too late, or you act on a sudden whim, and your whole life changes.

This was one of those times.

If Frankie had called five minutes earlier, I'd have ignored the phone because Marlo and I would have been in flagrante delecto — and nobody's as delectably flagrante as she is. I wouldn't interrupt that tune even if Jesus phoned me to sit in with his all-star band. But Frankie had better timing.

I was stretched out on the bed, basking in that post-coital sun that warms you all the way down to your scars. Marlo lay curled up against my side, her head on my chest, making tiny circles around one of my nipples with the tip of her fingernail.

"You're one of a kind," she said.

"Yeah," I said, "but what kind?"

"The good kind. The very kind. My kind."

She's inclined to see in me virtues I may not actually possess, which tendency brings back to my mind bad memories of child-like innocence taking the most savage beating you never want to imagine.

"Says you," I said.

She tickled my nipple with a butterfly-light kiss, and propped herself up on an elbow.

"The symphony wants me to renew my contract."

"Can't say I blame them."

"Ithaca College is offering me that teaching job. I could teach, and still play. And I like teaching. What do you think I should do?"

The part she didn't say was that if she took the teaching job, she'd be around full-time. Having more of her company might be sweet. Or it might be sweet for a little while, but ultimately, make us go sour faster. I suspected we had only so much allotted time together. We could use our time up fast, or string it out to last for a while. Like a bottle of 60-year old Dalmore single malt scotch. You want to have a shot now and then, savoring the magic hooch on very special ceremonial occasions? Or do you want to knock off the whole bottle in a one-night binge? Intensity or duration, the eternal quandary.

If my girl Marlo moved to town we would no doubt fuck ourselves silly for a time. But then, if it became a staple of our diet instead of a treat, we might only hasten the inevitable. Some things are better as fantasies than they are as realities.

"C'mon," she said. "What do you think? Give me some sage advice."

"I think the worst vice in the world is ad-vice," I told her, trying to sound like Mark Twain. "Go with your gut. Whatever you decide, it'll be the right thing. At least, that's what the fortune cookie said."

"Thanks a lot, Yoda. I'm starving, what's in your fridge?"

I'm thinking Mark Twain, she's thinking Yoda. There's that age gap thing I was telling you about.

She rolled off the bed, and unselfconsciously headed for the kitchen, affording me the pleasure of watching her tight gluteus marvelus samba down the hallway, a thing of true beauty to behold, especially with shiny traces of my semen gracing her thighs. She disappeared around the corner, and that's when the phone rang. Bereft of something a whole lot better to do, I answered it.

"Yeah?" I said, from a distant cloud.

"Hey, Kemosabe... Hey, it's Frankie." I'd already recognized his voice. And nobody else would refer to me as "Kemosabe."

Frankie's a kind of a sort of a friend, if you squint a little, and I don't have many. You have one person you call "friend," you're lucky. You have two people you call "friend," you're blessed. You have three people you call "friend," you're kidding yourself.

I'd met Frankie briefly in the joint, in another life. I guess we got palsy-walsy because he's Indian, like me. Only he's Apache. Me, my dad was half Lakota. The "Kemosabe" thing was our inside joke; it made sense while we were inside together. Frankie did a nickel. Never figured I'd see him again, because I never figured I'd ever get out. As I said, life is full of fucking surprises. One of them came in the form of a young, kick-ass lawyer looking to make her bones. I'll tell you that story sometime. It should be a movie. A spaghetti western. "A Fistful of DNA Evidence." Johnny Depp can play me. Ennio Miccone can do the score. Ah-ee-ah-ee-ah, wah-wah-wah...

10

Things were going bump in the kitchen.

"Hey, Frankie. Can't talk much right now, how about if I call you b——."

"She's in town, huh? I'll be quick. I need a favor — a huge favor, man."

"Such as?"

"I need to truck a horse out west. Issa's having some issues and I can't go off and leave her alone."

Issa was Frankie's wife. She was pregnant with what they hoped would be their first kid. She'd had a miscarriage previously. Issa didn't impress me as having been built to be a baby-maker, but what do I know?

They'd been working on getting her pregnant again for quite a while, which ain't exactly bad work if you can get it.

"Almost due, isn't she?"

"Almost."

"How far out west?"

"Way out west. Near El Paso."

"That's way out west, all right." Much farther west and you'd be in the Pacific Ocean.

I hadn't been out that way in a long time, and the last time hadn't been all that pleasant. There were no warrants out on me or anything. None I knew of, anyway. Even though I'd first met The Judge there, El Paso wasn't high on my list of places I wanted to go.

"They have horses in Texas, you know," I said.

"Not like this one, Kemosabe." He was pushing that "Kemosabe" shit a little too hard. "Lucky for me. He's got golden genes. This guy wants to splice some Arab into his remuda and he's willing to pay to play. Fuck knows we need the bread. Can you do this for me, brother?"

It's easy to get promoted from friend to brother when somebody needs a favor.

"Am I gonna have to wear a purple velvet hat and a leopard skin frock coat?"

He chuckled.

"It's informal," he said.

"Still a long way to go to get laid."

"Says you."

11

I suppose I agreed too quickly. Normally, I would have thought about the prospect more, but I didn't. On Monday Marlo would be heading back to Boston and the symphony, anyway, and I didn't have anything else cooking. I knew I'd have a case of the blues when she left. I always do. Never sure when I'll see her again. Never sure if I'll see her again. And she never entirely leaves. Her scent on a pillow. A long hair in the sink. Chinese take-out leftovers in the fridge.

A trip out west to play cupid for a horse would give me something to do, keep me occupied for a couple weeks, at least. Change of scenery, as they say, would do me no harm. I'd make the trip a vacation. Kick back, drink tequila, and work on my tan, I told myself, as if following a random whim.

"OK," I said. "I'm in. Kemosabe."

I hung up as Marlo returned, chewing the last of something; I didn't know what. My cock was napping peacefully against my belly, but she shook it awake. She started fondling it like a priceless Stradivarius she might never get another chance to play, and she began to get the same look on her face that she gets when she's on stage, wailing away on some finger-breaking Bach. Nice for me. I always enjoy a well-played fugue. She wrapped her thick lips around me and swallowed my cock all the way up to my armpits. I reached out and swung her hips around so I could join her for dessert.

Off we went to the Sabbat at a full gallop.

*Old Stewball was a racehorse*
*And I wish he were mine*
*He never drank water*
*He only drank wine.*
"Stewball"
Peter, Paul and Mary

# CHAPTER TWO:
# SPARTACUS JONES

Mares come in season in the spring or early summer so the foal will be born, 11 or 12 months later, when the grass is lush and the livin' is easy.

Most breeders use artificial insemination — unless the breed registration prohibits the practice, as with Thoroughbreds. Somebody collects the stallion's semen with an artificial vagina. He ejaculates about a cupful. They freeze it, store it, and ship it to customers for the vet to insert into the mare with what amounts to a turkey baster. This method has its advantages for the humans involved. Not real interesting for the horses.

Some breeders patriotically insist on no insemination without representation. They call that approach "live cover." Most them do "hand-breeding" where they typically drug the mare, bind up her tail up out of the way, and hobble her hind legs. With the mare trussed up, a handler brings the stallion in to do the deed, leads him away again as soon as he's done. No foreplay and no pillow talk. To me, hand-breeding steers a little too close to S&M date rape-porn.

I don't know why human beings think horses can't figure out how to make more horses without human assistance. They were doing it for a long time before we ever got here. Human hubris strikes again.

The best breeding method is pasture breeding, which is exactly what it sounds like. You put the mare and the stallion in a pasture

13

together for a few days and let nature take its course. The horses do the courtship dance. The mare flags her tail, or moves it aside, exposing her vulva. She'll urinate near the stallion. The stallion prances around, posturing with his head held up high. He nickers sweet nothings to her, nips her gently.

She squeals.

He nudges.

She squeals some more.

He'll sniff her urine to judge how ready she is to mate and, when the time is right, he mounts her. The foreplay lasts a lot longer than the play. If the actual intercourse lasts longer than about 15 seconds, the stud will find his name written in praiseworthy terms on the stall walls of the ladies' rooms all around the county.

Typically, the mare travels to board with the stallion, but in this case, with several mares to breed, the mountain was going to Mohammad. The mare's estrous cycle lasts about three weeks, but she's only sexually receptive for the first 5-7 days. So in horse breeding, as in so many things, timing is everything.

Thus the importance of me getting Frankie's stallion to the church on time. We had plenty of time to get there, though. I love it when people plan ahead.

In the still quiet before dawn, creatures on the night shift were punched out, but the day shift had not yet punched in. I stood leaning on the top rail of the split rail fence and gazed out at Frankie's pasture, where a dozen horses, most of them paints and appaloosas, were concentrating on transforming the lush green grass into horse.

I heard the screen door to the house slam shut behind me, and turned to see the ponderously pregnant Issa waddling in my direction bearing gifts in the shape of a large mug of steaming coffee. She made great coffee. Strong enough to strip the enamel right off your teeth. The mug was decorated with horses depicted in the old Plains Indian style. She made those mugs, herself. Had a wheel and kiln in the former garage, now her workshop. Did a decent amount of business, too. You'll see a lot of her stuff on the buckskinner rendezvous circuit.

People talk about pregnant women "glowing." I always thought that was maudlin bullshit, but damn it, there was Issa, glowing up a summer storm. Could be I was wrong about her and her baby-making destiny.

"You want to feel him?" she asked as she handed me the coffee. "For luck?"

"Not sure you'd want him to have my luck," I said.

She took my free hand gently, pressed my palm flat against her belly. Her hands were warm and soft. Her belly felt taut as a ripe watermelon.

"How do you know it's a him?"

"I just know," she said.

"Can't argue with logic like that."

I set the coffee mug atop a fence post, knelt down and kissed her belly. She laid a hand on my head to keep me there a moment, the way she might if I were kissing a little lower. I arose like a knight having received my accolade.

"You know, darlin'," I said, "where I come from 'mother' is usually only half a word, but it sure seems to suit you."

She gave me her brightest grin, and the glow almost singed my eyebrows.

"I think 'father' would suit you," she said.

A convulsive snigger erupted from my nose before I could catch myself. "Moving right along..." I said, reaching for my coffee.

She shook her head disdainfully, and finger-poked me gently on the shoulder.

"When are you going to drop anchor, sailor? Seriously."

"Seriously?"

"Seriously."

"When I find the right woman, I guess." I speak fluent cliché when I have to.

"And what, may I ask, is the "right" woman?"

"A beautiful, body-building nymphomaniac with an IQ of 220 who owns her own liquor store," I said.

"I know just the person," Issa said. She has a grin like a Cheshire cat.

"You always do."

"You're never going to find what you're looking for if you don't look."

The evil demon Jack sitting on my shoulder whispered in my ear and tempted me to go someplace with that. Tell her exactly where I was looking and how. Right then a sharp snort cut me short. Frankie

15

had arrived in the company of a majestic grey Polish Arab, prancing along beside him on a long lead rope. I assumed it was not Frankie who'd snorted, though you never can tell. They came up to the fence, and the horse tossed his luxuriant mane like a California surfer girl on the beach pretending to be oblivious to all the surfer boys tracking her with heat-seeking muscles.

"Kemosabe," Frankie said, "meet Spartacus Jones."

I offered my hand. Spartacus Jones sniffed my palm. The back of my hand. Processed my scent, nostrils flaring, then snorted wetly all over my forearm. Satisfied, he brushed my fingers with his nose, giving his lips a wiggle.

"Pleased to meet you, too, Pal." I said. "You just saved my life."

Issa poked me again, and went back to the house.

"How does he load?" I asked.

Load? He strutted right up the ramp and into the trailer like he planned on doing the driving himself. Took about two seconds. He gave me a head toss and a look that said, "Well, are we going or aren't we?" It's quite possible he knew that loading up on the trailer meant romance was in the offing. Horses are masters at knowing what happens before what happens happens. It's how they survive.

Frankie and I shook hands.

"I owe you big time for this." he said.

"I guess we're on our way," I said, and popped the driver's side door.

"Safe trip, brother."

"Wait!" Issa called from the house, and came speed-waddling over to us, hugging a large canvas bag, decorated with the same kind of horse figures that adorned the coffee mug. Another one of her creations.

"Hey," I said, "don't you be running like that."

"I made you some food. Meat loaf sandwiches," she said, a little out of breath. "Thanks for doing this."

"Your wife is trying to seduce me," I told Frankie. You'd understand why I said that if you'd ever tasted the woman's meat loaf. Any tastier and it would be on Schedule I.

"You better get while the gettin's good," Frankie said. "She don't take no for an answer."

We headed out.

16

We drove a couple miles along the curvy, unimproved road before we hit paved highway. Went past the old Miller place, and saw a "for sale" sign staked out there again. The place had frontage on the corner of Werner and Route 79. Greek revival farmhouse. New sixteen-stall barn. Couple of smaller outbuildings. An acre pond. 100 acres or so, in all. About 25 wooded, the rest in pasture. This parcel was the remains of what used to be a much bigger spread, but chunks of it got sold off over the years in a doomed effort to keep the family farm afloat.

Family farms don't float real well anymore.

Adam Adrian Crown

*On the road again*
*Just can't wait to get on the road again*
"On the Road Again"
Willie Nelson


# CHAPTER THREE:
# ON THE ROAD AGAIN


It's about 2000 miles plus a fine blonde hair from Ithaca, New York to Los Lobos, Texas, a flyspeck of a town about a hard spit down along the border from El Paso. You could make the haul in a day and a half if you had to.

I didn't have to.

No need to drive straight through, running on black coffee, no-doze and hubris. For a change, I was like a rolling stone and time was on my side.

There was no point in making the trip an ordeal, either for me or for the horse. I planned to take the slow and steady route. Make lots of stops along the way every couple of hours to stretch our legs and have some grass — the grazing kind, not the smoking kind.

We'd cut across western New York on 90 West and clip the northwestern-most tip of Pennsylvania. Then 71 South through Ohio. 70 West would take us through Indiana and into Missouri. Pick up 55 South to St. Louis, and the 44 West all the rest of the way through Oklahoma and most of Texas. Wind up on 80 West for the home stretch. Nothing to it. Piece of cake.

Once we left Ohio the terrain would flatten out and, being Spring, we'd go through the southern section of "tornado alley" during prime time for twisters. Storms can get interesting.

I decided to head out at first light, stop at dusk, each day. Should have 10-12 hours of driving time, with time out for breaks, so 8-9 hours of actual driving per day. Unless we ran into a problem.

So we had a plan, Stan. Couple days out. A week or so there for him to do his stuff. Couple days back. Good plan. Reasonable plan. The kind that makes the gods laugh.

I packed light for the trip, taking only essentials. In addition to Issa's highly coveted meat loaf sandwiches — did I mention she baked her own bread, too? A couple changes of clothes, a dog-eared copy of Captain Blood, by Raphael Sabatini, my colt 1911, in case I ran into a snake, and, of course, a shoe box full of Chet Baker tapes.

I'd gotten hip to Chet back when I was a kid, thanks to the bona fide beatnik dad of a high school pal. Baker was the crown prince of west coast cool jazz in the 1950's. Somebody once described him as James Dean, Frank Sinatra and Bix Beiderbecke all rolled into one. He was not only a superlative player of trumpet and flugel horn, but also a terrific vocalist. I think he played horn like a singer, and sang like a horn player. If you don't understand what I mean by that, don't worry about it. There's no way I can explain it to you, and like the man said, if you have to ask the question, you wouldn't understand the answer.

Sad to say, Chet had a lifelong love/hate relationship with his own kind of horse, the kind that bucked him off a lot and tried to stomp him a few times. The shooting kind. Heroin. And he dated cocaine occasionally on the side. I wonder sometimes what he might have done if he hadn't had the monkey on his back. Then again, some cats can only play when they ARE high.

Later on, Chet's career enjoyed something of a renaissance, but even though he recorded scads of great stuff in the '80's, most of it was scattered here and there on obscure European labels, practically impossible to find in the States. Took me a fair amount of time and energy to track his stuff down, but I think I finally got a copy of almost everything he ever recorded, and I dug everything I dug up. Including a cut of Elvis Costello's song "Shipbuilding;" Chet blows some tasty solo licks on that track. It's the only thing of his to ever get anywhere near the pop-top 40.

The Cool Jazz Prince checked out in the spring of 1988. In Amsterdam. An accident, they said. Heroin and cocaine were both found in his system. I guess he finally rode his horse habit out of town. There's a memorial plaque there now.

I suddenly realized that this trip would take me right past his hometown: Yale, Oklahoma.

Maybe I'd stop there on the way back.

Don't ask me what for.

About the artillery. You may be wondering if I was expecting trouble. Fair question. Here's the answer: I always expect trouble, because trouble always hits you hardest when it's unexpected. So I try to be prepared. The more prepared I am, the less trouble I get into.

The Colt was the standard sidearm when I was in the service, and I guess that's when we started going steady. It has what they euphemistically refer to as "stopping power." "Stopping power" means at 25 feet, a .45 caliber, 230 grain round slams into the target at a velocity of about 850 feet per second, with around 400 pounds per square inch of kinetic energy. That's a fancy way of saying a pistol like mine will knock a man on his ass, even a Sasquatch-sized man, even a highly-motivated, Sasquatch-sized man loaded up on drugs. Weighing about two and a half pounds, a 1911 has some heft to it. Only carries seven rounds, but you can reload in under a second, and I always pack an extra magazine or three, because trouble loves company and often doesn't travel alone.

Frankie had packed the trailer with some fine alfalfa-laden hay, topped off the 100-gallon plastic tank with fresh water and laid in a stash of carrots and apples because horse does not live by hay alone.

The trailer itself was an unusual item. Not your standard pull-behind horse stock trailer. This little darlin' had started out life as a Tioga mini motor home. A small fire had royally fucked up the interior, and Frankie had picked it up for pocket change. He'd stripped out the interior of all the fluff, keeping only the toilet closet, making space to carry a pair of horses, gear and provisions.

There was a storage space to hold a couple of hay bales, and a cubby above where you could store tack. The cockpit had a bench-type seat, so you could stretch out to snooze. With a tape player and coffee mug holder, it had, if not all the comforts of home, all the comforts I needed.

Separating the cab from the rest of the space was nothing but an aluminum bar, like a curtain rod on steroids. You could tie your horse to it, if you wanted, but I never tie a horse in a trailer. This open layout meant you could keep a close eye on your horse. It also meant the horse was practically riding in the front seat with you. He could watch the road, listen to the radio, breathe on your neck, tickle your cheek with his whiskers, and wiggle his nose against your head, if he was so inclined.

I had to wonder why I was mother trucking a horse halfway across the known universe. As I said, they have horses in Texas. LOTS of horses. Lots of real fine horses. What was so special about this one? He was a handsome devil, all right. He struck me as exceptionally alert, observant, eyes, ears and nose ever vigilant. Not because he was worried or fearful. He seemed relaxed and supremely confident. His was the vigilance of the dedicated leader.

He was ten years old, and sported hard slabs of lean muscle, and a chip on each shoulder, mantled in the sincere conviction that he was half James Dean and half Sean Connery, and crowned with a white plume of mane, which he wore like a badge of freedom. It was evident in his every movement, pose, and expression that he was the king, and everybody knows it's cool to be the king. Some people would call such a haughty air a "bad attitude."

Not me.

I call it "horse."

Spartacus Jones was no push-button pony, so broke and broken he'd let any asshole with opposable thumbs jump on his back and abuse him with impunity.

Nope. He was his own horse. He needed humans like submarines need screen doors, and he didn't give a fraction of a fuck about your opinion, because he planned on doing things his own way. He's what some call an alpha horse, the dominant stallion, the harem stallion, and the leader of the pack about whom the Shangri-La's so poignantly sang. A horse like that, you may never earn his respect, but if you do, it'll be worth the extra time and effort because you'll know you deserve it. A horse like that doesn't befriend easily, but when he does, you've got a friend for life.

Where a lot of people get in trouble is in thinking humans are smarter than horses. They expect the horse to be subservient to any two-legged who comes along.

Not me.

I've been around horses enough to know that when a man finally gets to the point where he's able to look at a horse as a true equal — he's vastly under-estimating the horse.

At every rest stop we hit, Spartacus Jones came prancing out of the trailer, the way a heavyweight champ dances into the ring. After taking quick stock of his surroundings, he gave the air a quick snort, and set to the more urgent task of grass recycling. Munchhorsin' syndrome, you could call it. He liked dandelions and could spot one at 50 yards. I found he preferred apples to carrots so I munched the carrots, myself.

I couldn't resist doing a few minutes of dancing with him, here and there. Went from the Groom Me Dance to the Follow Me Dance in record time. It was like playing one-on-one b-ball with somebody who was in great shape and loved going man-to-man, full court press. He read every nuance of my body language and knew what direction I was going to go almost before I knew it myself. Forward, backward, inside turn, outside turn, feint left, feint right, quick, slow, stop. He shadowed me step for step, move for move better than Ginger Rogers did Fred Astaire. I started to get an inkling why he might be worth cab fare. He loved being a horse and he was uncommonly masterful at the art. I could see the wisdom in passing some of those superb qualities on to future generations.

Wherever we stopped, he became the immediate object of adoration of children and little old ladies, and he bore their inexpert affections with the dignity and grace befitting a king. We must have taught a couple dozen kids how to offer apple pieces on out-stretched palm, how to stroke his neck. Nubile young women, too, were drawn to him, gazing at him in a manner in which only a rare few have ever looked at me.

Marlo looks at me like that.

Hell.

I missed her.

And missing her pissed me off at myself. What was I, a smitten sixteen? This wasn't my first rodeo. Dammit.

Men we encountered on the road, most of them, were more standoffish. Arms folded, teeth-sucking, non-committal glance, with an occasional grudging nod. They've had the joyful child kicked out of them entirely, and now they were uncomfortable around anyone they couldn't out-muscle or who had a bigger cock than they did.

Over the miles, Spartacus Jones and I got to know each other. I liked him. Couldn't help it. I think he liked me, too, though, like me, he played his emotions close to the vest. I'd say we got to be friends, and, like I said, I don't have many.

*And he carries the reminders*
*Of ev'ry glove that laid him down*
*Or cut him till he cried out*
*In his anger and his shame*
*"I am leaving, I am leaving"*
*But the fighter still remains*
                    "The Boxer"
                    Simon & Garfunkel


# CHAPTER FOUR:
# HONEYBOY PARKER


The first major leg of our trip, before dipping southwest, was almost due west. Before making that course change, I was seeing signs telling me how far it was to my ex-hometown, Chicago, if only I took an exit north.

According to Carl Sandburg:

"Hog butcher for the world,

Toolmaker, stacker of wheat

Player with railroads and the nation's freight handler;

Stormy, husky, brawling,

City of the big shoulders"

Yeah.

Never cared much for Carl Sandburg.

For me Chicago was Chi-town. The Windy City. Beirut by the Lake. City on the Make. The Cold Heart of America. Prurient Paris on the Prairie. Corruption Capital of the U.S. Chicago was the poster child for police brutality, political graft, organized crime, and several sub-varieties of miscellaneous motherfuckery. Sure, there's the Art Institute, and the Field Museum, Adam's Ribs, great jazz and blues, and the best fucking pizza you'll ever eat.

You know what?

They had beautiful woodwork on the Titanic.

25

Once I decided to keep my feet out of city limits, I had about as much urge to sentimental journey home as holocaust survivors have to take a nostalgic trip to Auschwitz. I wasn't going to head north this time, but I couldn't help remembering the last time I had. See, I would never have gone back that time, either, if I hadn't been obliged to return. I had a debt to pay. A debt of honor.

Some debts can be paid with money.

Some can't.

If you damage somebody's property, cast aspersions on somebody's reputation, hurt somebody's feelings, or do any one of a hundred other minor injuries, that's the kind of debt you can pay with money. Money and an apology, if it's a sincere one. Not "I'm sorry IF" bullshit. Or "I'm sorry YOU were hurt..." Those aren't apologies. They're cop-outs. An apology is "I'm sorry I did XYZ. I was wrong." Anything else, you can shove your apology up your ass. Apology aside, if you willingly and immediately make restitution, we can call it square. You prove your sincerity by never doing XYZ again. Ever. You do XYZ a second time, there isn't going to be an opportunity for a third time, daddy-o.

Drawing blood changes things. If you injure somebody physically, that's a different thing. If it was an accident, then you might be able to square the account with money. Maybe. Accidents happen, and they can happen to anybody. When a decent person hurts someone by accident, the knowledge that they've injured another person is, all by itself, a harsh and life-long punishment. A decent person is compelled to make restitution, if they can. So maybe.

When the injury is intentional, it's a whole 'nother ball game. Assault, or rape, or kidnapping or murder — no amount of money can ever make it right.

None.

In fact, even suggesting that you can atone for inflicting such a deep and permanent wound by coughing up a little long green is adding egregious insult to the existing injury.

That kind of debt can only be paid in blood.

When it's a debt payable in money, then you take the case to a great white lawyer and the offending party makes a trip to court.

When it's a debt only payable in blood, then you take the case to the street, and the offending party makes a trip to hell.

26

You probably never heard of Cleveland "Honeyboy" Parker. No reason you should have.

In his day, he was one of the finest and most under-rated middleweights around. Golden Gloves champ. Circumstances made him go for the short bucks in club fights, until nobody wanted to fight him. His bread-and butter was a left hook–right uppercut combination, and if he caught you with that short right hand of his, god and nine other white men couldn't save you. Like Terry Malloy, Honeyboy should have been a contender, but he never got a shot.

Except to the head.

In fact, he caught a lot of shots to the head, because the man knew no fear, never took a step back. It's a courageous way to fight, but courage takes its toll. By the time I met him, he hadn't been in the ring in a decade, was taking medicine for the headaches, and forgot things.

He had become a 170-pound cliché.

He owned a newsstand at State and Jackson, where guys would grab a paper and a quick shine on the way to work. I guess he did all right for himself. He wasn't starving and he had a regular place to flop. Plus he was working on his comeback.

Always working on his comeback.

If you got up early enough, you might catch a glimpse of Honeyboy doing roadwork in the deserted streets, in the quiet time between night and morning, long before the squares' alarms went off to summon them to the rat race. You might hear soft, steady footfalls echo down alleyways, his breathing solidly on the backbeat. You might see him pause to fire off a flurry of punches, the street light casting his shadow onto a concrete wall, making his phantom opponent look five times bigger than life, like the sword fight in an Errol Flynn movie. He was too much for mortal men: he fought giants.

Me, I didn't get up that early.

I used to see him at his newsstand. I didn't go there to buy a newspaper. Fuck the news. It's all bullshit.

I went there for the skin mags. I'm not talking about "Playboy," though he stocked that one, of course. He had a bunch of others, too. Most were big tit journals. Knight. Scamp. Rascal. Mammy's Mammaries. Humongous Teats for Infantile Losers. Similar titillating titles. Big tits were never my particular thing.

I liked the "French" magazines. No, not "Paris Match." The hardcore magazines, usually cheaply produced in black and white. Lots of naked ladies with legs spread wide open. You could teach a gynecology class with those mags. There were action mags, too. Like a fucking tutorial on fucking. Blowjob Review. National Geo-assfuck. Better Bones and Hard-ons. I forget the names.

Honeyboy kept these earthly delights behind the regular rack. They were wrapped in plain brown paper, like a pound of salami from Gold's Deli, which is appropriate if you think about it. Lord knows how many quarts of sauce I expended over those images.

Honeyboy's newsstand was like an oasis, and me and my few pals spent some time hanging out there. Watching chicks go by. Listening to him recount in detail each of his fights, many times over, and picking up boxing pointers that came in real handy more than once. He was both a mentor, and a cautionary tale. He wasn't very much older than we were, but boxers get older faster.

Like I said, he forgot things. My name, for example. Fortunately, I had it painted on the back of my jacket, along with two white dice coming up seven. Nice jacket. Black leather. A2 style, like a WWII flying ace.

"Hey, man," he'd say. "What's goin' on...?"

Then I would do a quick turn around, like I was looking behind me, so he could see my jacket.

"Lucky, my main man," he'd say.

We'd slap some skin, and all was cool.

Across the street and up half a block was Vinnie's Starlight Lounge. I didn't know who the fuck Vinnie was, and nobody else did, either. The Starlight had a bar, served sandwiches, occasionally featured live music; all to make the operation look legitimate, but basically, it was a strip joint — where all the strippers tricked. The stripping part was thinly unveiled advertising for the prostitution that was the club's real moneymaker. It was like an open secret. Everybody knew the score. Even the cops. Especially the cops, because they got paid off in both money and free pussy. The place was "protected." We watched some of those dancers coming and going, wishing we could be the ones who were going to be coming with them.

Sometime soon. Yeah. Save up your pennies, pal.

Anyway, I liked Honeyboy. He was like an older brother or uncle or something. Always glad to see me and always had something upbeat to say. That can mean a lot when you're a kid and the rest of your life stinks like an outhouse in Hell.

Eventually, I split. Got my ass out. Hit the road, Jack. Made Chi-town my EX-hometown, and the big EX stands for excrement. Went out to have adventures. Fight villains. Slay dragons. Rescue maidens — sort of. Never gave a thought to setting my feet down inside Chi-town city limits again. No more Sweet Home Chicago for me, daddy-o.

Until I the day I received a small brown envelope in the mail. There was no return address, but I recognized the handwriting. It was from The Judge. Inside were half a dozen newspaper clippings. Not page one stuff. A couple of column inches from somewhere way past page twelve.

Honeyboy Parker was dead.

According to his obit, he'd been the victim of a robbery gone bad. Street gang, the paper said. Police were investigating, the paper said. Yeah. Like the cops gave a fuck about a down-and-out former boxer.

Remember what I told you about the news.


I stayed at the Sheraton on Michigan Avenue. I like the view of the lake. I made the rounds. Let it be known I was interested in what happened to Honeyboy. Let it be known there was a little money to be had for the right info.

No immediate takers.

That told me something, right there. But I needed more.

More came in the guise of a square, gaunt woman of about thirty. She had a tight jaw and hard blues eyes, like somebody dealing with a lot of unspeakable private grief.

"Who are you?" she asked me.

"I'm the guy looking for the guys who did Cleveland Parker."

"You're not a cop,"

"I'm not a cop."

"What're you going to do when you find them?

"That's my business. Drink?"

I poured us a couple fingers of Jack Daniels. She sipped, I sniffed.

29

"It wasn't a robbery," she said.

"How do you know?"

She told me her story. It went like this:

Once upon a time there was a fairy princess named Rhonda. A wicked witch, jealous of Rhonda's beauty, condemned her to go-go dance, and strip, and give ten-dollar hand jobs at the Starlight Lounge. The current manager of the Starlight was a dapper psychopath named Tony Pentangeli, known as "Tony Angels" or simply "Angels." With his Tony Curtis looks, and bottomless wallet, he was reputed to be a cunt hound extraordinaire who never took "no" for an answer.

It came to pass that Pentangeli cast his eye upon princess Rhonda, and his soft smile and hard cash soon had Rhonda dreaming of white picket fences and PTA meetings. Little did she know that she was nothing more to him than a new cum-catcher, of which he would weary in a short period of time.

Pentangeli expressed his growing boredom with an increasingly frequent barrage of harsh criticism and surprise slap-arounds, for petty offenses, real or imagined.

Enter the noble Lucinda, come to rescue the fair Rhonda from Pentangeli's evil clutches. With logic, reason, begging, pleading, and, presumably, much wailing and gnashing of teeth, the noble Lucinda finally convinced the fair Rhonda that her "love" for Tony Angels was a non-starter and the smart move was to quickly and quietly get out of Dodge.

So, at the appointed hour, Lucinda was parked at the curb on her white charger — actually, in a yellow Mustang, the backseat packed tight with their meager belongings, and her back pocket with all the bread she could scratch together. There she waited for Rhonda to finish her shift, grab her check, and make off to the fabled realm of Tulsa, Oklahoma, there to live happily ever after.

But things went sour.

When Rhonda strode out the rear entrance to the club, Pentangeli was in hot pursuit, with angry, if unintelligible, words being exchanged between them. Then Pentangeli caught Rhonda by the shoulder, spun her around to commence a slap-around, but found his own face slapped instead.

As if by magic, Pentangeli's phony mask of matinee-idol suavite dissolved, revealing the ugly, demented face of his soul, normally only

30

seen on a portrait he kept hidden in the attic. There followed a slap-around of F-6 intensity.

Lucinda watched, paralyzed with fear. Pentangeli was numbered among the anointed untouchable, a "made guy," who must ever remain unfucked with.

All was lost.

As Rhonda slumped to the concrete, a hulking shadow charged across the street to intercede. It was a white knight in the form of Honeyboy Parker. Only few words were spoken between them before Pentangeli, presumably in a blind rage, was so ill advised as to throw a fist at Honeyboy. A split second — and a left hook-right uppercut — later, Pentangeli was sitting on his ass with a broken jaw, wondering, if indeed he was capable of wondering anything, whence came the Mac truck that had just smacked into him.

Like all victories of good over evil, this one was short-lived. No sooner had Pentangeli's ass kissed the concrete, than two — no, three goons came race-waddling out of the club, their ill-fitting suits giving each the appearance of 100 ponds of shit stuffed into a 50-pound bag.

Even with three of them, even with saps and brass knuckles, they did not remain unscathed in the fray. Honeyboy slipped and slid, ducked and dodged, rocked and rolled and with each bend of leg, with each turn of shoulder, he let fly punches that loosed like arrows and struck like mother-fucking cannonballs. It was Honeyboy Parker's championship round and he fought it like the true champion he was, with not fists alone, but with every bit of his unconquered, if ragged, heart and soul.

Right up until one of the goons got behind him with a sap.

In a trice, two goons had pinioned the dazed Honeyboy's arms, while the third goon started working him over.

Pentangeli got to his feet, wobbling, cradling what was left of his jaw. He dug into his pocket. There was a flicker of steel tongue, and Pentangeli stabbed Honeyboy repeatedly — twenty-two times, they say — until one of the goons stepped in to cool him out and backed him off. They lowered Honeyboy's body, and Pentangeli could not resist kicking the corpse, again and again, until one of the goons once more lulled him away. At Pentangeli's direction, the goons dragged Honeyboy to the curb and dropped him in the gutter. They then spirited away the limp form of Princess Rhonda, who was never to be seen or heard from again.

I poured Lucinda another one and she tossed it down all at once like she was pulling off a Band-Aid.

"What was I supposed to do?"

It wasn't for me to say.

"I loved her," she said. Softly. Under her breath. Almost unable to get the words past her quivering lips. Like she was saying a final good-bye.

I offered her the c-note I had promised.

"I don't want your fucking money," she said. "Are you going to kill him? I hope you're going to kill him."

It's a remarkable thing.

Predators never see themselves as prey.

Guys like Tony Pentangeli have the world by the balls. The regular rules that apply to regular people like you and me — well, like you — don't apply if you're a Pentangeli. You can do anything, get away with anything — as long as you follow orders, and didn't cross another made guy. If somebody lays a hand on you, even "disrespects" you, you have carte blanche to fuck them up to your heart's desire. You never rat, because if you do, everybody else in the gang will be after your blood. As long as you stand-up, the rest of the gang will rally behind you, lie for you, bribe for you, kill for you, and provide for your family if you go down. That's the way it is to be in the mob.

It's a lot like being a cop.

Almost exactly, in fact.

Pentangeli was easy to find. He wasn't hiding. Why should he? He was in the phone book. He kept up an honest front, like so many of his breed, and if you didn't already know he was a scumbag, you might never guess from superficial appearances. In addition to running the Starlight, he owned a legitimate business, a bakery, which made a believable cover for his more lucrative enterprises, as well as a truly excellent baguette, judging from the one I bought. Warm, right out of the oven. Bathed in butter. There's nothing like fresh-baked bread.

Picking Tony Angels out of a crowd was easy, partly because of Lucinda's excellent description, partly because of his thousand-dollar suit, which is atypical attire for bakers, and partly because he still bore the evidence of Honeyboy's hook-uppercut combination on his face.

One half of his mug was black and blue, now turning green and purple, giving his face a half-moon effect, and he had some kind of cast or something over the broken teeth.

Lucinda had given surprisingly detailed descriptions of the three goons, too. I was pleased to see distributed amongst them an assortment of cuts, black eyes and split lips. One of the goons was Pentangeli's driver. Another did collections. The third was a bouncer at the Starlight, where I became a regular, but invisible, customer. Pentangeli spent most of his time at the Starlight, in the office, way in the back.

Like most people, Tony Angels and his crew were men of regular habits, as predictable as a fine Swiss watch. Patterns. It's all about patterns. The deciding difference between predator and prey is this: the predator knows the patterns of the prey.

The bouncer was the easiest. Being not much smarter than a cinder block, he was but a beast of burden. Senior Bouncer was as far up the corporate ladder as he was ever going to get. I pretended to know him, called him by name, "Hey Tommy, wait up!"

He waited up.

It was the last thing he ever did.

I made it look like a mugging.


If you're going to do collections, you should always have a back-up man. Some guys are so established or so badass they decide they don't need one, but the other reason for a back-up man on the scene is to discourage the collector from skimming. This guy made his collections with a young kid no older than early 20's, doing the driving for him, tagging along on the pickups, learning the ropes.

I made this one look like a professional hit.

Small caliber. Two shots to the back of the head each. Left the cash.

I was a little sorry about the kid. But not too much. He wasn't a Cub Scout. You have to be careful about the company you decide to keep. For every choice, there are consequences.


The driver had a wife and three kids. Young kids.

Yeah. Regular guy. "Nice" guy. Family guy.

I decided to make as little mess as possible, for the sake of his family. If you drive a long, thin spike into the base of the skull, into the medulla oblongata, it does the job. Something like an ice pick. It's quick and there's not a lot of blood. Doesn't disfigure the remains.

When Tony Angels came home from the club, I was waiting for him. He should have had a dog, but he probably would have abused a dog, so it's just as well he didn't. No dog. No alarm system. He thought he was immune, see? Untouchable. Nobody would dare to rob him, and the cops would politely knock on the door with a warrant; none of that no-knock SWAT raid bullshit for a made guy. That's for people with no clout.

He wasn't a big guy. He was a small, nasty, ratty guy. He wasn't appreciably strong, either. Just ruthless. Not tough, only cruel. Not smart; only sneaky. He was the kind of guy who would beat a young girl to death. The kind of guy who would stab a better man twenty-two times while goons held the man's arms pinned behind his back. I'm glad he didn't have a dog.

Taped to a chair with a sock in his mouth, he whimpered like a little girl, when I slapped his not-yet-healed jaw. I instructed him on what a baseball bat could do to knees. And elbows. And a few other things. I went slowly so he could fully appreciate it, because I figured he'd never been on the receiving end. Perhaps I could provide him with an epiphany.

Then I tossed his pockets. The knife was in his topcoat. Cashmere topcoat. Custom-tailored. Top quality.

"Nice coat," I said out loud.

The knife was a classic design, spring release, "switch-blade." I took my time, let him feel each one, putting it in slow, letting him see his blood on the blade in between.

"This is for Cleveland Parker," I told him. "For the girl, too. Rhonda. But mostly for Honeyboy."

I have no idea whether he heard me, whether it registered, or whether he understood who the fuck I was talking about. Guys like Pentangeli, they kill people the way regular people step on ants.

Twenty-two times is a lot. I'm sorry to say he might not have felt the last few. I left him right where he was, but I draped his topcoat over him. I hated to get blood on that coat, though. It was a work of art.

That was my last visit to sweet home Chicago.

I don't miss it.

Adam Adrian Crown

*We wore old matador boots*
*Only Flagg Brothers had them with a Cuban heel*
*Iridescent socks with the same color shirt*
*And a tight pair of chinos.*
"Keepin' the Faith"
Billy Joel

# CHAPTER FIVE:
# THE WOLF LAKE BLUES

You go a little northwest of Chi Town, you find what the tourism bureau refers to as the "Chain o' Lakes" area. Cruising past the final turn-offs for Chicago, I couldn't help thinking about this crew I ran with for a while when I was a kid.

We were the mutt squad.

Mongrels of the earth. The reject brigade. "Those south side kids." Or even just "those kids." Yeah, Baby. Born fucking losers.

There was me and Doc. One-eyed Tico. The Rat. The Cicero Kid, Big Eddie G., and Bernie Schwartz. The seven delinquent dwarves. Count 'em up. As Lenny Bruce would say: 1 Spic, 2 Polacks, a Wop, a Nigger, a Kike and one half-breed Redskin. All afloat in a sea of lily white German and Anglo-Scotch-Irish Protestants.

Wolf Lake was about as Wonder Bread as you could get on the squaresville meter. Football heroes, Eagle Scouts, and cheerleaders who weren't that kind of girl. It was the land of Memorial Day parades, and flag-strewn 4th of July picnics, Thanksgiving pilgrims, and Christmas decorations all over town, like Frank Capra was the Mayor. Lawrence Welk was doing the soundtrack, and Norman Rockwell was capturing it all on canvas. At least, that's what was visible on the surface.

This little berg had one movie theatre, and only two decent restaurants, neither of them Chinese. Life revolved around high school sports, and the crème de la crème met at the Wolf Lake Shopping Center, before they were called "malls," where there was a Woolworth's with a soda fountain, a Jewel grocery, a Sears, the Town and Country clothing store, and an Ace hardware, along with a couple of storefronts that changed hands and signs about every week.

Still, small as it was, Wolf Lake had a good side of town — the north side — and a bad side of town — the south side, demarcated both physically and metaphorically by the railroad tracks running through the approximate center of town.

The north side had Inga's Steakhouse and Sabatini's Family Restaurant. The south side had The Wolf Lake Diner, aspiring to rise to the status of greasy spoon. The north side had most all of beautiful Wolf Lake. The south side had the part called Big Hollow Creek. The north side had the American Legion Hall and Wolf Lake Lanes bowling alley. The south side had Bruno's, a bar and pool hall. The north side had ranch house homes, and Greek revivals, and colonials. The south side had some tenement apartments, a couple blocks of run-down shacks, and a trailer park.

Don't ask me how I landed in this low-rent fucking Mayberry. My dad found work and we moved from the city, essentially overnight. I think I was twelve or thirteen — a city thirteen. A city thirteen is not the same as a suburban thirteen. Entirely different scale. The kids in Wolf Lake struck me as at least mildly retarded.

Except for the mutt squad.

We had nothing much in common with each other, but we had even less in common with the "good" people of Wolf Lake, the folks whom O. Henry called "fine upstanding collection plate passers and mortgage foreclosers." We were the poor, the ragged, the wretched refuse longing to breathe free — but breathing free is against the law. Outlaws flock together even more than birds.

Eddie G. — G for "Green"— was ¼ of the only Black family in town, the other ¾ being made up of his father, Tyler Green, who was the owner and chief mechanic at Green's Auto Repair and Towing Service; his mother, Louisiana, who was the high school librarian; and Trisha, his little sister. She was a smart, sassy thing, who was clearly destined to be a knockout, once she ditched the blue, rhinestone-studded eyeglasses and put a few womanly pounds on her tiny frame. We called her Chicklet, and she pretended not to like it.

Eddie G. hit his growth spurt unevenly and too soon, and it left him gangly and stiffly uncoordinated at the same time, like a cross between the Frankenstein monster and Scarecrow from the Wizard of Oz. He spoke in hoarse mumbles and would laugh at even your lamest jokes until he couldn't breathe.

Doc was an avant-garde techno-nerd, apparently the only human being capable of reliably operating the school's audio-visual equipment. He had a nose Cyrano would envy, and allergy-reddened blue eyes. He tinkered a little with a yard full of cars — well, more than a little — but he was a particular wiz at picking locks of all kinds, including handcuffs. He hung around with the cops some, and did them favors, like fixing their cars, or TV's or stereos. Some other favors, less benevolent, too. His affinity for the bullies in blue was a little disturbing, but he had a police scanner, knew the ten-dash radio code by heart, and always, always knew what the fuzz was up to, sometimes before they knew it themselves. Such information can come in handy. So who was using who? Too close to call from the cheap seats. He and I hung out because he had wheels, and I was adept at picking up chicks. Together we thus made an effective take-out-and-make-out team.

Colin "the Rat" (from "Ratkovic") was Elvis Presley's number one fan and the King's goodwill ambassador to Earth. He had every Elvis album and Elvis single ever released, and a collection of Elvis memorabilia, newspaper and magazine article clippings, knew all about the King's horses and the King's men. He was, in short, a walking encyclopedia of Elvis trivia. Unfortunately, he was also a talking encyclopedia of Elvis trivia, and didn't always know when enough was enough and he was being cruel to a heart that was true. He was on a campaign to scientifically prove that Elvis was better than the Beatles. He turned me on to the Ian Fleming "James Bond" novels. Those, along with the works of Richard S. Prather (Shell Scott, Private Eye), gave me some unrealistic expectations that would one day almost get me killed. His mom was sweet to me, always asked me if I'd like something to eat, no matter when we went to his apartment. Even if we had inadvertently walked in when she and her current boyfriend were otherwise engaged on the pullout sofa bed. She didn't seem to mind if I got a pretty good look at her ass, and she had a pretty good ass to look at.

One-Eyed Tico Santiago was a collector, too. Only his collection was second-hand "naturism" magazines from Scandinavia. His uncle was a subscriber, but his aunt didn't know it. Now, these magazines weren't really porn. No fucking or blowjobs. Not even erections. But the girls were completely naked. Not bikini naked, or sheer negligee naked, but bare skin, sun-clad naked. Further, the girls would typically be sporting a healthy, natural growth of pubic hair, the removal of which from "mainstream" mags like Playboy, kept an army of airbrush commandos steadily employed. Somehow, these girls' unsexy volleyball playing and sun tanning were sexier than the plastic come-hither teases of Playboy-type models. Besides which, many of the Scandinavian girls seemed to be around our own age. These literary masterpieces led to much speculating about whether this one might be what Melody Petersen might look like naked, or whether that one might look like Laura Hansen. And so on into the oui hours.

Bernard Schwartz was like our lawyer. Once, somebody called him "counselor," as a tease, but it stuck because it fit so well. I don't remember how he came to join us. He was Jewish, and therefore an outsider, like the rest of us. The town's token "kike," he and his mom had to drive all the way to Waukegan to go to temple. Don't know what happened to his dad. He never mentioned him. He was pensive and introverted and was a straight-A student, which naturally made him double the target. When we disregarded reason, he was equally adept at fully committing to insanity. But his madness was methodical. Bernie had the best and most devious mind of us all, knew all the rules and how to slip and slide around them. He could look at the most unreasonable situations reasonably, and then rationally decide to do something irrational in response. It was amazing. It wouldn't surprise me to learn that he actually did end up becoming a lawyer.

The Cicero Kid, we generally referred to as "The Kid," the way the Rat referred to Elvis as The King. The Kid was, like me, a relatively recent refugee from the Windy City, and he was the first kid I met who seemed normal to me. He was always hip to the latest dance, which made him the undisputed heavyweight champion of pick-up artists. He was dark, broodingly handsome, and he taught me many things, including that, for whatever reason, few women could resist a "bad boy." That vital piece of information was particularly good news for me, because trying to be a "good boy" was fucking killing me.

When I first landed in this dystopian fucking Mayberry, it was The Kid who axed me, "So. How the fuck did you land in this dystopian fucking Mayberry?"

"Just lucky," was my sardonic reply. It made the Kid laugh out loud. So The Kid started calling me "Lucky," and I guess it stuck because I wore my bad luck like a badge of honor, solid gold with defiance trim. It was cool. I ran with it. Even adopted Lucky Strikes as my brand of smokes. About me, much may be rumored but little is known, and I plan to keep it that way. What you figure out on your own, you figure out on your own. Good luck.

As I said, we mutts had little in common but our poverty, and the disdain lavished on us by the "good kids" of the "good" people of the town. Like Eddie G, I dug jazz and blues. Like Bernie, I enjoyed reading and thinking about what I'd read and what it might mean. I shared the Kid's interest in chicks, and Tico's enthusiasm for porn. I admired Doc's ability to use the cops who thought they were using him, and thereby stay one baby step ahead of John law. Our tastes, philosophies and beliefs were divergent, but on one thing we religiously agreed: the Football hero types were a ridiculous bunch of faggots and the chicks who fawned over them were stupid, stuck-up cunts.

The word "faggot" had a specific nuance. Allow me to elucidate. "Faggot," to us, wasn't exactly a homosexual. To us "faggot" referred to a particular kind of mincing, cringing ass-kisser. You know, that kid who reminds the teacher that she forgot to collect the homework assignment? That kind of sucking up would be faggotry. In the joint, it would be a guy who wasn't homosexually inclined, but performed homosexual acts for some bruiser in exchange for protection. Homosexuals were known as "queers," not nearly as smiley-faced a term as "gay," though, frankly, with all the discrimination against them, I don't see what they have to be so fucking gay about. Still, we didn't have a beef with homosexuals, not like the good Kids did. We all knew that Bruno, who owned the pool hall that served as our unofficial headquarters, was queer, even though he'd been a boxer and a decorated Army sergeant in Korea. He'd give you five or ten, or even twenty bucks if you let him suck your cock. I sure as hell wasn't the only one who picked up a little extra cash that way. It's hard to think ill of a guy who gives you a balls-draining blowjob AND pays you for the privilege. It would be ungracious.

For a while, we adopted as our unofficial mascot a boy whose actual name was Stewart, but who was otherwise universally known as "Suzie."

See, God fucked up.

Big time.

Stewart was supposed to be a girl, no question about it. Walked like a girl, talked like a girl, threw a ball like a girl, liked girly things. But you could say there was a fly in the ointment, and if you unzipped that fly you'd find a dick behind it. Plus, he seemed a little slow, or disconnected or retarded, or incredibly innocent. As bad as the hallowed halls of school were for the mutt squad, it must have been an indescribable hell for Stewie. He was always getting picked on, pushed around, ridiculed, teased in the most cruel and brutal way, and often the abuse came from so-called teachers, or in the blind eye of their presence. Poor kid was a pariah without a friend in the world.

Yeah. He belonged with us.

It happened in gym class. Baseball was the waste of time du jour. "Suzie" was getting the usual ration of shit from a couple of the football faggots led by the homecoming king heir-apparent, a red-faced clown named Randy, from the north side of town, of course, son of one of the town cops, of course, and it looked like Stewie would, as usual, wind up in tears. The Kid spoke first, as it was his custom to do.

"Hey, fuckwad," the Kid said. "Lay off."

"What's this — your girlfriend?" said Randy. A round of snickers from the Good kids, led by two of Randy's pals.

"No," said the Kid. "This is my sister."

He delivered that line so deadpan serious that, for a moment, he even had *me* believing Stu was his sister. I dug where the Kid was going, so I sang harmony a third above, as it was my own custom to do. I sidled over close to him, shoulder to shoulder and put my arm around Stewart.

"Yeah," I said. "His sister. My girlfriend. You want to make something of it, Jerk-off?"

Eddie G. croaked up next. "Dig, man, this here's my cousin. You got a problem with that, daddy-o?"

The other member of the mutt squad being present was the Rat. He picked up a Mickey Mantle Model, took a couple of test swings, stepped up to within home run range of Randy's noggin, and leaned on the bat as elegantly as Fred Astaire on a cane. He said, "Anybody ever tell you your fuckin' head looks like a fuckin' baseball? You better be careful, man. Like, it could get hit, like by accident, you know?"

Suddenly, Randy was on his own. No snickerers now, and his two regular back-up singers were giving him a lot of space to improvise.

"Can't you take a joke?" said Randy. Full astern. "I don't mean nothing by it."

"Now, that's righteous, brother," Eddie G. said. "I can dig it. You don't mean nothin.' Nothin' at all." Eddie G. could get real dark. You could hear Randy's dick shrivel up at 50 yards.

There's both strength and safety in numbers, especially when the numbers simply don't give a fuck. Shortly before the end of the school year, Stewie disappeared, moved away, I heard. I don't know what ever became of him. I hope it was something sweet, but I have a vague gut-level apprehension that says it was probably something awful. I hope I'm wrong. But my gut rarely is.

Small town cops don't have enough actual police work to do, so they have to make up shit. Consequently they spend a lot of time rousting undesirables, including juvenile delinquents like us. For a young man, "delinquent" meant he's learned how to say "fuck you," instead of "yes, sir," one of the seven warning signs of starting to think for yourself. For a young woman it meant she's discovered sex right on time, according to nature, but five years too early according to the law.

An exemplar of the latter was Angela "Cookie" Duncan. Cookie's sexual virtuosity was legend. The kind of virtuosity you achieve only when you love doing something and practice it all the time. I'm sure every one of us had some sort of sex with her at one time or another, but after she heard about the Stewie baseball incident, she was a regular squeeze to the Kid and to me, jointly and severally, as they like to say in the law. It was exceedingly cool. She amazed me most of all with her social and political savvy. There was a brain behind all that gum snapping, and she was smart enough to keep it hidden.

One early summer night, Eddie G. and the Rat got cornered by this cop, Pete Hannigan. Hannigan wasn't much older than we were. A former — you guessed it — football star, he joined the police because he didn't have the brains or the balls to do anything else. Take the biggest high school bullies and give them badges and guns and a license to do whatever they want. Yeah, real smart plan.

Hannigan stops my boys for no reason but to give them shit, just because he can. Eddie, always too uppity for his own good, tosses some of the feces right back at him. So Hannigan thumps him around a little bit. Not too much, and not where it shows. Enough to put bruises on him.

Eddie and the Rat met us at Bruno's and told the tale. Rat had a nasty purplish mouse going under one eye, and I could tell by Eddie's shallow breathing that his gut was hurting him where that coward had poked him with his nightstick. It wasn't the first time Hannigan had pulled this kind of shit, and he wasn't the only cop to do it, either. It wasn't even the worst such incident. It was just the one that fucking broke the fucking camel's fucking back.

There was another person present at Bruno's, who couldn't help overhear the story. Let me tell you about him.

His name was Nick. I didn't know his last name. Maybe he didn't have one. Or maybe he had a dozen of them. He was that kind of guy. He came blowing in with the summer wind. He dressed richly but quietly, black suit, white shirt, plain black tie. He always had his shoes shined, always had a Camel dangling from his lips, and he would cock his head like the RCA Victor dog to keep the smoke from getting in his eyes — eyes as blue and cold as the arctic sea — while he shot 8-ball. Never saw him miss, and I never saw him play against anybody but himself. Nick never smiled or frowned or gave any other outward expression of human emotion.

Rumors about him abounded. One was that he was connected to the mob. Another said he'd gotten kicked out of the mob because he was too blood-crazy. That particular rumor was certainly bullshit because the mafia doesn't kick anyone out once they're in. They send you on a sentimental journey you don't come back from. Still, even the idea was butt-clenchingly scary. Imagine what a guy would have to do to get booted out of La Cosa Nostra. What kind of evil shit would be over the line for those guys? Just sayin.'

Of all the wild-ass stories flying around about Nick, probably ninety-nine percent were bullshit.

This one isn't.

It happened in Old Town. Nick was leaving Mother Blues, at that time the premier club in the area, and becoming the focal point of the folk music revival. Impeccably dressed as always, he paused at the mouth of an alley to light up a smoke, and some young punk pulled a pistol on him, shoved it right in his face for the intimidation factor. Nick raised his hands. Not real high.

For an awkward elevator moment, they just stood there, frozen, two guys staring at each other.

One of them was extremely dangerous. The other one had a gun.

"What do you want, kid? Nick said.

"Give me your wal—"

He was going to say "wallet." He never got a chance to finish the word. The next thing he knew, he was on the ground, nose and mouth bleeding, stars buzzing around his head like angry hornets trying to suck him down the drain into unconsciousness. His right index finger throbbed and was bent at an unfamiliar angle. And Nick was holding the gun, aiming it at the punk's chest.

"Don't," the punk said. "Don't shoot me, man."

"Why the fuck NOT? You were going to shoot me..."

"No, I just wanted the money, that's all."

"Yeah, but if I didn't give it to you, you woulda shot me."

"Please, man..."

"Maybe I give you my wallet and you shoot me, anyway, huh?"

"C'mon, man, please..."

"Get the fuck up."

The punk lumbered unsteadily to his feet. Nick directed him farther into the alley.

"Move," he said simply. The punk moved. They went all the way to where there were trashcans and a rusty green dumpster against a wall.

"Turn around. Face the wall," Nick said, and the punk complied. "Now drop your pants."

"What?"

"I think you fuckin' heard me."

It was clumsy to accomplish with the broken trigger finger, but the punk managed to get his trouser undone.

"Shorts, too. All the way down."

"Please, man..."

"Shut the fuck up. Bend over and spread your cheeks."

"What? Jesus, I..."

Nick thumped him on the head with the pistol barrel. "Bend over and spread your cheeks," he said again. The punk complied, and Nick put the muzzle of the weapon up against the punk's asshole.

"You can take this gun or you can take my cock, but one way or another I'm gonna shoot something up your ass. Lead or cum. Which one do you want?"

"Please...don't shoot me..."

"Make a choice," and Nick pressed the pistol in a little more.

"The cock, ok? The cock. I'll take your cock!"

"You don't sound sincere. I think secretly, you want the bullet..."

"No, I don't. Please don't."

"You want the cock?"

"Y-yeah."

"Are you sure?"

"Yeah."

"Say 'please may I have the cock.'"

The punk said it.

So Nick unzipped and gave the punk's ass a quick pounding, right there in the alley, with all kinds of folks passing by a few yards away. When he was done, he sauntered away cold and calm as if nothing at all had taken place.

I happen to know this story is true, because the punk who tried to mug the wrong guy had a partner who was supposed to double-up on their chosen victim, but before the back-up man could get off the bench, Nick had changed the game. So the punk's back-up man went MIA, pissed himself and hid behind that dumpster until Hurricane Nick moved on. It was the back-up man's moment of truth, and he decided on a career change to the fast food industry. He's the one who recounted the tale, charitably omitting the name of the buggered mugger.

So Nick overheard Eddie tell us the story of Hannigan the Asshole Cop — but hey, "asshole cop," is redundant, isn't it? Nick slammed the 8-ball into the side pocket with a crack that sounded like a rifle shot in a phone booth, and started to rack the balls up again. He leaned way over to let cigarette smoke drift up unhindered and said, like he was absently thinking out loud to himself, "You don't want to get pissed on, you gotta get pissed off."

Nick's bit of koan-like poetry smacked me into a sudden epiphany. I guess I didn't need much of a push. I'm kind of long on grudge and short on fuse.

Suffice it to say, we made a plan.


Jokes and stereotypes notwithstanding, Hannigan spent most of his tour at the Dunkin' Donuts, half a block down from the train station, technically on the north side of town. Maybe he was there to stuff his ugly puss with pastry, or maybe he was there to try to get into the prime pussy of Diane Pesche, who waitressed there nights. Either way, his fat ass was predictably parked on a stool there at certain hours. Doc went in first, took his position on Officer Fatass's left, and struck up a conversation. "Hey, Pete," I heard Doc say, "you get a twenty on the speakers I told you about?"

Next, the Kid wandered in and paced back and forth along the counter, spending way too much time studying all the different kinds of donuts, like he was looking to boost something. Hannigan couldn't help but notice. So now the cop's attention was divided between Doc on one side and the Kid on the other. He was on the verge of giving himself a case of whiplash trying to track both. Thus pre-occupied, he had about zero attention left over to devote to what was happening outside, right behind him.

And what was happening outside right behind him was this: while Bernie and I stood watch, the Rat and Eddie G. hauled out some heavy-duty towing chains we had borrowed from Green's Auto Repair and Towing Service. They secured one end around the concrete base of a streetlight, which we figured wouldn't be going anywhere. They took the other end and slithered under the squad car with it, hooked it around the rear axle.

47

When it was done I gave the Kid the high sign, which, of course, Hannigan missed. The Kid bought a chocolate eclair and strolled out, with Hannigan eyeballing him hard for an excuse. Then Doc scooped up his bag of pastries and marched his donuts out of there a second later, leaving Officer Buffoon all alone and blue.

Doc did the driving. For this occasion, he'd selected a Chevy convertible he had been tinkering with. The rest of us piled in how best we could. I got shotgun. We pulled up next to the squad car, revving the engine, honking the horn. We figured it would get Hannigan's attention. When we had it, we leaned out and wildly gave him the finger, both fingers, to the accompaniment of a chorus of "Fuck you, Pig!" Pushing up our noses in porcine fashion, we yelled, "Oink! Oink! Oink!" We then hauled asphalt, peeling out, with a scream and a squeal, and a hardy hi-yo, Silver, leaving behind enough rubber for mortals to drive on for a month.

We didn't get to see what happened next, but we got to hear it.

With the flash of the blue gumballs flapping against the darkness, the wail of a siren rose — and then a terrible metallic clunk-chunk, engine whine, moan, groan, crash, and scraaaaaape! Then nothing.

Not a sound echoed in the sound of silence.

"Now, that's what I'm talking about, dig?" said Eddie G.

"Fuckin' A," said the Kid and the Chevy erupted into unrestrained jubilance. We laughed like madmen, gave each other skin all around, and then cruised away unhurriedly into the night.

The Kid copped an old half-gallon bottle of no-name Chianti, we scavenged up some French bread, a salami, and, of course, we had Doc's big bag of donuts. We drove out to The Point, a high spot overlooking Wolf Lake that was a notorious lovers' lane.

Tonight The Point was Valhalla. And there we celebrated and feasted like Viking heroes.

Tomorrow it would be Ragnarok. There would be holy hell to pay. All kinds of it. We knew it, and we would pay it, no matter what it was. But tonight, the mutts of the earth were the kings of the world. And whatever that would cost us, it was fucking worth it.

*Mamas don't let your babies grow up to be cowboys*
*'Cos they'll never stay home and they're always alone.*
*Even with someone they love*
> "Mamas Don't Let Your Babies Grow
> Up to Be Cowboys"
> Willie Nelson

# CHAPTER SIX:
# LOS LOBOS

"The wickedest town west of the Mississippi."

That was the title of a dime novel by Annabelle S. Ellis, published in 1890, and present-day denizens of the once-notorious outlaw paradise still took a certain perverse pride in it, as evidenced by the fact that somebody had reproduced the cover of her magnum opus as a 24x36 poster.

Unlike such famous Wild West towns as Deadwood, South Dakota; Tombstone, Arizona; and Dodge City, Kansas, the founding fathers of Los Lobos had no pretensions of being "civilized" or any apparent ambitions in that direction. It was a town of, by, and for desperados whose consuming interests, apart from evading the hangman's noose, were drinking, gambling, and whoring, not necessarily in that order. It was a place populated by loose women and hard men. The Tortuga of the American Frontier. At one time or another, Los Lobos had hosted such luminaries as Sam Bass, Johnny Ringo, Buddy Guinn, Henry "Billy the Kid" McCarty, and John Wesley Hardin.

That was the gospel according to Cal Hanshaw, mayor, town historian, and the owner and proprietor of Cal's Service, the only gas station for a hundred miles around.

I was running on fumes when I passed the signpost at the Los Lobos city limits. Population 750. It looked like a real old sign.

I pulled on to New Main Street from the travesty of a road that some would politely call "unimproved," and spotted the pumps. Before I could get out to stretch my legs, a stringbean scarecrow in faded green coveralls was at the nozzle, giving me a broad crooked-toothed grin. The name "Cal" was embroidered above one chest pocket.

"Fill 'er up for ya?"

I felt like I had time-traveled back to the 1950's.

Happy Days.

Whoopee.

"Thanks," I said.

He had a mop of sandy hair that looked like an awful toupee but wasn't, and bright blue eyes. His face was awash with concentric circles of wrinkles suggesting he laughed a lot. I made him for about 60-something. He was upbeat, open, and friendly in a way that automatically made me suspicious.

Without even asking, he checked the oil, wiping the dipstick on the rag that hung dashingly out of his back pocket and was dedicated to that purpose. Then he produced a spray bottle and tackled the windshield, which was coated with a heavy layer of dust and broken insect heroes on a last chance power drive.

"You here for the show?" he chirped. Like a friendly raccoon in a Disney cartoon.

"What show would that be?"

"Why, Old West Week, of course."

"What's Old West Week?" It was the kind of question you should never ask unless you've got a lot of time to listen to the answer. Mr. Mayor put on his town historian hat, and I subsequently learned more about Los Lobos than a sane man would ever want to know.

"The wickedest town west of the Mississippi" wasn't all that wicked, anymore. Wasn't much of a town, anymore, either. There was Cal's. Next door to that was a modest Best Western motel. Across the street was a greasy spoon called The Cantina Bonita. Next to that was the "General Store," that stocked the essentials from canned goods to 10d nails. A little farther down was "First Bank of Los Lobos." First and last. It also housed the post office. At the end of the block was the economic heart and lungs of the place: The Double L Brewery where most of the townsfolk were employed. Their big hit was "all natural"

50

Old West Sarsaparilla, which had become reasonably popular in the El Paso area, and helped keep the Los Lobos economy afloat. A root beer float.

The other principal industry in Los Lobos was tourism.

Somebody had had the foresight or dumb luck to preserve the original town buildings that had been constructed along what was now called "Old Main Street," which ran perpendicular to New Main Street at the north end, making the overall layout of Los Lobos into a "T" shape. These 19th Century structures were in mint condition. Some still had the out-houses in back, though a few had been re-fitted with more modern plumbing.

I'd be willing to bet that you've seen Old Main Street, but didn't know it. From the late 1920's on, it was a favorite location for shooting western movies, and still is. A lot of celluloid shoot-outs have taken place there. A whole host of cowboy heroes have ridden into the sunset on that street — literally, since it runs due east and west. A certain classic TV show filmed its opening credit scene there — a mythical duel between the tall, handsome marshal and some anonymous black hat.

I always wondered about that one. Action beats re-action. Because re-action has a ¼ second delay known as "lag time." Not to be confused with the piano music of Scott Joplin, lag time is the interval between your perception of the stimulus and the initiation of your response to it. A quarter of a second may not seem like much. It's not as deep as a well or as wide as a church door, but it's enough. It can mean the difference between dead or alive.

The code of the movie west says the Good Guy never starts a fight. But when you let the Bad Guy draw first, you're playing catch-up. If you can let the other guy slap leather before you do, and still be the one who fires first, you are one quick drawing son-of-a-gun. On the other hand, speed isn't everything. Sometimes, it's nothing. I think Wyatt Earp said it best: "Fast is fine. Accurate is final."

Movie genres come and go, popularity waxing and waning like the width of men's neckties. Theme parks live forever. Thus, Old West Days rode into town. It was a new wrinkle on an old idea. Part Disneyland, part rodeo.

Imagine a Renaissance Faire in cowboy drag and you've got the picture. Never been to a Ren Faire? You simply haven't lived. You could do all your research for a PhD in deviant psychology right on the premises, all the while swilling ale and gorging on turkey legs. Ostensibly, these faires are based on the old English fairs thence folks would assemble to market their arts, crafts, and produce, as well as to drink, feast, and gossip. Such events attracted a wide variety of buskers hoping to make a buck: acrobats, musicians, jugglers, and magicians. It was to prostitutes and pickpockets what a Shriners' Convention is today. Tournaments of arms were a common feature, the centerpiece of which was the joust in which anonymous penurious knights would hope to win fame, fortune, or a little of both. When a knight defeated his opponent in the lists, he won the vanquished party's horse and armor, which the loser could then pay a ransom to get back. In the 12th century, one of the most famous knights in history — William the Marshal, the Elvis Presley of chivalry — made his living from tournaments until he married money.

Modern Faires fall somewhere between the historical and the hysterical. Typically set during the reign of Elizabeth I, or her dad, Henry VIII, they are a hodge-podge of bawdy humor, tongue-in-cheek history, and pure fantasy. Carnivale meets Halloween in tights and kung-fu shoes, and speaking a very bad British dialect. The joust is still the featured event, performed by bold young pups — and a few old lions — in stunt crews like the Hannon Lees Action Theatre troupe. If you've got a joust and you've got beer, you've got yourself a Faire, especially when that beer is served by earthy wenches recruited for their buxomness and their penchant for exposing as much of their bux as possible without actually breast-feeding the customers.

In the Wild West version, the thrill of the joust is supplied in part by a gunfight re-enactment, and in part by the Cowboy Shooting Contest. Nothing much else is changed. The booze is still booze, the buskers still busk, and wenches — now dance hall girls — are still bawdy and buxom.

The scorching summer was not conducive to such shenanigans, so Los Lobos held its faire in the Springtime, which means it coincides with horse-breeding season, and when Spartacus Jones and I arrived, the merry citizens thereof were buzzing around like frantic ground hornets, making final preparations for the impending blessed event. Coming into town, we drove past a sprawling campground that had been set up to accommodate the deluge of tourists, re-enactors, performers, cowboy action shooters, and craftsmen who had been arriving for several days.

All the buildings along Old Main were included on the official list of historic places, according to the brochures.

You could slip into your Old West Days duds and time-travel, swaggering down the dusty trail, leaving New Main Street and its modern connivances behind, invisible to you until you needed them. A lot of people were willing to pay for that experience. Rooms in the turn of the century Hotel were booked up months in advance — as was every other spare room in town, vintage or not.

Apart from Old West Week, the other popular tourist attraction, according to His Honour, was the clump of mountains to the northwest. They weren't the Himalayas. They weren't even the Rockies. But they were plenty rugged enough. In the waybackwhen, they were famous for being an impregnable Apache stronghold. These days, they were rumored to be the last-stand habitat of a pack of wolves that had somehow eluded humankind's best efforts to eradicate them. No one had ever actually seen them. But there were signs. A paw print, here; some droppings there. A suggestive deer carcass. A distant howl too grand, too powerful, and too forlorn to be a coyote.

Environmentalists, conservationists, naturalists, and photographers, amateur and professional, made regular pilgrimages there to look for them. One of the locals hired out as a guide, which was a lucky thing, because those mountains were 2500 acres of such a tangled patchwork of treacherous trails, deep gorges, and twisted canyons that the place was known as El Labrinto, or as the gringos called it, "The Maze." I forget the actual name, the one on the maps. I think everyone else has, too.

Hardly a year went by, Hanshaw said, that some fool didn't under-estimate The Maze and over-estimate his outdoor skills, to get himself lost up there. The locals would posse up to make a search. Sometimes they found the missing party. Sometimes they found the remains. Sometimes they never found anything at all. Nothing goes to waste in nature.

There were all kinds of spooky stories and legends about The Maze, too. The kind of stories Boy Scouts whisper to each other that makes them huddle a little closer to the late-night campfire. Ghosts of lost conquistadors. Ancient treasure. Apache holdouts still living in the

Old Way, hiding out up there. Like those mythic wolves. The locals did nothing to quell such tales. Just the contrary. Those legends were a part and parcel of their tourism trade, and Los Lobosites — Los Lobocitos? Los Lobohemians? Los Lobozos? — delighted in purveying them, if Hanshaw was any indication.

After he was done filling my tank and my ear, he gave me directions to the Bonner Ranch.

I climbed behind the wheel and Spartacus Jones snorted wetly against my cheek.

"What is that guy, a Jehovah's Witness?" he seemed to say.

"Close," I said.

*Oh, I am a Texas cowboy, lighthearted, brave, and free,*
*To roam the wide, wide prairie, 'tis always joy to me.*
*My trusty little pony is my companion true,*
*O'er creeks and hills and rivers he's sure to pull me*
*through.*

"The Jolly Cowboy"
Traditional

# CHAPTER SEVEN:
# THE BONNER CATTLE COMPANY

The Bonner ranch — home of the Bonner Cattle Company, Inc. — wasn't hard to find. There was nothing else out there. It was about nine miles from downtown Los Lobos and about a zillion times bigger than the town, itself.

It was quite a place from what I could see.

The centerpiece was an enormous two-story house that looked like it might pre-date the war — the Civil war. A grand porch wrapping around as far as I could see. Balconies.

The house was surrounded by cow pens, paddocks, sheds, and fabricated steel barns. It was an odd mixture of antique and modern, like the jousters on motorcycles in Knight-Riders.

I pulled in near the house where a couple of cowpokes were jawing in the shade of that sprawling porch, and I climbed out. There was a warm dry wind blowing. Southerly.

Seeing me, they moseyed right over. First time I'd ever seen anybody mosey, but it was self-evident that that's what they were doing.

As they approached I could see that one of them was a rather slight, lean gent with a heavy mustache drooping over his mouth, hiding his upper lip. The ends were waxed into fine quills that pointed to his eyes. He wore brown jeans that made Carhartt's look like taffeta, a black shirt, sleeves rolled up to his forearms, a khaki vest, and a

55

stained, center-creased hat the color of the sand in Death Valley. A red silk bandana hung in limp folds around his neck. He had an air of quiet authority about him, like a glow emanating from a lifetime of acquiring expertise the hard way. Fair chance this was the boss, J.T. Bonner.

His companion, I realized only when we were in handshake range, was a woman, and much younger. Daughter? Granddaughter? She was a head taller than the old buckaroo, with a narrow build. She wore baggy cowboy jeans, faded to the color of the cloudless sky, a blue chambray work shirt, and a beat-up cattleman-style Stetson.

"Hi," I said. Almost said "Howdy." Seemed almost like a duty. A howdy duty.

"Howdy," she said. See? I told you so.

"I'm looking for J.T. Bonner." I directed that intro to the steely-eyed gent and started to offer my hand.

"You found her, son," he said.

Yeah. "Oops."

I hastily re-directed my handshake, hoping no one would notice what a presumptuous asshole I was.

"Ms. Bonner?"

"You can call me J.T.," she said, looking up at me sideways, smiling with one side of her mouth like Elvis, and shook my hand. Grip like a steel trap. Callouses. She was no hothouse orchid.

"You must be Frankie," she said.

"No, Ma'am," I said. "Frankie couldn't make it. His wife's about due. I'm Jack."

"Well, I guess that makes us about even, huh, Jack?" She cocked her head a little and grinned. Nothing shy about her now. "This here's Harmon. He's the best wrangler you're like to meet."

"She tends to exaggerate a might," he said as we shook hands. Another grip like the bite of a gator. My hand was taking a beating.

"Let's get you unloaded," J.T. said, "and I'll give you the twenty-five cent tour."

I checked Spartacus Jones into the honeymoon paddock, and learned he wasn't one for long good-byes. Without giving me so much as a "thanks for the lift," he pranced immediately over to the far side where a winsome filly was eyeing him from the adjacent paddock.

Can't blame him. I would have done the same, under similar circumstances. In fact, I'm reasonably sure I have.

On with the twenty-five cent tour...

Like many cattle ranches in the west, the Bonner Cattle Company was a family-run enterprise, and had been ever since Jeremiah Bonner immigrated to what was then Mexico in the 1830's. Like most such immigrants, Jeremiah was a farmer, not a cattleman.

The cattle originally brought to the southwest in the early 1700's came from Spain, and were intended to feed the missionaries and the Indians whom they had converted via fire and steel. As the missions spread north, crossing the Rio Grande, the Spanish made the acquaintance of additional Indians who weren't all that keen on being converts themselves, but didn't mind converting the missionaries into worm food.

Comanches for one.

Apaches, for another.

The native resistance eventually persuaded the owners of some of those land grants to head back south, and they left their cattle behind. The abandoned cows had to fend for themselves, and soon there were a fair number of mavericks wandering around.

For a time, there were so many wild cattle that there was no profit to be made raising cows. Anybody who wanted some beef could easily go out and get one of the wild bunch. There was no place handy to sell beef, even if you did raise some. Cattle were slaughtered for hides and tallow, not for the meat, which went to waste because it couldn't be preserved.

Then somebody got the bright idea to take the mountain to Mohammad. Some people say it was a Bonner. Whoever it was, the notion of driving cattle to market on foot started to catch on. Cows and cowboys hit the trail for New Orleans, St Louis — even all the way to New York.

During the Civil War, so many Texas men went into the Confederate army that once again the wild cattle herds flourished. The Bonner men did not join the Army. Though Jeremiah Bonner was said to be an abolitionist, he had no qualms about supplying the Confederates with a little beef now and again.

After the war, Texas was financially strapped, and the little money brought in from cotton just wasn't going to cut it. But there was a demand for beef in the East and North. The Bonners got the jump on the cattle competition, being one of the first to collect up wild cows and drive them to Sedalia, Missouri, fattening them along the way. It was a sweet hustle. Cows that were only worth about a dollar a head back home on the range, could fetch twenty dollars a head or more if they could be signed, sealed and delivered to the right market. Delivering them was labor intensive, but labor was cheap. The country was full of unemployed, homeless veterans for whom a dollar a day plus meals was big money. So if you had a herd of 2000 cows that cost you nothing, and you grazed them on grass that cost you nothing, and you paid 10 or 12 guys a buck a day for a month, then sold each of the cows for 20 bucks... do the math, daddy-o. You could make yourself some serious money.

And for about two decades, during the golden age of the cowboy, the Bonners did exactly that. Getting out early in the spring, foraging on the best grass along the trail, being the first outfit to get their cow piggies to market.

As the railroads expanded, the cattle drives dwindled, and by the 1880's, thanks to over-grazing, droughts, and severe winters that took a catastrophic death toll on the cow population, the party was over. Prices plummeted and there was an epidemic of bankruptcy. Add to that a recent influx of settlers who began taking up more and more of what had been "open range," or public land, and closing it off for their private use.

As circumstances shape-shifted, the Bonners displayed their uncanny ability to bob and weave. They started buying up all the grazing land they could afford. They gradually acquired nearly 250,000 acres. Those outfits that could do so followed suit. Those that couldn't folded.

Where I grew up fences were everywhere. Everybody's yard was fenced in, even if the yard was the size of a postage stamp. In Texas, not so much. They didn't have enough rock or wood, hedges required time and water, and smooth wire didn't hold in the stock. Then along came "Barbara Why're-You-Like-That."

Barbed wire, that is.

"Light as air, stronger than whiskey, cheaper than dirt, all steel, and miles long," proclaimed the street corner barbed wire hustlers. "The cattle ain't born that can get through it."

Overnight, folks went wild for the stuff. They took to fencing in all their acreage, large and small, including an appreciable amount of acreage that wasn't theirs to fence in. It was the Beatlemania of the 1880's.

Not everyone was in love with the idea. There were still a lot of Elvis fans. Especially the guys who owned thousands of cows but no grazing land for them to piss on. God had made the open range open, and they wanted to keep it that way. It led to some cross words. And a few crossfires.

Inevitably, the immovable object — in this case a fence — and an irresistible force — in this case a guy who needed to get his cattle to water — came face to face, and the confrontation was decided by a pair of wire cutters. That incident touched off a frenzy of fence-cutting, and for a short while, wire-cutters sold faster than hoola-hoops and some folks considered fence-cutters to be like the Robin Hoods of the range, defying the big ranchers who were presumably backed by big money from back East.

When the costs mounted, however, public sentiment turned against the wanton destruction of fences and the Governor was forced to abandon the one he was straddling. Speeches were made, chests were thumped, and laws were passed making fence-cutting a felony. That was the final nail in the coffin of the open range and the gypsy cattleman.

It worked out all right for the Bonners, though.

Once they had their grazing lands fenced in, they could sub-divide that, which made it easier to selectively breed, and to manage more cows with less labor. But ranching has always been a gamble. Prices go up and down, depending on the numbers of cattle on the market. One of the worst declines was in the fall of 1973. A great many ranches that had been home and hearth to several generations bit the dust of bankruptcy. The Bonners had nearly been one of them.

That's when Clive Littlefield Bonner — J.T.'s father — had his epiphany and decided to go organic.

It took a decade to accomplish it, but the Bonner Ranch became a leading supplier of grass-fed beef, grazed on certified organic land. No grain. No hormones. No antibiotics.

The Bonner Cattle Company capitalized on the growing demand, among those who could afford to pay a premium price, for clean, healthy, high quality, all natural and unfucked with meat.

Part of the appeal of Bonner "Open Range Brand" beef was the romance associated with traditional California-style vaqueros, working the herds from horseback. It harkened back to the days when things were simpler and more honest — back when food was bona fide food, not some frankenfood product fashioned in a secret lab from petroleum and nuclear waste.

The vaqueros were but a dwindling handful of rugged wanderers who were among the last real and true working cowboys in the United States. No ATV's or helicopters for the Bonner Cattle Company. The horse was, as always, the cowboy's most important vehicle, tool, and partner, equaled only by a well-bred cattle dog.

The Bonner remuda was easily one of the finest — if not the finest — in the West. So many generations of horses had been bred for their cow sense, that new foals now scarcely needed any education at all. Cutting had become an instinct. On one of those ponies, the vaquero was nearly reduced to nothing but an accessory for roping, doctoring, or branding.

The day-to-day operation of the ranch was in the hands of Judith Teresa Bonner, assisted by middle-child Laughlin Travis Bonner. No family in Texas is complete without a child named Travis. I think it's a law.

"We've got a room for you upstairs," J.T. said. "You just consider yourself like one of the family. We're not real formal around here."

"Sounds good," I said. "Much appreciated."

"I imagine you'd like to get cleaned up and such after being on the road. I should have thought of that before I went off filling your ear about the cattle business. I apologize about that. Sometimes I just run off at the mouth."

"Not at all. I enjoyed it very much. I learned something."

"Now, you need anything, jus' holler."

"Will do."

I was looking at a week or more with nothing to do but laze around waiting for Spartacus Jones to cast his fate to the wind. I planned to kick back and enjoy it.

Always make plans. That way the gods will always have something laugh about.

I slept late. It must have been almost seven by the time I rolled out of bed. Either it was an exceptionally comfortable bed, or I was a lot more tired from the drive than I thought. Getting dressed, I happened to glance out a window, and saw the long, tall figure of Harmon Cobb sally forth into a small paddock. It was made up of tubular steel sections, the way portable round pens are, but this one was much larger than usual and set up in a square. There was a stock tank in one corner, but the paddock was otherwise empty except for a dun pony, pacing, snorting, and stomping. Cobb went to the approximate center of the pen, opened up a folding chair, and stretched out in it, pulling his hat down over his eyes, and appeared to be intent on taking a nap.

Breakfast was long over, but Leticia Bonner, who was in charge of all things food-related, met me as I came down the stairs, and introduced herself. "How would you feel about some steak and eggs?" she asked.

"You're very kind," I said. "I don't want to make extra work for you. I was just going to go over and have a look at what Harmon was doing."

"He'll be there a spell. And don't you worry about making extra work for me. Shoot, the boys are always coming and going, and lots of times you got to catch a meal when you can. So the kitchen is most always open. How do you like your steak?"

There's nothing like steak and eggs for breakfast, especially when cooked up for you by someone who's handy with a spatula, and makes coffee you could blacktop your driveway with. She slid me the bottle of Tabasco, like nobody would be fool enough to eat steak and eggs without slavering it in mouth-blistering hot sauce, and just for the hell of it, I gave my food a couple poinks of it.

When in Rome, daddy-o.

I made short work of that meal, and when I was done, I said, "Ma'am, that may be the best breakfast I ever had." I made a note to buy myself some Tabasco sauce when I got back.

As Leticia had predicted, Cobb was still there when I'd finished eating, and I practiced my mosey over to the paddock. The sun was high and hot, and I adjusted my cap to shade my eyes. It was a baseball cap. Blue. Chicago Cubs. I wore it in lieu of a St. Jude medal. It was getting a tad ragged at the edges of the brim. Too bad there's such a thin line between broken in and broken down.

"You otter git yerself a proper hat, son," said Cobb softly from under the shade of his.

"Mind if I watch you work?"

"Suit yerself, son. It's gonna be like watching paint a-dryin.'"

And we fell into silence.

Cobb had not misestimated the process. He remained immobile in his folding chair while the dun, a mare, paced and wandered, had a drink, stopped to sniff the air, then wandered some more. From time to time she cast a wary eye at the motionless scarecrow in her paddock. Eventually, the dun's curiosity got the better of her, and her wandering brought her gradually closer to Cobb's chair, until the pony was standing within arm's reach. Then, quick as a cat, Cobb did — absolutely nothing. Kept his arms folded on his chest. Aggressively uninterested.

Finally, the mare sniffed him, and nudged him with her nose. And again.

Cobb shifted around, turning his back to her.

She nudged him some more. Nudged his hat right off his head.

He rolled slowly out of his chair, scooped up his hat, and replaced it as he walked away from her. She followed after him. Then he stood still a moment, until she bumped him again, and then he moved away from her. Soon, she was following him around the paddock wherever he went, however he turned. His moves away from her decreased in size, with the effect that she was now essentially remaining by his side. Now when she pushed against him, he didn't move, but pushed her back with his shoulder. Next thing you know, he had an arm over her back, and was giving her withers a lavish scratching. With the other hand, he rubbed under her neck, down on her chest, a place where bugs like to bite, but horses can't reach on themselves to scratch. She raised her head up enjoying the attention. After a bit of grooming, Cobb wandered away, and the pony stuck with him like a puppy. He let her catch up to him, and when she did, she got some more good rubbing and scratching.

When he finally called it quits and left the paddock, she followed him to the gate, and he reached back inside, offered her his hand, which she nuzzled.

"Care to fetch me a flake o' that there hay?" he said to me, nodding to a nearby bale.

I fetched it.

He shook it loose, and dropped it in the pen.

"Let's get us some coffee," he said.

"I sure like what you did with that pony," I said.

"Hellfire, that weren't nothin.' Ain't a female ever been born who could tolerate being ignored."

Instead of lying around, slothfully soaking up the rays, I spent the rest of my time on the Bonner Ranch following Harmon Cobb around like that pony had, and taking notes like mad.

Adam Adrian Crown

*Round,*
*Like a circle in a spiral*
*Like a wheel within a wheel*
*Never ending or beginning*
*On an ever-spinning reel...*
                "The Windmills of Your Mind"
                Noel Harrison

# CHAPTER EIGHT:
# EL LABRINTO

With Spartacus Jones having done his studly duties, I was planning to shove off for home on Sunday morning. The boys at the Bonner ranch were wrapping up the branding chores. Curiosity got the better of me and I decided to pop into town and have a look at their Old West Days. It was only a fifteen-minute drive. When I arrived, it looked like an RV convention, and parking was backed-up almost to Indiana. I found a spot on the outskirts.

As I said, what we have here is a cowboyed-up Renaissance Faire. Most visitors came into town from the camping area via New Main Street and they passed by The Emporium where they could rent or buy authentic attire appropriate to the time. The visitors who had reserved rooms tended to have their own wardrobe. Quite a number of town folk dressed up in their late 19th Century best, and portrayed a real or imaginary character from the glory days of Los Lobos. A few of them went with an 1880's counterpart of themselves: the mayor, Cal Hanshaw and his wife Lillian, played the mayor and his wife. Bob Rutledge, the part-time Chief of Police, played the town marshal. Clive Bonner was there, doing his bit for the town, playing the part of his own great-grandfather — or great-great grandfather — Cyrus Bonner, Cattle Boss. Any of the womenfolk who had the legs for it — or wanted to pretend they did — dressed up as dance-hall girls. Those that didn't simply portrayed wives and mothers, then as now, taken largely for granted. Most of the men opted for desperadoes or cowboys. Fundamentally, the townsfolk provided food and drink for the legions of visitors.

Some folks took on the vital role of cleaning up the town. And not metaphorically. A large crowd can generate an unbelievable amount of garbage in the course of a day. One of the few concessions to modernity was the strategic placement of 55-gallon garbage cans, that everyone pretended to take no notice of, simply accepting them as being invisible necessities. Willing suspension of disbelief they call that.

Actors depend on it.

So do politicians.

I have to say, there was one re-enactor who impressed me: Wild Bill Hickok. As far as anybody knew, James Butler Hickok had never set boot-heel in Los Lobos, but what the heck, the show must go on. And here was a fellow who took dress-up with deadly seriousness. From his boss of the plains Stetson, with its broad, straight brim and low, flat Spanish crown cocked jauntily atop his shoulder length curls, to the matched pair of pearl-handled .31 caliber 1851 Navy revolvers tucked cavalry-style — handles pointing forward — into an elegant red sash bound around his frock coat, he looked every stitch like the real deal. But it takes more than a costume to play the part, and this fellow wasn't just a clotheshorse.

He had the eyes.

The melancholy eyes permanently set in a stoney squint, always on the watch. Those eyes didn't belong on such a young man. They should have been worn by a man much older, a weary veteran who has seen too much blood, too soon and too often. It's a rare thing, those eyes, and common only among those who have fought on the front lines.

I know those eyes.

A killer's eyes.

Hickok didn't seem to do anything but stroll around town, casting a sardonic gaze at this or that. But his presence added a sense of brooding danger to the atmosphere of the show. I wondered who he was, what his story was. I decided I'd try to track him down after the show, and find out.

The day's festivities included a slew of Wild West entertainers who performed on an outdoor stage set up at one end of Old Main Street. Most of the "refreshments" were at the opposite end of town, so visitors had to traverse the entire street, past all the shops and crafts booths to get from the show to the chow and the booze, giving them multiple opportunities to impulse buy some memento or other.

Smart.

There were music acts, at least a couple of which were townsfolk, ranging from old timey stuff to modern country & western. There was a troupe of Can-Can dancers complete with squeals and flashing thighs. At high noon, down the street, was a "re-enactment" of the famous shoot-out between the town's turn-of-the-century marshal, known as "El Gato," and the notorious Buddy Guinn gang, all narrated by a famous cowboy poet. For the ladies, there was a fashion show, illustrating the tactical use of the bustle. For the gents there was a mustache contest, and some of the contestants would have given your average walrus an inferiority complex. For kids there was Trumpy the Rodeo Clown and his trick horse, Cochise. I had a feeling that the pony was a ventriloquist.

I guess the headliner was "Cowboy Dan McGrue," and his lovely and scantily clad assistant. Cowboy Dan didn't fret none about period-correct duds. He looked more like he'd walked straight off the set of a 1940's singing cowboy movie. He sported high-heeled boots, stovepipe chaps, a sky blue shirt trimmed out with silver fringe and matching embroidery, and festooned with sequins. He topped it off with a pure white 10-gallon Tom Mix hat. You had to be careful; if you looked directly at him for too long, you'd turn into a cactus. Costuming aside, he put on an entertaining show. He did some trick roping, some adroit gun-spinning, told a few terrible jokes that drew happy groans from the crowd, and finished up with some whip-cracking, using a pair of 8-foot snake whips, putting to the test the keenness of his eye, the sureness of his hand, and the gullibility of his assistant, who held a variety of small targets in her hands and mouth for him to whip crack.

A real crowd pleaser attraction, scheduled for the afternoon, was the Mounted Cowboy Shooting event that took place north of Old Main Street. Competitors with Cowboy Shooting aliases and costumes galloped their horses past a series of balloon targets, emptying out not one, but two, replica pistols with special loads. A pair of replica pistols ain't cheap. Not a hobby for poor folks. It was the functional equivalent of the Ren Faire Joust, with patrons forming cheering squads for their favorite pistoleros — and at least one pistolera.

Halfway up the street, in the restored saloon/cantina, was Amarillo Slick, who played your basic tinhorn card sharp, complete with satin brocade waistcoat and sleeve garters. He performed some of the best close-up card magic I'd seen since I'd caught Ricky Jay's act, to the oooo's and ahhhh's of the sardine-packed crowd. Three shows throughout the day.

It was right after the El Gato/Buddy Guinn shoot-out came to a close with designated extras carrying the five "dead" gang members from the street during a tsunami of applause — despite the fact that one of the blanks had misfired causing one of the bad guys to fall before he was shot. The hero quickly fired another round and the crowd went along with it. Across the street from me, I spotted Hickok, whose hard-bitten gaze never wavered.

The official photographer was about to take the official photograph of the event, and was herding performers into the street for a somewhat typical family portrait. Cowboy Dan waved, can-can girls showed thigh, Trumpy smiled, Amarillo Slick appeared to be pulling a Jack of Spades from Cowboy Dan's ear, and old Wild Bill stood impassively above them on the boardwalk, leaning against a post, not even deigning to pay the camera any mind, while the photographer snapped away.

"Thanks, pardners!" The shutterbug called to release them from their modeling duties. Then she turned around too fast and almost ran into me. "Oops! Sorry," she said. "Um, commemorative photo? 8 ½ by 11, suitable for framing. Only five dollars?"

"Sure, darlin'," I said. "I'll take one."

"Give me your name and address." She handed me what looked like a raffle ticket to write it on. "I'll have it to you by the end of next week."

"No hurry," I said.

I gazed over at Wild Bill, who hadn't moved a muscle, and thought again how talented this guy was, staying so perfectly in character. Cool as the Red Queen's dildo on a winter day. De Niro quality stuff. Then, all at once, he snapped his head to the left, intent on some calamity down the street, where New Main Street and Old Main Street locked horns.

I don't know why, but I followed his gaze and headed down that way. As I turned the corner onto New Main Street I saw her.

She was a mess.

Disheveled doesn't begin to describe it. Dirty face streaked with the tracks of tears. Sweat-stained clothes. Nut-brown hair in the tattered remains of a French braid. Faded jeans were torn at the knees, with blood dried on the fabric. Hands and forearms scraped, and thorn-scratched. Chambray shirt torn at the pocket. Her eyes were feverish, with a feral desperation.

"Can you help me, please?" she said.

Mark and Jessica were senior engineering students at UTEP. He was from Los Angeles. She was from New York City. They'd been dating for a few months, and decided that Old West Days was too cool to miss. On a friend's recommendation, they had come out early on Thursday, so they could get the ideal spot to pitch their borrowed tent. After taking a tour around the town, they decided that the trip would not be complete unless they hiked over to check out the "haunted" mountains that lay a few miles to the west.

El Labrinto.

No need to burden themselves with unnecessary baggage. Like water. Or food. Or matches. Or a goddam compass. No need to tell anyone where they were going. Have a quick peek, and come right back. What could go wrong?

They followed the official trail in as far as the sign that said: "Caution: Permit required beyond this point. Los Lobos County Sheriff." And then they went in a tiny bit farther, a hair past the point where the trail petered out. Jessica had gone off behind some brush to pee in privacy, and when she came back, Mark was gone.

At first she was mad, thinking Mark was teasing her. She called to him. Went looking for him. It was just a stupid game of hide and seek, she thought. When her shouts went from playful, to pissed-off, to pleading, and still went unanswered, she knew something was wrong.

Better get help.

Except in searching for Mark, she'd strayed far from the path, hadn't paid attention, and now couldn't be sure which way was back.

For the next forty-two hours, she'd stumbled and crawled up one dead end and down another, her only sustenance one 16-oz bottle of water. She finally found that sheriff's sign again — she had no idea how. But once she knew where she was, she had hobbled back to town as fast as she could on a badly sprained ankle.

She was now scraped, bruised, lame, exhausted, and dehydrated. And she was terrified that something even worse had happened to Mark.

This was not the first time someone had gone missing in The Maze, and the regular residents of Los Lobos knew what to do. While attending to the battered girl as best they could, giving her water and juice to drink, putting ice-packs on her swollen ankle, they did three things immediately. First they put in a call to the County Sheriff's Office about 30 miles away. Second, they sent someone out to fetch a guy named Kelly, who made part of his living as a guide, and who knew the Maze about as well as anyone did or could. Third, they put a call out to the Bonner Ranch to recruit some of the men for a search posse. After all, branding was in full swing and there was a whole lot of work to be done. It was no surprise that the call went unanswered. I volunteered to run out there personally with the news.

I broke land speed records in Frankie's trailer, and half a dozen cowboys mustered up to help with the search. More than one asked if anybody had sent for Kelly, and I told them that, yes, that had already been done. That seemed to close the deal. So the guys started hurriedly packing up their horses into trailers. Well, I sure as hell wasn't going to just stand there with my thumbs up my ass. I brought out Spartacus Jones, who again walked into the trailer without hesitation, casting me a quick look that said, "Let's go, Jack. Time's a-wastin'. You gonna drive, or what?"

The staging area was the foot of the mountains, where the official trail began. About half a dozen cowboys had come out, and were tacking up. I unloaded Spartacus Jones and followed suit, selecting the lighter of the two saddles stored in the tack cubby, and opting to use the halter for a bridle, doubling up a long lead rope to make reins. I've never been a fan of bits — bits are like a combination of handcuffs and taser — and it felt presumptuous and just plain fucking wrong to me to impose one on Jones, even the "gentle" egg-butt snaffle that Frankie

70

had aboard. Besides which, I couldn't see this particular horse taking kindly to it, going passively along with the idea. He was too proud, too smart, too strong, and too Horse. And this was no time to get into an argument.

The Chief of Police had come out, too. His truck was the official command post, but he obviously wasn't in command. Seemed like everyone was clearly waiting for something or someone to get the ball rolling.

Enter, Carlos Francisco de las Mercedes Kelly.

He was about thirty, rangy with a thick shock of jet-black hair that did whatever it felt like, and eyes nearly as large and nearly as brown as those of his pony, a fine paint mare. His skin was a deep reddish-bronze before it ever saw the sun, and he had a prominent, straight, sharp nose. Not a single thing about him suggested an Irishman straddling any recent branch of his family tree.

Where his left forearm should have been, there was a mechanical pincers/hook that he used with more dexterity than some people have with their own flesh and blood fingers. I wondered where he'd left that arm. And why.

He spotted me and came over. Actually, I think he spotted Spartacus Jones.

"I'm Kelly," he said. He didn't offer to shake hands, but he gave Jones a quick once-over with an expert eye. "I don't know you."

"I'm Jack," I said. I didn't offer a hand, either. When in Rome.

"Are you a cop, Jack?" Pretty impressive instincts for a human.

"Not anymore. Not for a long time."

"Ever do a search for a missing person?"

"Not in your neighborhood," I said. "But I catch on quick."

"Ok." Now he offered his hand and we shook. "That's a real fine horse you got there."

"We're just friends."

He almost cracked a smile.

"All right, listen up," Kelly said quietly. "It's been 48 hours. The missing boy is Mark Wasson, 21 year-old Caucasian, dark blonde hair, blue eyes, about six feet tall, weighing about 170. Last seen dressed in jeans, a blue and white plaid shirt over a white t-shirt, a navy blue baseball cap, and New Balance running shoes. He had no known supplies with him, so time is running out. If he's lucky, he found a stream. There are some running this time of year. He could be injured. Could be wandering around. Maybe both. Best-case scenario, he stayed put. But people tend to respond to being lost with anxiety and fear. So they're not thinking too well. Not making the best decisions.

"If he's been on the move for 48 hours he could be a long ways from where he was last seen. I've marked off the search area, based on my estimate of how far he might have gotten. You've got some natural features there that he's not likely to get past. That helps. That still leaves a lot of ground to cover. We'll take it step by step. If we don't bring him in by nightfall, we'll rally here and go out again at first light. If he hasn't had any water in 72 hours, this could turn into another recovery and not a rescue."

*Another* recovery?

I was starting to feel less than optimistic.

Kelly handed out a couple of radios and kept one for himself, gave everybody a map.

"Three teams," he said. " Frenchie, take a man with you and make your way up to the point. Walt, you take a partner and head down along the old streambed. Jack and me'll take the rest and string out from the middle trail. We're on channel 12. Check in every thirty, or if you find any sign. Sometimes the reception can be kind of shitty up here. In that case, three shots if you find something."

With Kelly leading the way, I took my place at the end of the conga line. We moved at a walk. For the next several hours, we tip-toed up, down, around, over, and through some of the most treacherous terrain I've ever seen — all of which Spartacus Jones traversed as easily as if he were ambling along in his own pasture seeking out dandelions or red clovers to snack on.

The Maze was no place for four-wheelers or such. To navigate that kind of ground you're going in on foot, or you're going in on horseback, or you're not going in at all.

It's true that a rescuer on a horse can carry more gear — first-aid bags, canteens, and so on — and go farther, faster, and for longer, than a rescuer on foot. It's also true that being tall in the saddle, a rider has a better, higher, longer view of the surroundings than a searcher on the ground has. And it's also true that, unlike a four-wheeler, your horse can refuel as he goes along. But that's not what makes a horse the ideal search and rescue partner.

72

The horse is a lot more than mere transportation.

Because a horse is a prey animal, he's tuned-in to the environment on an intimate level we can't begin to comprehend, and at a distance far, far beyond our paltry human perspective. In order to survive, the horse has to spot potential predators before those predators get within range, so he can do what the Great Spirit made him to do best: run like hell. A horse is always on the watch for trouble, will see and hear subtle things long before his comparatively retarded human rider ever will. The horse can even sense vibrations through the ground.

Dogs, being latter-day wolves, are predators and have a sense of smell that's somewhere between a hundred times and a million times better than that of a human. Horses have an olfactory sense as acute as most dogs or even better, and they can pick up the scent of a human on the air the way a schutzhund can. In addition to that, a horse can vary the aim of his nose from ground level to about seven feet high, and a horse can adjust the angle of his reception over a greater range than a dog can without moving his body. Now here's the clincher: dogs track upwind toward the source. By using all his senses synergistically, horses can also detect a threat that lies downwind.

When you're a search rider, your job is simple: stay out of the horse's way, and pay attention to what your horse tells you. To stay out of his way, you have to lose everything that would interfere with his natural intelligence, including bits, spurs, tie-downs, and your pompous human conceit. You let him move along picking his own footing — which allows you to use both eyes to look for sign of the missing person. If he wants to lower his head, you let him do it. If he wants to raise his head, you let him. If he wants to pause to look or listen, let him. Let the horse take the wheel, and don't be a backseat driver.

Paying attention means paying attention. Every sniff and snort, every cock of an ear or turn of the head, every pause, every sidestep, your horse is talking to you, telling you details about the world you live in that you'd otherwise miss with your own puny eyes, ears. and nose. In other words, the horse is the star of the show; you're nothing but a roadie.

There's something that mounted search and rescue riders know that every horseman should understand: a good horse isn't trained; a good horse is cultivated.

73

A good horse is one who is still a horse.

Most people ruin their horses. Most people want to micro-manage the horse until he won't sniff, snort, or fart unless you tell him to. They beat all the horse out of the horse. They want a horse that's dead to the world, a hairy robotic extension of their own petty egos. They want a horse that can't or won't think for himself, a horse whose intelligence and will must be always subservient to the "superior" human.

They call that "bomb-proof."

I call it slavery.

And if the horse is the slave, you know what that makes you?

If you answered "the master," then stop reading this book and go put your head in the oven.

The correct answer is "an asshole."

You want complete control with immediate, unquestioning, unhesitating obedience?

Buy a fucking motorcycle.

No matter where you go, no matter what you do, you interact with the environment. You disturb it. You leave some trace of yourself behind, and take some trace of it with you. That's the whole basis of forensic science, as any "CSI" fan can tell you.

When you search for a missing person, you don't just look for the person; you look for clues. There are dozens — hell, hundreds, and possibly thousands, of signs the person leaves behind, tiny changes in the natural state of things that result from that person's interaction with the environment. A man on foot, for example, taking about a twenty-inch stride, leaves at least 3000 signs per mile. The trick is to see them, and to see them before you trample them. And to figure out what they mean.

However, the day was wearing thin and nobody had yet picked up any sign of the missing boy. Not a bruised patch of grass, not a broken branch, not a thread of torn fabric, not a discarded gum wrapper, not a footprint, not insects clamoring over a recent urine deposit.

The future wasn't looking real bright.

In fact, it was looking darker by the minute as the sun slumped ever lower in the sky.

I was starting to think that the next place we'd be searching would be thin air and I almost missed the message. I asked Spartacus Jones to turn left a little and head back up the trail, and felt resistance. Instead of smoothly responding to my suggestion, as he had been doing until now, he suddenly went completely mule, and ignoring me, halted, cocked his head, and flared his nostrils, tasting the air deeply.

I'm embarrassed to say it took me a second to read him.

"Let's go look, then," I said, stroking his neck.

I alerted the other searchers, and we headed down a steep decline, sending waves of dust and stone down ahead of us.

There are some places even horses can't go, and young Mark Wasson had fallen into one of them. A thousand men shoulder-to-shoulder could have combed the area and still missed him.

He was barely conscious. Had a nice gash on his skull, and looked overall like somebody had dropped him into a blender. He drank some water, and asked, "Where's Jessica? Is she ok?" I made a point to remember to tell her that was the first thing he said.

It took some fancy rope-knotting, and some hauling from a saddle horn, but before too long, Kelly was on the radio saying, "All units, this is Kelly. We've extricated the subject and are transporting him now. Apparent head trauma, but subject is conscious, alert, and oriented. No other apparent injuries. What's the story on that medivac, Amos? Over."

"Kelly, Amos. Chopper's on the way. Over."

By the time we got back to town, Old West Days was winding down to Old West Night with none aware of the little drama that had been played out off stage as they kicked off the evening festivities. Hey, the show must go on.

I found some apples at Cal Hanshaw's store and Spartacus Jones and I ate a toast to his success on the search. He washed his down with water from the tank in the trailer. I washed mine down with a Los Lobos Sarsaparilla.

Tasted damn good, too.

Adam Adrian Crown

*Please allow me to introduce myself*
*I'm a man of wealth and taste*
*I've been around for a long, long year*
*Stole many a man's soul to waste.*
"Sympathy for the Devil"
The Rolling Stones

# CHAPTER NINE:
# WHEN THE DEVIL COME TO TEXAS

It was time to shove off.

Spartacus Jones had performed in spectacular fashion, J.T.Bonner couldn't have been happier about it, Frankie would be getting a nice fat check, and I was getting ready to hit the road. I'd come to like the place, though. Felt good being there. Not sure why.

Bonner surprised me with what she called "just a little something."

A hat.

It was a hat, like the HMS Queen Mary is a "boat."

This was not any old hat, but a handmade, 100% beaver fur hat. The kind of indestructible hat that a working cowboy could wear come sun, rain, snow, or stampede. A hat like that wasn't an article of clothing; it was a tool. And it pays to buy the best tools you can afford. A hat like that would be a long-term investment. Cost a rank and file cowboy about a month's wages, and was worth every red cent. This one was the color of sun-bleached bone. Almost white. The brim was flat, four and a half inches wide, with a tall, open crown. No curls, dents, creases or greasy kid stuff. A narrow grosgrain ribbon of matching color, finished in a bow.

"I don't know what to say," I said.

"No need to say anything at all," she grinned. "But if you have a mind to, you can say it to Harmon. It was his idea."

Harmon Cobb was sitting on the porch in his customary spot, one foot propped up against the porch rail, so he could rock back and forth like he was in a rocking chair which it wasn't. I moseyed over — I was fairly well skilled at moseying by now.

"I hear I've got you to thank for this," I said, holding up the hat like Vanna White showing the contestants what they'd won.

"Feller's got to have hisself a proper hat, son. You give it a dip in that stock tank yonder, and you can put some shape to 'er."

I did as he suggested, got it soaked, and returned with it.

"Got time to set a spell?"

I was all packed up. Nothing left to do but load Spartacus Jones into the trailer and be on our way.

"Yes, sir," I said, took the chair next to him, and started to massage a slight curl into that sombrero brim.

Cobb gave the world an unhurried 2000-yard circumspection, and sipped his coffee. He took a quiet moment, like a conductor getting ready to cue the orchestra to board the train, and then he took a deep breath and launched himself into his story. He told it like it was an epic Homeric poem he was reciting from memory, and in a way, that's what it was.

This is how it went:

"God willing and the crick don't rise, I'll be ninety-eight years old in a few days time. Some of the boys are fixin' to have a big doin's over it. Feller asked me t'other day how'd I live so long, and I told him I was too ornry to die, but truth to tell, I never give it much thought till he asked.

"Got all my own hair — white though it may be now — and all my own teeth, too. I can outwork three fellers a quarter my age and my pecker still shoots as straight as my old Colt .44.

"I been cowboyin' all my life, catching, herding, breeding, and training horses mostly. Workin' cattle some. It's hard work. Honest work. Been smoking a sack of tobacco every day since I was old enough to roll my own. I like my coffee black, my whiskey straight, and my women soft.

"I'm up before the sun just like I been for the last eighty years or so. I've outlived three fine women, five sons, and two daughters. I've outlived all my closest friends and all my worstest enemies. But I ain't no fool. I know my time's got to be a-coming, even if I can still ride all day and dance all night. So I'm tightening up my cinch and such, fixing to go when it's time. And since I'm the last living soul who knows the tale I'm about to tell you, I reckon it's all right and high time to git it offen my chest."

He gave me a sidelong look, to see if I was listening. I sure as hell was.

"You see, I was just a boy when the devil come to Texas.

"I was born and growed up in Los Lobos. At one time it was known as the wickedest town west of the Mississippi, and folks was kind of proud of that. By the time I come along it weren't all that wicked no more and weren't that much of a town no more neither.

"Some time back, a whole lot of cattle come through Los Lobos and a whole lot of outlaws, too. Just a hard spit from the Mexican border, it was a fine place to lay low if you had loot in your saddlebags, fire in your belly, and men on your trail. But them days was gone now. The James Boys and the Youngers, John Wesley Hardin, Billy Bonnie, Bill Hickok, Butch Cassidy and his Hole in the Wall gang, the Sundance Kid — them boys was all done. Onliest thing left was the stories folks told about them. Not much rustling, horse thieving, bank robbing or such to be done anymore and outlawing was purt near a dead profession. Except for a few sad old-timers who didn't know their times was past. I reckon I always figured I was born just a might late.

"My daddy got his fool self killed in the Spanish War. Hell, it didn't hardly last more than a hour and not but a handful of our boys was killed in it. My daddy was one of them. I weren't a year old yet, you see. So I never rightly knowed him. Seen a pichure once though. Handsome cuss, he was. Reckon that's where I get my own good looks, hey?"

Cobb winked at me to let me know he was just joshing me a might.

"By the time I was old enough to play with my pecker and get it right, I was the man of the family, though the family was just me and my Ma. To make ends meet she took in boarders. Now, I found out later that some of them boarders got a might more than a soft mattress and a plate of beans, but I don't fault her for that none. She was

79

providing for me the best she could and besides, a woman's got herself certain needs. I reckon it helped her feel less lonely for a bit.

"Now, you wouldn't think, what with the Spanish War and all, that folks in Los Lobos would elect themselves a Mex for town sheriff. I reckon you ought to know how that come about. On account of he's the one who faced down the Devil.

"Eduardo Alvarez had a little spread not far from our place. A real horseman he was, from a family of horsemen going back generations. Could be all the way back to them conkeestadories. Learnt most of what I know about horses from him. Got the rest directly from the horses.

"Anyways, he was a little sweet on this here Rujales girl whose folks owned the feed and livery in town. Always a-walking her here and there, like to think she might not find her way around without him. Church and such — them Mex's is cathlickers and real serious about it.

"One day, one of them Guinn boys from the Circle K ranch — Buddy Guinn I believe it was — got out of hand. It's a known fact that nothing can make a fool — or a corpse — out of a man faster than the combination of whiskey and a firearm. You get full of whiskey. You get full of yourself. And you're apt to get full of lead in the end. That there's natural arithmetic.

"This little señorita was on her way to church — don't know why Alvarez weren't with her at the time. Old Buddy Guinn decided he wanted to be friends. Lots better friends than the girl had herself a mind to be. Grab led to slap, slap led to push, push led to scratch, scratch led to a torn dress and the free sight of one of the sweetest looking teats I ever seen on a woman, including my Caroline, god rest her.

"Right then, Alvarez shows up.

"He and Buddy have a few words. Buddy swings on Alvarez, but Buddy's awful drunk and I don't believe he'd a been able to take that Mex even on his best day. As it turned out, Alvarez gave Buddy quite a pommeling. Did it in a right gentlemanly fashion, with his fists. No kicking or suchlike.

"Drunk as he was, Buddy wasn't so drunk that it didn't sink in that he was getting the worse of it. Should have quit right then and there. But he was packing his six-gun, a Smith and Wesson, if I recollect. What happened next was as predictable as getting wet in the rain. Sometimes the hand pulls the gun. Sometimes the gun pulls the hand.

"Buddy drew down on Alvarez.

"Now, to bob the tail of this story some, Alvarez took Buddy's gun away from him and whipped him with it something awful, didn't ease up 'til that young hothead of a cowboy was curled up, whimpering like a puppy dog.

"Then Alvarez picked Buddy up, dusted him off and asked would somebody take him over to Doc Miller's to get cleaned up. Couple of the boys stepped up to help Buddy along.

"That might have been the end of it and right ought to have been, too.

"'Ceptin' ole Buddy was a-carrying a hide-away gun and he pulled that out and took a shot at Alvarez's back afore anyone could keep him from it. Alvarez turned around and right as Buddy's second shot went wild, breaking the window of Mrs. Simon's Ladies Tailoring, he fired one clean shot right 'twixt Buddy's eyes. I reckon poor old Buddy was dead before his ass hit the dirt. Sad thing. He got just what he come begging for, though. Hell of a thing, gittin' shot dead with your own pistol. I reckon there's a lesson there.

"I remember real clear how Alvarez knelt hisself down beside Buddy Guinn and checked to see was there any life left in the boy. Then, real gentle, he closed Buddy's eyes, and mumbled something or other, saying a little prayer for the lad who'd just tried to kill him, and you'd a thought he'd lost his best friend from the way his eyes wetted up. I believe that right there was the very moment I decided to make Eduardo Alvarez my adopted Pa.

"Sad to say, that there weren't the end of it, neither.

"Them Guinn boys didn't take kindly to no Mex shooting down one of their kin, and they posse'd up and headed out to Alvarez's hacienda afore Buddy was settled in his grave. They surrounded the place round about midnight and took to shooting it out with him. Purt near a dozen of them boys and Alvarez all by his lonesome. Shot it out till sunup. The Guinns must have plunked a bullet into every square inch of Alvarez's cabin, from every angle you could shoot from. When they was done it was tattered as a old whore's lace hanky.

81

"About that time the Sheriff — amiable old cuss named McCall — come riding out to see what was what. It was all quiet right then and the Guinns naturally figured they must have got Alvarez so they never bothered theirselves to look inside to make sure of it. Lit out with a string of Alvarez's horses afore the Sheriff could face to face with them.

"I don't suppose as the Sheriff was mighty surprised that it come to this, knowing them Guinn boys as he did. But I'd reckon he was mightily goll-darned surprised to turn around and find Alvarez a-standing in what was left of his doorway without so much as a scratch on him.

"Spooked that Sheriff something terrible. How Alvarez lived through that flashflood of lead that broke every dish in his cabin, tore up his mattress, shredded up his clothes where they was in the trunk, and busted up two new saddles all to hell and gone, nobody could guess.

"That was when some folks took to calling him "El Gato" — which in Mexican means "the cat" — on account of he must have nine lives, you see. They say the Mex's made up a song about him. Them folks love to sing and they'll make up a song about most anything.

"Alvarez wanted the sheriff to bring the Guinn boys in, as any man would rightly want done. McCall weren't about to face those lads all by his self and he weren't like to get much help, folks knowing them boys to be quick on the trigger like. Truth to tell, McCall up and quit on the spot, leaving the town without any law at all. If Alvarez wanted him some justice, he was on his own for it.

"Now, nobody knows what happened next, exactly. But it's a true fact that Alvarez went out to the Circle K spread and somehow got the drop on them boys, one by one. He hog tied 'em up real snug and took 'em out someplace real private — took his string of horses back, too.

"What was said or done between them boys that night only they and God knows and they're all gone now and God ain't telling. You'll hear a lot of different tales told of it. And they're all horsemanure, plain and simple, on account of nobody seen it and nobody knows.

"All them boys got themselves back to the Circle K the next day, nary a mark on any of them and nary a word from any of them. It was downright peculiar. There was never a lick of trouble between El Gato

— or just "Gato" as the gringos called him — and the Guinns ever again.

"Truth to tell, Alvarez's grandson, or could be great-grandson, it was, married up with a Guinn girl. Course, not him or those particular Guinn boys would any one of them live to see that, but I did. Just goes to show, you can't never tell how things will go in the long run.

"A lot of folks had seen how El Gato handled his self with Buddy Guinn, real cool like, with a deadly hand and a tender heart, and word got around as how he'd settled things with the other Guinns and not a shot fired. With the office of sheriff empty thanks to old McCall's real sudden retirement, folks was getting a might nervous about not having proper laws to break, and they figured Alvarez was the man for the job. Mayor called a town meeting, put it to a vote and quick as that, Eduardo Alvarez got his self elected. Town Sheriff. Paid upwards of ten dollars a month, if I recollect.

"Me, I sort of reckoned myself Gato's un-official deputy. My duties was to follow him around like a lost pup, pestering him with questions and generally making a nuisance of myself. I was real dedicated to doing my job, too.

"And, being gentle as he was, he took to letting me go about it. I reckon he knew about my Pa. Lord, how I studied on that man, looking to walk like him, talk like him. I must have been quite a sight. But I don't regret it none. I could have done me a lot worse for a man to take for my example.

"It ain't just any man who can stand toe to toe with the Devil and have the best of it."

Cobb paused long enough to hand-roll a cigarette, and offer me the makin's, which I declined. He scratched a wooden match against the heel of his boot, and cradling the flame from the breeze, touched it to his smoke. He took a deep drag and blew it out with calculated satisfaction.

"The Devil hath the power to take a pleasing shape," he said. "Least wise that's what the Good Book says, if I recollect. Ain't done much bible reading in a while, not since my Maria Teresa passed. If ever the Devil took his self a pleasing shape, it was the night he appeared as the man who called his self Foster. No first name, mind you.

"He come at the proper time, I can tell you. It was August. There was a dry spell a-going on, drier than any scorcher anybody could recollect and it was intolerable hot. So hot that cattle and horses were shriveling up weak and dying. Felt as if the whole town was like to dry up and blow away. Hot as hell I'd call it.

"So the Devil would naturally feel right to home.

"We was in the Longhorn Saloon right after sunset. I believe I was near abouts ten years old. We'd just come from doctoring one of Gato's mares, a beautiful bay name of Corazon. She was weak and wistful from the heat. Horses don't fancy the heat. They can take the cold, but not the heat. I was setting with Gato, studying on the way he ate his steak. I knew he was a-worrying about that mare.

"That's when the Devil strode his self in.

"He was lasso lean with a face as gaunt as a mid-winter wolf. His eyes was as blue and clear and cold as a January morning, and they took in everything in one glance. His mouth was broad as a snake's and full-lipped and had a cruel set to it. His hair was corn yeller under his black, straight-brimmed Stetson, and longish, calling to my mind that arrogant fool Custer. His face were shaved clean as a baby's bottom as if to show off a scar that run from one corner of his mouth down the side of his chin. Wore a real fine black suit, he did. The like of which you might see on a preacher or a undertaker. Or the undertaken. Had a new Colt tucked into a belly holster, up on his left hip. You could just see the butt of it peeking out. The mark of a true pistolero.

"A lot of men still carried guns in them days. Most boys will wear their firearm on their leg. It's out of the way while you're a-working but still handy enough in a pinch. A belly holster is real subtle like, can't hardly tell if the man is going heeled. And it's easy and quick to get to. A man who carried his hand cannon in a belly rig, was like to fancy killing enough that he always wanted to be ready so's he could to do some.

"One thing that struck me peculiar was Foster's spurs. I'd have figured him for some fancy kind of silver spurs. His was just brass and steel. You could see the rust on them in places. They still jingled a tune when he walked, and he had that loose-hipped gunslinger gait that sends the ladies running for their smelling salts. Like he scarce weighed anything at all and what he did weigh was all pecker.

"I recollect he said to Freddie the barkeeper something like, 'May I have a bottle of your best whiskey, please. And a new deck of cards, if it's no trouble.'

"Never heard a man talk like him before or since. Seemed to whisper like, but you could hear him strong and clear, like his voice come from someplace else. Like them ventriloquist fellers used to do, you see. And it was too damn perfect. The way a play-actor talks. It weren't natural-like. Put a chill in my bones, I don't mind telling you.

"Soon as he come in, him and Gato traded a glance, real casual-like. A body'd think they didn't even see each other. But, truth to tell, I believe they both knew right then and there that they was going to have it out sooner or later.

"Foster got his self a bottle and a deck and, there not being much else to do, men come right over and sat in with him for some card-playing. Poker was the favorite back then. Every man fancied hisself a poker player. Dang few was correct about it.

"I suppose it ain't much of a trick for the Devil to win at cards. Foster won. Most always.

"The boys kept on a-playing him, no matter how much they lost. Could be the more they lost, the more they played. It was like they couldn't help theirselves. Before the night wore out there was quite a crowd collected to watch the goings on. Too hot for sleeping anyhow.

"Around about midnight Jed Honeywell left the game a-shaking his head and stopped by Gato's table.

'I've never seen a man win so much, Sheriff.' (Folks always called Gato "sheriff" when they was a-wanting him to do some lawmanin') 'It's downright — sacrilegious!'

"You see him bottom deal?" Gato asked, bottom-dealing meaning cheating in general, you see.

"Hell of it is I was dealing myself. He's good. He's real good. I mean he's real damn good."

"Gato shrugged and took a swallow of coffee on account of his doing his drinking only at home. 'Then don't play', he said.

"Jed grumbled and staggered out. Most of the boys did a fair bit of drinking along with their card playing which is a fool thing to do, but they done it. Foster drank up his fair share too, except to him it was like water. Didn't seem to worry at him one single bit.

"The Long Horn had three fine whores to brag of. They had names like Marie and Antoinette and Jezebel to make theirselves sound more wicked and exotic-like, I reckon. Didn't figure Martha, Sally or Caroline would put the lead in a man's pencil. They done some singing and some dancing but that was mostly to get the fellers worked up enough to go upstairs with them. I run errands for them ladies from time to time and they always treated me real nice.

"Now, the fact is, the Devil is hell on whores.

"After Foster had his fill of card playing and whiskey-drinking, he collected up his winnings, tossed enough back down on the table to buy a round of drinks for the house, and headed upstairs. Not with one of them girls. Or two of them girls. But with all three of them girls.

"I had me some idea what to do with one of them — I seen horses breed and such — but three? It was more than my young imagination could bear. Purt near wore out my arm a-thinking about it. And I expect I weren't alone on that score. Many a mouth hung right open for watching him take all them girls up that long staircase.

"I don't know exactly what he done with them whores, but the next day they all three of them looked real peaked like they was plumb wore out. All the paint in the world couldn't liven up the pallor of their cheeks, nor put a light in their eyes. Not even the gay satin or velvet ribbons they took to wearing round their necks could make them seem more lively.

"In the morning, Foster was gone.

"Nobody seen him leave, as far as Gato could find out by casual asking. Hadn't put his horse in the livery neither. Now, men do like they do and they don't all do alike, so nothing much was thought of it. Leastways, not till the next night when Foster come back again and done right like he done the night before. And did likewise every night, night after night for — I don't recall how many. But it seemed like quite a spell to my young mind.

"Not a body took much notice of the Apache who come to town right about then.

86

"Mex's and Injuns come and go all the time along the border. Gringos tend not to see them and when they do, tend to think all Mex's and all Injuns look pretty much the same, like to can't tell one apart from another. I don't agree, of course. That's ignorance a-talking. I didn't hardly know no better at the time, neither.

"Even back then, there weren't no mistaking this here Injun for any other.

"Rugged-looking buck he was. Good-looking, I reckon, in an Injun kind of way. Like his face was chiseled out of stone. He was a Mescalero, if I recall — was wearing a derby hat and a duster. I could see his trouser legs when that duster swung open — striped pants the like a banker might wear. No boots; moccasins. Tall moccasins, though, so they was kind of like boots. Had this here fringe all around the top.

"Anyways, he come into the jailhouse while I was a-studying on how Gato wrote his letters.

"'Afternoon, Sheriff,' he said, his voice low and smooth like clover honey. Talked his English real good. Then he turned to me and smiled a tad. 'Afternoon, deputy,' he said to me.

"I liked that Apache right off.

"'What brings you to Los Lobos, Señor?' Gato asked it real friendly-like. Funny thing, I can't rightly recollect now whether they started talking Ingles or Español. It didn't matter none to me as I could do one or the other about as well.

"'I'm tracking a man,' the Apache said. 'Sometimes he calls himself Foster.'

"Mind if I ask why?"

"'Telling why might take some time.'

"Gato pointed to a extra chair. 'I have some time.'

"The Apache pulled up that chair, straddled it and spun us his tale. It was quite a tale, too. Like a rattler's.

"His name was 'Watches-Much-Sky' which got whittled down in Spanish to just 'Tanto,' and which to my ear sounded sort of stupid that way. But that's how them things goes.

"According to him, Foster come to the Apache Reservation near Sumner a few years back. Started taking up with some of the Apache women. They'd a-been having themselves a dry spell then, too. And it brought along some kind of wasting disease that struck down cattle and horses and people, alike. That sort of thing happens pretty regular on the reservation, though. It ain't no good of a place to live. Especially not if you been used to running free up in the mountains, hunting and fishing as you please and not having to kiss some Injun Agent's fat ass for a cup of wormy cornmeal.

"This here wasting sickness put down their women. Especially the women that Foster was knowed to have been with. Watches-Much-Sky's older sister was one of them.

"After she was buried, she appeared to Watches in a dream and in that dream, she said she was aching with heat and thirst, and asked him could she drink some of his blood.

"Watches woke up scared witless, and was sure that it had been a medicine vision, not just your regular penny-candy dream.

"Injuns is big on visions, you see. Somehow he knew that his sister's spirit and the spirits of some of his other folks had become slaves to this here Foster. They couldn't go on to the next world on account of that.

"So Watches took to hunting Foster down. On his trail purt near three years now, just missing him here and there. Closest he come to him was in Mesa Redondo. Got close enough to see Foster shoot it out with William Rawlins in the Redondo Hotel saloon.

"William Rawlins was known as 'Texas Bill.' He was a real pistolero, famous for his quick-draw and fancy shooting. Had done some lawmanning in Oklahoma where he'd put enough men in the ground that the rest quit trying him out.

"Foster shot Rawlins dead.

"'You mean to say that Foster out-drew Texas Bill?' Gato was getting set to be impressed.

"'No,' answered Watches. 'No, he didn't. I saw it. Texas Bill was faster.'

"You're saying Bill missed him?

"'No.'

"I don't understand, amigo. What are you saying?

"The other man was faster and shot Foster here, Watches explained, touching his fingers to his heart. 'It was as if the bullet was nothing. My eyes saw this.'"

It was quite a tale, all right.

"Suppose you find this man? asked Gato. Then what?

"'I must kill him.'

"Gato drew a deep, slow breath as he was like to do when he was about to say something important. 'Mister, I'm sorry for your sister and for your people, but I can't let you come to my town and kill a man who hasn't done anything here, as far as anyone knows.'

"'Your horses and cattle grow weak, do they not?' asked the Apache.

"We're in the middle of a bad drought..."

"'He takes your women and they grow weak, too,'" he added.

"I wouldn't know about that."

"'He fears the light of the sun. No one has ever seen him except in the night.'

"That doesn't prove much, Señor. Men work the range days, do their drinking at night."

"'He is not a man.'

"'So you say. I hope you understand that your story is not an easy one to believe.'

"'I understand,' Watches nodded. 'You must understand that this one must die.'

"Perhaps. But any killing to be done in Los Lobos, my friend, and I'll do it myself. It's my duty here. Not yours."

"'Examine your horses, Sheriff. Look for dried blood. Like the bites of flies but much bigger. Examine the women, too. Here,' he pointed his fingertips at the side of his neck.

"'If I am wrong...' he shrugged. 'If I am right, you will need these.'

"He dug into his pocket then and took out a handful of bullets and pressed them into Gato's palm. I only got a glimpse of them, but they looked to me like they was made out of silver.'

"I don't mind telling you this Injun's story spooked me up my spine, down to my heels and back again. Not Gato, of course. He took it cool and calm as you please. Said nary a word about it all next morning, just set there quiet like, comforting his Corazon. She was doing mighty poorly and I reckon that put everything else right out of his mind. She wouldn't even eat a bite of carrot. Gato put a little salve on a couple sores he found on her neck and headed into town.

"He went right over to see Toby at the telegraph office and I naturally went along with him.

"'Here's the message,' Gato told Toby. It was a purty detailed description of Foster right down to that chin scar. And asking was there any warrants out on him. 'And this is the list of people I want you to send it to.'

"Toby let out a low whistle and pawed at his walrus mustaches like an old, grey dog.

"'That's quite a list there, Sheriff. Gonna take some time...say, are you paying for this or the town or...'

"'Tell them it's urgent,' Gato nodded. 'Send the bill to me.'

"'Yes, Sir, Sheriff. I'll get right on it.'

"By sundown, Gato had got some of his answers.

"When Gato was fixing to head over to the Long Horn to see was Foster there, he told me to stay put at the jail. 'Take care of things here,' was what he said, but I knew he was trying to keep me out of harm's way. I believe it was the only time I willfully disobeyed the man. I give him a head start, then followed along. I watched the whole rodeo by poking my fool nose around the corner under the swinging saloon door. By the time I got to peeking in, Gato was a-standing up facing at Foster.

"Foster was sitting at what had come to be his usual table. He had a pile of winnings in front of him, and the Long Horn's three whores hovering around him looking sort of blank and pale, eyes kind of feverish, like to recall a rabid fox. Foster tossed his self down a hefty gulp of whiskey like it were sarsaparilla."

"'I'm going to have to lock you up, Mister,' Gato was saying."

"'Me?' said Foster, grinning like a wolf. 'Whatever have I done?'"

"There's a warrant out on you for the murder of William Fenimore Rawlins."

"That was a fair fight, Sheriff."

"That's for a jury to decide. You'll be my guest until the federal marshal can come and take you back to stand trial."

"Foster eased his chair back and stood up too, in no particular hurry. Folks got away from him like fleas a jumping offen a wet calf.

Then he smiled. It was a queer kind of a smile. Smug like. A man who knowed his self a secret.

"'I'm sorry, Sheriff,' Foster said. Still grinning. 'I'm afraid I'll have to decline your gracious hospitality.'

"That was all there was to say."


"In my life, I've seen many a man die. Some of them from a bullet. A few times from my bullet. I seen them die fast and I seen them die slow. I seen them die easy and I seen them die-hard. I seen them go peaceful as a babe at momma's teat, and I seen them die a-choking and fightin' for one more breath.

"I never seen a man die the way Foster died that night.

"I've studied on it on many a sleepless night since and I come to figure that it worries at me so on account of how he stood there, calm as you please. So confident he was chafing right up against cocky. You'd a-thought Gato weren't even heeled.

"And then, in the time it takes to skin leather and fire, which ain't much time at all for any kind of pistolero, that smug-like set was all gone out of him and his face went plumb pale, and it was all a-twisted like barbed wire. His eyes bulged out the way a horses eyes are like to do when a mountain cat pounces on his withers, or when he smells smoke in a barn.

"Foster's mouth stretched out real wide open but not one sound come out. He let his gun drop from his fingers and took to clawing at the wound like he was fixin' to dig that bullet out of his chest with his bare hands.

"This weren't a man in pain, even gutshot pain.

"This weren't a man afeared to die.

"This here were a man a-looking into the maw of hell itself, with tortures beyond a sane man's mind to imagine, a-waiting for him. And the knowing of it filled up his face with a kind of soul-ripping terror that was so deep you like to pity him. He looked right into my eyes, and I pert near wet myself.

"The moment Gato's bullets tore into Foster's body, a stink something terrible come into that room like it were leaking out from the holes in Foster instead of blood. Weren't no way to mistake it; it was the putrid stink of dead and rotting flesh. And it was powerful strong. Like to made me puke.

91

"Then, real slow, Foster sunk back against the bar and down to the floor, mouth a-gaping open, a look of horrorfied surprise left hanging on his face.

"And that was the end of that.

"Mostly.

"Gato had a couple of fellers heft Foster's body over to Smalley's Funeral Parlour. I noticed how their noses wrinkled up at the smell of him. As they carried Foster out, Gato picked Foster's pistol up offen the floor and tucked it into his waistband. That was the last time I saw it and I never could figure what become of it. Back at the jailhouse, Gato took the cartridges out of his own .44. Two was spent; four wasn't. He gave me one.

"That there bullet was sure enough made of silver."

"It rained that night a cool, clean rain, down from the mountains. It sprung things back to life quick as a cat can catch cream. Grass greened up, Corazon took to dancing and prancing, and even the Long Horn's three whores seemed to get their color back.

"The next morning, it being Sunday, I was fixing to go to church with Gato like I often done, though the truth is I ain't much for psalm-singing and never was.

"We was just out the jailhouse door when Mr. Smalley the undertaker come a-running up with a look on his face I never seen afore.

"'Sheriff, -y-y-you have to come quick,' Mr. Smalley's mind was galloping hard but his tongue was trotting easy. 'I just...I don't know what to...just come, Sheriff. Come right now!'

"At the funeral parlor, Mr. Smalley showed us the casket where he'd laid out the late lamented Mr. Foster. It was empty.

"Not entirely empty.

"Foster's clothes was in it, all buttoned and buckled like they should be, but there was no body in them. Only the shadow of a body. A shadow made out of dust.

"Gato told Mr. Smalley to fill the casket with rocks and bury it just the same. Smalley weren't much inclined to do that, but Gato told him it was the only way he'd be paid, so that more or less inclined him."

Cobb examined the bottom off his coffee cup, frowned at it, tossed the cold dregs off into the dirt.

"Flappin' yer gums is thirsty work," he said. "I believe I'll get me another cup."

But he didn't get up. Sat and stared into the empty cup a moment. Then turned his head slightly, barely enough to look at me out of the corner of his eyes.

"If you was to go to the old cemetery in Los Lobos, you could find Foster's grave, if you had a mind to. And you could dig 'er up. But you won't find no bones. There ain't nothing buried there but rocks and I'm the last living soul who knows what fer.

'Ceptin' you." He pointed a finger at me to put a period on it, and stood up, stretched his back.

I got up, too.

He reached out to me and I thought he wanted to shake with me, but as I took his hand, he pressed something into my palm.

It was a bullet.

"Adios, son. You be safe on the road, and take care of that pony. He's a good 'n."

Then he went inside, and I went to load Spartacus Jones.

Later, after I got back and squared things away, I went down to a jeweler who has a shop on the Ithaca Commons, and I showed her that bullet.

She said it was made of silver.

*I won't take all that they hand me down,*
*And make out a smile, though I wear a frown,*
*And I won't take it all lying down,*
*'Cause once I get started I go to town.*
"I'm Not Like Everybody Else"<br>The Kinks

# CHAPTER TEN:
# HALFWAY INN

I hate walking in, in the middle of something.

It's awkward.

You don't know what's going on and you can't always be sure things are the way they appear to be, even if your gut is usually right, like mine is.

One time, when I was a kid — I must have been 5 or 6 — I came in — unexpectedly, I guess, and dashed upstairs to the room I shared with my older sister. Unexpected, see? Yeah.

I didn't expect her to be laying across the bed with her pants off while our step-father leaned over her with his pants puddled around the ankles of his work boots like dirty khaki foam on a sea of old floorboards. I was stunned. And puzzled. I didn't know what to do or say, stay or go, sneeze or bleed. The old man looked at me with those beer-bleary eyes as he finished pumping, pulled out, and finished by jacking off on her ass. All the while he looked at me like my being there didn't matter at all. Like to him I wasn't even really there. Like he was proud of fucking that little girl and wanted to show off his semen shooting on her back. A symbol of power. Ownership.

Funny, I hadn't thought about that in a lot of years. Not since I'd split the old man's head open with a wine bottle and split town heading for place or places unknown. I thought of it now, though, as I walked into the "bar and grill" of the Half Way Inn. "Thought" is the wrong word. It flickered through my mind, just under the surface of my memory where I couldn't really see it, but could feel it was there. Like a shark skimming by, bumping me a tiny bit to see if I was edible.

I had pulled off the interstate to make a sentimental journey, and wound up dazed and confused somewhere near the actual geographical middle of nowhere, and with a storm rumbling vague threats like a belligerent drunk. The pale red neon that said "Dick's Half Way Inn," was like an omen — I had my head about halfway up my ass, navigationally speaking — and I quickly decided to humor the gods and duck in there. If nothing else, I figured I might be able to get directions back to the interstate. As I pulled in, the wind changed moods, took on a cold edge, and a splatter of raindrops hit my windshield like a burst from an AK and beaded on the road-grimy glass. I parked on the far side of the lot near a pavilion that hovered over a couple of picnic tables. There was only one other vehicle in the lot. A new Caddy.

There were no signs of any recent picnic-related activity and I didn't figure there would be that many picnickers tonight, so I made myself right at home. The pavilion was about 15 x 20. I had plenty of rope in the truck and quick as I could, I hauled those two picnic tables out of the way, and strung up two strands of rope around the 6x6 posts that held up the roof. The roof was plenty high and clear span which was perfect and no one had mowed the lawn recently so there was plenty of grass, too.

I popped open the trailer and brought out Spartacus Jones. He was glad to be out. Didn't care for being confined. Pranced and jigged some to celebrate, make sure everything still worked. I roped him in inside the pavilion and after he tasted the wind to assess the coming storm, he set to trimming that grass down. He wasn't a big drinker, but I drew off 5 gallons worth of water from the reservoir in the trailer, setting the bucket against a post, and tossed him a flake from our stash of hay.

With Spartacus Jones settled in for the time being, I headed for the alluring lights of the Inn.

Sign said "Bar & Grill," and "Rooms." I was primarily interested in the "bar" part. Another sign said "Karaoke Every Saturday Night."

Karaoke. Great. I had arrived at the garden spot of all Nowhere. I said a silent "thank you" to the spirits that it was Friday night and not Saturday.

I stepped inside as rain starting coming down by the tubful.

And that's when I walked right into that middle-of-something I was telling you about.

The folks in the bar (and grill) froze in mid-action, like kids playing "red light-green light," to give me the once over. I felt like a cowboy, stumbled on to the set of a John Ford western.

Dominating the scene was a nasty piece of work. He was about a super-middleweight weight, in his 40's with prematurely steel grey hair in a jarhead haircut, deep-set blue eyes. Lean as a last-minute excuse, he had a permanent scowl and a scar that hyphenated one brow. Expensive suit. No tie. Oversized hands. Canine mouth like the Big Bad Wolf.

He stood looming over a 20-something woman. Her hair had been dyed and fried so many times it had no recollection of its original color or texture. It was currently blonde. She was runway skinny in tight leather pants and a loose low-hanging top that showcased her silicone tits. She wore enough make-up to share with those less fortunate. Her hazel eyes were feverish, there was a ring of blood around one nostril, a smear of it across her mouth, and she cradled her cheek with the palm of one trembling hand as if Mr. Steel Grey had just bitch-slapped her.

Which he had.

Seated at a table that was awash with beer bottles, glasses, and plastic serving baskets were a couple of other guys. One was Italian-looking. A cruiserweight. Bald on top, earring, and what he thought was a dapper mustache. He was enjoying the show that Mr. Steel Grey was putting on, almost as much as he'd enjoyed tearing the wings off of flies as a child. He had the huge biceps and the matching chipmunk cheeks that identified him as a steroid abuser. So he came on like a tough guy but he was really a chickenshit little weasel. All his "tough" was on the surface. No balls. He was wearing a black polo shirt, tight at the sleeves to show off his arms, and untucked to not show off what was either a large tumor, or a piece he was carrying on the right side of his waistband. He was dangerous because he was a coward. When you're a coward, everything's a threat. Cowards tend to panic early and shoot first.

The other character was a different matter. He was beefy, built like a defensive linebacker. Had to be 260 if he was an ounce. Cheap suit. Wedding ring. Stubby fingers. Hands like paws. A little red-faced with dead, detached eyes, and an expression absent of affect. I knew the look. He didn't give a fuck. He'd kill you without hesitation, and without remorse, not because he enjoyed it, but because you were inconvenient. In his way. Like an ant on the sidewalk. Nothing personal, see?

I don't know what's worse: a guy who enjoys inflicting pain, or a guy who's indifferent to the pain he inflicts. For the former, it can be an end in itself. For the latter, it's a means to an end. The difference is too close to call from the bleachers.

Behind the bar was Aunt Bea's evil twin. Once-blonde hair piled up into a matronly Gibson girl bun that had gone out of style a century earlier. Dirty apron over huge breasts. Cigarette dangling from the corner of her mouth. Sleeves rolled up revealing biker tattoos on both forearms. Hazel eyes busy, calculating. Very cool. I'll bet she had some stories to tell.

Just the six of us. The place was otherwise empty. Cozy.

"Help you?" Aunt Bea said.

The rest of the cast awaited my next line with tense anticipation.

"Kitchen open?"

"Just burgers."

"Burger's good," I said, and as I crossed to the bar, the denizens of the Half Way Inn recovered from their suspended animation, with me now the center of their attention.

Great.

I perched on a barstool.

"Drink?" asked Bea.

I perused the bottles on the shelf.

"White Horse, neat," I said. White Horse. Another omen. The spirits like to fuck with people.

Bea was fast and loose with her booze. I like that in a bartender. I tossed down the Scotch before she'd returned the bottle to its place, which was demarcated by a thick crater of dust.

"Whoa," I said. "Don't you go too far with that, darlin.'"

She poured me another, easily a double. I think it may have been quite a while since anyone had called her "darlin.'"

"Is it ok if I use that picnic area you got out there?"

"Use it for what?"

"Camping' out with my pony."

"You clean up after yourself. I don't want piles of horseshit out there."

"You'll never know we were there. I promise."

"I guess that's all right. How do you want that burger, Cowboy?"

"Medium should do it." Ordinarily, I'd have been inclined to kick the shit out of anyone who addressed me as "cowboy," but, after my visit to the Bonner Ranch, I was starting to mellow on that, and she spun it like it was French for "lover," so I let it lay. Besides, it was my own damn fault.

It was this hat. Let's face it: it's a cowboy hat. A damn fine hat. A generous gift. A perfect, comfortable fit. I liked that hat. But a cowboy hat, after all.

"What'd ya want on it?"

"Give me everything you got."

That made her grin.

"Think you can handle everything I got?" She gave me her version of bedroom eyes.

"Only one way to find out," I said.

She raised her head and bellowed to the room at large in a voice that only large women can have. "You folks ready for another round? I'll be in the kitchen for a bit."

She set everyone up with drinks and left the bottle of White Horse on the bar by my elbow. "Go ahead and help yourself if you get thirsty."

I gave her the wink-nod combo platter. "Much appreciated," I said.

Then I focused on my drink and did my best to mind my own damn business with three goons staring holes in my back.

My best didn't cut it.

There was a mirror on the wall behind the bar shelves. I don't know why bars do that. Make it look like they have twice as much booze? In this case it allowed me to observe the goings on behind me without having to turn around and look, and I didn't want to turn around and look. Mr. Steel Grey ambled up to me in an overly jaunty way, leaning back, hips jutting forward like his dick was way too strong for him and was pulling on the leash. The guys at the table watched closely like they were expecting some entertainment.

He leaned on the bar next to me, gave me a direct stare like he was intent on memorizing every detail of my face because he'd never seen one like it before and it was puzzling. He was close enough that I could smell the whiskey on his breath. Close enough that I could spot, under the tip of his nose, a faint trace of something that could have been powdered sugar, but wasn't. He was close enough that I knew he was testing me, invading my space with a silent threat, testing to see who had the bigger dick. But I never show mine unless it's necessary.

When you're faced with a threat, there are four possible things you can do.

You can run and hope that the threat can't run as fast as you can.

You can yield, and hope that yielding will be enough to mollify the threat. Give the mugger your money and hope he won't knife you anyway. Let the rapist fuck you and hope he doesn't kill you. Kiss the cop's ass with "Sir's" and hope he won't beat you, taser you, or shoot you anyway.

You can posture, try to make yourself look threatening, and hope the threat won't call your bluff. Puff out your chest. Talk shit. Call names. Insults. Give warnings about what bad shit you're going to do to the threat.

Or you can fight – by which I mean to unleash a raging maelstrom of such overwhelmingly relentless fury that the threat will cease to exist.

Me, I don't run, yield or posture.

I do nothing.

Until it's time to do something.

And when it's time to do something, I do it all. Pedal to the floor, no foot on the brake, all-out, no-holds-barred, one of us dies. Possibly both of us. But you, for sure.

For me, it's not a volume knob that you can adjust perfectly, degree by degree. For me, it's a toggle switch: it's either off or on. No in-between's.

I know this about myself, and knowing it keeps me out of a lot of mundane trouble. If it isn't worth killing the guy over, then fuck it. It isn't even worth fighting about. But you step on my blue suede shoes, baby, and I'll do everything I'm capable of doing to cause you to regret that step with profound sincerity.

The advantage I have over most people is that I have this knowledge. I know what dark and bloody deeds I'm capable of. And it scares me. It scares me more than anything my antagonist threatens me with. But it also appeals to me, the freedom in letting go, turning it loose, like a horse who loves to run, and you have to work like hell to hold him back, keep that wild urge in check. You give him his head and let him gallop as hard and fast as he wants, taking you wherever he wants to go.

When some minor league jack-off is running his mouth at me, he has no idea what he's fucking with. I've got the equivalent of my .45 always in my pocket, cocked and ready to rock. All I have to do is squeeze the trigger. He doesn't know it, but I know it. And knowing it lets me be relaxed enough to control the situation. All his posturing doesn't threaten me, because if I need it, I've got the trump card to trump all trump cards.

In the current situation, since it wasn't necessary to act, it was necessary NOT to act. So I ignored him. I figured that would prompt him to up the ante, or fold.

He didn't fold.

"How you doing there, Cowboy?" he said.

Fucking hat.

"Let me buy you a drink?"

I didn't like him. I didn't like whatever was going on. But I don't particularly like getting mixed up in other peoples' shit, either. Only a fool stops to throw a stone at every dog that barks at him. I decided to play it light, be non-confrontational.

"Thanks," I smiled. "I've got one."

"How about a raincheck? After you get some food in you? How's that sound?"

"Sounds ok."

"Good. We're having a little party. Thought we'd invite you to join the celebration." He put on a toothy grin, but it was all mouth, nothing in the eyes. The eyes were the eyes of a dog wanting to bite, looking for a reason. Still testing.

"What are you celebrating?" I said.

The question stumped him for a moment. He turned to the rest of his entourage.

"Hey," he said, "the cowboy wants to know what we're celebrating." That elicited a chuckle from the dapper mustache, a wince from the young woman, and nothing at all from Redface.

"Leave him alone, Dutch," the woman begged.

"I ain't bothering him," Steel Grey Dutch objected. "I'm just being friendly. I ain't bothering you, am I, Cowboy?"

The Jets started singing in my head, "Boy, boy... crazy boy. Stay cool, boy...."

"No," I said. "You're not bothering me."

"There, see?" he told her, spreading his arms wide in innocent supplication. "I'm not bothering him." Then, to me, he said, "I guess you could say we're celebrating Friday night. We're just high on life, know what I mean?"

That was so funny that dapper mustache almost gave himself a hernia trying not to laugh out loud.

"Lee was just gonna sing us a song to celebrate. Right, Lee?"

"Please, Dutch," she cranked up the whine.

"Bullshit. The cowboy'd like to hear you sing – wouldn't you, Cowboy?" He used the word "cowboy" but he obviously meant, "faggot." He was trying to get a rise out of me, but I wasn't taking the bait. You press, I disengage. Now you see me, now you don't. That damned elusive pimpernel. I looked the woman called Lee right in the eye, connected with her.

"If she wants to sing, I'd be happy to listen," I said to her.

"There you go," said Dutch. "Sing for us and I'll do something nice for you." There was only one nice thing he could do for her. It was written all over her. She didn't want to sing. She didn't want anything but a fix. She needed to score. Needed it bad. And Dutch was her candy man, keeper of the crack. Still she hesitated.

"Sing," Dutch demanded roughly, making it sound like "suck it, bitch," which indeed was the literal translation. He was gifted at speaking those two languages at once.

She kept her eyes glued to mine.

"I'll sing something for you," she said to me.

She approached the tiny karaoke stage like she was walking up the steps to the guillotine. Dutch nudged me with his elbow, gave me a grotesquely exaggerated wink. Not enough that she was going to suck him off. He wanted me to watch her suck him off.

My ears started feeling hot.

Then the music started up. A slow-dancing dirge. A twangy country arrangement so heavy on pedal-steel guitar, that I didn't recognize the song until Lee launched herself into the lyrics.

She sang:

"I'm a fool...to want you. Just a fool...to want you. To want a love...that can't be true. A love that's there...for others, too..."

I was doubly surprised. First, that the twanging country thing in my ears was one of my favorite songs, a song I'd played many, many times, myself. I had the Chet Baker version somewhere amongst my tapes in the trailer. The second surprise was that this palpably burned-out chick could really actually sing. And I mean SING.

Her voice was clear and strong and, while she sang, it seemed to hold the full torment of her pain at bay by letting it out, giving it a shape and sound, an expression of her own choosing, under her own control. I knew exactly where she was coming from. She sang directly to me, as if we were alone in the room.

Suddenly, we weren't strangers anymore.

Fuck.

"Time and time again I said I'd leave you," she sang, and I could feel a fist squeezing my heart. "Time and time again I went away. But then would come the time when I would need you. And again, these words I'd have to say: Take me back; I love you..."

Everyone in the room was silent and still, under the spell of the singer and the song. Aunt Bea had brought out my burger in a plastic basket with some potato chips and a sliver of pickle on the side, set it on the bar and now stood enthralled, unwelcome tears welling up in her hard eyes as Lee finished.

"I know it's wrong. It must be wrong. But right or wrong I can't get along...without...you."

The music twanged itself out and for a moment, there was nothing in the bar but the echo of the song. With Lee's eyes and mine still locked together, I put my hands together for her. I slid off the barstool, and clapped some more. She deserved a standing ovation in my book. She understood what I was saying. Aunt Bea joined in enthusiastically. Dapper mustache joined in, too. Dutch didn't like that, his eyes darted to each of us in turn, our applause a shocking betrayal. He had lost control and had to regain it.

"Bobby," he summoned, and dapper mustache perked up like a pet Doberman. Dutch nodded in Lee's direction and Bobby dug something out of his coat pocket, walked it over to her. I didn't see what it was. Didn't have to. Lee took it and rushed out without a word, and Bobby sauntered back to his chair.

Dutch spun on his stool to face me.

"Not bad, huh, Cowboy?"

"Not bad at all," I said. I had the most delightful image of shoving my hat down his throat.

I dug into my burger, and Dutch got bored with me and joined his pals at their table.

"How's that burger?" prompted Aunt Bea.

"A work of art, darlin'," I told her between swallows, "If this was any better, it would be illegal."

That seemed to please her. She twisted me up a smile.

"You gonna want a room?" She asked.

"I think I'll camp out next to my pony. I need to keep an eye on him."

"On a night like this? He must mean a lot to you."

"He does."

"A cowboy and his horse, huh?"

"I guess."

"Well, if you need anything — anything at all — I'm in 101."

"Much appreciated." I told her, pretending to be obtuse in regards to the anything she was offering.

As I polished off the last of the burger, I heard Dutch say, "You about ready to join us for that drink, Cowboy?"

They were ranged around their table, now, the four of them. Dutch reached over, grabbed a chair from another table and pulled it over.

"I've been saving you a place," he said.

Without my asking, Aunt Bea poured me another double and slid it to me. I took it and went over to the table.

"Thanks," I said to Dutch. "I guess I could have one more before I turn in."

A peal of thunder shook the windows. I didn't know if the spirits were trying to warn me, or were laughing at me.

"You've got to let me buy you one back, though," I added. Dutch laughed. There was no humor in it.

"I'm Dutch," he said. "This is Bobby and George. And you already kinda met Lee."

Lee had returned feeling no pain. She was in a languid, drowsy condition some might find sexy. Not me.

"I'm Johnny," I said, because my name was none of their fucking business, and I straddled the chair. Dutch did all the talking for his ensemble.

"What brings you to our neck of the woods, Johnny?"

"Passing through."

"Where you headed?"

"East."

It was all superficially friendly and civilized small talk. But he was jabbing, testing my reflexes, looking for an opening. He wanted information. I wasn't giving him any. That pissed him off, but he kept that frozen smile aimed my way. Nobody else entered the conversation.

I drank the drink he bought me. And he drank the one I bought for him. Lee was out of it, but gazed at me as if trying to catch my eye, a pick-up gaze I ignored.

Dutch checked his watch again. He checked it a lot. I wondered who or what he was waiting for.

"Let's play some cards," he said, like a bored child coming up with a bright idea on a rainy indoor play day. Bobby groaned. George remained impassive. "You play poker, Johnny?"

It wasn't as simple a question as you'd think.

See, I used to enjoy playing cards. Back in the waybackwhen. During my ill-spent youth. When I was a city cat. Seems like about a thousand years ago, now. I wasn't a terrific player. A shade better than average, maybe. Maybe not.

There was a small group of friends, or friendly acquaintances. Friendly enough that everyone's marker was good, and no one would ever dream of welching on a bet. They got together quite often, almost always on a Saturday night. There were a dozen or so members of this group, three or four of whom were "regulars." All but one were male. Other than that, it was quite diverse. Several, like my boss, were black.

One was openly (at least within the group) gay. Italian, Irish, Hispanic. It was like gambling at the UN.

I was invited to sit in by my then boss, SWML. I'm not sure why. I think he regarded me as he would a stray kitten he'd decided to feed and look out for. I suspect that comparison is more apt than I'd like.

I was the youngest guy in the room — and the dumbest. I had recently earned the nickname "Billy the Kid," which was not intended to be complimentary — but not altogether a condemnation, either. My boss sometimes addressed me as "double-o," as in double-o-seven, Bond, James Bond. That gives you an idea of how melodramatically I played myself, how little I knew, and what a source of amusement I must have been for the older, and more experienced. In general, the attendees at the game called me "kid," but not in an insulting way. Hey, I was a kid. They were introduced to me by their first names, and so I addressed them that way. Except for my boss. I called him "boss." Not very original, I know.

When I say "cards," I mean poker. And when I say poker, I mean straight poker, with 5-card stud as an occasional change of pace. It was the understanding. No liar's poker with 3's, 6's and 9's wild. Nothing like that.

Different players hosted the games, at their homes or hotels, and the ambience varied considerably. One night might be black-tie, sipping champagne, listening to jazz greats on the stereo. Another night might be jeans and sneakers, steak sandwiches and beer, with the boxing match on TV in the background. Sometimes it was pizza. On one occasion, a member who happened to be a great cook made huge pans of lasagna served with Chianti. Always lots of cigars. Exquisite cigars. From Cuba. Illegal or not.

These weren't terribly "high stakes" games. I don't think I ever won or lost more than a thousand dollars, of an evening. I learned a lot of math by playing poker. Learned to figure the odds based on how many people playing and so on. Learned a few other things, too. Learned a lot about reading people, about the way they so often unconsciously reveal themselves, if you watch carefully. An unconscious behavior that reveals a man's thoughts or intentions, that's called a "tell."

I learned how to cheat. I learned how to spot a cheat. I also saw what happened to guys who got caught cheating. So I paid extra special attention to how not to get caught.

One night, a steak sandwich and beer night, I was dealt a royal flush. Spades. I played the hand reasonably well and walked away with a decent pot, to the hoots and complaints of all the other gentlemen present. My boss shook his head. "Billy, Billy, Billy..." He said, produced a Cuban from his pocket and stuck the end in my mouth. "My man. You're buying everybody breakfast."

It was a great moment. Probably still a story told in certain circles. The trouble was – how do you top that? It's like having sex with Sophia Loren. Everything after that is anti-climactic. Haven't played much cards since. Still hoping to meet Ms. Loren.

"Poker?" I said. "Thanks, I don't play." I feigned a yawn, excused myself and headed for the door. I could feel eyes on me all the way out. Whatever was going on, I didn't like it, and I didn't want it to involve me.

Like St. Mick says, you can't always get what you want.


I'm a light sleeper.

And my ears never sleep at all.

Even with the wind up, when Spartacus Jones fired off a soft, breathy snort, it alerted me. I was stretched out across the seat of the cab and I shifted slightly to facilitate access to my pistol, should it become necessary. I had the windows open. I like to have a breeze in my face while I sleep.

"Hey, Johnny?" she said. She had a green sweatshirt wrapped around her, was carrying a small over-night bag.

"Hey, Lee," I said, and sat up.

"Could you give me a ride?"

I slid out of the cab, tucking my Colt into my jeans behind my back.

"Where to?"

"Anyplace but here."

"What about your friends?

"They AIN'T my friends."

No, I didn't really think they were.

"Ok," I said. "You can ride along."

"Thank you, thank you," she gushed. "Um...could we go now?"

"Right now?

"Please?"

I understood the urgency in her voice. I'd heard it before. No way I could say "no."

"It'll take me a minute to load him up," I said.

A minute was too long.

The door of the inn, blown by the wind, cracked hard against the frame. Moe, Larry and Curly came stumbling out.

"Lee!" shouted Dutch. "Where you goin', Lee? It's not very polite to leave without saying good-bye." His tone and manner told me he was freshly coked up.

"Oh, god," Lee whined.

Spartacus Jones snorted and shook his mane.

Dutch and company closed to within a few yards. Close enough for some things, not close enough for others.

"You're up early, Cowboy."

"Day's half over," I shrugged. "The early bird gets the worm."

"Yeah," said Dutch, "but look what happens to the early worm."

Dutch grabbed Lee by the arm and she struggled with him. I instinctively poised to spring in his direction. Both his playmates produced pistols and aimed them my way. As Dutch and Lee struggled, her overnight case popped open, and out spilled neat bundles of cash. Not bundles of twenties. Bundles of C-notes. It was more cash than she'd need for overnight in any case.

"Pick it up," Dutch ordered in his suck-it-bitch tone.

Lee picked the money up.

"Put it in the case."

She put it in the case.

"Now let's go have a quiet little chat, just you and me."

"What about him?" asked Bobby hopefully, jerking his thumb in my direction.

"What the fuck do you think?" growled the Big Bad Wolf. And he pulled Lee by the arm, back to the inn.

Well, fuck.

They had the drop on me, as they say in the b-westerns. Both men were armed with Glocks. I had to get them closer to me, or I'd have to go for my .45 and hope for the best, but at this range, the best was looking none too good for me.

I needed a distraction.

I got one.

I don't know who it surprised more, them or me.

Spartacus Jones bellowed in his hoarse whisky voice, like Rod Stewart but two octaves lower. He reared up, flailing his front feet like he was at the gym dog paddling the speed bag. Reaching over the rope I'd strung up, he struck Bobby's head several times in rapid succession, and those blows split the goon's skull open like a ripe pumpkin. When he fell, Spartacus Jones continued to stomp on him, the way he might any other snake.

While iceman George was trapped for a split-second in the inaction of surprise, I pulled my Colt, cocked the hammer, and dropped to my belly in the mud. George recovered himself quickly, and reflexively fired where he'd last seen me, which was now well over my head. I put four slugs into his chest and belly. It was more than enough.

I took his Glock — didn't see where Bobby's had gone — and stuck it in my waistband for back up. Then I headed for the inn.

I hadn't quite reached the door when I heard the unmistakable blast of a shotgun. I crept inside carefully, ready to rock.

But the fat lady had already sung. A 12 gauge Winchester pump aria.

Lee was on the floor. Petechial hemorrhage in the eyes, and her head was cocked at an unlikely angle. I checked for a pulse, checked again. But there was nothing I could do for her.

Dutch was sprawled across an overturned table, with a huge hole in the center of his chest, about where his heart would be, if he'd had one. Getting hit with the blast from a 12 gauge loaded with "00" shot is like getting hit with about nine .38 calibre slugs all at once.

Aunt Bea was still aiming the shotgun at Dutch.

"Easy, darlin'," I said. "It's ok."

She was wearing a filmy thing that was intended for a much younger, much more slender woman.

"I ain't no fragile flower, Cowboy," she said.

No, indeed.

"That son of a bitch," she muttered. "Is she dead?"

"Yes."

She didn't ask about Dutch.

"Son of a bitch." She lowered the muzzle of the shotgun. I checked Dutch for a pulse, too, though it was obviously pointless. I filled Aunt Bea in on the two other bodies at the picnic area. Then I noticed something hanging half out of Dutch's inside jacket pocket.

It was a badge case.

Well, fuck.

I flipped it open. He wasn't a local cop.

I showed the badge to Aunt Bea.

"Son of a bitch," she said again. "You don't want to be stickin' around here, Hon."

"No, Ma'am, I do not."

I searched Dutch's body. Found a Glock in a waistband holster. It was a Glock party; The whole neighborhood was carrying one but me. I took his and stuck it in my jeans. Then I wiped my Colt clean, pressed it into his hand, making sure to get his finger on the trigger. I routinely wipe down ammunition when I load a weapon, so I wasn't worried about my prints on spent shell casings or on the magazine. It was a lousy trade, my Colt for his Glock, but I could always pick up another one.

Aunt Bea watched me dress the scene, went over to the bar, set down her shotgun and poured herself a shot of JD. "Better saddle up, Cowboy," she said.

"What about you? " I wasn't terribly inclined to leave her holding the bag for this mess.

"Hell, don't worry about me, Hon," she said with absolute conviction. "Farley and me go back a long ways. But his wife don't know."

"Farley?"

"That would be Sheriff Farley."

"Before the cops get here," I said, "you might want to have a look in that overnight case."

"That right?"

"Trust me on that one, darlin'," I said.

110

"C'mere," she said. A smile pulled at one side of her mouth. "I like it when you call me "darlin.'"

Sometimes, if you look real close at an older woman, you can glimpse the young girl she once was. Look deeper and you can see the young girl she still is. I went to her and when I was close enough, she wrapped herself around me, kissed me hard, like she was a long time between kisses, kissed me with her whole body and soul. It was a damn good kiss.

"Too bad you got to go," she said. "But you better get."

"Give me ten minutes to head out?" I asked.

"Oh, hell," she said, "I'll be in shock for at least that long. Poor thing that I am."

I saddled up. I packed Spartacus Jones into the trailer and managed to drive out without running over the bodies. As we were turning onto the highway, we passed another car turning off of it. It was a dark SUV. Four guys in it. I had a feeling they were headed for the Halfway Inn, and they were late. If they were carrying the load of dope that I suspected they were carrying, they weren't going to be pleased with what they found when they got there. Not if Sheriff Farley was on the way.

Never did get to stop off in Yale to visit the birthplace of my man, Chet. I guess I'll have to do that another time.

The remainder of the homeward journey was relatively uneventful. I pondered what had gone on in Spartacus Jones' mind that he decided to pummel Bobby into chitlin's. Had he read that goon's body language? Smelled aggression on his scent? Gotten a sign from Allah? Why stick his neck out for me? Why do that? Not something a lot of humans have done, or would do. The horse answer was simple: he considered me a member of his herd. And woe betide the predator who fucks with a member of his herd.

When we got back to the emerald city, I told Frankie I wanted to buy Spartacus Jones.

He quoted me a price that was way too high.

I didn't care.

*Can't look at hobbles and I can't stand fences*
*Don't fence me in.*
"Don't Fence Me In"
Ella Fitzgerald


# CHAPTER ELEVEN:
# MAGIC DOG FARM


It's funny how things work out.

When I was a kid, one of the worst things you could call somebody was "farmer." As in Shit-kicker. It was synonymous with hick or rube, which meant stupid, a sucker, an easy mark. Lots of unsavory jokes about hicks in the sticks getting their kicks with an assortment of domesticated animals and inanimate objects.

If you done told me when I was in knee pants that one day I'd buy a farm, I'd have slapped the lips right off your mouth.

I guess the joke's on me.

That's ok. It's not the first time.

Frankie and I did the deal.

Signed the papers. Shook hands. Drank a toast. Danced a mambo.

Now I had a horse — or should I say, he had me. But I had no place to put him, neither paddock, pasture, nor Norwegian wood. Frankie offered to keep him until I found a suitable place, but I was spending most of my time at Stevie's Ark anyway, so I stashed Spartacus Jones there. I didn't want to board him at all. I wanted to be with him. Close to him. All the time. I had to find us our own place. I already had a place in mind.

113

They say the three most important things in business are location, location, and location. Location was why I bought the old Miller farm.

It was far enough away from town that it was quiet, on a road that had almost no traffic, but still got plowed by the county in the wintertime, and was sandwiched in between state forests that were not going to be "developed" anytime soon.

The whole area was thick with deer, opossum, raccoon, squirrels and foxes. A mixed pack of coyotes and wild dogs could often be heard late at night, like keening tormented banshees, from the direction of the reservoir. Occasionally, a black bear would blunder into human contact, cruising for garbage. You might rarely catch a glimpse of what had to be a grey wolf. And once in a great while, after a rain, you might even find a cougar paw print in the soft mud of the old Bald Hill logging road.

My nearest two-legged neighbors were three quarters of a mile away, over the river and through the woods, Roger and Stevie Sanders, at Stevie's ark.

Stevie's husband, Roger, was a music prof at Ithaca College where he taught the guitar, both classical and jazz, and also music history. Although his super-power was Spanish music of the 16th century — which he played on vihuela and lute, as well as on guitar — he had uncommonly versatile chops and could as easily manage some dirty delta blues when the occasion warranted it.

Oddly enough, about five or six years earlier, I had picked up his CD, "Memories of Spain." Tracks included tunes by Luis de Milan, Alonso Mudarra, and Luis de Narvaez, along with several of Roger's own compositions, all played on a Spanish guitar of the period, the kind with five courses of strings. His original piece entitled "Campeador," which featured a brooding melody over a dissonant minor chord progression, became a favorite of mine.

Now, suddenly, he's my neighbor.

You just never know.

Off in the exact opposite direction of Stevie's Ark, about three miles, was Frankie and Issa's place. Momma, Poppa, their five horses, three dogs, two cats, and their brand new son, a 9 pound 5 ounce bruiser whom they named Tatanka. And a partridge in a pear tree.

114

Frankie was a blacksmith, but he never shod horses anymore. He gave what he called a "mustang trim," keeping the horse barefoot, and hoof healthy. He trimmed Stevie's ponies and she vetted his. I was happy to be dealt in.

So I had horse people to the left of me, horse people to the right of me, valley and timber, state forest behind me and across from me. Neighbors close enough to neigh for help when help was needed, far enough away so it ain't nobody's business if I do. We were like in-laws through our individual marriages to the Horse, and we shared most of the same ideas about horses and our relationship with them, a point of view I'm tempted to call "the Indian Way," so I will. (I'm a Wilde man; I can resist anything but temptation.) This set-up was about as close to actual family as I'm ever likely to get. Family of the two-legged variety, anyway. It was perfect. Damn perfect. Almost like it was all foreordained or something.


My spread was mostly flat, with a few low hills, hills about as steep as a wave that a 10-15 knot wind might kick up. Roughly 75 tillable acres were currently planted with grasses, the better to make hay with, my dear.

There was an outdoor riding arena, a small indoor arena. Paddocks. Pasture. A quarter acre pond. The rest of the acreage was wooded. A shallow stream ran through it, and another smaller spring-fed pond. 103 acres, total.

The property included a sprawling Greek revival house, white with black shutters. Five bedrooms and 2 1/2 baths. Full eat-in kitchen, formal dining room, living room with a fireplace, study/office, laundry room/mud room. Where I grew up, that's not a house. That's a hotel.

The original house and barn had been built in the 1840's, back when they built things like they gave a fuck, and the barn was a classic gable-roofed structure of such titanic dimensions I took a quick look around for icebergs. You could have housed a medium-sized circus in the hayloft. Like the other barns, it was painted dark red, and had a metal roof that, in summer sun, would be too hot for even cats from Tennessee. The house had sprouted a couple additions over the decades.

There were three additional barns.

The newest barn was a horse stable and was only very recently built by the now-previous owners, who had intended to expand the scope of their horse habit into a grander commercial venture, a boarding operation offering lessons, and trail rides, and yada-yada. It was a good plan. Gave the gods a real good laugh.

The stable was about as modern as conventional stables can get, I suppose, with all the features that make it convenient for humans and hell for horses. 10x10 stalls — too fucking small. In prison, my cell was 6'x'8'. Theses stall weren't a hell of a lot bigger than that even though the average horse is five times my size. Walls between almost up to the ceiling minimizing social contact — and being alone is a horse's worst nightmare. Bars across the front, on the sliding door and on the little window that gave access to toss in hay or fill the grain feeder. No way for a pony to stick his head out and look around, see his pals. Automatic waterers set up high, instead of down low the way a horse naturally drinks. Sets of crossties anchored at intervals. Cross ties are a great way for a horse to break his neck. The whole shebang was about constraint and control, and constraint and control are all about fear. More about that shortly.


It's amazing what cold, hard cash can do.

I thought the real estate agent's eyes were going to pop out of her head. We had obviously lived in completely different worlds. She had the sellers' power of attorney, and, as they say in the real estate biz, the sellers were "motivated," which means they had their ass in a sling and had to unload the property pronto. That's an ideal situation for the buyer to negotiate the price down. I hate to haggle. Maybe because I stink at it.

Once, in Mexico, I bought a shoulder holster from a guy who told me his asking price, expecting me to wrangle awhile. My counter-offer was higher than his original ask. He was kind of stunned. But the article was well worth it and I felt like he was under pricing his work. If I'd haggled over it, I would have felt like a cheapskate. A chiseler. If I'm going to steal something, I'm going to fucking *steal* it, and steal it honestly. I'm not going to chisel. That's strictly for punks.

116

Anyway, before I could even start talking, the sellers' agent lowered the price. I hadn't said a word. She went on to extoll some of the property's virtues — mostly about the house which is what most normal people would have been most interested in, I guess. I took a breath to accept the offer, and she lowered the price again.

"Ma'am," I said. "Could you just tell me how much they want for the place? Bottom line?

She told me.

"Done," I said.

So, being armed with cash, I thereupon went from zero to close-the-deal-and-move-my-ass-in in under 60 seconds. No banks, no mortgages. There were no liens, no encumbrances, easements, no rights-of-way. No hits, no runs, no errors. On my end, I'd already had my lawyer give the deed a close read, make sure I had all rights and title with all the frills and none of that greasy kid stuff. The purchase took a huge chunk of my settlement money, just over a third. I had my mouthpiece form a not-for-profit corporation and I donated almost all the rest of the money to that. Even at the lowest standard rates, the principle would generate enough interest to cover the house nut, to operate the farm and care for at least a dozen horses for about the next hundred years.

Technically, I had just created a horse rescue, and the 501c(3) status made the operation tax exempt. Fuck taxes.

That wasn't the end of the story; that was the beginning.

Horses are like potato chips: one isn't enough. They're social animals and they need company. They'll make do with dogs, cats, goats, sheep, birds, or even humans, in a pinch. But for a horse there's nothing like the company of another horse. I can dig that. So I decided to take the "overflow" from Stevie's Ark. Stevie got quite a chuckle out of that.

Before long, Spartacus Jones would have a herd of rescued pals to hang with.


Here's something a lot of people who have horse fantasies don't think about: good horse-keeping is a lot like having a long-term relationship: no matter how good it is, there's always going to be a certain amount of manure you have to deal with. Might as well just accept that and anticipate it.

A 1000-pound horse will pass manure a dozen times a day, about 40lbs worth. That's about 9 tons per year, if I did my math correctly. Throw in a couple of gallons of urine per day, and that comes up to a nice round 50 pounds of raw waste to handle. PER day. PER horse.

If you want to plan a successful crime, start with your get-away. And make sure you have a Plan B, or you don't have a plan at all. A Plan C and a Plan D are not a waste of time. Shit happens. Start at the end, work your way back. Never get into anything unless you know how you're getting out. That's a pretty good habit to get into, and the principle also applied to my new situation.

On a horse farm, if you don't have good manure management, things can really go to shit fast. Odors, flies, parasites, water pollution, locusts, pestilence, famine and the end of civilization as we know it may ensue. I picked Stevie's brains on it, did a little on-line research, and made a plan.


Let me tell you something about prison.

Prison is a lot easier once you give up hope.

When all your appeals are used up and that ugly yellow-green door slides shut on you for the last time with a soul-chilling clang, you have to accept that this is your life now. Not a stopover, or a side trip, or a detour through hell. Hell is now your permanent fucking address. Might as well make the most of it.

Took me a while to figure that out.

I recommend you take it one day at a time.

Don't look forward to anything, don't think back on anything; the despair will drive you nuts. But you better find something to do. Idle time crawls by. It makes your sentence feel even longer.

I worked in the library, in the laundry, and in the cafeteria. Apart from that, I worked out intensely, read books voraciously, and listened to other cons carefully.

About half of the poor bastards I met in the joint had done nothing more than smoke a little weed, maybe sold a reefer to a friend. Thanks to Rockefeller's mandatory sentencing laws, these harmless hash heads who hadn't hurt a hamster were doing longer stretches than

118

many of the murderers, rapists, con men, counterfeiters, arsonists, gang-bangers, pimps, thieves, and jerks-of-all-criminal-trades who composed the rest of high society on the inside.

Like most people, criminals are often proud of their work and consider themselves professionals, even experts, conveniently ignoring the minor point that they had not been expert enough to elude the cops — who weren't, themselves, exactly Holmesian quality geniuses. I was polite enough never to bring up that point.

Most everybody likes to brag about his work, likes to be respected. So I listened and they liked that I listened. It was a sign of respect. Asking advice is a sign of respect, too. "Suppose a guy wanted to do so-and-so or such-and-such. What do you think is the best way to do it?"

Respect opens a lot of doors.

But, unfortunately, no gates.

Criminology is the scientific study of the nature, extent, management, causes, control, consequences, and prevention of criminal behavior. You could say that's what I was doing, an internship in criminology, except for the "prevention" part. After almost a decade of taking notes, I'd accumulated far more knowledge about crime than I'd ever learned on the street, or at the police academy. I deserved a Ph fucking D. I never thought I'd put it to use because I never thought I'd get out.

But enough about being buried alive.

I mention this about prison only to explain how it came to pass that when, on the night of the first day the old Miller place was mine, that nice new fancy-ass, high-tech horse barn had an unfortunate collision with fire, after which the fire state investigator concluded that the cause was "undetermined." Possibly due to faulty wiring.

Golly, what are the odds?
To be fair, the investigator wasn't completely comfortable with that. He wasn't stupid. But his dog found no trace of any of the accelerants she'd been trained to detect. And there was not a whiff of any other evidence, either. No multiple points of origin. Nothing like that. Maybe his gut told him it was arson. Fuck his gut. Here's something I learned the hard way: quoth the sage; there's what you think, there's

what you know, and there's what you can prove. Where the law is concerned, the only thing that matters is what you can prove.
The insurance company grudgingly had to pony up, so to speak.
That was fun.
I hate insurance companies.

So I built my manure composter on the bones of the late lamented maximum-security multi-stall barn. It was a good spot, far enough from water sources so any run-off would be filtered by grassy fields where the plants would consider it a real treat. The surviving poured foundation was of suitable size. I added three concrete walls and a couple of partitions, organized it so I could use the tractor to turn it. Bada-bing.
The compost was exquisite. Do it right and you kill off all the wee beasties and unwanted seeds, leaving fertilizer so rich you could write a song about it, and maybe I will. I could have given it as Christmas presents to local gardeners. What I didn't give away, I could spread on my own fields. You could almost hear the grass giggling. Free pizza.

It was summertime. The livin' was easy. I don't know about the cotton, but the pastures were lush. There was still a lot of work to do to make the changes I wanted to make, but with manure management taken care of, and plenty of good forage, my hacienda was ready for my pony to come to his new home. I could take my sweet time with the rest of my honey-do list while he settled in.
I barebacked Spartacus Jones up from Stevie's to his new digs, ponying along with us a little paint mare named Shyla who'd been smitten with him. Spartacus Jones: the Errol Flynn of equines. I turned them out in the honeymoon paddock and the Lord said it was good.

A short time after that, I initiated the place with a farm-warming, featuring a couple of tons of chicken wings, plenty of pizza, mounds of egg rolls, and a couple cases of hooch. Frankie and Issa, Stevie and Roger, and B and J made the scene, as did some of the local cats I played with regularly, and the chief audio wizard from Electric Wilburland, over in Newfield, where I like to record my stuff. I'm not by nature gregarious, but this was nice. Issa brought her home-baked bread and I discovered I wasn't the only one who was crazy about it.

120

She also gave me an over-sized coffee mug with a likeness of Spartacus Jones painted on it, but she'd added a few magic signs and symbols, decorating him up like an old Lakota warhorse. I still have that mug.

The only person missing was The Judge. She was a Texas horsewoman from way back. But our extra-curricular activities were of such a nature that we had decided it best if we avoided unnecessary contact, just in case the law was watching.

Or listening.

These days, legal or not, constitutional or not, government minions are reading your emails, tapping your phones, tracking your movements via cell phone and the GPS in your vehicle. They know who's naughty and who's nice better than Santa Claus. And not just criminals or "terrorists." Every fucking body. See, in a police state, everybody is a criminal because everything is against the law. You better do something about that. Anyway, The Judge was there in spirit.


It was Issa who asked me what I was going to name my place. Their own farm was waggishly called, "Back Acres." I hadn't given it much thought before, but I did now.

What's in a name?

Everything, Old Bard.

Names are important. A bard in the hand is worth two in the bush.

Your name doesn't just tell other people who you are; it reminds *you* of who you are.

It can define who you are. It's both a calling card and a mantra.

The Lakotas had got that one right. Names were individual and descriptive. They had meaning. They didn't have a hundred guys all very different from each other and all named "Bob." To the Indian a name was a spiritual thing. To the Wasichus, it's only evidence of ownership. It's the difference between who ARE you and who OWNS you.


I had to come up with not just a good name for my place, but also the right name.

Maybe Dream Chief would whisper something in my ear. After all, it was his prophecy I was fulfilling. He'd first come to me, in a

121

recurrent dream, after I tried to eat fire, and I bit off more than I could chew. Specifically, a lamp cord. I was four or five years old, I guess. Maybe younger, I don't really know. It was an electrifying experience. It should have killed me, they said. While recovering, swathed in bandages and unguentine, I read a little, and slept a lot, during which time Dream Chief kept me company.

Dream Chief had so many wrinkles in his face, he looked like someone had crumpled his head up into a ball and then tried to open it up, lay it out flat and smooth again, and when he smiled, the wrinkles consumed everything but his broad equine teeth. Wispy, snow-white hair terminated in two thin braids. He scat-sang to himself in scratchy falsetto, spoke to me in an unknown tongue that I nevertheless understood, and was always accompanied by his pure white pony, whose proud prancing and snorting marked him, I realized now, as close kin in spirit to Spartacus Jones.

As I healed up from my extensive burns, Dream Chief's visits became less frequent, but he never gave up on me entirely. He still showed up sometimes, when I really needed him, and many times since then Dream Chief visited me in my sleep, walked with me, teasing me gently, and always leaving me the inscrutable parting advice, "Go where the arrow points to the rainbow." Took me a long time to figure out what that meant, because I'm not as smart as a horse.

Dream Chief's intermittent pestering, and family legend that I was fathered by a half-breed from out west, from Lakota country, led me to do a lot of Indian-related reading, especially in the joint. I read everything by Vine Deloria, Jr. "Lame Deer, A Seeker of Visions, by Doug Boyd. Rolling Thunder. The Cheyenne Way. Black Elk Speaks. I discovered that the traditional way of life, of the so-called Sioux, matched up pretty well with my own take on things. There was a lot in their philosophy and religion that I found fundamentally sound, and the harmonics reverberated in distant corners of my soul, where they echoed on into infinity. It was a way of life that was predicated on individual freedom, with each person following his or her own special "medicine," walking a path unique to him and no one else. They understood the alikeness of everything in creation, the inter-connectedness, that all things that exist are part of one great big

122

cosmic family. Mitakuye Oyasin, they say. "All (are) my relatives."
That belief influenced every word they spoke, every move they made.

I tried to imagine what that life must have been like.

I couldn't. Not really.

But I still tried. In wistful, melancholy moments. In lazy afternoon
dreams. Sometimes in songs I wrote.

Imagine this: you get one quick glimpse of your true love across a
crowded dance floor. She smiles at you, and you run the gauntlet to
reach her, but by the time you get to where you saw her, she's already
gone. You look for her, down the hall, near the lady's room, in the
garden. But you never see her again. Now, you carry forever the
memory of a love you never knew. That's how the Old Ways were to
me.

I'll give you two examples.

One is the word "Lakota," and the other is the word "Wasichu."

"Lakota" is what the people known to the general American as the
"Sioux," call themselves. It means something like "allies," or
"friends," or, loosely, "guys like us." Which means, to take it a little
further, "all those who live like we live, believe what we believe, and
value what we value."

"Wasichu" is a word used disparagingly to mean "White Man."
But it doesn't literally mean "white" (the word for the color white is
ska) or "man" (the word for man is wichasha). It means, "takes the
fat," that is, "a greedy person."

To me, that's huge.

The Lakotas defined people not by their appearance, but by their
behavior.

Where do I sign up?

I first considered naming my place "Magic Dog Farm."

I'll tell you why.

According to Anglo-European historians, the horse originated in
North America, but went extinct there, wiped out by over-hunting. The
horse was then re-introduced to the continent by the Spanish
conquistadors in the early 16th Century, and it had been so long since
horses had wandered the plains there, that the memory of them went
extinct, too.

123

According to the Lakota, the horse did NOT go extinct in North America, and they did NOT get the horse from the Europeans. They had had horses for many generations long before the Spanish ever set their greedy, murderous feet on the continent.

Somebody once said that history is a collection of lies written by the winners to justify what they did to the losers. I'm inclined to believe the Lakotas' own account of their own history.

You go ahead and believe whatever history you want.

What you choose to believe isn't going to change the Truth one iota.

According to Lakota history, before the gift of the horse, the people traveled on foot, hunted on foot, fought on foot. Sometimes they employed dogs to help carry their meager belongings on a travois hitched up to their canine companions and dragged along behind them.

When Wakantanka sent them the Horse everything changed.

Everything.

And I mean revolutionary change.

Traveling on horseback, the Lakotas could now cover greater distances in less time, extending their hunting range. Hunting on horseback, they could outrun buffalo, eat well all summer, and store a lot of dried meat for the winter. Fighting on horseback, they could make quick hit-and-run raids, like the sudden attack of angry ground hornets, and they would one day be described even by their grudging enemy, as "the greatest light cavalry in history."

They became a horse culture. The horse became sacred to them. A gift from the Creator, Wakantanka, and a gift beyond compare. The horse came to be a central figure in their world, their religion, myths and rituals and legends. Even today Lakotas speak about the horse nation and the Lakota nation being one and the same, one tribe, one family, like Siamese twins joined at the spirit.

When the Horse came to me, it made an equally radical change in my life. It revolutionized my way of thinking, my way of doing, my way of feeling, my way of being. I would be a different man today, if not for the Horse. And I don't think I'd like him very much.

The Lakotas, on first encountering the horse, compared this strange beast to something they already knew, the same way the

Anglos would one day refer to the automobile as the "horseless carriage."

The Lakotas called the horse "t'shunka wakan."

T'sunka is the word for dog.

"Wakan" can mean strange, mysterious, holy, magic, weird, unusual, special, or sacred, depending on the context. "Wakan tanka," for example is usually translated as "god," but actually means something like "the great, sacred mystery."

Connect the dots and you get "t'shunka wakan."

Voila, Magic Dog Farm.

It wasn't just a good name.

It was the right name.


I tried sleeping in the house, I really did.

Elegant place, but I swear those people in 1850 must have been life members of the Lollypop Guild because the bedrooms were so small the mice were round-shouldered. I tried sleeping in one. Then another. Like Goldilocks looking for the bedroom that was just right. I didn't find it. I guess I spent too many years in a 6x9 room. For the moment I was happy to camp out in the paddock with Spartacus Jones and company, look up at the night sky, listen to the music of the late shift, but summer wasn't going to last forever.

I started thinking about re-modeling. I could open the place up. Take out a wall here and there, maybe cathedral the ceilings.

I took a few preliminary measurements to make sketches to make plans.

Then I took them again.

And again.

Something wasn't right.

Either I didn't know how to use a tape measure, or those measurements didn't add up. The interior measurements and the exterior measurements didn't match.

It was a real Twilight Zone moment.

I finally figured out why, and maybe I'll tell you that secret sometime. For now what's important is that my discovery decided me to leave the house the way it was.

But I had a Plan B.

I don't even open my zipper without a back-up plan.

This one had come to me courtesy of Dream Chief.
In the dream, we were walking across the verdant, limitless prairie, accompanied, as always, by his prancing white stallion. A red-tailed hawk whistled hoarsely overhead and I looked up to see it soar effortlessly across the sky, riding the wind toward high mountain majesties, purple in the distance. "He goes to the sees-far place," Dream Chief said to me in a language I don't speak but somehow understood. I watched the hawk circle its way to the highest peak until it was just a tiny dot, and then disappeared. Behind me, Dream Chief's pony started nuzzling my ear with his wet lips.

I woke up to Spartacus Jones standing over me nuzzling my ear with his wet lips. One of his whiskers went up my nose and tickled.

My Plan B was to go to the sees-far place. Take the high ground. The highest ground I had was that massive old barn.

So I sketched out a plan to convert the lower part of the barn to a three-sided shelter, and the loft above into my living quarters, and I just caught myself, lucky you.

I was about to launch into a dry dissertation on re-modeling that only a carpenter could love. I'll spare you the hammers-and-nails details. If you're really interested, you can always dig up some old episodes of This Old House. Suffice it to say that, thanks to a former hippie named Kiki, who was the Johnny Appleseed of solar energy, I wound up with a place that wasn't exactly off the grid, but if the grid ever went down, it would be a month before I'd notice.

I built a deck that wrapped around all four sides, with stairs at either end. It made a great place for sunbathing and it doubled as additional shelter for the horses, who like to stand in the shade of it and chat. Added lots of glass on the south side, sliding patio doors. Skylights. The plumbing was beyond my skills, so I brought a pro in to do that part. Likewise some of the wiring.

I added a few clever touches all my own. Storage spaces that didn't look like storage spaces. A contraption for bringing up firewood that I based on the lifeboat davits on my old ship, and using the bucket of a retired wheelbarrow. A feat of engineering I'm pretty proud of.

A house is a project that's never quite finished. There's always more tinkering to do. But there's a hell of a lot of work to do on a horse farm, season by season, as well as daily routine. I got my crib to the point where it was comfortable, functional, and put a period on it.

That done, I turned my full attention to setting up my paddocks so the ponies could live as close to their natural way as possible.

Horses had both literally and poetically saved my life, and I owed it to them.

It was a debt of honor.

And that's the kind of debt you always have to pay.

Adam Adrian Crown

# PART TWO:
## The Film Noir Cowboy

*When you believe in things*
*that you don't understand, then you suffer.*
*Superstition ain't the way.*
                    "Superstition"
                    Stevie Wonder




# CHAPTER ONE:
# TRUE BELIEVER


I was a city kid.

To me, "wilderness" was a parking lot with no slot lines laid out and painted on the pavement. I had only one encounter with "nature," in my ill-spent youth, but it was significant. It happened in a round about way, one of those big fucking surprises in life that catches you flatfooted, because you had no clue it was coming. Those are the worst. And sometimes the best.

It's not fair to judge your behavior as a child by the standards you have for yourself as an adult. You're just a kid. You don't know anything. All you have to go on is what the people around you say and do. Would you condemn yourself as a baby for wetting your diaper, just because you wouldn't normally piss in your pants now as an adult? Nope. Not fair. But it's an easy trap to fall into.

Even though I know it doesn't make sense to feel this way, I can't help feeling embarrassed that once upon a time — you'd never guess it, now — but once upon a time, I was a true believer, a "patriot," in the worst possible sense of that word. I was like the love child of Yankee-Doodle Dandy and Captain America. If you cut me, I'd have bled red, white, and blue. It makes me cringe now. Makes me feel sick to my stomach. Makes me angry. And sad. But it's true. But I know why it was true, and that's some consolation.

Adam Adrian Crown

See, my childhood environment was chaos. My father was Mr. Arbitrary and my mother was Mrs. Capricious. It was a roiling stew of forbidden sexuality and sudden violence. Unreasonable and unpredictable. My mother was always displaying herself naked, and while she condemned the penis as an evil predatory beast, in practically the same breath she'd give mine a dirty smile and assure me that I would have a lot of girlfriends. My "father" was all over my half-sister Kay from the time she was a little girl. She, in turn, gave me an intensive tutorial on sex when I was five or six. Then I showed my little half-brother some of the tricks that she had shown me, and the beat goes on.

Speaking of beat, I'd have a hard time remembering a day when I didn't get a beating for something, usually for nothing. And when I wasn't getting pounded physically, I was getting hammered emotionally either with ridicule, or the most degrading kind of micro-control over every move, every breath, down to the smallest imaginable detail. Like which drawer to put your socks in and the only right way to fold them and they better be folded that way. Of course, the only right way varied, and whatever way you folded them, it was always the wrong way.

It was a real drag to be small and weak and always afraid, at the mercy of parents whose mercy was sliced thinner than Artie Pugliese's garlic — which he sliced with a razor blade.

I wanted to be big, to be strong, to be courageous — but I wasn't. Except when I lost myself in a book or a film, dissociated from myself to inhabit the hero. El Cid. Robin Hood. Zorro. Errol Flynn. John Wayne. I wanted to be anybody but me.

Every day was filled with dread and despair. This was the way things were, and there was nothing you could do about it.

It was a lot like being in prison.

I know. I've been in prison.

The main difference is that in prison nobody pretends to love you while they're torturing you.

In prison, there's only one thought that makes any sense, only one idea worth clinging to with all your might, only one thing that enables your spirit to survive another day: the dream of somehow getting OUT.

132

Scarcely more than a decade after the end of WWII, still hung-over from "the good war," everybody loved a soldier. Saw them all as "heroes," though very few actually were. Military-type parades were popular on Memorial Day, and the Fourth of July, and military-style color guards were included even on Thanksgiving, Christmas and Easter — as well as being carted out on any and every other possible occasion. When actual soldiers weren't available, they'd use ex-soldiers like guys from the American Legion, or budding soldiers: Boy Scouts. Never Girl Scouts. The game was strictly balls or better to open.

In school, I excelled in music class which consisted of a weekly hour or so of patriotic songs (and the occasional "negro spiritual") among which was this little ditty penned by Noel Gay:

> There's something about a Soldier,
> Something about about a Soldier,
> Something about about a Soldier,
> That is fine fine fine!
> He may be a great big general,
> May be a sergeant major,
> May be a simple private of the line line line!
> There's something about his bearing,
> Something in what he's wearing,
> Something about his buttons all the shine shine shine!
> Oh, a military chest seems to sooth a lady's best,
> There's something about a Soldier that is fine fine fine!

In all those old war movies — the half propaganda and half recruiting film — strong men, stonily facing the enemy and gallantly embracing death, had great appeal for me. Sometimes death looks a lot like being free.

Uniforms, and rank insignia, right there on your arm made it clear who belonged and who didn't, and where you fit in, who you were responsible for and who you were responsible to. On top of that, I was apparently a sucker for the pomp and circumstance of marching. A large number of people working together in a unity of purpose and skill, as opposed to every man for himself. And dressed in pretty sharp uniforms, too.

Now, when it comes to uniforms, it's hard to beat the Marine Corps. Unless you're riding with Napolean's hussars. That's for me, I thought. I couldn't wait until I'd be old enough to join up. Then I'd be big and strong and fearless, and be part of a family, a brotherhood of big, strong, fearless men. I learned the Marine's hymn — and I mean all three verses. I read all about them. Guys like Sgt. Major Dan Daly who lead a detachment of out-gunned, out-numbered marines in a counter-attack at Belleau Wood in World War One, rallying his men with "Come on, you sons of bitches! Do you want to live forever?"

One Marine I didn't know about was General Smedley Butler. It would be years before I would read his little book "War is a Racket." Too bad. I should have started with him.

I was the perfect mark.

In part, because the "hero" fantasy has great appeal to the small, weak, and fearful, and in part simply because the military represented order instead of chaos. There seemed to be a rational structure to it. Chain of command, you know? Rules and limitations that applied to everyone. Superior officers were not allowed to strike their subordinates. That alone was a step up from my situation. The guy in charge had earned his rank, was qualified to be in charge. So you could trust him. Just sit back, follow orders — you didn't have to try to parent yourself. And there was an inviolable code you could count on. All for one, one for all. Semper fi. Or so I thought. Remember what I said about being a kid: you don't know shit.

Anyway, I grabbed at that patriotic crap the way a man falling off the Sears Tower will grab at fog. I pledged allegiance to the flag like it was the sermon on the mount, and once I accidentally said "amen" at the end. The other kids laughed at me. I didn't even care.

If I wasn't old enough to join the Marines — or the Navy (I was a bit fickle because I liked ships) — at least I could join the Boy Scouts. That was a step in the right direction, see? Soon as I turned 11, I signed up with the nearest Scout Troop. The Scoutmaster was a guy named Dave Milligan. Square jaw. Buzz-cut hair. Deep-set eyes with sleepy lids. Ears like the bells of trumpets sticking way out from his head. Faded blue tattoos all over his forearms. Navy motifs. He had two sons who were members of the troop. Dave Junior was a carbon copy of the old man but without the tattoos. He was an Eagle Scout, and Dad was getting him prepped to go into the service as soon as his 18th birthday rolled around. He was straight-arrow, button-down, ivory soap. Honor student. Nice kid, but he could give you a toothache if you stood too close.

The younger son, Donny, was entirely different. Soft, round features, limp blonde hair. Slight lisp. Black horn-rimmed glasses too big for his face, and they kept slipping down so that he was constantly poking himself between the eyes. He was clearly the runt of the litter, didn't measure up to his older brother, and Big Dave was always riding the kid. I think scouting was his father's attempt to "make a man out of him," to lure him away from the realm of books, and initiate him into the world of fight, fuck, and football. It wasn't going well.

I jumped into scouting with both feet. Memorized all the baloney, went to all the meetings, marched in parades, went on overnight camp-outs, yada-yada. Busted my hump hustling lawn-mowing jobs or anything else I could to scrape together enough bread to buy a 3rd-hand uniform shirt from the second-hand store. And a hat. You've got to have the hat.

That first winter of discontent, there was a big event for which kids in each patrol built a dog sled — only we were the dogs that pulled it. Froze our asses off that weekend in record cold temperatures trudging through record deep snow. On the upside, I learned how to treat frostbite.

I sold so many Christmas wreaths, and flag kits, and whatever else the scout troop was hustling, that I actually was able to finance two weeks at a Boy Scout summer camp in the wilds of Wisconsin. Two weeks playing toy soldier, camping out — and, best of all a couple hundred MILES away from my parents. That's two weeks with NO beatings. Two WHOLE weeks. Guaranteed. It wasn't salvation, but it wasn't nothing, either. It was like finding a walk-in refrigerator in hell, and ducking in there for a quick wank.

Camp Ma-ha-ko-pe was located on 1500 acres of woods way up in the wilds of northern Wisconsin, not far from the Bad River Ojibwe Indian reservation. It was the most beautiful place I'd ever seen. Thick forest. Five spring-fed lakes. All kinds of wildlife from mouse to moose.

And quiet.

If you wanted to, you could find a secluded spot on the nearest lakeshore — less than a hundred yards from our campsite — and stretch out in the sun, with nothing in your ears but the leaves whispering secrets in the wind, and sparkling wavelets tickling the rocks with their Irish step dancing.

In quiet like that, if you listened, you could hear the earth's heartbeat.

With luck, yours entrained with it.

You became the earth.

The sky.

The wind.

The water.

You had all the answers to all the questions you never even knew you had.

I'd never before experienced such a moment of indescribable peace, completeness. As if somehow the whole fucking mess made sense. As if it all was just the way it was supposed to be, and everything would be all right.

Although I'd catch a glimmer of this feeling from time to time, at sea, or even in the arms of a lover, I wouldn't have that powerful, all-consuming kind of experience again until I was adopted by a horse.

The camp was actually two camps situated one on either side of Lake Chippewa. Each camp had its own dining hall, where we had most of our meals, a trading post, where we could purchase Scout gack and nick-nacks, and a collection of campsites. The campsites on the west side of the lake — cleverly designated West Camp — were named for legendary — meaning bullshit — frontier heroes: Boone, Bowie, Cody, Carson, Crockett and that pantheon of scoundrels from American mythology. West Camp was the newer and smaller of the camps.

The campsites in East Camp, the original camp, were named for Indian Tribes: Sioux, Comanche, Mohawk, Menominee.

Our campsite was designated "Cheyenne." It was nestled deeply in the woods, on several levels of hilly terrain, and was the most isolated from the other campsites, which was okay by me. It could accommodate maybe 30-40 campers and two different troops could share it. But that summer, we had it all to ourselves.

The camp circle — actually more of a twisted up trapezoid — was spread out around a central fire pit. It had one shelter and one latrine. Our 10x10 tents were set up on wooden platforms, which were in turn set upon cement cinder blocks, because it rains in Wisconsin, and it can rain hard when it does. Wash away lesser camping facilities in a flash.

Each tent had two cots, heavy and sturdy, made of steel. There were holes in the bottoms of the legs for bolting the beds in place, and I suspected they were Navy surplus. The springs were such that any movement on the bed — such as breathing — made a noise like a thousand mice singing the Hallelujah Chorus in a key and a range that the human ear was not made to handel. The mattresses had seen better days, too, but were adequate to put sleeping bags or bedrolls on top of.

My tent mate was Bobby Badasino, and if you've guessed that he was universally known as "Badass," you're getting into the spirit of the season. It was a moniker he embraced with enthusiasm, however unrealistic it might have been, him being more smartass than badass. He was a pudgy kid with bug eyes, heavy lips and one eyebrow — none of which were his most distinguishing feature, as I will confide shortly. He played the accordion, which I considered to rank just above the kazoo in the hierarchy of musical instruments, no offense to the lovely ladies of Spain whom I adore. A year or so older than me, Bobby had been to camp before. I think the scout leaders tried to team up the new kids with veterans.

Our digs were on the far side of the campfire, deepest in the woods and farthest from the Scoutmasters' tent.

Settling in for our first night in camp had one awkward moment to negotiate. Ever since my sister, Kay, had taught me how to masturbate properly (and a few other earthy delights), jacking off had been a regular party of my nightly routine. Like brushing my teeth. Only a lot more fun. I wasn't greatly inclined to suspend the practice for two weeks.

Twenty two hundred was lights out, and we slipped into our sleeping bags. After a decent interval, I sought out my cock to rock myself to sleep.

No way.

Even a modest stroke set off the alarm springs of the bed like everybody in the D block of Alcaseltzer was making a break. I tried it a couple of different ways, but there was simply no way to build up the necessary head of steam when moving in slow enough motion to defeat the alarm. I was pondering my predicament when Bobby whispered, "Hey, Johnny. Do it standing up, man. That's what I do."

I say he whispered, but his voice was always a little too loud and his whisper sounded loud enough to me to be heard all the way to West Camp. But it also sounded like good advice and I didn't have a better plan. I went to the foot of the bed, facing the tent opening, and went to work. I could see the soft glow of the last campfire embers where the scout leaders were still hanging out, and I could hear their voices swinging soft and low, just as though you had me on your knee, which was not well enough to make out what they were saying. The day had been warm but the night was cool. We'd left the sides of the tent rolled up and that now allowed the evening breeze to caress the trees — and my bare flanks — tenderly.

I typically took my time with this ritual, letting it find its own footing, like a good trail horse, but on this occasion discretion compelled me to abbreviate the episode. But even when it's short, it's still sweet.

I crawled back into bed, riding the wave of relaxation that followed in the wake of the exercise.

"Hey, Bobby," I whispered.

"Yeah?"

"Thanks."

"You're welcome. That work ok for you?"

"Yeah."

"Cool. G'night."

The daily routine of the camp was unhurried. Reveille was early but not too early. 0630. Yup: fucking bugle. A little before 0800, all the troops assembled for the raising of the colors, which in my ill-informed state of mind was like taking communion every morning. Troops took turns doing it, and I, of course, volunteered to be part of the 4-man detail it took to raise Old Gory with the proper degree of pomp under the circumstances. I got a good look at the other troops. Some were dressed in Boy Scout drag right down to their socks.

138

Others were more motley. I looked like the rag-picker's son. That kind of thing eats at you after a while.

Once the flag was safely flapping in the breeze, we took an hour for breakfast. Scouts took turns serving their troop's tables, doing cleanup.

From 0900 to noon we worked on scout stuff. Merit badge skills. We had lunch a little after noon, and went back to do more scout stuff. Retreat was a little before 6PM. The same troop that raised the flag that morning would lower the colors in the evening. Following retreat, we had an hour for dinner. It's worthy noting that meals at camp were jovial affairs and typically included songs, skits, and stories, led by the counselors. This was a bizarre change from the screaming, shouting, and slamming that had always been a part of my meals at home, and it took me a while to adjust.

After dinner we went on stargazing night-hikes, had free time, or a troop campfire with more songs, skits, jokes, and scary stories.

Taps was at 10PM. In your rack, get some sleep, do it all again tomorrow.

I learned a lot at camp that summer.

Learned some "scout craft" which included things like map-reading, backpacking, and outdoor survival skills, and yes, you CAN start a fire by rubbing two sticks together. Learned basic first aid, too.

But most importantly, I discovered the rifle range. That's where I wound up spending every minute I could. I learned basic firearms safety and marksmanship and I found I had a strange talent for making pieces of lead go exactly where I wanted them to go. I could do it with arrows too which appealed to the Indian half of me. Could also do it with knives and hatchets. Never could do it with a baseball, though. Or a basketball. Not sure why that was. Maybe I just didn't give enough of a fuck.

The counselor who ran the range was a former gymnast named Scott. He was dark, like me. We looked like brothers. He sported a New York Yankees baseball cap and favored white shirts with cut-off sleeves, worn loose and open, exposing the lean muscle of arms and belly. He was patient with instruction and lavish with encouragement and praise. It was another shock to my system.

On the firing range, he was more strict than concrete but off the range, he was infamous for practical jokes he pulled on a tight-assed counselor named Sweeney — even though when the deed was discovered, Scott was a mile away, high and dry. Ever put your boots on in the morning to find them full of chocolate pudding? Did you know that there's a way to fill a toothpaste tube with Elmer's glue? Did you know that they make six-foot long rubber snakes that look very realistic? Did you know it's possible to sneak in on a sound-sleeper like Sweeney and put bright red lipstick on him without waking him up?

I think I had a boy crush on Scott. If a Boy Scout could start a fire by rubbing two sticks together, I couldn't help wondering what kind of fire you could start by rubbing two Boy Scouts together. I regret to report that I didn't have the chance to find out. He was beautiful and kind and I liked him a lot.

Yeah, I learned a lot at camp that summer.

One night, I even learned something about elephants.

As I mentioned, we were supposed to hit the rack at 2200 and get to sleep because reveille was at 0630.

Sometimes we had other plans.

One of those plans called for Bobby Badass to entertain us with his famous elephant impression — famous, that is, to a select few, one of whom I became by virtue of being his tent-mate. Outside the half-dozen or so kids in the know, it was more secret than the combination to the lock on the back door of Fort Hard Knox.

Shortly after lights out, the enlightened sneaked into our tent from the rear; we had already pulled the tent sides down. At the appointed hour, Bobby pulled a blanket over himself and turned his back to us, like a magician hiding the key to the trick. When he turned around, he draped himself in the blanket, using it like a monk's hooded cloak. Illuminated only by the spotlight of my palm-covered flashlight, it was revealed that Bobby had pulled the pockets of his shorts as far inside out as they would go. Those were the elephant's ears. The elephant's trunk was Bobby's penis, dangling out from his fly. His foreskin looked like the mouth of a balloon at the end of his dick, as if that would be the place you'd blow for a blowjob.

Ok. Elephant. Cute joke. And that's that.

Except for one thing.

That cock didn't belong on a kid. It belonged on a man.

And not your average man, either.

Bobby's penis was not just precocious, it was pendulous. It was profoundly, ponderously, preposterously prodigious.

His cock was to cocks what Cyrano's nose was to noses, and to describe it merely as an elephant's trunk would be wasting a grand opportunity, and lament forever after the things one might have said:

Maritime:
It was a lead line for sounding the depths of the navigable waters of the United States — or a lifeline for a man over-bored.
Medieval:
It was a battering ram for crashing through castle doors.
Piscatorial:
It was so big he used it for fly casting and caught a 30 lb. rainbow trout
Olympic:
It was so big Bobby could pole vault with it. He could enter it in the Javelin event — by itself.
Athletic:
It was so big, he once used it to hit a grand slam in Little League.
Literary:
It was a bigger dick than Moby.
Taxonomical:
It was too big to be a dick. It was a Richard.
Igneous:
It was so big, the Chicago Fire Department deployed it for high-rise fires.
Geographical:
It was so big, it had its own area code, two zip codes, and three time zones.
Geological:
It was so big, there was still snow on it in July.
Academic:
His dick was so big, he could be ten minutes late for class, but his dick would be on time.

Scholarly:
He could be in English and his dick would be across the hall taking notes in History.
Recreational:
It was so big he could hoola-hoop with it — with multiple hoops.
Patriotic:
It was so big, the VFW used it as a flagpole on Memorial Day.
Architectural:
It was so big he could fuck an elevator shaft — but only with lots of lube.
Arboreal:
It was so big, you could tell how old he was by counting the rings in it.
Anatomical:
It was so big he could use it for anal and oral sex at the same time.
Historical:
It was so big, it could have saved everybody who went down on that Titanic — and it would TAKE that many people to go down on it.

These are things we might have said to describe Bobby's penis, had we not been so awed by the elephant's trunk that all we could do was gasp one unison big-dick gasp.

Keep in mind we were only 11 or 12 years old. Some of us hardly had two pubic hairs to rub together, and for some firing off rounds of ejaculate was purely sementic. What we were witnessing was a marvel second only to a UFO landing.

But the show wasn't over.

With expert hip gyrations, Bobby swung the elephant's trunk side to side, back and forth, around in circles — cockwise and counter-cockwise — and even managed something of a figure-8. These acrobatics he accompanied with muted elephant trumpeting.

It cracked us up.

And trying to keep quiet, so as not to be discovered by the adults, made it even funnier. The scoutmaster's son, the younger one, the one with the lisp, was in the audience and he had one of those laughs that not only carried for miles, but was enough to goad even the most mirthless into racking guffaws. As soon as he got started, we had to put a pillow over his face for security reasons. That made everyone laugh harder, including him.

Houston, we're approaching gut-busting territory.

Imitation is the sincerest form of flattery, and several of the lads decided to make it a herd of elephants. Sometime, you really must get a few guys together and see if they can swing their cocks in unison. The Full Monty meets the Flying Walendas.

It was also a chance to look at other guy's cocks and display our own. Some of those trunks stopped swinging and started looking like Uncle Sam on those posters that said "I want YOU..."

Inevitably, the look-out whispered that the scoutmaster was coming, doing his rounds, and the guys swiftly slipped out the back of the tent whence they came, like mice scurrying back under the stove when you turn the kitchen light on.

It was Donny who wrote the wicked and daring postscript to the Night of the Elephant. A subsequent evening campfire featured one of the most popular skits: scouts doing impressions. Everyone was fair game and someone did John Wayne, and somebody else took a crack at Humphrey Bogart. A couple tried Elvis on for size. But the best were impressions of other scouts, people we knew. Dave Junior did an impression of his dad, made all the more hilarious by their physical resemblance. Somebody did sourpuss camp counselor Sweeney. But the piece de resistance was Donny's impression of Bobby Badasino. Hit by a bolt of sudden inspiration, Donny left the fire circle and ran to his tent to return with a white turtleneck shirt. He pushed the sleeves inside the body and pulled the shirt over himself just far enough so that the neck of the turtle was on his head like a hat. Then he swung himself from side to side, doing the elephant trumpet solo.

A certain group of scouts went berserk. We laughed so hard we cried. We rolled around on the ground like we were on fire. We laughed so hard we couldn't breathe. And we couldn't stop.

Meanwhile, the rest of the troop, watched our antics in bewilderment so complete that they nearly achieve a zen state of what-the-fuck? "I don't get it," they intoned like a Greek chorus. "What's so funny?"

We were in no position or condition to explain it, and I have no idea if they ever found out.

So I learned a lot at camp that summer.

Some shooting, some hooting. Camping and tracking, hunting and trapping. Learned a little about bear and wolf, deer and fox, rabbit and raven, eagle and elephant.

And I learned something about fear, too.

It was the day of the swim test.

We trekked down to the waterfront early in the morning in swim trunks and hiking boots. Towels around necks. Giddy. Woke up some of the birds. Chill in the air. Smoke on the water. A fire in the sky.

We cued up on the floating dock to await our turn. There were some scouts taking the advanced test — 100 yards with specified strokes required. But I was just taking the "basic " test. Not much of a test. Jump off the dock. Thrash your way over to the marker and back, any way you could do it. I don't know how far it was. Not very far. 50 feet or so. Camp counselors were there with long poles you could grab on to if you got in trouble. I watched the other guys do it. Piece of cake.

Until it was my turn.

I stood on the edge of the dock of the bay and looked into the water's dark grin, and I couldn't make myself jump in. I wanted to, wanted to like all hell. But my body would not obey. I froze, trembling, despite myself. It's what they call "paralyzed with fear." That's not a metaphor. That's literal.

It wasn't that I didn't know how to swim. I could swim just fine in water that was shallow enough for me to touch bottom. I should have been able to do this. No matter how deep the water is, you only swim in the top two or three feet, right?

I was terrified.

All I could do was cry, and cry I did.

And just as I couldn't make myself jump in the water, I couldn't make myself stop crying.

Sourpuss Sweeney was on hand and tried to help me out, but I was wretched and inconsolable, and he didn't know what to do. There wasn't anything he could do. I was afraid, and ashamed of being afraid. It was the worst humiliation possible. I thought I would die, and I was afraid that I wouldn't, and I'd have to live with the shame of it.

I understand now why I was afraid. I had been taught to be afraid. Afraid of everything and afraid of everyone. More than that, I didn't believe that, if I got in trouble, anyone would save me. Oh, they might stand there and yell at me while I drowned. If I got a cramp or panicked I was on my own, and I didn't know if I could save me.

I couldn't act, couldn't jump in, because I didn't have the motivation to do it.

I didn't have the motivation to do it, because I had no expectation of success.

I had no expectation of success because I visualized disaster.

I visualized disaster because I believed disaster was inevitable.

I believed disaster was inevitable because all the evidence I had, all my experience was disaster. Failure which led to ridicule which led to humiliation.

You know what most people fear most?

It isn't death.

It's public speaking.

Embarrassment.

I didn't take the swim test that day.

The following day, I spent the morning at the rifle range with Scott. I fired some excellent groupings. The other scouts had already left, knowing that lunch was in the offing.

"Wow," Scott said gazing at my last target. "Look at that. Right on top of each other. That's good shooting, Jack." He signed and dated the target. Then he shaded his eyes and squinted up at the sun. "Man, it's a hot one today." It was, indeed. We were both wearing shorts. "Hey, let's go for a swim." He cuffed me lightly on the shoulder. "You've earned it. Come on."

There was no way I could say "No" but my heart and mind raced to find a way out. I didn't want him to know my ugly secret.

He took me down to the waterfront almost at a jog, keeping up a steady stream of chatter so I couldn't squeeze an excuse in edgewise. Because everybody else had gone to chow, the waterfront was deserted.

145

"What a perfect day," he said. "This is going to be great. Thanks for coming with me. I always like to swim with a buddy," he said, pointing to the markers. "Just from there to there and back again. What do you think?"

I didn't say anything.

Coincidentally, the distance he suggested was the same as the distance required for the swim test.

We left our shirts and shoes on the sand, having decided to swim in our shorts, not having swim trunks with us. The pleasant thought of us skinny-dipping flickered through my imagination. I followed him down the dock to a spot where there was a ladder. I climbed down it after him into the water, but I clenched the rail so hard I'm sure my fingerprints are indelibly embossed on it. My discomfort must have been so obvious that even Brother Ray could have seen it.

Scott stopped clowning around and put a hand on my shoulder.

"I'm right here, Jack," he said. "I won't let anything happen to you. I promise. Trust me. Trust me. Whenever you're ready, you go and I'll go with you. Just go slow. You know how to breaststroke? Just do that. It keeps your face out of the water and doesn't take a lot of energy. Plus it's quiet. Not a lot of splashing. In case you ever have to sneak up on somebody." He wiggled his eyebrows at me and it made me smile.

I let go of the ladder and swam with Scott beside me, talking to me as we went. "You're doing great. That's a strong stroke you've got. You're good at this one..."

Things like that.

Out to the markers and back.

We rested. Like a late-night DJ, Scott filled in the silence with soft conversation about different things. Sports. School. Girls. I think he was trying to find out what he could use to help motivate me. After a few minutes he said, "Want to do it again? I want to do it again. Will you go with me? Please?"

I'd have done about anything for him.

We swam it again.

We swam it a couple more times.

Then we took a moment, perched on the dock where we could dangle our feet in the water, and Scott talked some more. Finally he said, "Hey, we better get going or we're not going to get any chow at all. You want to do one more? On your own? I want to watch you."

I swam it on my own.

I don't remember it in particular, but I know I did it, I must have, because I went on the Bad River canoe trip and you had to have passed the swim test to do that. But I don't recall the details. I remember the sand feeling warm on the soles of my feet when we grabbed our stuff and headed for the dining hall.

The thing I remember vividly though, is not the later victory, but the earlier defeat, the salty taste of those hot, bitter tears. And the fear, that deep, over-powering fear that inundates the best of you. That's as fresh as yesterday. I hated that feeling, hate it still. Don't ever want to feel it again.

FDR had it right.

The thing I fear most is being afraid.

I guess I've spent my whole life dealing with that moment of incapacitating terror as a 12-year old on the waterfront. In retrospect, I think I've done a lot of foolish things just to prove to myself I wasn't afraid, to try to eradicate fear from me forever.

The trouble is, you can't do that.

Fear is like rust.

It's always there, waiting for a vulnerable spot to take hold of — and humans are just noisy bags full of vulnerable spots. Courage isn't the absence of fear, quoth the sage, but the conquest of it.

Yeah.

But not ONE conquest.

A continual, never-ending series of conquests, every moment of every day for as long as you live.

Everyday is Thermopylae.

The maintenance of your soul is like maintenance of a ship.

You can never turn your back on rust, never paint over it and move on. It will corrode the steel underneath even though the surface looks fine with a touch up now and then. But eventually, that rust will eat away all the steel underneath and there won't be anything left but layers of rust under a thin coating of paint.

The hell of it is, nobody's a hundred percent one hundred percent of the time.

Nobody.

Not you.

Not me.

Sometimes you might do well, you act, if not heroically, at least not disgracefully. Other times, you don't do so well. What makes the difference between a hero and a can of sauerkraut? I'll be damned if I know. Catch somebody at the right moment, and they're capable of incredible feats of courage. Catch them at the wrong moment...?

Sometimes you're the hammer.

Sometimes you're the nail.

Last day of camp was Saturday morning breakfast, everyone in camp together in the dining hall. The usual songs and skits that accompanied meals were foregone and instead there were awards and benedictions from the camp staff, much handshaking, and picture snapping and fare-thee-wells.

Scott called me up and presented me with my marksmanship merit badge, like it was a big deal. Like I was somebody special.

Outside, as I was heading out, he caught me once more. "Take care of yourself, Jack," he said as we shook hands.

"You, too," I said, and he laughed.

"Come here, kid."

He hugged me and I hugged him back. I hated to let go, but I managed it.

A wave and a smile and he was off at a jog.

Then it was just the long bus ride back to hell.

Now, after all this time, here I am with my own place and, in addition to pastures, I have acres of woods, with streams, ponds, and filled with all kinds of wildlife, from mice to deer. I could conceivably hunt, gather, and garden myself to complete self-sufficiency and almost never have to interact with another human unless I felt like it — which would be fine with me.

And now, there's no long bus ride back to hell.

Just a short walk back to my digs and the company of horses.

It's not heaven.

But it'll do.

*Bang bang, you shot me down*
*Bang bang, I hit the ground*
*Bang bang, that awful sound*
*Bang bang, my baby shot me down*
"Bang Bang"
Sonny and Cher

# CHAPTER TWO:
# TWO SHOTS, NO CHASER

## I.

Dominic Caputo, Junior, was the head of the local plumbers' union, even though he wouldn't know a pipe wrench from a pipe dream. He was a chubby fellow, and jolly as the fat man's stereotype demands, proof of which was that he was always asked to be Santa at the Christmas party. He had a certain superficial charm, deceptive, if you didn't know how to look — and most people don't. In his early forties, his hair was starting to thin and he'd begun to style it in what was destined to become a terrible comb-over, but he was all smiles and compliments with the wives, and they were forever telling his wife, Angela, what a prize husband she'd caught, him with those liquid brown "bedroom" eyes — what the Japanese would call "sanpaku."

Angela sometimes longed to refute them but bit her tongue because the revelation would have been too personal, and too painful. But wouldn't Dominic's admirers be surprised to know that they hadn't had "normal" sex since Marie was born. At first, Dom playfully said it was birth control, but she knew that wasn't true. And now it was always her mouth or her ass, and she was smart enough to pretend she enjoyed it that way. If she wanted some satisfaction herself, that was between her and her dildo while Dom was "at work."

Marie (named after Caputo's mother) never hesitated to proclaim to any who would listen that she had the world's best dad. Who could blame her? He'd just bought her a classic Mustang convertible for her high school graduation present, and had set her up in her own off-campus apartment at the college that was her first choice. No dorm rooms for her. Or part-time jobs, either.

A stranger, upon meeting him, would take him for nothing but a happy, hard working, if overweight, family man.

To those who were not strangers, Caputo was known as "Little Cap," his father, and the Dominic Senior, being "Big Cap." In Italian, "caputo" means "big head," and sometimes they were known as "Big Head" and "Little Head," when not within earshot, or even "Big Dickhead" and "Little Dickhead," whispered under the breath and only with the closest and trusted fellow discontents, for neither Dominic was known for his easy manner or sense of humor. To his face, Dominic was addressed as "DJ" (for Dominic Junior), and riffs and permutations based on that. With Dominic Senior, it was simpler.

They just called him "Boss."

Dominic Jr was the idiot of three sons, like Fredo, but with a long sadistic streak and a short fuse. Even though first-born, DJ was never going to reign over the family business. That would fall upon his younger brothers, one of whom was about to receive an MBA from Cornell University.

But DJ had his talents.

He was adept at persuasion by artfully inflicted pain. He was also artful at killing. A master of the gun to the back of the head, the knife across the throat, the icepick in the ear. As the go-to enforcer for the Augusto crime family, he had killed enough people to be on the CDC's Causes of Death index, right after "cancer." Despite his happy-go-lucky front, even associates tiptoed around him they way you might around a large vicious dog.

DJ had a secret.

A deep secret.

Deep and deadly.

He liked young men.

Or at least, he like using young men for his sexual gratification.

Mafiosi are not renown for either a progressive philosophy or a forgiving nature, but they are known for being strict Catholics, if you skip the part about robbery and murder. Since homosexuality was as anathema to Catholic doctrine as garlic to a vampire, the cosa nostra crew could indulge in beating, torturing, or killing a fruit, faggot, or queer, with the Church's tacit blessing and ready forgiveness, to the extent that any of them really cared about either one. Evil men will always find some excuse to do what they had always intended to do in the first place.

DJ, having beaten up a few fruits in his day, was well aware that his unwanted compulsion could buy him a bullet in the head — or much worse — if anyone ever found out, so he took great care that no one ever would. He resisted the awful urge with heroic effort (he claimed), but there were times when the thing was overwhelming. He could not control himself. He didn't want to want it. He couldn't help it.

There were dozens of places DJ could to find available partners of the kind he liked — college kids between 18 and 22 — and Dom knew them all. It wasn't hard for him to meet lads who were happy to hook up with a generous daddy. Obviously, he couldn't risk the possibility that any of them might later come forward, might "out" him, might destroy him. He had to protect himself and protect his family. So each time, when he had finished with his current "date," Dominic would kill him, and dispose of the body in such a way as to never be found. In pieces. And in different places. He knew all about disposing of bodies.

However, when he killed his victims, (he said) he did it as quickly and as painlessly as possible. Usually by snapping the neck. He'd never tortured them or made them suffer, as he might have on a "business deal." See? He wasn't all bad. Really, he wasn't. It was this compulsion of his. It was like a disease. He was every bit as much a victim as the boys were (he said) — probably even more.

Dominic Caputo murdered at least nine young men. The youngest was 16, the oldest, 21. All nine were reported as "missing persons" by family and friends. He may have murdered as many as 30. He probably would have murdered many more.

But he fucked up.

Big time.

He broke his own rules, and everyone knows that breaking your own rules goeth before a fall.

151

It was in early December. Angela had gone to visit her parents; Marie was still away at school. He had the house to himself. He did something he'd never do. Why in hell did he do that? He brought someone home.

It was a Craig's List hook-up. It was short notice. It somehow seemed... simpler. After the sex, he'd broken the kid's neck, easy as a twig, with his powerful hands. He then used assorted power tools to disassemble the body in the bathtub, letting the blood swirl down the drain. He packed the pieces into several large green "industrial strength" plastic garbage bags, and meticulously washed and disinfected the tub. He shuffled the bags out to the trunk of his Cadillac.

Things might have gone trippingly for our hero, if only 15-year old Julie Baldini, from a few blocks over, and her secret boyfriend, Tommy Cagney, 14, who didn't even live in this neighborhood, hadn't decided to fuck, right there against the old oak tree across the street from Caputo's house. It was bold. It was daring. It was dark already. But Julie had eyes like a cat, they said, and when one of the bags caught the corner of the Caddy's bumper, and when it tore open, and when that severed arm spilled out onto the driveway with a cold, wet SMACK, she saw it as well as heard it — and heard Caputo muttering, "God damn it..."

"Holy shit!" she shouted a whisper into her preoccupied boyfriend's ear.

"What? Did I hurt you?"

"No, stupid. Shut up. Look."

DJ was fumbling desperately, stuffing some body parts back into the bag as others fell out. It was almost comical.

"Holy shit," whispered Tommy. "Is that...it looks like...holy shit."

No sooner had the caddy left the driveway, than Romeo and Julie were hastily rearranging their clothes while sprinting down the street — a more challenging feat for Tommy who still had a raging erection that resented both interruption and confinement.

The kids almost didn't go to the cops because they knew it would put them in deep shit. They attended different schools. Julie, daughter of a dental surgeon, attended upscale St. Martin's, and Tommy, raised by his waitress single-mom, was going to old and decrepit Warrick

Junior High. Julie was Italian and Catholic. Tommy was Irish and Protestant.

EEther, EYEther, toe-MAY-toe, toe-mah-toe.

It's the stuff of Shakespeare plays.

They had both lied to their parents about where they were going that evening, who they were going with, and why. Julie was supposed to be at basketball practice. Tommy was supposed to be at band rehearsal. They weren't supposed to be together, they certainly weren't supposed to be fucking, and both kids were convinced that their parents would kill them. Nevertheless, Tommy insisted that they go to the cops about what they'd seen, and Julie didn't take all that much persuading.

A cop named Franz caught the case.

DJ didn't have to be a genius to know that this was an earth-shattering event and his tenuously constructed house of cards was about to get hit by a huge kamakazi. The fat lady pulled into his driveway and started warming up her vocal cords. The worst part for Caputo would not be getting made as a cold-blooded killer, but being "outed" as a queer. That by itself was enough to get him whacked in the joint. But he also knew too much about too much and if he went to prison, he wouldn't survive a week. Plus he didn't want to go to prison.

DJ's father sent along an attorney who charged more per hour than a circus-full of hookers who only drank vintage champagne, but he was more interested in keeping DJ quiet than keeping him out of prison. If nothing else, DJ had the survival instincts of a predator and he knew that he had to do something, and he had to do it fast.

So DJ went to the Feds.

He offered to provide the FBI with detailed information regarding more than two dozen organized crime murders. Names, places, dates. Who did what. Who ordered who. He was privy to this information because he, himself, had been the button man on a number of these killings, had assisted with others, before or after the fact. All this could be theirs in exchange for the one-time, low, low price of blanket immunity. Blanket immunity would mean that he would not be prosecuted for ANY crime he mentioned in his statement or the one he was currently charged with.

The Feds had no idea that, in addition to organized crime hits, Little Cap had murdered a whole bunch of young men for his own personal, sexual reasons. They assumed that the murder that he'd been caught both red-handed and red-faced with had been a contract killing. In their enthusiasm to take down some significant O.C. dignitaries, they pulled out all the stops, and before you could say, "witness protection" ten times fast, they had struck a deal with the Devil. They were quite pleased with themselves, and confidant that they had just gotten the bargain of the century.

Until DJ gave his statement.

# II.

I watched the video. It was enough to turn the tequila in your bones to Margaritas.

"He's a piece of work," I said.

"Isn't he, indeed?" drawled The Judge.

I poured us each another shot of Jose Cuervas, took mine to the window and stared out over the townhouse roofs towards Collegetown. She tossed her shot down and poured herself another. She was a two-fisted drinker when she drank. She never did anything half-assed.

Caputo confessed to multiple murders on that tape. Murders both business and personal. He talked about them like he was describing his high school football career. Game by game, play by play. Who won, who lost, who played, who coached, who fucked the cheerleaders. He threw in a few amusing anecdotes. Like the time his back-up man, Vinnie Carlucci, slipped on some blood and fell on his ass so hard he let out a huge fart. Merry little moments like that. I'll spare you those.

There were no bodies to recover.

He was the best disposal man you'll ever find, even if he did say so himself. But he gave a full accounting, descriptions, names. He'd later identified photos provided by the families of his victims. He confirmed the fate of their beloved sons and brothers as if he were confirming that, yes, he'd found their dog dead on the highway and had given it a decent burial. He was doing them a favor, giving them closure. Because he really was a nice guy, see?

"If he goes into witness protection," I said, "there's going to be more bodies wherever they put him."

"He claims he only killed them so he wouldn't be exposed to his family," said the Judge. She wasn't talking about his family; she meant his "family."

"That's because he's a fucking liar," I said. Not sure how I knew that, but there was no doubt in my mind. Instinct told me he wasn't a stone killer — that is, someone who feels nothing when they kill. This guy pretended to be stone cold, but in reality, he enjoyed it. He wasn't just killing for the practical reason of eliminating witnesses. It was fun. Lots of fun. Probably sexual fun. That meant he wasn't going to stop unless and until somebody stopped him.

Statements, grand juries, testimony, indictments, trials.

These things take a little time.

While waiting for Caputo to sing his spotlight solo in court, the Feds had him stashed in a hotel. They had an army of men protecting him, most of them blended in as well as Tupac Shakur at a Klan rally. His location was the most widely known secret in town.

I myself was ensconced in a studio apartment in an apartment-hotel across the street and down a few doors, about 200 yards away. With a Remington 700 mounted with a Bushnell scope, at this range, it wasn't a difficult shot. The four-round magazine gave me three rounds more than I anticipated needing. Only thing that made the shot challenging: Caputo was sure to be surrounded by bodyguards on all sides. But unless they assigned an agent to ride piggyback on his shoulders, I was fairly confident that from my 7th floor position, I'd have enough of an angle to afford me a clean shot. If I didn't get one, that was that. I wasn't going to shoot up the street, or risk hitting innocent bystanders, or federal agents.

There's always a Plan B.

If you don't have a Plan B, then you don't have a plan at all.

But not this time.

Once he sang his abominable aria for the court, the Feds would whisk him away to another life in another place, and he would be as difficult to find as an honest politician.

So no Plan B.

One single roll of the dice, all or nothing.

I would get a phone call at least thirty minutes before they moved Caputo from the hotel to the courthouse. Guaranteed. I figured it had to be somebody on the inside, someone close to the operation able to access the information, and pass it on without rousing suspicion. I wondered who it could be. A cop? Somebody with the D.A.? A Fed? A well-placed janitor? No way to know. The Judge knew a lot of people.

So I waited.

Three days now.

Just me and a copy of Marcus Aurelius' Meditations.

Except for one other thing.

Directly across the street from my position was a building offering "Luxury studio, one-bedroom, and two-bedroom apartments." The apartments I could see from my vantage point each had a small terrace. Enough space for a couple of people to have a cup of hot coffee together on a Sunday morning, after some lazy sex, or some champagne on a Saturday night, leaning against each other, looking out over the twinkling city lights.

When I'd first set up, I was checking the focus on my scope and I happened to pan by one of those terraces. And that's when I saw her. She was sitting at a computer console, facing the terrace, and so facing me too. I could see her perfectly through the open sliding glass door that separated the terrace from the rest of her apartment. Separated by four lanes of traffic, two curbs, and the sidewalks, we were not more than seventy-five feet apart. Through the scope, she seemed close enough to touch.

I'm not sure what it was that caught my imagination. The impish, turned-up nose, the slightly slanted set of her green eyes, the way she had a pencil tucked behind her ear. Maybe it was the way the grown-out bangs of her pixie-cut dirty blonde hair fell into her eyes. She wore a plain athletic grey sweatshirt about four sizes too large for her, and dungarees that were way too tight. Barefoot.

She reminded me of a little girl I'd had a hopeless crush on when I was about seven or eight. I'd followed my pre-pubescent heart-breaker around for years, like a lost puppy, even forcing myself to go to school on the chance that I might see her, say hello to her, be blessed by her sweet be-dimpled smile. Once or twice I was so blessed, and her smile made the effort more than worth it. I guess I wasn't a precocious child when it came to social skills and the opposite sex. I've learned a lot since then. Sometimes, as the country song goes, I wish I didn't know now what I didn't know then.

Books, books, books.

Piles of books. Stacks of books. Stacks on piles and piles on stacks. All over the place. Surrounding her like phony marauding Indians circling a wagon train in a late night B western. The scope allowed me to make out some of the titles: The Anatomy of Human Destructiveness by Eric Fromm. I knew that one real well. The Encyclopaedia of Erotic Art by the Drs. Kronhausen. William James. D.H. Lawrence. Abraham Maslow. A five language dictionary. All of them with numerous strips of paper sticking out to mark particular pages.

She had armed herself with yellow legal pads, reams of them. She flipped pages, jotted notes, consulted books, flipped them closed again, and pecked furiously at the keyboard like Beethoven on acid, pausing only to brew herself some more coffee, or disappear briefly, presumably to get rid of it.

Eric Fromm and D.H Lawrence? What the hell could she be writing?

While I waited, I watched her work. I don't know why. It's not like I was hoping to catch a glimpse of her in her underwear. There was something about her. Some combination of the familiar and the exotic. If the breeze was favorable, I could detect sounds coming from her apartment, the scrape of a chair, the clink of a spoon in a coffee mug (that wasn't sugar...what was it?), the low murmur of a breathy tenor sax on her stereo. The audible detritus of her life, leaking out into the world.

She didn't go out, but she appeared to be on a first-name basis with a variety of take-out restaurants. She didn't answer the phone, though it rang a lot. She stared at it while she let her answering machine take a message, but I never saw her play back any of the messages. She finally disconnected the phone from the wall.

The court kept bankers' hours, so in the evening I could go out for a quick run, grab a paper, whatever. On the third night, I did part of my cool-down walk past the entrance to her building. I buzzed a few people on the top floor, and when they answered, I said into the intercom next to the mailboxes, "It's me." Somebody buzzed me in. I explored the first floor layout, and calculated what apartment she must be in, and returned to the mailboxes. The name on hers was "J. Arthur." Smart. No way to tell if the tenant was male or female.

That night, I read awhile, but I'd read Meditations many times before, and it could not hold my attention. I doused my lights, and sat behind my tripod at the open window, and watched her work, late into the night. I recognized the music seeping faintly into the muggy night air. Kenny Burrell. Midnight Blue. She played it over and over.

When I finally turned in, I gave her one last look. Her lights were out now, too, and, at first, I didn't recognize her shape, couldn't distinguish her from the other shadows. But she was there. The city's artificial starlight reflected from her skin. I could just make out the swell of a breast, the sweep of a hip as she leaned on the terrace railing, looking up at the night sky.

What was she thinking about? What was she searching for? The Big Dipper? A shooting star? A friendly UFO pilot bringing secrets of the cosmos to share? After a moment, she gathered herself up, turned away, went back inside, with an unhurried, hip-rolling gait, as if listening to a silent samba. The curve of her back, the fullness of her heart-shaped buttocks, burned into my brain, and I can see it vividly, even now.

"Sweet dreams, J. Arthur," I said softly, and stretched out on the bare bed. But I slept poorly, restless, my own dreams unsettling.

Something woke me around 3:00 A.M. I'm not a deep sleeper. A loud car engine could do it. A door slamming. A leaf brushing my window pane. A mouse pissing on a cotton ball. In this case it was the relentless pounding of an angry fist on J. Arthur's door, accompanied by drunken, unintelligible shouting.

I sat up, instantly wide-awake. I went to the window, peered though the scope, and her light snapped on. She came into view wrapping a white terry robe around herself. She went to the door, but didn't open it. She spoke to the person on the other side, but I couldn't hear what she said and she had her back to me so I couldn't read her lips. But her body language shouted out loud and clear: it wasn't a pleasant conversation. It was an argument. A heated one. She ended up

158

pleading, pleading, pressing her palms to her temples, backing away from the door the way you'd back a way from a coiled diamondback you'd almost stepped on.

Then it stopped.

Quiet.

She crept closer, looked through the peephole. Then she turned, lay back against the door and sunk to the floor, face in her hands, shoulders shaking, chest heaving, sobbing.

I was suddenly embarrassed.

Felt like an intruder.

I turned away to give her back her privacy. But I couldn't get it out of my mind, and couldn't get back to sleep. I cleaned and oiled the rifle, dismounted and remounted the sound suppressor, wiped the scope lenses with cleaning solution and thin paper. Rubbed each bullet casing free of any fingerprints, and re-loaded. None of which actually had to be done again.

The next morning, J. Arthur and I were taking a coffee break together — me in my place and her in hers. She'd been working feverishly at her desk since dawn and now sat back to read what she'd written, sipping coffee from a blood red oversized mug.

Atta girl. Stay focused. Don't dwell on whatever is going on with you and the door-pounder.

But it didn't last.

Around 10:00 the pounder came back. It was a re-play of the previous night. But this time I very clearly caught one thing she said. Somewhere between a whisper and a scream. "For God's sake please leave me alone! PLEASE!" Once again her tormentor finally went away.

On impulse, I focused on the street below, on the entrance to the building. Only two people exited there at about the right time. One was a dumpy lady dressed as if for the Mad Hatter's tea party and courting a tiny, yipping dog that resembled a rat with a lousy haircut and a cough.

The other was a man, around 30 years old. Hunky, strapping lad. Reddish-blonde hair, cut real short. Walked with the long, quick strides of the terminally pissed-off. No one else came out. Could her sparring partner live in the building? That was a possibility. Could he have gone out a different exit? That was possible, too. But my gut told me this was the guy, and I rarely argue with my gut anymore. It's been right too many times.

J. Arthur slumped in her chair, head down on her desk, her shoulders shook, and I knew she was crying.

Over the next three days, this scenario repeated with minor variations. The argument through the door, the shouting, the pleading, the tears. There was nothing I could do for her. I don't like it when there's nothing I can do.

On the fifth morning I had just stepped from the shower when the phone rang. A male voice I didn't recognize told me they'd be transporting Caputo to the courthouse at 0800. Then he hung up. No conversation, just information.

I felt a slight adrenaline arousal in the quickening of my heartbeat, palms perspiring more. It can be a subtle thing. I checked my watch — plenty of time. I had a light breakfast just to have something in my stomach, and took up my firing position. I focused in on the hotel entrance and waited.

I had done some executive protection work, myself. I have to say that I don't think I'd have gone about this the way these guys were doing it. They go by the book, which is fine, unless the opposition has read your book. Never assume everybody thinks the same way you do.

At 07:53, three dark, late model Ford Sedans pulled up in front of the hotel entrance.

The Feds always drive the latest vehicles, got to give them that. And why not? They weren't spending their OWN money. Tense men in plain suits, conservative haircuts, and sunglasses emerged from the cars. They might as well have blown a bugle.

At the same moment those car doors slammed, the door pounding across the way began yet again. I put a blanket over it, tried not to listen. I had to keep my focus. I'd made a commitment. I'd given my word.

I fine-tuned my scope. Flicked off the safety. Dug deeper into my shoulder, laid my finger alongside the trigger housing. Any moment now, they'd bring him out. It would be a tight shot. I'd need perfect aim. I had to filter out the angry shouting, the mournful begging.

I can do that.

I could do that.

I had to do that.

160

When they appeared at the entrance and started down the stairs, I slipped my finger lightly onto the trigger, and nothing in the world existed but Caputo's balding pate, and the men floating in and out of focus, all around him. I took a breath. Let half of it out. Perfectly balanced, perfectly focused.

Until the scream.

The scream and the unmistakable sound of splitting wood. The sound of somebody taking down a door. Jarred me loose from my plan and I swung the rifle around and zeroed in on J. Arthur's place.

He had gotten inside her apartment.

My gut had been right, as usual. It was him. Reddish-blonde hair and all. Seeing them together was stunning. He dwarfed her. Had to be six-three or six-four. Two-twenty, if he weighed an ounce. He stormed in, arms gesturing wildly, coming after her like a twister, and demolishing everything in his path. He swept books off a shelf, kicked another pile for a field goal. Knocked over her desk, sending computer and papers flying. He closed in on her slowly, deliberately, enjoying her fear and making it last. She hugged herself and backed away from him. There was no angry shouting now, no pleading. The arguing was all over. Dogs don't bite while they're barking — and they don't bark when they bite.

I spun back over to the hotel. They were approaching the cars. A few more steps, a few more seconds. I would have a narrow, but clear, shot.

Then I heard something large and made of glass shatter, and I knew without looking what had happened. I whipped my scope back to J. Arthur's and right back to Caputo, and in less time than a heartbeat, I realized what I had seen. He had thrown her or punched her through the partially closed balcony door. She was leaning against the terrace railing, blood streaming from her scalp, like a beaten fighter hanging on the ropes, praying to be saved by the bell. But there was no bell. Her attacker was behind her, closing on her like a shark, reaching for her with one hand, the other raised up high, clutching something shiny and heavy, poised to swing it down on her with maximum force.

I did something then that I couldn't do again in a million years, if you paid me a zillion dollars to do it, even if my own life depended on it.

I fired.

Two shots.

The first at J. Arthur's terrace, the second at Caputo's head.

I didn't aim. No time to aim. If I'd thought about it, I wouldn't have done it, but I wasn't thinking about it. Something else was operating that weapon. Something way beyond instinct. At that moment, everything unfolded in ultra-slow motion and because everything slowed down, I had more time. Otherwise, it would be impossible to operate the bolt action as fast as I had to. Somehow, J. Arthur and her attacker, and Caputo and his victims, and the bodyguards and me, we were all intimately connected, performing a ballet we'd rehearsed an infinite number of times. We were all exactly where we were supposed to be, exactly when we were supposed to be there, carried along on invisible flood waters, connected by an invisible thread, coming down the tracks in adjoining cars of the cosmic choo-choo — hell, I don't know, pick a metaphor you like.

At this angle, the first shot exited the skull taking the medulla oblongata of J. Arthur's assailant with it, resulting in instantaneous motor paralysis. He fell heavily back, like a great old tree, his eyes wide with astonishment. The object in his hand was a large bookend. Brass, I believe.

As quickly as I could — which is a lot quicker than most people you'll ever meet — I spun back to Caputo, saw the shine of his thinning hair bobbing in a sea of bodyguards, and squeezed the trigger again, and instantly, his head grew a dark hole half an inch above the temple and then disappeared from view. His protectors sprang into a frenzy of drawn guns, sweeping the street in all directions and looking up, scanning the surrounding buildings for indications of the assassin's location.

On her terrace, J. Arthur was pulling herself together. She was holding one arm to staunch the flow of blood from a cut. Nose and mouth were bleeding — from a punch, probably. And one eye was rapidly swelling to a mere slit. But she'd survive.

She ignored the worthless meat lying on the deck behind her and stepped out on the terrace toward me, leaned out over the railing, searching all around for, I assume, the source of that bullet. For a moment, she seemed to look directly at me.

I doubt that anyone heard the loud slaps the shots had made with the sound suppressor attached — silencers don't really "silence" a firearm. Still, I didn't waste any time packing up and getting out, ditching the weapon, in pieces, down the incinerator chute.

I put in a call to the Judge.

"I tried that recipe you gave me," I said. "I think I just fucked it up."

The police were baffled, bothered and bewildered.

It doesn't take a hell of a lot to baffle them.

They couldn't connect the dots.

They questioned J. Arthur, but they never charged her with anything. The Judge would have had her back if the cops had gone after her. It was amusing to see the Judge trying to be cross with me over it. She wasn't convincing at all.

The authorities, enfin, concluded that the Caputo murder was a mob hit, and that the other death was a bizarre accident of some kind. A stray bullet. Freak coincidence.

You and I know there's no such thing as coincidence.

But I don't mind letting them think what they want to think.

Adam Adrian Crown

*And when I hurt*
*Hurting runs off my shoulder*
*How can I hurt when holding you?*
"Sweet Caroline"
Neil Diamond

# CHAPTER THREE:
# WORTH TEN THOUSAND WORDS

Sometimes, I started feeling like if I had to spend one more fucking second in Hicksville, USA, I was going to explode all over somebody. See, my family had made the big move from the City to the Sticks, but I really hadn't, not emotionally. My heart still had a mailbox on Tobacco Road.

Wolf Lake was an oppressive sea of lily-white, cookie-cutter sameness. I felt like I was drowning, desperately clawing my way to the surface to catch a breath of air. Whenever I could pull a little bread together, I'd sneak out and slip away, like William Holden in Stalag 17, right under the Nazis' noses, hie me back to Chi me where I could breathe, and recharge my batteries.

I'd take the train to Union station, staring out the window as it rocked and rumbled along, the wheels clacking out a back beat on sections of track. I watched desperately for signs of life, as verdant rural grass transmogrified into film noir greys and blacks of concrete and asphalt. It was like watching a time-lapse movie of a garden growing. I welcomed the sight of the first tall building the way a sailor lost at sea would welcome the sight of a large flock of birds.

I grabbed a coffee at the news stand in Union Station, near the Jackson Street exit, glanced over the headlines, lit up a Lucky with a snap of my Zippo, then skipped up the stairs to emerge like Plato's prisoner, out of the cave and into the sunlight.

The scent of summer in the city at State and Jackson is a potpourri of auto exhaust, sun-baked asphalt, sweat, perfume, cigarette smoke, and food aromas from the Palmer House leaking out into the ether. It was the scent of adventure.

Everybody else was on their way to or from work, busy buzzing around doing something or other. Me, I was just adrift, free to wander wherever the trade winds took me. I liked to make my first stop Sam the Shoe Man, the Gene Krupa of the shoeshine. You could hum Sing, Sing, Sing in your head while he soloed with that wax, rag, and brush. When he was done, anybody who looked directly at your feet would turn to stone. You could only view the reflection on your shield.

If I had the bread, I might take the L up to Wiggly Feel, and watch the Cubs try to play. I'm not really a baseball fan. It's just about the most boring game ever invented, except, of course, for golf. It's a complete waste of time. That's its appeal. It's pure escapism. It has no relationship to anything in the real world, outside its artificial environment. Baseball skills don't transfer to anything else, they have no survival value. (Although once, I did use a Mickey Mantle model to slam a certain gent's head for a stand-up triple. That's another story) Once upon a time, they say, before business corporations monopolized it and ruined it, baseball was played just for fun. Baseball was, to humans, what Frisbee is to your dog.

There's something radically indolent about a mid-week afternoon ball game. To stretch out in the sparsely populated stands with a dog and an ice-cold beer while the suckers were busting their asses to make some rich guy richer. Normally, I hate beer. But this is different. It's ritual. Like communion. The dog is the wafer, the beer is the wine, the body, and the blood of The Bambino.

Other times I might take in a movie. The State-Lake Theatre was my personal favorite. The Art Institute was another favorite hang-out, when I was short of funds.
Or I might just occupy a bench near Civic Center, near the Picasso monster. Pablito once said "Art is whatever you can get away with." I guess he proved his point. It was a great spot to people-watch. I confess I focused primarily on female people. There's something about

the fabric of a thin summer skirt stretched taut across the primal jiggle and sway of a woman's ass, that reminds me of the primal jiggle and sway of the sea. And there was good sailing at Civic Center. Across the street, on the corner, was a deli that sold terrific pizza by the slice. Good spot to take a long lunch.

The details of my downtown itinerary varied depending on the time of year and my state of scratch. Sometimes I could disappear for a whole weekend, knowing my mother would be working and didn't give a fuck, and my father would be drunk and didn't give a fuck.

On the particular occasion I have in mind, it was late Fall. Thanksgiving had thankfully come and gone with no more injuries than usual, but the Christmas slaughter was now closing fast. Holidays always meant more stress, more yelling, plate-smashing, more beatings arising from spontaneous combustion. But to be fair, I was no longer subjected to physical abuse. The last time my old man had laid hands on me, I parted his hair with a beer bottle. A full one. Not sure who was more surprised, him or me. After that, I made sure he knew I always carried a knife on me.

I had spent the day downtown, having cut school, but Fall temperature fell and landed on exceptionally wintry, and since I had no place to stay, no money, and was underdressed for it, I grudgingly grabbed the 6:10 back to the Planet of the Squares.

Looking out the window of the train, the lights of the city, like a million multi-colored fireflies, gradually diminished, until they disappeared entirely, and there was only blackness. My coach was once again a pumpkin; my horses, little white mice.

Frigid and forlorn, I made my way to Bruno's where One-Eyed Tico and the Cicero Kid were engaged in a game of 8-ball. Bruno went back into his "office," which was what he called his spartan one-room living quarters, and brought me out a mug of black coffee. Bruno was a pretty cool guy.

Tico and the Kid traded skin with me, but there was something funny going on. They had the look and manner of a pair of cats who had stuffed themselves on canary and were now afraid to belch for fear of revealing inculpatory bird breath.

167

"What?" I said.

"What what?" said The Kid

"Should we?" said Tico to the Kid.

"What, right now?" said the Kid to Tico

"He looks like he could really use it."

"Yeah, but it ain't Christmas yet."

"Right. Is it Chanukah? It could be for Chanukah?"

"I don't know. But he ain't Jewish…"

"HEY!" I said. "I'm IN the fucking room."

"Be cool, man," said The Kid. "All's cool. Like, trust me."

Tico and the Kid exchanged a nod.

"So like, you dig that Jensen chick right?" said the Kid.

He knew the answer to that, so why was he asking? Caroline Jensen. Blonde. Shy. A little too much space between her two front teeth added to her charm. She was one of the "good" kids from the proper side of the tracks, but didn't use that as a bludgeon every time she opened her mouth like most of them did. Plus, I'd caught her looking at me in class. She was well known to be and much celebrated as an "A" student. Funny thing, when a "good" kid got A's, their name was in the paper. When one of us mutts got A's nobody fucking noticed. The school figured it was a fluke, just luck, or proof that we'd cheated. Under those conditions, it doesn't take long for you to say fuck it and quit trying, and most of us had.

But that wasn't her fault.

She was as much a prisoner as we were.

Different cell block, that's all.

"I guess she's okay," I conceded. I'd long since learned never to let anyone know what you really think or feel, and sometimes I was even guarded with those I considered friends.

"I got something for ya," said Tico, and he reached out and slapped his palm down on the green felt. When he withdrew it, he left behind what I first thought was a playing card. It wasn't. It was about 3x5 inches, but it wasn't an index card either. It was a photo print, face down. Serrated edges. "Merry fuckin' Christmas, 'manito," Tico said as his acne-ridden cheeks spread into a wide grin.

I picked up the photo.

It was Caroline Jensen.

Naked.

It wasn't a great photo.
It was a little out of focus, and under-exposed.
But it was her.

She was framed in the center of a narrow corridor, standing sideways to the camera, face and upper body turned toward it. She appeared to be either picking up or putting down a white towel from or onto a wooden bench behind her. The ends of her hair appeared to be wet, straggly and darker than the rest of it.

What I took to be somebody else's arm reaching blurrily across the foreground obscured part of her midsection, but not her slender arms and legs, not the slight rounded contour of her buttocks, not the almost perfectly flat chest, not the wisp of pubic curls. Puberty had attacked her unevenly and late, and was nowhere near finished with her yet.

"Holy fuck," I said. "How'd you get this?" Obviously, it was taken in the girls' locker room.

"Santa Claus," said the Kid.

Untrue.

It wasn't Santa at all. Just one of his devious former-elves, cut loose for drinking on the job and fondling too many little dollies. Wally, the school custodian. Doubled as a bus-driver. He was a big, brawny circus bear of a man, laden with a bulldog underbite and occasional stutter, who slushed his "s" like a west Texas tent-show preacher. Renown for his amiable disposition, he always had a smile and a good word for everyone.

It seems that Wally — called "Walter" only by the uber-prissy Mrs. Trautmann, the vice principal — had either found or created one or more peepholes into the girls' shower room from the adjacent furnace room and storage closet, with which it shared walls. According to my smug benefactors, Wally had amassed quite a collection of photos over his long tenure as jack-of-all-janitors at the school, developing and printing the film himself, for obvious reasons.

The Cicero Kid had accidentally discovered one of the peepholes when he and Becky Clark had sneaked into the storage closet to make out. He'd wisely kept the secret to himself, pending an opportunity to use the knowledge to some advantage. Investigating further, putting two and two together, the Kid had caught Wally red-handed, jacking off while peeking into the girls' showers after volleyball practice. They had quickly cut a deal in which Wally agreed to share in exchange for the Kid's discretion, a sucker deal if there ever was one, but what choice did he have? The Kid getting an eyeful of Wally's artwork, had negotiated the provenance of Caroline's portrait to extend to me. I was deeply touched that the Kid, under those circumstances, would think of me. That's true friendship.

I had lots of Playboy centerfolds to fuel my fantasies. And some Scandinavian nudist magazines by way of Tico's uncle, and even some hardcore rags to saddle up with. But this photo, this was different. This was somebody I knew, somebody I saw all the time, somebody I talked to. That changed the meaning of the photo, as much as the photo changed the meaning of my knowing her. I now knew something about her that others didn't know, and even though she didn't know I knew it, it made me feel, somehow, closer to her. Like we shared a secret. I don't know why, exactly. It's not like SHE had given me a pic of herself to masturbate over.

Nevertheless, having seen Caroline naked, I felt a strange connection to her that I didn't have with anyone else, except maybe with my sister. I found myself being nice to her for no apparent reason, and was inclined to act as her defender, her protector, her champion, or some silly shit like that.

Yeah, I know that doesn't make any sense.
When it comes to sex, love and rock & roll, what does?

*These are tears from a long time ago*
*I got these tears from a long time ago*
*I need to cry 30 years or so*
*These are tears from a long time ago*
 "Thirty Years of Tears"
 John Hiatt

# CHAPTER FOUR:
# VENDETTA

## I.

You go to the corner of Third Avenue and Lincoln, kitty-corner from the new Rite-Aid drugstore; you'll find Lupo's Hardware. It's a modest place, one of the few not to have been devoured by the big-box chains, but it has just what you need, depending on what you need. The proprietor was technically a locksmith by trade, the guy you run to when you lose your keys, or need to change your locks because your lover went ballistic, or because you want to get into something you weren't intended to get into. If an item could be locked, Lupo could open said item. He's also a wiz with alarms. He can design, install, and maintain a system for you that will transform your humble abode into Fort Knox. That's not his best feature, though. The most remarkable thing lies below the surface.

Some call him a navajero.

Loosely translated, the word means something like "knife-ist." If you're a Marvel Comics fan, you might say "Knife-man." He doesn't wear a cape, doesn't sport tights, and doesn't display his jockeys on the outside of his clothes. But he can make knives do things. Odd things. Impossible things. And if you ever see him do those things you'll swear it's his super-power. That, and his ability to consume espresso.

171

A well-made knife is an excellent tool. It's versatile and effective. Its shark bite is quiet, unlike a gun with a "silencer," which minimizes, but does not eliminate, the report. Knives are inexpensive, so they can be discarded without hesitation. They are available virtually everywhere. They require no maintenance, are easy to conceal, and are legal to possess with no "registration" or "background check" required. A knife has two limitations. First, it's strictly a close-quarters weapon. Second, you have to know what you're doing. You need the kind of skill that only comes with patient, loving practice.

I'm no stranger to the knife. I know where all the arteries are and how to get to them, and make you wish I hadn't. But Lupo is on another level of consciousness entirely.

Take knife throwing, for instance. It ain't rocket science, though physics comes into play. All it takes is a little practice. Lupo, though, he's the Cy Young of tossing a blade. He can make a knife dance, make it drop, make it curve; make it arrive with the speed of a world-class fastball. I've seen him bury an Arkansas toothpick three, almost four inches deep into a pine log from 25 feet away. Had a hell of a time getting the damn thing out.

He keeps knives the way some people keep salt-water tropical fish. Knives of all kinds. Long ones, short ones, fat ones, thin ones. Blondes, brunettes, and redheads. Sheath knives. Switchblades. Knives that can spring-fire the blade out of the handle like a crossbow, but with less noise.

I once asked him what he thought of the "butterfly" knife.

"Paisan'," he said, "I don't think about them at all." He owned one, though, kept in a drawer along with rubber bands, a ball of string, a corkscrew, and some expired condoms.

Some people assumed that Lupo, being Sicilian, he must be mobbed up at least knee deep, but they were wrong. Like me, he was too much a loner to play well with others, and not greatly inclined to take orders from someone simply because they had managed to ass-kiss their way up the chain of command. However, he would sometimes let people assume whatever they wanted to assume, and use their assumptions to his advantage. Nevertheless, despite being an "independent," he knew a lot of people.

He was hard, rugged, experienced, and just a little bit nuts. The wrong guy to fuck with, but the right guy to have on your side, the rightest possible guy if you had to get into someplace where you weren't supposed to be, the kind of place where the opposition was numerous and had to be eliminated quickly and silently, the kind of place you might not get out of again.

The kind of place where I was going.

## II.

She had reappeared, like a magician's assistant, about two weeks earlier.

I hadn't seen her in a whole lot of years. Maybe longer. Not since she'd left me high and dry south of the border, down Mexico way, and I could still hear the church bells ringing. But when I opened the door and saw her standing there, with her raven hair, and slightly manic gleam in her eyes, when I felt the scent of her slip from my nostrils into my brain, stirring my nether regions awake like an old dog catching a whiff of beef bone in his dreams, it felt as if no time had passed at all. As if we'd been having a late supper and she'd excused herself to hit the ladies' room. She looked the same as when we'd parted company. Maybe she had an extra wrinkle now; maybe she had a couple additional pounds. Maybe I did, too.

We stood there silently for what might otherwise have been an awkwardly long time as old forgotten feelings surged through me like a devil-tide, sweeping away all obstructions in its path.

"I found him," she said.

She didn't mean Jesus.

I knew who she meant, and I knew what she meant. And I knew why.

You might as well know, too.

The last time I'd seen her, lo these many years ago, was in sunny Mexico. She helped me conduct appropriate memorial services for recently fallen comrades, and afterward we'd struck up something of a friendship, insofar as a relationship based on cheap booze and blistering sex can be called a friendship. Her name was Dolores, but she called herself Linda and everyone knew her as Nancy.

On meeting her, I had a sense of a turbulent undercurrent beneath her placid surface, some ghost of Christmas past she couldn't quite shake, some demon closing in on her, taut, heart-shaped ass. But I'm

173

not one to pry. Far be it from me to look a gift whore in the mouth. She proved herself creatively carnal, carnally creative, and in my current state of mind, who could ask for anything more?

During one of our breaks between rounds — she was ahead on points and looking at a victory by knockout before the final bell — we wandered out to find food, because man does not live by bed alone. In flagrante delectable, she had pounded my pubic bone with such ferocity I felt like I'd been fucked by a sledge hammer, and I now felt so bruised and sore, even pressing my loin chops against her well-padded ass elicited a wince of sweet pain. I wasn't ready to throw in the towel, but I had staggered back to my corner wishing I had a better cut-man. So I happily agreed to the respite.

We wandered aimlessly through the streets awhile, so seemingly drunk on love that we made elderly men weep, stout matrons smile, and children giggle. With my arm glued to her shoulders keeping her tight against me, and hers around my waist, with her hand in my back pocket absently cupping my ass, we must have looked like a pair of horny teenagers experiencing their first real romance — which was about the farthest possible thing from what we were. We were long past our teens and we were more in lust than in love. I bought her a flower of deep, dark red. It emanated a fragrance of vanilla. I don't know why I did that.

When we paused to buy some tortillas, I spotted the Mutt and Jeff odd couple down the street, behind us, but didn't give them much thought, being lost in the dizzying influence of l'amour. One of them, tall and built like a football hero, was blonde with a jarhead haircut and a prematurely receding hairline. The other was shorter, heavy, but not fat, shiny black hair, thick and slicked back. Both wore sunglasses. Both dressed in casual, somewhat loud and unstylish tourista clothes that looked too new, fold creases still in them, fresh out of the package or off the rack.

If I'd been firing on all cylinders, I might have picked up on that tell sooner, seen other discrepancies, and been immediately on my guard. But when you've been cunt surfing for too long, and guzzling tequila like you could get a doctorate in dipsomania and you were preparing to defend your dissertation, it can shave the keen edge off your lightning-like reflexes.

By the time I finally made them, I was reacting instead of acting, and barely eked away from the bull's horns by a hair on my chinny-chin-chin.

They made their move near the mouth of an alley.

BAM!

Only it happened a lot faster than you can say "BAM!"

Jarhead jumped me from behind, wrapping his meaty arms around my neck and head, intent on putting me into a sleeper hold, possibly choking me out permanently. Greasy went after my paramour with a foot-long Bowie that Freud would have had something to say about.

That's when it finally dawned on me.

Their shoes.

Not tourista shoes. Comfortable sensible shoes.

Cops' shoes.

I can be slow, but I'm not stupid.

I reached down and grabbed Jarhead's testicles and gave them a hard squeeze and twist, doing my best to rip them from his crotch, and my grip is fairly strong. Seizing the moment, as well as his balls, I torqued my head around enough to take a nice big bite out of his forearm. I'm afraid I ruined his faded eagle-ball-and-anchor tattoo. Its semper would never be fidelis again.

"Ah! MotherFUCKer!" I believe he said.

I can't be a hundred percent sure of what happened next. A blur of frantic action lasting only a few seconds. I think the combination ball-buster and arm-bite bought me a little slack in time and space, and a little slack was all I needed. I started machine-gunning elbows behind me, aiming at Jarhead's face or solar plexus or anything else I could destroy. I heard and felt one of those elbow swings crunch into the soft cartilage of his nose, which allowed me to spin out of his grasp. His conflicting reflexes couldn't decide whether to buckle forward to guard his genitals, or rear back to protect his face. I took advantage of the opportunity presented by his moment of indecision and threw some odds and ends at his throat. One of those miscellanea connected with his trachea to satisfying effect.

He stopped thinking about me.

While he'd been trying to crush my windpipe, close off my carotid arteries and/or break my neck, I'd felt the gun in his waistband digging into the small of my back, and now I flipped up the hem of his baggy, flowered shirt with one hand and snatched his piece away with the other. A Colt 1911. My favorite. I interpreted that as a favorable omen.

They say you don't appreciate what you've got until it's gone. Air is one of those things you take for granted until you can't get any, and with Jarhead now experiencing the wonders of anoxia to a sophisticated degree, he no longer posed an immediate threat.

I turned my attention to my compañera.

She was keeping Greasy embarrassingly at bay by throwing kicks at his groin and swinging her handbag at him like the founder of a new martial discipline.

Purse-jitsu.

Her unexpected ferocity, plus Jarhead's sudden reversal of fortunes, had stunned Greasy into inaction for perhaps a quarter of a second too long. I had a gut feeling that Jarhead's Colt already had a round in the pipe, and I decided to test my theory. I cocked the hammer and fired off a shot at Greasy, but as I did, I slipped on something — dog shit, I think — lost my balance and fell on my ass. I blame the poor dog shit, but it's possible I just tripped over myself. Adrenaline can fuck with such unsung bit players as your balance and your manual dexterity. My danse macabre sent the bullet into Greasy's thigh instead of into his chest as intended. Still, a .45 slug in your thigh will definitely demand your full attention for at least a moment or two. He went down clutching the wound tightly with both hands, face contorted, growling. Which pleased me immensely.

With the world spinning, my eye suddenly got snagged on the ring gracing Greasy's finger. Third finger. Right hand. Familiar somehow, that ring. I knew I'd seen it, or one just like it, before. Sometime. Someplace. But I couldn't remember where or when.

Fuck it. Not important at the moment.

"Run!" I yelled. Cunningly brilliant plan. The gentlemanly thing would be to stay behind while the lady got away while the getting was get-able, and prove to my new playmates they were as mortal as Socrates. And that's exactly what I intended to do.

"No!" she yelled back. "Come on!"

"Run, dammit!"

"Come ON, dammit!"

Sweet thing, but she could be a bit of a nag.

I peripherally glimpsed a car fast approaching. A dark late model Ford.

That did not bode well.

"Fuck, Baby! Come ON...ÁNDALE!" She added a staccato string of high-velocity Spanish expletives. I didn't catch all of them, but I found the general timbre persuasive, and I decided to ándale.

So we bolted.

Behind us, I heard the car screech to a halt, and lots of bi-lingual swearing and sputtering.

We ran faster.

We ran helter-skelter, careened one way then another, around corners, in and out of buildings.

Ran like hell was following right on our ass and gaining ground. Which it was.

# III.

For every action, there's an equal and opposite reaction.

So the effect of smacking your elbow into the 10-pound mass of bone that is someone's head, is much the same as the effect of someone smacking a 10-pound rock into your elbow: it hurts.

It was a cinch we couldn't go back to my hotel, so we ducked into the nearest dingy dive we could find and afford with what we had on us. One of those anonymous places where they rent rooms by the hour and you need picture I.D. if you're Andrew Jackson. I had enough in my wallet to get us a room, some booze, and some ice. I wrapped some ice chips in my handkerchief and massaged my elbow with the stinging cold. Keep the swelling down.

My querida was still wide-eyed and breathless, but this was no time to indulge in the alluring sight of those deeply heaving breasts, those soft, cozy, comfortable...

Well, maybe for just a second. You've got to stop and smell the roses.

"Look, I'm sorry," I said. "I don't know who those guys were, or what the story is, but I'm guessing I pissed somebody off. I'm sorry I got you mixed up in the middle of whatever the fuck is going on."

She took a slow belt of hooch, draining the glass, and poured herself another.

"Thanks," she said. "but you don't have to apologize. They weren't after you. They were after me."

"I beg your pardon?"

She laid the story out for me.

I'll lay the story out for you.

In the early 1980's the people of El Salvador, the tiniest and most densely populated country in Central America — Dolores's country — were being crushed under the brutal heel of a fascist government. A guerilla movement consisting of a coalition of resistance groups arose to fight that oppressive government. The motley crew eventually became known as the FMLN, for "Farabundo Marti National Liberation Front."

Don't worry about remembering the name.

You can think of them as the rebels. Or the Minutemen. We can call the extreme right-wing government oppressors the "Redcoats."

As usual, the United States rallied to the side of the Redcoats, thanks to Democrat Jimmy "The Carpenter" Carter and Republican Ronald "Hollywood Ron" Reagan — which illustrates how fundamentally different the two monopoly parties really are.

In addition to M-16's, Coca-Cola and Playboy magazines, Uncle Sam supplied the Redcoats with special training in "counter-insurgency techniques" at a place called "School of the Americas," located at Fort Benning, Georgia. By "counter-insurgency techniques," is meant torture, kidnapping, rape, and murder. Of course, the official story claims they never taught any such thing. They claimed that the training emphasized due process and human rights and brotherly love. Peace through macramé.

Uh-huh.

So you can imagine how embarrassing it would be for them when the actual torture manuals later came to light. Water-boarding. Sexual sadism. Stuff that would gag a maggot. I don't know how a human being can even think up that shit. Your tax dollars at work, daddy-o.

One of the graduates to proudly wear the SOA ring was Colonel Ernesto Narvaez — known as El Tiburón, "The Shark" and not for his toothy smile or his cold, dead black eyes. He commanded Atlacatl Battalion, a unit named, incidentally, for a famous indigenous warrior who fought against the brutal oppression of the invading Spanish in the 16th century, which makes for a dizzying combination of irony and déjà vu.

The little town of Santiago — her little town — was located on the fertile banks of the Rio Blanco. Life should have been sweet for the 600 or so residents. But there were rumors of rebels in the mist. A rebel hiding out there. Or someone who might be a rebel. Or a rebel sympathizer. Or someone who knew someone who knew a rebel sympathizer. Or someone who had farted during the national anthem. Wicked men will always find a way to justify doing the things they had planned on doing all along and call it macaroni.

When the grim reaper came riding into town, Dolores was dallying in a cave not far from town, playing "show me yours and I'll show you mine" with a nimble young lad named Jorge, who had dreams of becoming a lawyer and ridding his country of injustice.

Their flirtation saved both their lives.

Temporarily.

Colonel Narvaez came to town with his troops in force. Over the next three days they systematically tortured and murdered everyone in Santiago.

Everyone.

The women, of course, they repeatedly raped first — if you call girls as young as eight "women." The soldiers laughed about how tight those young ones were, and bragged about how their massive, manly cocks had torn their tiny vaginas apart.

Many of the children, even infants, they strung up by the heels and slit their throats. Narvaez left not a man, woman, or child alive when his troops burned the town to the ground at the end of the third day. Among the dead were Dolores' father and mother, a brother, and two younger sisters — as well as uncles, aunts, and cousins — almost everybody is related to almost everybody else in such places.

Dead men tell no tales, but surviving witness can be a pain in the ass. My haunted lady and her boyfriend, who watched from a distance, as the nightmare unfolded, couldn't do a damn thing to stop it.

But tell the tale, they did.

The news of the massacre ripped through the country like a hunting knife through a rusty screen door. The government claimed no knowledge of the incident, and regretted that they had no way to find out what unit had been involved, or who had been in command. In any case, if such an atrocity had actually happened, the bloody deed surely must have been the work of the communist rebels.

However, both witnesses could identify the insignia worn by the soldiers, and could describe in detail the commanding officer, whose face they would never be able to exorcise from their nightmares as long as they lived.

For Jorge, that wouldn't be a very long time.

Within two weeks of coming forward with the story of the massacre, he disappeared without a word. Without a trace. They found his car, ignition on, but run out of gas.

Dolores's survival instinct took over, and with the help of some Catholic nuns (who would themselves later fall victim to one of the infamous death squads), she managed to slip out of the country one step ahead of the snapping jaws of El Tiburón, to find herself in this cheesy motel room with me.

"Narvaez knows eventually we will win," she said. "And when we do, there will be a reckoning. He knows I can identify him. So he has sent men to find me. I thought I had... Now, I better disappear, querido. Before someone else disappears me."

"Easy, I said. "Take it easy. Don't panic. Let's think it through. See if we can come up with a plan."

"They almost killed you. They tried."

"Almost only counts in horse-shoes and hand grenades," I said. "This isn't my first tango in Paris." Okay. I probably didn't say anything quite so slick. But something along those lines, I'm sure.

"Are you crazy? Why would you do that? Why get involved...?"

"I just hand-castrated one guy and ruined another guy's ballet career. I think I'm already pretty involved. And they don't seem like the forgiving type."

"No," she said. "No, they're not."

I applied some more of that hooch to my elbow internally. Tasted like gasoline spiked with tabasco sauce. What the fuck had I bought?

Sometime during the long conversation that ensued, I suggested that instead of waiting around for Narvaez to come and make her into a lamp, a wiser plan might be to go on the offensive, track this fucker down in his own crib and put a bullet into some select part of his anatomy.

An attack would be the last thing he'd expect.

180

He expected her to run, to hide, to get as far away from him as possible. Hold still. Look small. Don't draw attention. That's prey behavior, and the predator counts on it. The predator knows the patterns of the prey and as long as the prey follows those patterns, follows those rules, the prey is fucked.

If you're the prey, well, then fuck that. You better play by a whole different set of rules.

You can turn the tables on the predator. You can abandon the nature of prey, and adopt the nature of the predator. You can let go of your patterns, and you can learn the patterns of the predator just as if the predator were prey. In fact, when you do that, you transmogrify the whole scene. The poles reverse. Up is down. Day becomes night. Night becomes day. Prey becomes predator, and predator becomes prey.

Your prey.

See, the predator doesn't know the game has changed, has no idea what's going on. He has never in his wildest imagination ever entertained the notion that he, himself, could be the hunted. He still thinks he's the hunter.

By the time he realizes he's not the one doing the hunting, it's too late for him to catch up. It's a thing of beauty to behold. Like cosmic ju jitsu with a twist of lime.

It's a madman's world. The big fish eat the little fish. The little fish eat the tiny fish. The tiny fish eat the teensie-weensie fish. The predator believes he's the biggest, baddest fish in the briny blue, perched way up there at the tip-top the food chain. He doesn't expect his prey to turn out to be a great white shark named Bruce.

The idea made Dolores smile with half her mouth. Or it could have been the booze.

"I wish," she said. "If I could...find him. Find him alone, without his army. If I could do that..."

"What?"

"I would kill him," she said. "Slowly."

My kind of woman.

We drank a toast to the idea. The stuff wasn't so bad after you'd drunk enough of it. Probably cauterized your taste buds.

Then we indulged in each other again, in the dead of night hours. But this time, not the famished ravaging of the starving man who wants to eat everything all at once and a lot of it.

This was different.

Slow and soft and tender.

Gentle and easy.

We went into the abyss together, wrapped in each other's arms, holding on tight, tighter, wanting to never let go, and knowing that we would.

I awoke to a golondrina chirping just before dawn, and it reminded me of the saddest song I know. My jacket still hung on a chair back. My cigarettes still lay on the table. Jarhead's pistol still snoozed under the pillow.

But she was missing.

Missing.

She'd taken the rest of my cash with her. Not exactly a fortune. A few bucks short of a grand. I didn't care about the money. Money is easy.

On the pillow, she'd left the flower. Wilted now, but still smelling faintly of vanilla.

## IV.

The next thing that happened, it's kind of a funny story, if I tell it just right.

So, yeah, she left me swinging in the wind like a limp dick, but not *with* a limp dick. To prove to myself how little her split and splitting mattered to me, and because I had time, money, and the inclination, I waltzed around the border, stumbling from dive to dive like a former champ kissing the canvas for upstart tomato cans on the downslide of his noble career. But she was a hard act to follow, and none of the chicas bonitas I offered a shot to were quite up to the task. I rode a merry-go-round of boozing, fucking, and gambling for a week, maybe two. Possibly three.

I was floating a few inches above gravity one night shortly before it would be the next morning, musing to myself with forced jocularity, trying to remember what street my shitty hotel was on, but for some reason only able to recall the lyrics to "Old Stewball" (was a racehorse, and I wish he were mine; he never drank water, he only drank wine…)

They appeared out of nowhere, which is to say my guard had been so low; I hadn't noticed them following me. They cut me off in an alley, the way a good cutting horse isolates a cow for doctoring, but they weren't concerned for my health. Like a chump, I let them surround me before I knew it.

These guys weren't all local boys out to play mug-the gringo.

Even in my bleary state of mens in recto, I recognized the two goons she and I had so recently danced with. I was pleased to see that Greasy had what appeared to be a painful limp. A bullet will do that.

The third guy was a wiry kid, looked like a local. Oily hair and nasty bad teeth.

Back a bit stood a clean-cut mope around thirty years old, broad of shoulder, narrow of waist, intent of gaze. I made him for the General because he wasn't interested in being in the front lines.

Feeling cavalier, I spouted a quote from one of my least favorite assholes. "Hurrah, boys!" I said. "Now we've got 'em."

It went over their heads. Except for General Clean Cut. He smirked. He got it. Which meant he was one twisted son of a bitch.

I wiggled around and managed to get my back against a wall, so I had that going for me at least. But four guys is one too many, and in my present state of crapulence, four guys was four too many. Two of them flanked me on either side. Lieutenant Leg Wound came in close from the front. With a wave of his right hand, a CLICK of the blade, and a hearty hi-yo Silver, he made a knife appear. Wicked navaja with a six-inch blade. A light from someplace glinted from the edge as it snapped open.

I put my hands up in what is universally recognized as a gesture of surrender.

"Nice," I said. "Can you do card tricks, too?"

"Smart ass, huh," he grunted. "Nobody likes a smart ass."

"Aw, c'mon," I said. "*Some* people do."

He pressed the point of the knife up under my chin, just hard enough to draw a bit of blood. "I'm going to enjoy this," he said. He put the true edge of the blade just below the notch between my clavicles, and traced a line down my chest. Just enough pressure to cut through my undershirt and my skin. I hardly felt it at first — that knife was scalpel-sharp, and I'd already self-administered considerable anesthesia. But a moment later, it started to sting.

There's something about the prospect of a premature autopsy that is exceedingly sobering. My head cleared immediately. I felt like that panicking soldier in all the B war movies whose commanding officer bitch-slaps him out of having a nervous breakdown. "Thank you, Sir," I thought. "I needed that."

"Who the fuck are you?" I said. "What do you want?"

I didn't really care what he wanted. I only cared about what I wanted, and what I wanted was to get him talking. See, your typical reaction time is about a quarter of a second. But if you're running your mouth, that slows way, way down. Half a second. Even longer. A lot can happen in half a second.

He grinned and started telling me in substantial detail what he was going to do to me. It involved the knife, his dick, and something about shitting down my neck.

My hands being up, they were already in reasonable proximity to the knife, and on the hinterlands of his peripheral vision.

While he was waxing eloquent, I abruptly shot the edge of my right hand — yeah, the "karate chop" edge — as hard and as fast as I could, across my chest and to the left, aiming at the wrist of his knife hand. At the same time, I jerked my open left hand across my chest and to the right, aiming for the knife. I got it, too, but grabbed enough of the blade to open up a deep cut on my palm. I still have the scar from that. But no plan is perfect.

My right connected with his wrist momentarily ruining his grip on the knife, and my left grasped the knife and pulled it from his hand.

It took a LOT less than half a second.

Before he had quite understood what had just happened, I reversed direction and brought his knife, now in my left hand, in a wide, sweeping arc to my left.

His neck happened to be in the way.

The sudden warm spurt of his blood hit me in the face like a soft, patty-cake jab, but went into both my eyes, temporarily blinding me, because blood stings like hell and you instinctively squeeze your eyes shut.

While I was sightless as Sampson, some phucking philistine hit me with a ton of bricks and I went where nobody knows you: down and out.

I don't know how long I was unconscious. One could argue it had been all my life, but that's another tale.

I awoke tied to a chair, arms behind me.

No blindfold. No gag.

That's not good.

I didn't move, didn't want to let anyone know I was back from Birdland. I listened intently, couldn't hear shit. No people talking, no traffic noise, no nothing. The smell of old oil and gasoline told me this place was or had recently been a garage.

Somebody doused me with ice-cold water, and I came up sputtering.

Then the festivities began.

The crew from the alley was present, and so was another guy, a fat Hispanic with a cheesy mustache and a cheap-looking suit. He did the talking. General Clean Cut took on the Bardian task of matching the action to the word, punctuating each question Señor Cheesy Mustache asked me, with a smack across my face, or a driving punch to my gut.

It was old school. Nothing scientific or sophisticated.

Sometimes, Clean Cut would take a break and one of the other Hardy Boys would come off the bench.

"Give me the other guy," I said to the substitute, after a particularly vicious slam to my belly. "You punch like a girl." I don't have anything against girls, and I know some who can punch, I just wanted to piss in his face. He replied with a wicked hook to my cheek. I looked up at my interrogator, and shook my head sadly. I said, "Good help is SO fucking hard to get these days, isn't it?"

The questions themselves were meaningless to me.

Guns.

Who got them the guns?

Where is the woman?

How'd they get the guns?

Who bought the guns?

Where is the woman?

Who smuggled them down to the rebels?

Where is the woman?

Same questions, over and over and over.

And I answered the questions truthfully, over and over and over.

"I don't know what the fuck you're talking about," I said. Until I finally said, "I don't know what the fuck you're talking about, and if I DID know anything, I wouldn't tell you, hijo de puta, tu follador..." I sang them an aria containing every Spanish curse word I'd ever heard.

Understand, I wasn't trying to be a tough guy.

I might have told them the answers if I'd known them, or I might have made up a convincing lie. Or even an unconvincing lie if I thought it would save my skin.

But when you know they're going to kill you, you have nothing to lose by telling them to go fuck themselves. Most dangerous opponent there is, is someone who has nothing left to lose.

The party could have lasted hours or it could have lasted days. I couldn't tell you. Eventually, Señor Cheesy became convinced that I knew nothing, or that I was going to say nothing even if I knew it. Maybe he was bored. Maybe he was out of time. Maybe he was out of patience. I don't know.

He gave Clean Cut the nod and said, "Get rid of him."

I landed heavily in the bed of a truck where they tossed me like a sack of garbage and covered me with a tarp that stank of rotten fish. Hands tied behind my back. Feet bound tightly together. I hurt everyplace I had a place. Stabbing pain on each inhale, a pretty good sign of busted ribs. Coughed a lot and coughing hurt all the way down to my toes. I winced with every bump and pothole that sent a jarring wave of pain through me. My mind raced with desperation. What was I going to do? I would have to make a move — I wasn't just going to lay down and die, wasn't going to cooperate. I'd go down swinging, if I could manage any kind of a swing at all.

If.

It was a long drive. And quiet. Through the tarp, I could feel the warmth of the sun, alternate with the cool of shade. Once, I though I heard the faint warble of a swallow far away. Could have been my imagination. La Golindrina. Perfect. I chuckled mirthlessly, but not much because it hurt to do that, too.

The truck finally purred to a halt. Must have been at least 20 or 30 minutes' drive. Clean Cut dragged my ass out of the truck, and lowered me to the soft, grassy ground. It was lovely and secluded wooded pasture area, and the air smelled fresh and sweet. Great place to graze horses, or have a picnic, or dispose of a body.
It was time to make my move.
But I didn't have one.
This was it.
My next move would have to be in another life.
Maybe I'd be reincarnated as a complete fucking idiot.
That would be a step up.
While waiting for the bullet to kiss the back of my head, I started humming La Golindrina to myself. Not exactly a move. But it was all I had.
I felt a tugging at my feet, and the ropes binding them suddenly loosened and my feet were free.
Then I felt the cold steel of a blade against my wrists, and though my hands were numb, I felt the pressure lessen and the ropes disappeared.
Clean Cut rolled me over, sat me up with my back against a tree trunk. He squatted down beside me. He lit up a cigarette, took a drag, and then stuck it in the corner of my mouth. Lit another one for himself.
Whiskey-tango-foxtrot?
He looked over what was left of my face.
I looked him over too, as best I could, considering my eyes were swollen almost shut. I noticed he had baby-blue eyes. And a tiny crescent-shaped scar high on one cheek. He wore a plain, thin gold wedding band. His voice was a higher pitch than I would have expected. An Irish tenor.

"Listen," he said. "Get the fuck out of here. You show up here again, and it's MY ass, see? So this is a one-time offer. Don't fuck it up."

He laid a small wad of folded bills on my lap, stood up, closed his knife and slipped it into the back pocket of his pants.

"You're about a mile away from a doctor," he said, pointing down the road with his whole hand in platoon-leader fashion. "If you can make that."

"I'll make it," I told him.

"All right. Don't forget what I said." He turned back toward the truck, paused and looked back at me. "Semper fi, Mac," he said. And drove away.

I managed to drag my whipped ass to the little town a mile away. Took me a while. I moved so slowly, so gingerly, I had your average tortoise look like he was doing the Ali shuffle. It wasn't much of town, either. But they did indeed have a doctor.

On my interminable crawl, I had time to think, and this is what I thought about.

Years back, I joined the Coast Guard.
It was an extension of my anti-war activities.
Rebel without a clue.
Basic training was at Cape May, New Jersey.
On our first liberty, a couple of other seaman recruits and I pooled our resources and made a wild dash to Atlantic City to feed, fuck, and frolic for a weekend. It was a frenzy.

That Saturday night, we got so jovially drunk, we could scarcely hold each other up as we reeled and rocked down the street. Somehow arose the salty topic of tattoos, and my mates both decided they wanted to get one. There was a lot of braggadocio about getting the head of their dicks tattooed. Maybe a scorpion? Me, I didn't need a tattoo. I just went along for the ride.

We wandered into a place where the tattooist was a middle-aged blonde with the air of a biker babe about her. Confronted with the prospect up close and personal, all the chatter about how cool a dick tattoo would be at first glans totally petered out. While the mates went tattoo shopping, flipping through pages and pages of designs, in

3-ring circus binders, I sprawled out in a vacant chair. I could say I fell asleep, but the truth is, I passed out.

When I came to, much later, I discovered that I had a brand new Marine Corps tattoo on my forearm. Eagle, ball, and anchor with a flapping banner that bore the marine motto "Semper Fidelis."

See, I hated the fucking Marine Corps and every macho, Nazi, bullshit thing it stood for. For me, they were no better than mafia button men, only no self-respecting wiseguy I knew of would work that cheap, and the mafia never hits women or children.

So, naturally, my mates thought that paying Momma Biker to pen a Marine Corps image on my arm was the funniest fucking practical joke ever invented. They howled like deranged monkeys when I saw it there, sending me into an inebriated fuming fit of "FUCK! FUCK! FUCK! FUCK! FUCK...!" Sounded like a chicken with Tourette's syndrome.

I immediately asked the matron how to get that goddam fucking thing removed right away.

But I didn't get it removed right away.

This was back before lasers could do the job easily and relatively painlessly, not that I give a fuck about a little pain. I thought about tattooing over it, or turning it into something else or…

I just didn't get around to it.

I meant to, meant to do it a dozen different times, but, one reason or another, it never happened.

So.

Clean Cut was a Marine.

He saw that old tatt on me, and made me for a former Marine. And in a bizarre gesture of "brotherhood," he'd spared my life. A beau geste from one brother Marine to another brother Marine.

And so now, I'm stuck with that damn tattoo.

It saved my life and removing it now feels like it would be extremely bad juju.

You have to admit, that's a real knee-slapper.

# V.

In Chicago, where I grew up, there's a saying: "Fool me once, shame on *you*; fool me twice — and they find your body in the trunk of your fucking car."

They'd worked me over pretty good, and I took the time necessary to heal up. But I heal pretty fast, which is a lucky thing for me, considering. There was a payment due. Sometimes, you do somebody wrong, you can square it with money. Other times, all the money in the world won't square it.

Only blood will suffice.

Blood for blood.

This score that had gone so suddenly and completely sour, the one that cost me three friends, was still unfinished business.

I had to finish it.

Olivia was still living alone in her sprawling Tudor style home in Coddington Heights, over-looking the lake. Bank executives get paid well, very well, but not quite that well.

She wasn't home when I came by that afternoon.

I let myself in.

I figured I'd have at least a couple of hours to wait. I gave the place a good once-over, then raided the fridge. All kinds of yummy stuff in there. Though she ate out a lot, she liked to cook and she was good at it. She ate well. I found some leftover quiche, and a variety of wines, but after my extended binge south of the border down Mexico way, I'd decided to lay off the hooch for a while. I opted for coffee. She had six kinds. Organic, naturally. I picked the French roast, and brewed some up.

It was 1630 when her Mercedes pulled into the circular cobblestone drive, and I made myself invisible.

She swept into the house like an Arizona dust devil, kicked off shoes, peeling off clothes. In the kitchen, she snatched a Chablis from the fridge and poured herself a large one. She barely paused, swirling around the kitchen island, to head for the shower. Hurricane Olivia.

I waited.

The glass shower walls concealed little. She was fifty and sufficiently fit that she was frequently mistaken for a 30-year old. A few grey hairs, a few lines in her face. Her business-like helmet of blonde hair was darker when wet. Her pubis not shaved, but neatly trimmed.

Stepping out of the shower, she slipped into a thick white cotton robe, gave her hair a quick toweling, and went to her closet. She extracted a very slinky red dress and laid it out on the bed.

"Hot date?" I said.

She spun around like I'd hit her ass with a cattle prod.

"Jack! Oh, my god. Jack, you're alive!"

"Hell of a thing, isn't it?"

She rushed to me and pressed herself against my chest, wrapping her arms around me tightly. She had strong arms.

"I thought you were dead," she said, almost a whisper. "Baby, I thought you were dead."

"Stiff upper lip," I said.

She let go of me and without taking her eyes off mine, sidled over to her bedside table and picked up the phone. Still looking directly into my eyes, she punched up a number. It rang twice.

"Martin," she said, "it's Olivia. I'm afraid I have to cancel. Yes, something's come up. No, I'm not going to be available."

I could hear a man's voice on the other end, but couldn't make out the words. She hung up on him. All done without altering that focused predatory gaze with which she burrowed through my eyes into my soul. Absolutely crocodilian. Fortunately for me, my soul was wearing a burrow-proof vest.

"Miss me?"

"Miss you? Are you crazy? Miss you? God... that doesn't even begin to cover it." Followed by another big hug.

"Why don't you show me?" I said.

She had a teardrop-shaped head with a wide mouth and equine teeth, lips not full, but not too thin, either. Her hazel eyes were large, round, widely spaced, and slightly canted, topped by unplucked brows, one of which she arched mischieviously at moments like this one, giving her the look of an evil little pixie.

Up went that brow, and a smile tugged at half her mouth. She set to work demonstrating how deeply she'd mourned for me.

191

She knew what I liked and went right for my id, bitch-slapping my superego to cry in a corner. She could do some cute tricks with that wide mouth. She could suck your cock, she could suck your balls, she could do both at the same time.

This time, she pulled out all the stops, and gave me a full-body massage with every nook and cranny of herself. Just to show she was all mine, and always had been, and always would be. It was a very convincing act. There are two kinds of women I enjoy fucking in the ass, and she was — or pretended to be — the first kind, the kind that loved that more than anything else.

I still had some aches and pains from the beating I'd gotten not many weeks earlier, but I heal pretty fast. Anyway, it wasn't anything I couldn't work around, especially since she was doing most of the work.

We humped our way through most of the kama sutra, and a couple of twists you won't find in that playbook. During brief time-outs, she fed me champagne, Russian black bread, caviar, and other such delicacies.

When that had run its course, she lay stretched out on the bed, like an indolent cat, and I sprawled back in a chair, put my feet up on the edge of the bed, and lit a smoke. She gazed at me dreamily, adoringly, lovingly, and smugly. She was working her magic and she was sure the magic was working.

But here's the thing about magic: once you know how the trick works, you can never be fooled by it again. Unless you're a complete fucking idiot. I flatter myself that I am not quite complete.

"I'm curious," I said. "How much was it?"

"How much was what?"

"Come on, Baby," I said. "Don't treat me like a sap."

Too late. She had treated me like a sap. But then, I had acted like a sap. A sap is as a sap does, and I'd done it so perfectly they're going to start naming maple trees after me.

See, she was the one.

The heist had been her plan, from start to bloody finish. She recruited me by making me feel everything I needed to feel, telling me everything I needed to hear. It's not that I was an easy mark. I'm not. I've run a few games, myself, and I can spot a hustle from the opposite coast. I play it close to the vest, never reveal anything about myself I don't absolutely have to reveal. I keep a cautious distance, and I always look both ways before crossing. So I'm not easy to sucker-punch.

But she was exceptional.

One thing that made her exceptional was her ability to read another person and instinctively know exactly who to be, what to say, and which buttons to push to manipulate that sucker into doing her dirty work. She was a shape-shifter par excellance, the chameleon's chameleon with no natural color of her own, only the pattern of her current surroundings.

Me? Yeah, she read me like a book — that was written in braille on my cock.

Her other exceptional quality was her ability to lie convincingly. She was, without peer, the best liar I've ever encountered. No fidgits. No little "tells." No nothing. Because she experienced none of the internal tension, the conflicted emotions of fear, shame or guilt that hit the jackpot on the polygraph machine by increasing your heart rate, or respirations, or blood pressure or perspiration. She didn't show any of these emotions because she didn't feel them. She didn't have them. She was like a person who's color blind. It's not that they refuse to see red, or choose not to see green, they can't. They don't have that tool in the box.

She didn't have emotions that a human being normally has. Cold-blooded as any reptile you'd care to pick.

But, you know, to take a color-blind person and put them behind the wheel at a traffic light, and they know that when the top light comes on you stop and when the bottom light comes on you go. They are to that extent able to mimic the behavior of color-sighted drivers. From the outside, just watching their behavior, you might never know they were faking it.

Olivia was adept at faking it.

There were some telltale discrepancies, inconsistencies, inappropriate "emotional" responses, either over-reacting or under-reacting, and these should have tipped me off, but they didn't because I couldn't see them.

Being the target of a psychopath like Olivia is like having a cop pull you over and shine that bright fucking flashlight in your face. You can't see what's beyond it, what's behind it, all you can see is the light. It's only when they shine the light on somebody else, when you can view them from the side, that you can see them for what they are.

Assuming you're still alive when they're through with you.

So, yeah, the bank job was her thing. Being a trusted bank officer she was in the perfect position to do it — a position she got only because she fucked the bank president — so he never checked out her bogus credentials and hired her. And she was able to fake her way through that, too. For long enough, anyway. She set the score up, she was the inside man. She was the one who filed the official report, too. So she was the one who inflated the alleged take by almost 200 per cent. It followed that she was also the one who burned us, getting my three friends killed, with me missing out on my own funeral by a hair. A thin blonde hair.

There was only one reason for her to do all that.

Money.

She'd been embezzling from the bank. Once a routine audit turned up a discrepancy — and it would sooner or later — the feds would descend on the scene with an army of forensic accountants, and she'd be fucked.

She needed the robbery to cover up the money that was already missing, to claim it had been taken in the heist. My guys and me, we were her puppets — and then we were loose ends.

A fragment of a Scottish ditty floated through my brain: "The time for piper-payin' comes soon. Remember then who called the tune."

"What do you mean?" she said, with just the right cock of head and pout of lips to feign a mixture of puzzlement and hurt feelings.

After parrying that accusation like Scaramouche, she effortlessly segued right into a chorus of "How Great Things Are Gonna Be Now That We're Together Again." I let her sing all five verses while I got up and slowly dressed. Launching into the coda, she slithered off the bed for the big finish, mamboed over to help snug and settle my tie. Wrapping one arm around my neck, she let herself drape across my chest. I pulled her even closer. When she felt something very hard press against her, she knew immediately what it was. Her

Shirley Temple smile curdled around the edges, and her eyes widened. Was it surprise? Fear?

I could practically hear her mind racing, as she desperately searched my face for some hint of exactly the right lie to tell. But there wasn't one.

Maybe she was going to beg for mercy.

Maybe she was going to say she was sorry.

Maybe she was going to insist that she loved me.

Maybe she was just stalling for time.

"Jack," she said, looking deeply into my eyes, giving her best impression of emotion.

I shot her.

Just once.

In the heart.

If I were in a clever mood, I'd mention what a tiny target her heart was, but I don't feel clever. I don't feel anything. Maybe I learned that from her. Maybe not.


Slipping into some latex gloves, I went about staging the scene.

I laid her out on the bed, like I was tucking her in for the night. I'd already taken all the rest of the bullets from the clip — that's "magazine" for all you prissy, anal-retentive gun fetishists. I pressed the rounds against her fingertips, then, carrying them in my handkerchief, dumped them into the top drawer of her bedside dresser. Next to her reading glasses and a vibrator. I pressed the pistol into her hands reversed, as if she'd had both hands bracing the grip and had pulled the trigger with her thumbs. The gun itself had long ago been stolen, but it was clean, no bodies on it. The serial numbers were still on it.

I took that second champagne bottle out of the fridge, dumped half of it down the sink, ran water after it for several minutes. Half a bottle is about what she'd drunk from the bottle we'd finished, so this would match what the medical examiner would find in her blood. The empty I took with me when I left.

Only a lazy or incompetent investigator would readily buy this as a suicide. Women almost never kill themselves with a firearm. I'd considered using poison, but giving it to her this way, abruptly, with no hope of reprieve, was too appealing to resist. Of those people who do suicide with a firearm, very few shoot themselves in the chest. Too easy to fuck it up.

So, yeah, if I were investigating the scene, I wouldn't wrap my arms around suicide and give it a big kiss.

But a lot of cops are lazy, and not a few are incompetent.

No reason to suppose Inspector Javert would be dogging the case.

I removed every trace I could of me ever being present.

I had considered taking her off, getting whatever swag she'd skimmed and stashed, in her safe or probably in a Swiss account, but that would have sullied the whole thing.

This wasn't about money.

This was about blood.

Blood for blood.

## VI.

"Jackie, paisan'," Lupo said. "Are you looking to take down a score?" Like a proud papa witnessing his son's first erection. I hated to burst his bubble.

"It's not a score," I said. "It's a vendetta."

I told him Dolores' story. What had happened to her. All about El Tiburón.

Lupo's espresso coffee made cocaine seem like chamomile tea. Might as well have been mainlining that caffeine. I hate needles.

He sipped thoughtfully, as he studied the satellite map of the estate. Not a palace, but a fair-sized place on five acres. Between what Narvaez had gotten from the U.S. when he fled El Salvador, and what he'd stolen and socked away during the twelve years of civil war, he was able to set himself up handsomely. Now he played the role of the respectable businessman. Imports/exports. Pillar of the community, you know. Donor to charity. Sponsor of Little League Baseball. Only his hairdresser knew that his imports/exports included cocaine, military weaponry, and human beings. Probably, he split the take with the C.I.A. The spooks use funds derived from such enterprises to underwrite activities for which Congress, for political if not moral reasons, refuses to provide official funding,

"How do I get in and out of here?" I asked. "Preferably without getting killed."

"How many in the opposition?"

"Four, for certain. Could be six. Possibly more." I had gotten a rough idea of the risk from staking the place out, watching the hired help come and go.

"How many more?"

"Maximum? Not more than a dozen, total. Probably. I think."

Lupo chuckled, shaking his head, and pinched my cheek like a doting aunt.

"This is why I love you, Jack, " he said. "You think? Who are you, Jackie Chan, now? You're going to need back up, my friend."

"Anybody you'd recommend?"

"Oh, please. Who the fuck do you think?" He polished off his espresso, then asked, "What's my end?"

"There's a safe. Full of rumors. You can have whatever's inside, if you're willing to take pot luck."

"Give me a day," he said. "Two days."

So concluded the business portion of our chat.

Out came the Anisette.

# VII.

Dolores and I spent the next two days getting ready for what we were going to do. We also took a little time to get re-acquainted, and everything proved to be right where we'd left it when she'd split on me in the lurch at El Fleabag Supremo in Old Mexico.

In the interim, the rebels had won the day. Sort of. In exchange for a full and frank accounting of their unspeakable atrocities, the rebels had extended an amnesty to the members of the army death squads. I guess they did it to get some kind of "closure." People could finally know for certain what had happened to their disappeared loved ones.

Amnesty?

What the hell did they think happened to their loved ones? Obviously they'd been murdered. Did these folks think the death squads had been keeping the missing on ice, like prisoners of war, feeding them, housing them, etc., for five or ten years? A blow-by-blow account served no purpose I could see — even if the bastards told the truth about the vicious things they'd done, the torture, the rape — unless you were going to hold them accountable.

They should have dragged every one of them out into the town square and given them a Mussolini party for all to see. Then the next batch of murdering sons of bitches might think twice before pulling the same shit. Forgiveness isn't much of a deterrent.

Fuck amnesty.

Narvaez may have been a ruthless psychopath, but he wasn't a terribly smart one. He made the mistake a lot of people make when they need a bodyguard. He picked guys who were massive, aggressive, and ugly. Now, that's probably all right if you're a narcissistic pop star who wants to make an impression on over-enthusiastic fans and determined paparazzi. It's not such a great choice if you think someone's sincerely out to get you.

If that's the scene, then you want somebody who is focused, flexible, and has an unfettered imagination. Remaining focused is critical because most of the time nothing is going to be happening, and it's natural for your batteries to run down from the boredom. You get tired. You get tempted to cut just one teeny little corner, take one itsy-bitsy little thing for granted. And that isty-bitsy little thing will be the one itsy-bitsy little thing the opposition is waiting for. Complacency kills.

In the waybackwhen, I'd once been called upon to be a part of a security detail protecting a certain individual in a hospital on the west side of town. It was on short notice, and as our taxi driver jousted his way through downtown traffic, my boss — let's call him Sam — hastily filled me in so I could relieve the first team, a pair of moonlighting cops, at the end of their shift. When we arrived on the scene, we found one on-duty man with his ass parked in a chair outside the principal's room, reading the Tribune. His partner had wandered off somewhere taking a leisurely piss, which situation pissed off my boss something furious. Everybody knows that the bodyguards' best weapon is a good bladder.

Sam breezed right past the idiot in the chair and checked out the room to make sure the principal was still ticking. Then he tore that hapless flatfoot a new asshole the size of Crater Lake.

"What do you think you're doing?" he asked the cop, who, at this point hadn't even had the good sense to get up off his ass.

"What do you mean?"

"I mean what the fuck do you think you're doing?" His choice of words startled me. My boss fucking never used fucking profanity. "You think you're being paid to catch up on your fucking reading?"

"I, uh, I thought..." the cop stalled.

"No, you didn't. Why are you out here?"

"It's the only way in. Nobody can get past me."

"Un-huh. Anybody go in there in the last four hours?"

" A doctor. Nurse. Cleaning lady."

"Oh? " my boss growled at him. "Names."

"I don't know, they..."

"Then how do you know who the hell they were? You don't think the bad guys would be smart enough to steal a lab coat? Never assume that your opponent is as stupid as you are, officer. Your services won't be needed any longer. Your partner's, either, wherever the hell she is."

"You're FIRING me?"

"You're lucky I'm not firing AT you."

"Any questions?" my boss asked me, as my predecessor scuttled out with his tail between his legs.

"Just one," I said. "How do you think the Cubs will do this year?"

So, yeah, the ability to focus and stay focused is important.

See, when cops bodyguard somebody, they get paid even if their principal gets killed. And they still have a job Monday morning. If a private bodyguard's principal gets killed, it's bye-bye pay day; au revoir reputation; adios future clients; and buon giorno, "Do-you-want-fries-with-that?"

Flexibility is equally important because conditions can change about six times in a heartbeat, and you have to be able to adapt faster than you can think. That's where imagination comes in, too. Action always beats reaction. The only thing that beats action is pre-action. If a bodyguard is playing catch-up, chances are his client's already as good as dead, barring the direct intervention of an all-knowing and merciful god. It's much, much better to anticipate the opposition's moves. That's where imagination comes in. No plan is perfect, including yours. You have to know your weaknesses, how to beat your own security, figure out ahead of time the ways the opposition could pull it off, and give the tiger no place to put his claws. As the fortune cookie said.

199

Narvaez picked guys who were huge, strong, and mean. Had he picked guys who were focused, flexible, and imaginative, I'd be dead.

# VIII.

As it turned out, my surveillance had been accurate: there were only six. Four outside, two inside. The gig was almost too easy. Lupo scarcely even broke a sweat. He disabled the alarm system in less time than most people take to light a cigarette, and then relieved three of the bodyguards of their duties.

Permanently.

I gave the others the immortality test, myself.

They failed.

I located the former Colonel fast asleep in an upstairs bedroom. He wore one of those little masks over his eyes, the kind people use when they have sleep problems. I wondered fleetingly if his difficulty sleeping involved a conscience, but then I immediately chided myself for the thought. I knew he didn't have one. I woke him up by inserting the muzzle of my pistol into his mouth and slapping his face lightly. When I pulled off his blindfold, his bloodshot eyes were wide and wild like those of a trapped mustang. I cuffed his hands behind his back and yanked him out of bed. He wore boxers and an a-shirt to bed, and the shorts slipped down under his paunch while the shirt rode up, exposing a bit of his hairy lower belly.

I got him situated in a chair, took the two-way radio from my jacket pocket, and keyed the mic three times. Waited a moment. Then repeated the signal. Dolores answered, keying the mic twice, then once.

"Listen," Narvaez said. "I have money. I can give you money. A LOT of money."

"Fuck your money," I said. I hate it when people try to buy me. Renting me is a different matter.

Dolores needed only a few minutes to make her way from our staging point to the bedroom. Meanwhile, Lupo located the safe and went to work. He didn't bother to ask Narvaez for the combination. Didn't need it. With what he found inside and the free weapons he collected from their recently departed owners, he seemed content.

When she arrived, Dolores took a moment to study the former colonel like he was something odd that her cat had puked up.

"Who are you?" he said. "Do I know you? What do you want?"

"Santiago," was all she said.

For the first time, fear worked its way into his face, and he revealed himself to be, under his superficial layer of machismo, what every sadistic bully is: a sniveling coward.

She killed him.

Slowly.

It took all night.

Adam Adrian Crown

*I'm in a world of trouble*
*I don't know what to do*
*I'm supposed to be one woman's man*
*But I am in love with two!*
"The Street Corner Hustler's Blues"
Lou Rawls


# CHAPTER FIVE:
## THE STREET CORNER HUSTLERS' BLUES


Friday the eagle flies.

At the end of the workday, the guys who worked in the warehouse went steppin' out, for which purpose they brought a change of clothes. Garment bags were hung from open locker doors like stockings by the fireplace in hopes that St. Nick would soon make the scene.

My first week on the job, it caught me flatfooted, and I wound up looking like a hillbilly hick at a City Slick Convention. Nobody said anything, but the guys averted their eyes like their grandma had absent-mindedly wandered out of the kitchen naked. It was bad enough I was the only "white" guy on the dock (Yeah, I'm half Native American, but I don't go around with my birth certificate pinned to my shirt). I didn't want to be the only rube besides, and I know what to do when you're in Rome.

The following week, I came prepared to strut my stuff in suit and tie. It was classy stuff, too. Quiet and tasteful. Timeless elegance that I'd picked up working at James Menswear over on State and Jackson.

Well, I guess my idea of flash and their idea of flash were the el-twain that never shall meet. Pop, the elder statesman of the gang, looked me over, sucked on his teeth, and took a long drink from something wrapped in a brown paper bag.

"You better have some of this," he said and offered me a drink. It was blackberry brandy.

Thereupon entered the Tweedle-dee and Tweedle-dum of street corner hustler cool, Lester and Head. Lester fancied grey leather. Head preferred silk. It went well with the scar that ran the length of his face.

They regarded me with unbridled horror as the rest of the crew filtered in, spread out around me, straining to keep straight faces. The name Custer came to mind.

"Man, oh, man" quoth Head with much shaking thereof, "Did you just get out of prison?"

Lester chuckled, tried to make it sound like a cough so as not to offend. But didn't try all that hard.

"Sincerely, my brother," Head said, "You best get you down to see Mr. Johnson."

"Yeah, babe," said Lester. "You best go in that door marked 'Emergency.'"

That was the straw that broke the camel's dam back. The locker-room erupted into laughter, chortles, guffaws, chuckles, snickers, and hoots like a page from Roget's thesaurus. Much slapping of skin all around. Even Pop succumbed. Then Tiny (biggest guy in the crew, of course) joined in with a laugh that should have belonged to someone 5 years old and female, and that was like dousing a fire with gasoline. Head was laughing so hard he was crying.

So was I.

What else could I do?

Mr. Johnson was the proprietor of The Gentleman's Emporium, on the northeast corner of 47th and South Parkway, kitty-corner from the Walgreens Drug Store. He was possibly the most dapper man who ever soft-shoed the earth. Made Fred Astaire look like that gawky kid in the ill-fitting tuxedo at the junior prom. "D.W. Johnson," it said in gold lettering on the shop window. Ironic that he should share initials with a world-class filmmaker who was also a world-class racist, but god has a sick sense of humor. Rumor had it that Mr. Johnson had been quite a hoofer in his youth, performed on stage doing tap, and he still had a few moves on tap that you won't find on YouTube.

The manikins on display promised all manner of sartorial splendor inside, awaiting the man of wealth and taste, if he would but answer the call to adventure.

I kept adventure on speed dial.

I went right in.

It was a world of white-on-white shirts, sharkskin suits; silk ties in hues no rainbow ever dreamt of, artificial diamond stickpins, alligator shoes, and snap brim fedoras. As I entered, Mr. Johnson emerged from a curtained-off area behind the counter.

"My good man," he said with the precise delivery of an A-trained thespian, or a Jamaican cop. "How may I be of service?"

I introduced myself. I told him I was looking for something different, but I wasn't sure quite what. He listened to my tale of whoa, while looking down at his own mirror-shined shoes, nodding his head sympathetically like he was hearing my confession.

"I see, I see," he said like he'd heard all these sins before. "Tell me young Mr. Lucky," he said, "do you prefer the bold Viking princess, the dark, brooding Greco-Roman temptress or the fiery Scot-Irish lass?

"I beg your pardon?"

"Do you like blondes, brunettes or redheads?"

"Um, well..."

"Or perhaps you fancy the mystique of the Orient? Or the sacred womb of mother Africa?"

"Do I have to pick just one?"

"No, my good sir," he said, favoring me with a puckish grin, and wagging his finger like Argos's tail. "No, you do not. Now, tell me this. You're meeting a beautiful woman for dinner. You're waiting for her at the bar. The menu is comprehensive and money is no object. What do you order to drink while you wait?"

What the hell...? But I decided to roll with it.

"Campari and soda," I said. "With a twist of lime."

"Ahhhhhh..." he smiled with great satisfaction. Like I'd just passed my final exam on the meaning of life. "Now, what do you order for dinner: the steak, the chicken or the lobster?"

"Surf and turf?"

"And for the lady?"

"Whatever she likes."

He was making me hungry.

"Very astute," he nodded with approval. "One more thing. You're at the Playboy Club playing poker. It's after hours. What are you drinking?

"Scotch," I said, "but...um..."

"Yes?"

"I wouldn't be caught dead at the fucking Playboy Club."

His laughter boomed like the report of a 20-pound culverin or the bark of a Great Dane. It came from way down South and shook the windows. It was like a .45 going off in a phone booth.

"Allow me to suggest some items for your consideration," he said.

The next Friday, at quitting time, I slipped into one of the toilet stalls with a working door to get dressed, and I made sure I was the last one out of the bathroom. I knew the guys would hang out in the locker-room until the clock struck midnight and it was time to punch out. I could hear them rocking and rolling as I approached.

And I was sure they could hear me coming from the new cleats of my mirror-polished Cuban-heeled shoes.

The lads, in their finery, were warming up for the game as I entered casually, and sauntered across the room to my locker, every eye in the place tracking me in awe-struck silence.

I was wearing a black sharkskin suit, white on white shirt with a tight tab collar and French cuffs, a narrow white satin tie and blood red pocket puff, with one of Mr. Johnson's imitation diamond stickpins holding the tie in place, and diamond cufflinks at my wrists in the likeness of dice, one die a four, the other a three.

From the shelf of my locker, I brought forth a fine black snap-brim fedora, and the crowd said "Oooooooooooo," like I had produced the Crown Jewels. It's called a snap brim because the brim can be worn up or down, though most people wear it down in front and up in back, and you can "snap" the brim down into place with a light touch of the finger.

Mr. Johnson had taught me a little trick. Nothing earth shattering. Something with a little style. See, with a bit of practice, you can snap the brim of your snap brim down with a savvy snap of your fingers. Of course, don't fuck it up or you might as well pratfall on a banana peel.

I set the fedora into place, held my breath and finger-snapped the brim perfectly. It popped into place like a member of the US Marine Honor Guard slapping his rifle to "present arms."

And the crowd went "Ahhhhhhhhhh..."

I turned nonchalantly, and surveyed the bloody field of stares and gaping mouths.

206

Standing, arms folded, way at the back was Pop, giving me a smile and nod usually reserved for the moment to see your baby boy's first erection.

"So," I said to the breathless throng, "you guys going out to work on your cars or what?"

Pop started to chuckle and Head joined in, and just like that it was Cheshire cat chagrins all around.

"Motherfucker," said Head. "Gimme some." He offered me his palm and we traded some skin. "Me 'n' Lester going over to Big Shirley's. Want to come?"

Big Shirley's was small club renown for hot chicks and cool jazz. Big Shirley herself could wail like a downhearted frail in jail.

"Like, lead on, McDaddy-o," I said.

We killed the night at Shirley's.

It was quite a scene.

Maybe I'll tell you about it sometime.

But right now, what brings all this to mind is something the impeccable Mr. Johnson said to me.

I had gone down to get a new shirt because I'd gotten blood on the one I had and it's impossible to scrub that shit out. When I got to the Emporium, there was a sign on the locked door that said, "Gone to Lunch." I remembered him mentioning that a lady named Mabel at the Parkway Diner made the best chili in the known universe, so I skipped down the block thinking he might be grabbing lunch there.

He was, and invited me to join him for a "sumptuous repast" of chili and biscuits made by Mabel's very own talented hands. He called her MISS Mabel, when he introduced me as his friend, Mr. Lucky.

"How lucky are you?"" she asked me.

"I have moments, Ma'am," I said. My boyish charm at full - throttle.

"I imagine you do," she said.

The food was simple and delicious, the conversation light. Mr. Johnson was a jazz aficionado, and knew who was in town and playing where. Eddie Harris at the Congress Hotel. Stanley Turentine at the Sheraton. Lou Rawls in Old Town. And so on.

When the check came, we both reached for it.

"Most gallant of you," he said, giving it the French emphasis on the second syllable, "but I must insist. I invited you. When you invite me, then you can pay."

"All right," I said. "Thanks. Is it permissible for me to leave the tip?"

"It is," he bowed.

I left 20% plus a penny. You tip only a penny, it means the service really stank. Add a penny to your tip and it means the service was excellent. I learned that from my mother, the waitress. Funny, the things you remember at odd times.

Walking back to the shop, I couldn't help but notice that Mr. Johnson seemed to know every woman we passed on the street — each of whom he addressed formally; Miss Berry, Mrs. Benton, Mrs. Lewis — and each of whom addressed him as MISTER Johnson, and in gentle, crooning, purring tones that could only mean one of two things: either they all thought he was a newborn baby, or they knew him intimately in some other, more biblical manner.

I remarked on his apparent popularity while I was looking at shirts.

"My dear Mr. Lucky," he said, "The difference between rape and rapture is salesmanship. You can't sell anybody anything they don't already want to buy. I'm not selling you a shirt. I'm selling you style. Elegance. Class. I'm selling you the you whom you deeply wish to be. Easiest sale since Eve and the apple. Every lady wants to see herself as attractive, desirable, and capable of inciting a man's passion. I merely assure each of them that it's true. Because it is."

I didn't fully understand that at the time, but it sounded profound so I filed it away for future reference.

Turns out, I referred to it a lot.

*Yippie eye-ay, Yippie eye-oooh*
*Ghost riders in the sky.*
> "Ghost Riders in the Sky"
> Stan Jones and his
> Death Valley Rangers

# CHAPTER SIX:
# OLD WEST DAZE

It was hot and humid as the Devil's armpit.

Not a good day to be a horse.

See, horses cool themselves by sweating; as the sweat evaporates, it has a cooling effect. They'll sweat 15 or 20 quarts an hour when it's cool and dry, and as much as 30 quarts an hour when it's steamy. That's a little over seven *gallons*. Only about 25% of that sweat goes for cooling them off, as opposed to 50% for a human, so you can't go by how you, yourself, feel. Horses are hit harder by the heat. They lose four times as much salt, too, and that has to be replaced.

Humidity slows the evaporation rate way down, and a horse can quickly get over-heated — and that can lead to hypotension, colic, and kidney failure. All it takes is for his body temperature to go from the normal 100 degrees to 105 degrees. And that can happen in 15 minutes of moderate exercise, when conditions are wrong. A pony's working muscles can reach 110 degrees. That's the temperature at which muscle proteins begin to cook.

Horses heat up a lot faster than they cool down, too. Rinse them with cool water and scrape off the excess. Rinse and repeat that over and over, and it takes ten minutes of that to bring his temperature down a mere 2 degrees.

So when it's summertime and the livin' is easy for you, it ain't so easy for your horse.

It's ten times worse. Always remember that.

The best thing to do is not to get in trouble in the first place. Calculate the risk by adding the temperature and the humidity together. It ain't rocket surgery. If it's 85 degrees and 45% humidity, the net effect is 130. If it's *under* 130, you're probably good to go, assuming your horse drinks enough water. Over 130, you start running into trouble. If it gets to 170, just fucking forget about it. You need to cool it — and cool your pony, too. Good time for a swim or a hose-down.

So on this particular day, I figured Spartacus Jones and I would take a short ten-minute ride over to a small, spring-fed pond on the northwest corner of the pasture and have us a swim. We didn't bother with tack. I just looped a lead rope around his neck. We took off at an easy amble. Real easy. Several turtles passed us honking their horns and giving us the finger.

Even slow and easy, he was sweating pretty good by the time we got to the pond. I slid off his back at the water's edge and bent over to pull off my boots.

I don't know why I did that.

My back was to him and I guess my ass offered an irresistible target.

While I was balancing on one foot to get off boot number two, I suddenly felt his nose under my butt, and before I could do anything about it, he picked me up and tossed me into the pond. And I mean he really sent me sailing! Horses have strong necks and I flew through the air with the greatest of ease. Splish, splash I was takin' a bath and I came up sputtering a hearty hi-yo Silver and snorting pond water out of my nose.

And then he laughed at me.

Yes, he stretched his nose to the heavens, and bawled out a long, whinny in his whiskey baritone, like Tarzan yelling his war cry in the jungle. He shook his mane like Paul McCartney singing "She Loves You."

Hell, I had to laugh, too.

I like a horse with a sense of humor.

He strutted into the water to join me. I stripped off my soggy jeans and socks, threw them up on the bank, and we spent the rest of the morning playing in the pond like little kids, splashing at each other, racing each other from one side to the other.

We must have been quite a sight to see on the way back, him with his dripping mane and tail, and me carrying my still-wet clothes under my arm, wearing nothing but my hat and my boots. But there was no one there to see it.

Probably just as well.


After turning Spartacus Jones out in the main pasture, where he would no doubt regale the other ponies with the story of Jack's Big Bath, I checked my mail. There was a package, a little battered and tattered, and delayed in delivery, having been sent to my old address first.

I had forgotten all about it.

It was from "L. Brodie Photography," according to the label. I didn't recognize the name, but I didn't hear any ticking so I opened it. Inside I found a letter attached to the front of an 8.5 x 11 folder, labeled in bold black type, "Los Lobos Old West Days."

Ahhh. Ok. I remembered now.

There in all its glory was the "handsome photo suitable for framing," finished in sepia to give it an authentic "period" look, a la Matthew Brady. On the back were the names and, as appropriate, contact information for the various acts and actors appearing in the commemorative public relations portrait. I gave it a quick and casual once-over, but immediately spotted the problem.

Wrong photo.

No doubt taken in a preceding year and accidentally mixed up with the current year's photo. That's not a hard fuck up to make, especially if you shoot about the same set-up in the same location against the same backdrop with the same talent year after year.

During my hitch in the service, I knew a Ships' Cook First Class named "Smitty," who had served on half a dozen or more ships over his career. A cook's work is never done, and the cook often foregoes liberty in order to do it. For a lifer with no family and few other interests, who didn't drink, smoke, swear, gamble, or cavort with loose women (or men) it wasn't much of a sacrifice, I guess.

211

Smitty kept a scrapbook with photos of himself in all the places he'd been — and the ships he'd been on — but all those photos were, to the untutored eye, identical. There was Smitty, in close-up, smiling and waving with the hull of the ship forming a blurred backdrop. Now, to be fair, some of the hulls were painted white and some were painted black, so there was that. But no other scars, tattoos, disfigurations or other identifying marks were apparent. Nevertheless, Smitty could point to one photo and say, "Oh yeah, that's on the Duane, down near Cuba," and then point to an identical photo and say, "That one's off the coast of Alaska on the Northwind..." For a long time, I suspected he'd created the picture album as a wry prank, a twist on the left-handed monkey wrench, or the magnetic bearing grease," and that Smitty's deadpan descriptions were all part of the joke.

Teasing of all kinds did run rampant on the ship I sailed on. It was a way to maintain your sanity in an insane situation. But as I got to know Smitty better, witnessed his apparent incapacity for guile or irony, I was compelled to reassess that opinion.

Of course, I could still be wrong. It's possible Smitty was not a bumpkin at all, but a comedic genius and the master of all masters of the put-on, and even these many years later he's STILL putting it over on me. If that turns out to be the case, I tip my hat, and bow with sincere admiration.

But I doubt it.

I decided to give the photographer a call and straighten it out. It went something like this.

"Hello?"

"Ms. Brodie?"

"Yes."

"Brodie Photography?"

"Yes, that's me.

"Hi. This is John Flynn. We bumped into each other in Los Lobos. Old West Days."

"Oh, yes. Hello." Spoken like she remembered who the hell I was.

"Right. Well, I just received this beautiful photo you did and I wanted to compliment you on it. You do fine work."

"Well, thank you. How nice of you to call and say that."

"You're welcome. I mean it. I really like it.

"I'm glad."

"There's one thing though," I said.

"Oh? What's that?"

"Well, I was expecting a different shot. I was wondering if this one was from last year or something, by accident.

"No, that's not possible. This is my first year doing Los Lobos."

"Oh. Well, I'm sure you took more than one shot, right? You bracketed? Then you picked the best one. Nobody yawning, sneezing or blinking at the wrong moment?"

She laughed. "Are you a photographer?"

No," I said, "but I have some experience yawning, sneezing, and blinking at the wrong moment."

"I see," she chuckled. She had a cute chuckle. Like a little kid's.

"Would it be possible for me to see those other shots? I was hoping you could do a custom print for me of the one I'm looking for. I'd be happy to pay you for your trouble, of course."

"Well, sure. It's no trouble. I could do that. But really, they're practically identical."

"I understand," I said.

I was pleasantly surprised that she preferred to shoot on film, since the whole rest of the world was snapping away madly at Thompson digital machine gun pace in hopes of catching just the right shot, a kind of photographic reconnaissance by fire. I mentioned it.

"I use a digital camera, too," she said. "I like it for some things. But I use it the same way I use my film camera. I see the image in my head first. Then I make it happen. It's hard to explain."

"On the contrary," I said, "I think you explain it very well.

In the end, she agreed to send me a contact sheet of all her photos from the Los Lobos shoot, and we settled on a reasonable price for any custom prints I wanted.

A week or so later, I received the promised contact sheet — in fact, a bundle of them. The images included the "official" family portrait, and shots she had taken of the various individual acts and characters. She also had taken a lot of shots of visitors in mufti, enjoying the show. In all, I counted at least three to four hundred photos. Possibly more. I didn't make a count. Because they were in 35mm format, I dug out my loupe magnifier to examine them closely. Felt like I should be wearing a deerstalker cap.

I went over each image on each contact sheet.

Slowly.

Carefully.

Repeatedly.

After my eyes started crossing, I dredged up a grease pencil and went through the process again, marking off each shot as I eliminated it. It was like doing a room-by-room search of a huge hotel, clearing each room one at a time, then marking the door with an X.

There's no other way to say it: Wild Bill Hickok did not appear in any of the photos.

I double-checked the list she had sent me, a list of every act at the event, professional or amateur, a complete list because she'd made it her job to get shots of everyone. It included the name of the act and the person or persons who were involved. It included various characters and the names of the "re-enactors" who portrayed them. It included all the folks who had competed in the single action shooting society event, their real names and the names of their personae. She had also taken shots of visitors who had rented wild west drag, or had shown up in their own — the better to expand her custom print market.

Wild Bill wasn't on the list.

I made a call to His Honour the Mayor, Cal Hanshaw. He didn't know about anyone appearing as Hickok, either, but he promised to ask the other organizers and mangers of the event.

A couple days later, he got back to me.

Nobody knew what the fuck I was talking about.

So.

Who the hell had I seen whom NO ONE else had seen, who didn't appear in any of those pictures, even though I know damn well he had stood right there and had to have been photographed?

I'm sure there's a perfectly logical, rational explanation. You figure out what it is, do me a favor: let me know.

*When you're alone, and life is making you lonely*
*You can always go*
*Downtown.*
                    "Downtown"
                    Petula Clark

# CHAPTER SEVEN:
# THE WOLF LAKE BLUES REDUX

Some people called it the suburbs.
I called it the sticks.
I hated it.
For me, it was the Chateau d'If and I was Edmond Dantes.
Whenever I could save up a couple of bucks, I'd hop on the Milwaukee Road and in a little under an hour and a half, I'd be at Union Station, a short stroll from the lights and life of the Loop.
If I was particularly flush, I'd grab a dog or a hot pretzel from a street vender, maybe attend high mass at one of the cinematic cathedrals. If I were tapped, then I'd just walk. Up and down the streets. Looking in windows. Studying people. Watching. Listening. Being broke in the city was still better than being flush in the sticks.
The city has a pulse. You can feel it. It's the sum total of the traffic and the people. There's action, passion, heat, tension. Things continuously happening. Horns honking. Buses moaning forward. Radios. Conversations in a half dozen or more languages. There's a rhythm. A groove. You could almost dance to it.
Wolf Lake didn't have a groove.
Or it didn't have one that I could dig.
It was too square, too straight, too on the nose. It was a rigid march in 4/4 with no backbeat. No syncopation. It was a small town groove for small people with small minds. People who never ever

colored outside the lines. It fit me like a straight jacket that was two sizes too small.

"Downtown Wolf Lake" was an oxymoron that only actual morons could use without a sneer and a thick coat of irony. When you got there, there was no there there. No downtown, no uptown. Hell, hardly any plain town town.

Sure, there were a few blocks — small town blocks, not city blocks — either side of the train station where there were shops and offices and such. But there was no heartbeat. The place was like standing water in an old tire track: narrow, shallow, and stagnant. The regular citizens of Wolf Lake were Stepford zombies with no true natural passions, only the artificial, imitation passions of patriotism, beer, and football.

The only glimmers of anything I could recognize as life were on the south side of the railroad tracks on the "bad" side of town. Where the poor and wretched dwelled. Where the devious and wicked congregated. Where the hard and violent dallied. Where I felt at home.

The most attractive thing about the Wolf Lake Diner was that the food was cheap and there was a lot of it. If you knew what to order, it was pretty good, too. It's hard to fuck up, say, steak and eggs with a side of hash browns. The meat loaf was okay, the roast beef sandwich, served with fries, was good. The biscuits and gravy was worth killing for.

On Saturday nights, the kitchen was open until 1am, the legal limit, if you cared about legal limits. We didn't.

It was shortly after midnight. I was washing down my biscuits and gravy with some bitter black coffee and a smoke, when Joy Roberts sashayed in. She was a tall, scrawny kid, with ratted beehive hair and an unfortunate resemblance to Mick Jagger. Because she was one of those girls who loved to fuck, and wasn't very particular about the identity of the fuckee, she was widely considered a slut, or worse, and the "good" girls shunned her like she caused pimples.

I'd seen her around plenty, but we hadn't fucked. Not sure why we hadn't. No particular reason. Just logistics, I guess. But I'd heard about her, flirted with her a little and she made no effort to dispel the notion that she was the good time who was had by all. My band had played some gigs in town. We were just doing top 40 rock & roll, covering the most popular tunes on the charts as best we could with guitar, bass, drums, and organ. Maybe one or two things I'd written, myself. I hadn't written very much at the time, and what I had penned was pretty. Pretty awful. But it fit right in with the emerging groove that was making the scene. I'd noticed Joy at a couple of our gigs; because there was no way you could miss her. She hit the dance floor like one of the furies, and remained there from our first note to our last.

That chick could dance, man.

It's not just that she knew all the latest dance fad stuff, but that she made up her own moves. She didn't dance the dance; she created the dance as an extension of herself that was hers and hers alone. She danced like her life depended on it. Maybe it did.

I dug that.

Even on the clinch-and-shuffle slow tunes, when she grabbed some sap to be her partner, obviously she was the one who was doing the dancing, even if the moron hugging her thought he was leading.

It was a gas.


She spotted me as soon as she came in the squeaky door of the diner and we locked onto each other. A faint smile rippled across her eyes. We were both after the same thing. She strutted her stuff over to my booth. She was wearing white go-go boots and a miniskirt that was almost a belt. Black Harley jacket, the kind with all the zippers, bells, and whistles. Pink lipstick. She licked her lips with the tip of her tongue. Some people apparently think that's sexy.

"Hey, Lucky," she said.

"Hey, Joy."

"Any chance I can bum a smoke?"

I dug out my pack, juggled it so a butt stuck up for easy bumming and she plucked it out. Pink fingernails to match her lips.

"Thanks," she said.

I pulled out my zippo, whipped it open and thumbed up a flame. She leaned in to get a light, rested her hand daintily on mine as she did. I snapped the lighter shut and pocketed it like Paladin spinning his six-gun into the holster. She picked a tiny piece of stray tobacco from her lip. Glanced around.

"You waiting for somebody?" she asked.

"Yeah," I said. "You."

That was the right answer.

She smiled again, complete with teeth, slightly off-center and slid into the booth next to me, immediately resting one hand on my thigh.

"Want something to eat?"

"Yeah," she said and gave my thigh a meaningful squeeze. "But I'll just have coffee."

I got her some coffee. She took it black, too.

We sipped coffee while our eyes played slap and tickle.

"I was gonna head over to Bruno's to shoot some stick." I said. "Want to come?"

"I'd love to come," she said. Her double entendre was as subtle as a cannon in a canoe, but I didn't mind. We were both on the same page and with the fuck now being a foregone conclusion, the hunt was over and we relaxed.

In the city it doesn't matter how far anything is because it's all only a bus ride or L train away. Here in sticks, there was no bus, no L, no taxis, and the sidewalks weren't that great, either. You either had wheels or you walked, and I didn't have wheels. So I left the diner with Joy hanging on my arm with both hands, leaning on my shoulder, and we struck out for the pool hall a few blocks away.

The first street we crossed, Dickie Nichols came cruising by in his new, cherry red Corvette, a birthday present from daddy Dick. You could hear him coming because he had the radio turned up to a blare and the Rolling Stones were bemoaning their inability to get no satisfaction. Bobby Gillis, whose old man was some kind of honcho at the bank, was riding shotgun. The vet slowed down to a crawl.

"Hey," Dickie said, turning the radio down just enough that he could talk over it, "Come on with us and we'll have some fun."

I assumed he was addressing Joy.

She ignored him in a loud voice.

"C'mon," he said. "Ditch this loser. It'll be a good time, I promise." He waved a condom packet at her as proof.

We reached the other side of the street with Dickie still tracking us.

"Hey, I said to Joy, "You want to go with these guys?"

"Hell, no."

"You heard her," I told Dickie. "Buzz off."

"I'm not talking to you, punk," was his witty reply. Then to Joy he said, "C'mon," Two cocks are better than one, right?"

She spun around toward him like she was a fast-draw expert. "Oh, fuck you," she said. Somewhere between a laugh and a shriek.

"Fuck you, skank," and he gave her a single finger salute.

"ASSHOLE!" she yelled, and pulled free of my arm so she could return that salute with both hands. "Fuck you!"

Dickie peeled away, tires screaming, leaving behind enough rubber to drive on for a week. Joy waved her double fingers at him as he roared away. "ASSHOLE!" she called after him. Then he squealed around a corner and disappeared, leaving her hanging in the wind, and suddenly self-conscious as a nun caught giving a blowjob. She lowered her guns, and straightened her clothes.

"Well," she said, "*that* was lady-like."

"Don't worry about it," I told her and offered her my arm.


Bruno's was practically empty. Bruno was behind the bar washing glasses. Cigarette in the corner of his mouth, rising smoke making him squint.

"Hey, Bruno."

"Whatcha up to, kid?" he said.

The only other person in the place was set up at the farthest of the six tables, in the corner. Brent Brasser. Currently feeding quarters into the jukebox. Long, dirty blonde hair, greaser style, only grown out longer. Cool blue eyes. Button nose. He was a renegade. Technically, he was one of the "good" kids, but he preferred hanging out on the wrong side of the tracks. I didn't know him well. He was a straight-A student. We had Latin class together. He'd turned me on to Shell Scott, written by Richard S. Prather. He nearly always wore a turtleneck, or a scarf or some kind of bandana. That was to hide the scars from when his father had tried to strangle him.

We traded nods across the room, and I started to rack up balls on the first table.

Outside, a car pulling in swept the room with a glare of headlights.

Two cars.

No, three.

While I was chalking up, I heard car doors slam outside.

A moment later, Dickie came swaggering in, with Bobby right behind him. And behind them, four more guys. Tony Montante, built a like an ox and almost as smart. His lanky pal, Pete. Plus two guys I didn't know.

None of them normally frequented Bruno's. Maybe they all got a sudden urge to shoot pool?

They more or less surrounded me.

"You need a little lesson in manners, punk." Dickie curled his lip into a snarl. Part Elvis, part junkyard dog.

"I don't think so," I said.

"Well, I do. You and the skank both."

"Watch your mouth," I said.

"Yeah? You gonna make me? C'mon, punk, make me." He punctuated that taunt by poking his finger into my chest. I hate that. My old man used to do that. Hate it. "C'mon," he said again. "Why don't you make me?" And he poised that damn finger to poke my chest again.

See, here's the thing. No matter how tough you are, no matter how good you are, when it's six against one, you're going to get your ass kicked. No doubt. The only question is, what is it going to cost them to do it? For chrissakes, don't let them kick your ass for free.

In the elongated fraction of a second between Dickie cocking that finger and his actually launching it at me, I experienced a sudden moment of clarity and calm. I became acutely aware of being in that very place at that very time. The sloshing and clinking of Bruno washing glasses. The crack and thunder of Brent making the 8-ball break. The smell of stale cigarettes and whiskey and Old Spice. The speck of a mustard stain on Dickie's shirt. The faint stirring of air from the fan in the opposite corner of the room. The Righteous Brothers on the jukebox crooning "You've Lost the Lovin' Feelin'."

Dickie cracked a nasty smile as he launched that fucking finger at my chest the second time. But I saw it coming from a mile away and it came toward me so slowly, like it was burrowing through some cosmic molasses, that it gave me all the time in the world, and long before it landed, I broke my cue across his face. Cracking his smile a second time, you might say. It was a stunningly unexpected thing, and it shocked Dickie's crew into a frozen moment of inaction. Personally, I found it supremely satisfying, a thing of self-validating rightness, reassurance that the world was a place of truth and beauty.

Too bad truth and beauty don't last long.

"...You've lost that loving feeling," sang Bill Medley, "Now it's gone, gone, gone..."

And with that, my moment of grace was gone, too, vanished like a garage in the desert heat.

I didn't have a plan, and shit happened fast.

I may have gotten a couple more good licks in. But they were all over me, and somebody grabbed my arms, and somebody else got an arm around my neck, and Tony Montante was throwing short hard uppercuts into my gut, and all I could do was grunt and yell, "Fuck you!" It's hard to be eloquent at such times.

Then, suddenly, it wasn't six against one.

Joy, bless her heart, jumped up on Tony's back and started to beat his ears, scratch at his face, all the while shouting her Valkyrie battle cry, "You asshole!"

Then, for no reason you'd probably understand, Brent Brasser came sailing in. He actually climbed up on one of the tables and launched himself into the huddle of action like somebody crowd surfing at a rave. All the pins went down in a cursing tangle, I got one arm free and was winging punches, kicking, trying to get that arm off from around my neck before bad things happened.

But it was Bruno who made the real difference. Bruno's a rugged guy. Not a really big guy. Big enough. But big, and strong, and tough are three completely independent variables. A decorated Korean War combat veteran with a shitload of medals and scars. He came out from behind the bar, and a moment later bodies were flying through the air in all directions. "Get the fuck out of my place," he growled. "You don't come in here and fuck with my customers, you little prick!"

As quickly as these bad boys could get to their feet, they scrambled out the door.

But not Dickie.

Bruno caught Dickie by the belt and pulled him back, pinning him against the wall. "Not so fast, badass."

"You know who my old man is," warned Dickie. Talk about desperation. Wrong card to play with Bruno.

"Sure," said Bruno. He waggled his fingers. "Give me your keys."

"My keys?"

Bruno swatted him across the head.

"I think you fucking heard me."

Dickie dug into his chinos, handed over his car keys.

"You want these keys? You tell your old man to come get 'em. Now take a fucking hike."

Dickie took the prescribed hike, and Bruno locked the door behind him, turned the sign from "open" to "closed."

Joy straightened out her clothes, primped her hair a little. "Well," she said. "*That* was ladylike."

"Don't worry about it," I said. I would have smiled but I think I had a split lip. So I winked at her. She winked back at me. Then I did smile, and I was right: my lip was split and it hurt like hell.

"You okay, sweetheart?" Bruno asked her. "Why don't you go get cleaned up?"

Joy headed for the head.

"How about you two? You okay?"

"Great," said Brent. Blood was running freely from his nostrils.

"I'm fine," I said, but I felt like I was going to puke. I could taste blood in my mouth and couldn't see much out of my left eye.

Bruno produced some ice wrapped in a bar towel and he gave it to Brent to put on his nose. A second towel and a bottle of Jack Daniels were for me. While he applied the alcohol to my face, I applied it internally. Brent got a dose too. For medicinal purposes only, of course. Bruno also took a belt of it, just to steady his hand.

"You owe me for that stick you broke," Bruno said to me.

"I'm good for it," I said.

"I know are, kid," he told me. "I know you are."

Joy came back from the bathroom as Peter and Gordon came on the jukebox begging to be locked away so they wouldn't have to stay in a world without love.

"Oh, I *love* this song," Joy said, and proved it by singing along, bopping and grooving like she was the third member of the Peter and Gordon trio. It was contagious, I guess. I started to sing along, and Brent joined in, too. Bruno grabbed Joy by the hand and she spun into his arms, and out again, and they danced to it.

Yeah.

There we were: two bloody juvenile delinquents, fresh from a rumble, singing, "I don't care what they say, I won't stay in a world without love," while the town slut hoofed a tango with the queer war hero.

You couldn't make up shit like that if you tried.

Adam Adrian Crown

*Come on over to my house, Baby*
*Nobody home but me*
*I've got a lot of kisses I can spare*
*Come on and get 'em 'cause I don't care*
　　　　　"Come On Over to My House"
　　　　　Julia Lee

# CHAPTER EIGHT:
# WOLF LAKE NOCTURNE

Joy and I left Bruno's and hoofed it to her house at a slow amble, once again with both her arms again wrapped around one of mine, her head against my shoulder. You see couples do that in the movies and on Hallmark cards, but it's a fucking awkward way to walk. We did it anyway. It required a certain amount of coordination, and we'd helped polish off most of that bottle of Jack Daniels of Bruno's so our coordination was unfettered but imprecise. Maybe we leaned on each other just so we wouldn't fall down.

Her living room looked like the set from Leave it to Beaver, and we sprawled out on the sofa, where we had a deep French kiss with dueling tongues, and she put my hand on hers.

"I think I have a fever, she said. "Maybe you should take my temperature."

"You're sure nobody's going to walk in on us?

Joy's parents were out of town for a couple of days. "They're visiting my brother," she explained.

"I didn't know you had a brother."

"Jeff. Jeffrey. He's the good child. It's his graduation."

"College?"

"Boot camp. He's in the fucking Army."

"Fuck," I said.

227

"No shit."
"How come you didn't go along?"
"Why do you fucking care?"
"Just curious."
"Yeah, well, remember what happened to the cat. And you don't have nine lives."
"Want to bet?"
"Hey, are we gonna fuck or what?"
You can probably guess what my answer was.

But first some foreplay.
"Dance with me," she said, suddenly jumping up and reaching out a beckoning hand to me.
"Whatever you want," I said.
"You're sweet." She had a good smile. I liked it.
She bopped over to the hi-fi and selected some .45's, slid the stack onto the tall spindle, and gave the play knob a twist. The first single plopped down.

Like I said, I'd seen her dance.
I wondered what would come next. It was anybody's guess.
She could Boogaloo, Bristol Stomp, and Bunny Hop. She could Watusi, Chicken, Monkey, Strut, and mash a mean potato. She could frug, hitchhike, and shimmy. She could come on, baby and do the locomotion. She could out-twist a double-decker Chubby Checker, out-swim Johnny Weismuller, and had created her own lewd Monkey/Jerk combo that looked like she was stroking a five-foot long penis.
Me, I was going to have to fake it.

She sucker punched me. Out came the strains of Pepito by Los Machucambos. Two accoustic guitars, snappy bongos, a chick singer, Julia Cortes, with back-up boys Raphael Gayoso and Milton Zapata.
And it was one-two-cha-cha-cha at the old ball game.
Not what I'd expected.
I tried to follow her groove. It's not like I'd never seen the cha-cha before. I wasn't raised on Mars. But it wasn't something I

expected to hear on the hi-fi of snow-white Wolf Lake's baddest bad greaser girl.

She danced it sly and slinky with hips that bumped and rolled. She wagged her tight little tail like Lassie when Timmy showed up with a steak bone.

I dug it.

"Hey, that's good," she said. Clearly surprised. I wasn't sure whether to be flattered or insulted. But now, I really wanted to fuck her so I went with flattered. "Wow," she went on, "you know how to move your hips. Guys are so tight-assed..."

Next up was Patricia, by Perez Prado, heavy on the Hammond organ, punctuating brass, a little on the cheesy side, like the soundtrack to a Mexican porno flick. Fuck it. She wanted hips, I gave her hips.

The unlikely last chapter of this Latin musical trilogy was Itsy-Bitsy Teenie-Weenie Yellow Polkadot Bikini by Brian Hyland. Silly song. I think maybe I actually played that one once someplace. But I don't recall when or where. Probably had PTSD from the experience. But it did have a more-or-less cha-cha groove.

Anyway, Joy made it work, and I worked it with her. She sang along with parts of the chorus ("one, two, thee, four, tell the people what she wore..."), trying to make it sexy, over-acting by three furlongs. Nothing's less sexy than someone trying to be sexy, but I was loopy enough not to care, Hang on, Loopy, hang on!

I have no idea what song came on next because at the end of that one, she fell laughing into my arms, we fell back kissing onto the couch, and then fell fumblingly to work, unbuttoning buttons and unzipping zippers.

Joy's body was long and narrow as a flimsy excuse. Not to say scrawny, but not an extra ounce of fat on her. Teacup breasts with puffy nipples. A square-shaped ass that was harder than softer. Maybe from all that dancing. The hair of her cunt was mustang wild, and was probing the perimeter of her soaking wet crotch, reconnoitering her panties for an escape route.

We went around the bases as a formality. I went down on her like I was on Death Row and she was my last meal.

"Oh, Lucky," she said. "Oh…god DAMN, yes!"

She bounced from orgasm to orgasm like a flat stone skipping across a lake. She lay liquid and dreamy afterward, shuddering with little after-shocks.

Pulling me up toward her, she found my cock and rubbed the head against the soft mouth of her vagina, to guide me in.

I took that for consent.

These days, you'd have to call your lawyer, and you still can never be sure.

At some point, while I was slip sliding away, I realized that she was being surprisingly docile about it, uncharacteristically passive, letting me do all the fucking. I didn't mind that. But I realized she was no longer with me. She had gone from languid, liquid, and dreamy to passed out.

"Hey," I said, and shook her shoulder to rouse her.

No dice.

She was out for the count.

I, on the other hand, was still on fire, with the need raging through my brain like a California wildfire. Maybe, in my inebriated state, I convinced myself that she wasn't quite unconscious. Or maybe the little head was dong all the thinking and it wants what it wants when it wants it.

So I went ahead without her.

Surprisingly, it isn't all that easy to fuck somebody who's absolutely limp. Limbs flop freely and get in the way. It's a creative challenge. But I managed it. It was a Wizard of Oz ejaculation: great and powerful. I lay beside Joy afterward, pressed snugly against her back, and left my cock inside her until it withdrew of its own accord.

In the morning, Joy was awake before me.

"Hey, Lucky," she whispered. "You want coffee? I made some coffee."

"Sure," I said. Maybe hot coffee would purge the morning-after sludge from my mouth.

"I kind of punked out on you last night, didn't I?"

I shrugged.

"Sorry about that," she said.

"It's okay." I filled her in on the festivities she'd missed.
"You fucked me while I was passed OUT?" she said.
"Um..."
"You know what that MEANS?"
"Well..."
"It means you OWE me one, you bastard."
She decided to collect forthwith.
I always pay my debts.

Joy collected what I owed her. She charged me interest that was on the upper end of the juice loan scale, too. But I didn't mind.

Afterward, we stretched out side-by-side on her bed. Her room was full of stuffed animals. Dozens of them. Rabbits, mostly. I suppose I could go somewhere with that. I lit up a Lucky Strike and we shared it, trading drags back and forth.

"So Lucky smokes Luckies," she said with a giggle. "I shoulda guessed.

No candy-ass menthol filters for you, huh?" On and on she chattered.

Maybe she was nervous or something. I wasn't really listening. I was thinking.

I looked her naked body over with cold, post-coital objectivity. Man, she was one skinny chick! Like scrawny. I mean, if she could flap her shoulder blades, she could fly. Lying on her back, her breasts almost disappeared, like guys ducking their heads down in a foxhole. Hands and feet too big, like on a puppy. Skin so white she was almost blue. Auburn pubic hair dense, wild, and wooly. Like Sascrotch. All tolled, she was one of the homeliest girls I'd ever met. She wasn't quite on ugly street, but she was in the crosswalk.

"You want to go downtown with me?" I said.
"Sure," she said. She sat up, spun around on her butt so her head was toward my feet and vice versa.
"Not *that* downtown," I said. "Down*town* downtown. The city."
"Really?" she said.
"Sure. Why not?"
She brightened like I'd offered her a basketful of kittens.

231

"That would be fab," she said.
"Cool."

The trip required a quick cleanup and some fresh clothes. We showered together, and that resulted in, shall we say, a small delay. She opted for black: black jeans, tall black boots, black turtleneck sweater, black leather biker-type jacket. Full metal jacket on the make-up. We swung by my house. No one was home. So I was in and out quick. My black "downtown" suit, white shirt, black tie, and my black leather coat. And the little wad of cash I had stashed for just such occasions. We missed the train in Wolf Lake and had to hustle over to catch up to it in Ingleside. From there, we took the yellow brick Milwaukee Road to the city of odds.

By the time we made Union Station, we'd made a plan.
First we'd take in a flick. "The Sand Pebbles" was playing at the State-Lake Theatre. Other options included the spy spoof "Our Man Flint," and the cold war satire "The Russians are Coming! The Russians are Coming!" We settled on a drama called "The Chase."

Joy nearly wet herself with giddy enthusiasm. "I fucking LOVE Robert Redford," she said.
"He's okay," I conceded. I was more of a Brando fan. "The Wild One," you dig?
So that was the plan. It was a long film, and the ending made Romeo and Juliet look like a comedy. Still, great flick.
We grabbed the L train and rode it north to pig out on the world's greatest pizza, Sicilian, deep-dish pizza. You can't eat more than one slice of that or you'll pop your belly like a balloon and fly around the room.
After that, we headed over to Wells Street.
Old Town was the scene. Cutting edge of the folk revival. Hippie headquarters. Counter-culture Central. My favorite place was Mother Blues.
On this cold December night, bluesman J.B. Hutto blew up the room with his raw ragged vocals and soulful slide guitar. He did Evenin' Train, Ain't it a Crying Shame, My Soul, and Stompin' at

Mother Blues.  You can say a lot with just 12 bars, if you've got something to say.

We caught the last train from Clarksville at 2am. Wasn't another one until 8am, and we didn't have enough bread to stay in the city overnight. The train was more or less empty. We had a whole car to ourselves, and considered fucking our way back. When we pulled in, Wolf Lake's one and only taxi was sitting there, motor running like he was waiting for us. Figured we might as well grab it. The night had gone deep-freeze. Colder than a free kiss from a five-dollar hooker. Spent the last of my roll on the tip.

We got out at Joy's house, and I gave the taxi a farewell wave.
"Wait," Joy said. "What about you?"
"That's okay," I said. "I feel like walking."
One shivering goodnight kiss, and the coach turned back into a pumpkin.

It was 13 degrees and my ears burned by the time I got home, where everybody was asleep and didn't notice me slip in.
Good thing 13 was my lucky number or I might have gotten frostbite.

Adam Adrian Crown

*Let me root, root, root for the home team*
*If they don't win it's a shame*
*For it's one, two, three strikes, you're out*
*At the old ball game.*

"Take Me Out to the Ball Game"
Jack Noworth

# CHAPTER NINE:
# TAKING THE WORLD SERIOUS

On the day hell froze over, I was in the city which brought me to be hunched over a double scotch, musing to myself about the condition my condition was in. Summer was still hanging on, like a washed-up fighter rallying in the championship rounds, and it had been all sunshine, and balmy zephyrs outside during the day. So naturally, I'd sought out the dark, dank dungeon of Nick's bar. The place was mostly empty. Everybody was out frolicking in the mid-60 degree weather. Fuck'em. Fine with me. Where joy most revels, grief doth most lament, know what I mean?

The ballgame was on TV. Last game of the Series. But I wasn't paying much attention. For me it was just white noise. I don't really follow baseball. Played some when I was a kid, wasn't very good at it. Was going to play Little League ball one time, but that plan went south in a nasty way and I guess it soured me on the game. I don't hate it. I just don't give a fuck.

Nick DiMusio, known as Nick the Mouse, was tending bar. He's quiet and quick, with clever eyes, like he's always on cat watch. He and Olie Pederson, a retired CTA bus driver, were having one of their usual political discussions, po-tay-toe/po-tah-toe, and I filtered it out. Olie was as archetypical of the strapping Scandinavian Viking as you could possibly be and still be a paunchy, middle-aged, balding black guy.

I had sipped about halfway through my second double, having tossed down the first one to cauterize my wound, when Shorty strutted in. He was a nimble, bandy-legged little Italian gnome with sleepy eyes and thick brows arched in a permanent state of what-the-fuck-is-going-on. As if he'd just arrived from some other planet and couldn't believe the stupid shit he saw here on earth, and it left him stunned speechless.

Respecting my privacy, and not wanting to appear overtly queer, he slid onto a stool a few places away from me.

"Usual?" Nick asked him.

"Why not?" said Shorty.

Nick set him up with a shot of bourbon, filled to the brim. Then he floated back over to continue his pointless debate with Olie.

Shorty dug out a smoke, stuck it in the corner of his mouth and started patting himself down. I had my Lucky's and my lighter already on the bar, kept a butt burning to provide self-illumination. I tapped the Zippo lightly on the oak, tattooed with generations of stains and scars, and when Shorty looked over, I slid the lighter across the bar to him. He snatched up the lighter like an easy grounder, smoothly as the legendary Arthur the center Fiedler for the Boston Red Pops. He flipped it open, tilting his head sideways to keep the start-up smoke out of his eyes, a gesture so odd I wondered if he had learned it from one of the pigeons in the park. He returned my lighter the same way I'd sent it, adding a wink and a nod and a hearty Hi-yo, Silver. I gave him a nod of "you're welcome," and we were square.

He pointed at the TV and raised his brows even higher.

"Six to four, Cubs, bottom of the eighth," I reported like I was informing the relief helmsman of the course heading.

Shorty nodded some more.

Just then Rajal Davis got a huge home run hit off Chapman, knocking the ball well over the left field wall, bringing Guyer home from second, to boot.

"Six-six," noted Shorty. The way you'd point out to a guy that his fly was open.

"Shit's about to get interesting," I heard Olie say.

Nick made book on the side. I wondered what the line was on the game.

Going into the ninth, they all turned their attention to the game, and I pretended to follow suit. But I was thinking about something else. I had a thing to do. It was going to be ugly, and it was going to be painful. But not for me.

The Cubs pissed away a chance to score at the top of the ninth, Chapman returned to the mound, pitched his ass off, three up, three down. So the game would go into extra innings. It had clouded up a little, and a rogue cloudburst resulted in a rain delay before the tenth inning.

It was enough time for Nick and Olie to pick up their argument where they'd left off, and insult each other, with Nick calling Olie a bleeding-heart liberal, and Olie pronouncing Nick a fat-cat conservative. Or maybe it was the other way around. Sometimes you can't tell the players apart without a program.

Shorty regarded them with an extra measure of disbelief, evident in his head shaking.

"You guys are fuckin' nuts, you know that?" Shorty suddenly said.

"What do you mean?" said Nick.

"What do you mean, what do I mean? What did I say? I said you're fuckin' nuts. That's what I said. That's what I mean. Fuckin' nuts."

"What're you talking about?" said Olie. "Why are we fuckin' nuts?"

"Let me ask you something," Shorty said after a sip of bourbon. "You ever know anybody who was one hundred percent right about everything all the time?"

"Yeah," said Olie with a bitter snort. "My ex."

"No, no, no, no, no," said Shorty, wagging it away with his finger. "She only *thought* she was one hundred percent right about everything all the time. That's why she's your *ex*. 'Cause if she actually *was* one hundred percent right about everything all the time, you would take her tight little ass to Vegas, hit the blackjack table, and retire to the French Fucking Riviera on your winnings. Now, am I right or am I right?"

"Okay. I guess you're right," Olie conceded. "I don't know about the Riviera part, though."

"Close enough. Look," Shorty went on, "you guys are baseball fans, right?" It was a rhetorical question. "Okay. Who's the best hitter in the game?"

"Right now, or of all time?" asked Nick.

"All time. Any idea?"

Nick and Olie looked at each other like kids trying to telepathically cheat on a history test.

"Ted Williams?" Olie shrugged.

"Good guess." Shorty turned his gaze to Nick. "What do you say?"

Nick toyed with a bar towel. "Lifetime or single season?"

"You pick."

"I'll go with Ted Williams.

"Holy fucking Christ," said Shorty with a shocked hush in his voice. "You fucking guys actually *agree* on something?" His brows were getting a real workout. "Holy fuck. Alert the fuckin' media."

Shorty glanced over at me to see if I had an opinion, but I wasn't getting involved.

"Well, my fine fucking feathered friends," he said, "it might interest you to know that Ted Williams' lifetime average was .344. Ty Cobb's lifetime average was .366. Highest lifetime average ever."

"Ty Cobb?" said Olie.

"Ty fucking Cobb," Shorty confirmed. "Now, Ted Williams best season was in 1941. He hit .406. But Rogers Hornsby hit .424 back in 1924, and nobody's beat that yet. Had a .358 lifetime record."

"Okay," said Nick. "So what? What's your point?"

"I'm getting there. Don't fucking rush me. Who's the highest paid player in the game today?

Olie and Nick looked to each other for the answer and came up with bupkis.

"Jason Werth," said Shorty. "He's making 21 million fucking dollars a season. That's 21 million. With an M. For Mother-fucking Million. With a twenty and a one and a million. Know what his batting average is? .267 lifetime. Best season .300 in 2012."

"Okay, okay, Mr. Baseball. I still don't see what you're getting at."

"Batting .300; batting .424; batting .358. What does that actually mean? It's a fraction, right? Out of so many times at bat, the guy gets so many hits. You divide one by the other, carry the one, pi times the radius squared, e pluribus unum, one if by land, two if by sea, and you get a percentage. We say .300 and that's a pretty big number sounds good. But what it actually means is that the guy only gets a hit 30 per cent of the time... 1/3 of the time. When a guy steps up to the plate, his job is to hit the fucking ball, right? If he gets a hit, we could say he made the right decision, did the right thing. And if he doesn't get a hit, we could say he made the wrong decision, did the wrong thing. That means the greatest hitter in the entire history of fucking baseball was only right 34 percent of the time, lifetime average, or 42 percent of the time, single season. They were right *less* than half the time. Not even 50/50. Fuck, if you always bet heads on a coin toss, you'll be right 50 percent of the time. THIS guy Werth is only right 26 percent of the time and he's pulling down 21 million bucks. For being WRONG about 75 percent of the time."

Olie frowned and rubbed his bald spot. "Yeah, but —"

"Yeah, but?" said Shorty, cutting him off at the pasta. "But, but, but, but, but. What are ya, a fuckin' golf cart? Yeah but nothing. Now, you guys are always going around and around and around about this issue and that issue. Abortion. Gun control. Taxes. Health care. The latest stupid fucking war. No matter what the issue is, you, sweet prince (he pointed at Nick) always take the so-called fucking liberal position. Always. 100 percent of the fucking time. And you, my brother duck, (he tapped Olie's chest very lightly with a fingertip), you always take whatever the fuck the so-called fucking conservative position is. Always. 100 percent of the time. Now, we have established that NO ONE is right 100 percent of the time about *anything* — not even about something they are extremely good at, like hitting a fucking baseball. In fact, if you're right not even half the time, you're such a fucking genius you wind up in the Hall of Fame, and you get paid more money than you could ever spend unless you dedicated the rest of your life to buying completely silly shit."

Shorty had them on the ropes now, and kept hammering them with combinations.

"So pick an issue. Any issue. Look at it. Remember it. Put it back in the deck. And if you think it through, look at all the angles, look at all the evidence pro and con, wrestle through all that shit, it only stands to reason that *sometimes,* on *some* things you gotta wind up taking the so-called conservative position, and *sometimes*, on *some* things you gotta wind up taking the so-called liberal position. Ya *gotta*. Because nobody is 100 percent right about everything all the time. Right? But you're in your little liberal box, or your little conservative box. So you can't actually be thinking about shit at all. If you *always* take the liberal position, or you *always* take the conservative position, simple logic forces me to conclude that one of two things must be true. Either you're both full of shit, or you're both completely fuckin' nuts. Since you do seem wholly fucking sincere in your belief that either the liberals or the conservatives, respectively, are 100 percent right about everything all the time, ipso fatso, I'm compelled to conclude that you're both fuckin' nuts."

Shorty then took a dainty sip of his drink. I think he was luxuriating in the effect his ejaculation of oratory had had on certain mouths — rendered dumbly agape by the onslaught.

"Any fuckin' questions?" he said.

In the bewildered silence that followed, Olie and Nick turned toward each other grudgingly, like embare-assed lovers trying to make amends and not knowing how to start.

"Holy shit," said Olie.

"Yeah," said Nick.

"So what you're saying," Olie said to Shorty, "is that we have to start thinking outside our fucking boxes."

Shorty tossed down the remainder of his hooch, smacked a bill down on the bar and stood up to take his leave. He laid an affectionate hand on Olie's shoulder, and reached out the other to squeeze Nick's arm.

"Think outside your fuckin' boxes?" said Shorty. "My friends, Romans, and countrymen, I'd be happy if you just start thinking outside your fucking asses."

And with that he was gone.

The tenth inning commenced and the Cubs won the World Series 8-7.

*I'll be your mirror*
*Reflect what you are, in case you don't know*
"I'll be Your Mirror"
Lou Reed

# CHAPTER TEN:
# MIRROR, MIRROR

Once Old Dream Chief visited me in my sleep to teach me that everything that exists in the world — horses, dogs, mountains, the ocean, the rain, and even other human beings — was a mirror, reflecting back to you who and what you are.

There are mirrors and there are mirrors.

I remember the funhouse mirror in the carnival that showed a hilariously distorted image.

And a shattered mirror reflecting back a hundred splintered faces.

So the value of a mirror is that it reflects a perfect image, one that is true. Further, it reflects only what is there in the present moment. It neither anticipates an image, showing it before it arrives, nor lingers on an image after it's gone.

No mirror is more perfect than a horse.

One of the things that horses are best at is reading people, even at a distance.

Whether it's your body language, your scent, the electro-magnetic impulse of your heart, or some combination of these things, or something else entirely, horses have a most uncanny ability to

241

perceive the mental-emotional — dare I say spiritual? — state of a human being with dead-on accuracy.

They know what you're thinking and feeling often better than you do yourself.

They pick up minutiae of *being* about you that you, yourself, are not consciously aware of, the way a good poker player knows when you're bluffing by picking up your micro-tells.

In an instant, a horse knows you better than your friends, your family, and your lovers.

Knows who you are in the deepest, most secret corners of your heart.

You *have* no secrets from a horse.

You can't fool a horse, con a horse, lie to a horse.

He sees you naked right down to the bare bones of your soul.

Then he reflects that back to you.

The truth sucks.

You're walking around like Dorian Grey, smooth-talking the whole world, getting by on your looks, your charm, your superficial appearances, your "image."

But up in the attic is that ugly portrait that displays every blemish and flaw, every selfish moment, every thoughtless cruelty, every petty fear, every brittle weakness.

And horses have the key to the attic door.

You probably won't like what the horse shows you about yourself, because you're a human being and most human beings aren't worth the fuck it took to produce them.

It'll be you without all your bluff and bullshit.

Once he shows you to yourself, once that truth hits you in the face like a stiff Larry Holmes jab, you know either you have to change, or forever accept that you're an asshole.

And change is difficult and terrifying.

But I think being an asshole is worse.

Keeping company with horses, I get to see myself through their eyes. And I'll change whatever I have to change until I like what I see.

Maybe that's why Dream Chief bade me to go where the arrow points to the rainbow.

Maybe he knew, somehow, that it was my last shot at redemption.

*I can't stop – I can't stop*
*It's like lightning striking again…*
"Lightning Strikes"
Lou Christie




# CHAPTER ELEVEN:
# LIGHTNING BOLTS AND NUTS


There are moments that change everything. Experiences so profound, so deep, so moving that they change the course of your life forever. It becomes a reference point and you divide your personal history into two parts: your life before that moment, and your life after that moment.

I suppose, if you think about it, every moment is a defining moment.

I think about what would be different if I'd done that instead of this, said no instead of yes, turned left instead of right, arrived five seconds earlier or five seconds later. Every moment is a defining moment for the moments that come after that.

But some changes are bigger than others.

Some choices have greater impact than others.

Some experiences are so assumption shattering that you can never go back to the way you were before. You can't turn around, backtrack, pick up that other road you didn't take. Once you stretch your mind, it never shrinks back to its original size.


I divide my life into two parts: Before Spartacus Jones and After Spartacus Jones. I could say before and after Horse, but since he embodies all that is Horse, and undertook to be my long-time mentor, he personifies that change. Everything that came before was prologue, things I needed to do, feel, in order to be ready for his appearance. It's that thing about "when the student is ready, the master appears." It's possible that everything happens exactly when it's supposed to happen. Everything is a natural and foreseeable consequence of what went before — if only we are able to foresee from the right vantage point.

The idea makes me queasy.

It's impossible to describe what it's like to get hit by lightning. That's what I call it, getting hit by lightning. Spiritual lightning. It's paradoxical. You lose yourself, and by losing yourself, you find yourself. Don't ask me how that works. I haven't a clue.

First of all, the lightning thing defies analogy, simile and metaphor. The experience is not like anything else. My calling it "lightning" is a puny attempt to wrap words around it, but all words are inadequate, if you don't know the experience yourself, and superfluous if you do. It's like trying to explain jazz. If you have to ask the question, you won't understand the answer.

Second, it's self-validating. It's a truth you can hold onto tightly because it's self-evident. It's beyond question. In contempt of denial. You can take it to the bank. Like when your ear hears just the right lick and it goes right to your soul. You don't have to think about it, because it sounded perfect. You know it when you hear it. It's instinctive.

When I say you lose yourself, I mean you shitcan all the petty egotistical bullshit that you define as "you" in the normal, everyday world. All your attitudes, beliefs, and demographics that give you your social identity are suddenly schmutz. Your age, race, religion, size, and shape are meaningless. There's just the You that's at the core of you, the you without which the rest of "you" would mean even less than it does, to you or anybody else. The spark of you. The essence of you. The very thought of you, my love.

Third, it's the ultimate. It's got more punch than George Foreman's right hand. It's the shit. The bee's knees. The fox's socks.

246

The cat's meow. Jiztastic. It's cooler than cool, tighter than tight, badder than bad. It's beauty beyond beauty, right beyond all rightness or anything you've got left. Ain't no mountain higher, ain't no valley lower, ain't no Truth truer. You think an orgasm is intense? This is orgasm to the billionth power. It's the most alive you're ever going to feel.

It's good. It's pure benevolence. It's all the different kinds of love there are all rolled up into one, and then given a huge dose of steroids. It's clean, honest, unadulterated, non-GMO, organic, and grass-fed. It's joyful as your first kiss, playful as foreplay and exuberant as your maiden-voyage fuck. It is the way it is because it can't be any other way. It's simple. Naked. Elegant and effortless.

It's the answer to all questions. It crosses all your t's, and dots all your I's, even the third one. It's perfect balance, perfect justice, perfect perfection in which even imperfections are perfect. It reconciles all opposites, unifies all contradictions, integrates all the various parts into a coherent whole, and connects all the connections. It makes order out of chaos. Falsifies all dichotomies. Synergizes all your synful synergies. It homogenizes past and future into the Right Fucking Now. It is constant, yet ever-changing; eternal, yet fluid. It includes everything and lacks nothing. It's whole and complete; it needs nothing but itself to be itself, writes its own rules, lives by its own laws, like a B-movie anti-hero.

There's only one drawback to this experience: It'll drive you nuts.

Here's what I mean. Back when I was a kid, a young teen-ager playing in my first real band, we played a gig that was...hell, let's say "fantastic." People dug it with a backhoe. Applause, cheers, screams. A tsunami of adulation that was 180 proof. Girls begged us for autographs, tore buttons from our coats, threw personal items of their own onto the stage. It was completely fucking nuts. And it was wonderful. The thing is, where do you go from there? That's about as good as it gets, see? After that, everything is kind of a letdown. But that crazy gig, kept me going for YEARS, hell, DECADES, on a quest to dance that dance just one more time. And it ain't gonna happen. I know that. But I keep remembering it, I keep hoping for it, keep needing it. Just one more little taste. One more good one like that, and I'm done. Which is pretty much what every washed-up fighter dreams, isn't it?

So.

Once you get hit by lightning, you want to get hit again.

You try to remember how it happened, recapture it by repeating the sequence of events like a cloud jockey going through his preflight checklist. But you can't force it. You can't make it happen. You can't control it. The only way to take control is by letting go, and letting go is the toughest thing in the world. Doing is easy; NOT-doing is hard. But you can't help it. Once you've been a rainbow-rider and your eyes glimpse what's behind your face, you'll hunger for it, you'll do anything to get it even if you have to chew your own foot off to escape the trap we jokingly refer to as reality.

For me, that means I keep getting back on the Horse.

Every time I do, I get a miniature, cliff notes version of lightning.

Just a little tickle.

Enough to keep me on the quest.

*What you want*
*Baby, I got it*
*What you need*
*Do you know I got it?*
　　　　"Respect"
　　　　Aretha Franklin


# CHAPTER TWELVE:
# R-E-S-P-E-C-T


"Respect" is one of those words than can mean anything the speaker wants it to mean. Like "love." And "terrorism." And similarly, it's quite often a self-serving euphemism. Some people say "respect," when they mean fear. Certain self-described "horsemen" use "respect" to mean instant, absolute obedience. My old man decided he was going to make me "respect" him by beating me to a pulp everyday. It didn't work. And coercion doesn't work on horses, either. Sure, you might be able to coerce a certain behavior out of somebody. But don't ever turn your back on them.

Me, I define "respect" as a feeling of deep appreciation and admiration for someone or something elicited by their unique abilities, qualities, or characteristics. For a horseman, that means appreciating and admiring the unique abilities, qualities, and characteristics that make a horse a horse. Respect comes from understanding and non-judgmentally accepting the horse's true nature. In order to do that, you have to know your own true nature as a human being, and comprehend what's the same and what's different, what words are common to both the equine language and the human language, metaphorically. On top of that, you have to get to know this particular horse to see how he expresses his true nature. In my opinion, if you don't do that, you're not a horseman; you're just a rider.

The horse "respects" a human being instinctively from out of distance, and he's got your number individually at ten yards. The horse reads you like a book because, as a prey species, he's had that skill honed to a fine edge over thousands of years. Despite the horse's knowledge of human nature, for some inexplicable reason, many horses seem to enjoy human company, and resist stomping us into chittlin's. Don't ask me why. The Old People have a story about that. (Basically, the creator saw how puny and stupid humans had turned out, so the creator took pity on us and sent the horse to be our mentor. Unfortunately, we're incredibly slow learners.)

Respect comes first. Then trust. Trust happens when you know the true nature of the horse AND you know the character of this particular horse. On the flip side, the same goes for the horse: she knows your nature as a human being, and knows your character as an individual. You earn trust by being consistently respectful, i.e., by being trustworthy. It takes a long time to build trust — and just one careless second to destroy it. That's why you need patience to play with horses. If you're not a patient person, change. Or stay the hell away from horses.

After respect and trust comes affection. You can't really love anyone whom you don't know well. You can be infatuated or "IN love" with them, but that's a whole lot more about YOU than it is about THEM. I think affection is the natural outgrowth of a good relationship — one based on respect and trust — in which you accumulate an abundance of shared experiences of all kinds, but especially intimate experiences. The first rule of affection is "Give a lot more than you take — and be damn careful about what you take."

When you have a relationship built of respect, trust and affection, anything is possible. Spartacus Jones taught me that.

*And the wayward wind is a restless wind*
*A restless wind that yearns to wander*
*And I was born the next of kin*
*The next of kin to the wayward wind*
                "The Wayward Wind"
                Patsy Cline


# CHAPTER THIRTEEN:
# SPARTACUS JONES AND THE WIND


You've heard the expression, "run like the wind?"

Maybe you know the book, King of the Wind, by Marguerite Henry.

According to Bedouin legend, Allah created the horse from a handful of the south wind and enabled the horse to fly without wings, and bound victory in battle to the horse's forelock. So you could say the horse is kin to the wind. I am, too.

The wayward wind.

Spartacus Jones is no young pony anymore. He's not in his best condition, got a touch of arthritis here and there. We go out for a little ride; he's in no particular hurry.

Takes his time.

No urgency. No Pavlovian work ethic. Just strolling along, whistling a tune. But every once in a while, he gets in a mood. Most often it's on a cool, cloudy day when the wind is up, tugging at his mane, tiny whirlwinds dancing up dust as they spin across the earth like Valkyrie, teasing and taunting.

He gets in this mood where he can't keep still, paws the ground, paces, tosses his head, like a boxer getting ready to answer the opening bell. He gets in this mood where he just wants to run. And when he does, I turn him loose and let him fly. His gallop eats up ground the way an alcoholic going off the wagon tosses down tequila.

251

The world becomes a blur and I lean forward, floating over his back, feeling the powerful pounding of his hooves under me, each one lighting on the ground just long enough to spark off of it again.

When he gets in this mood, he could run forever and just might, except there is no such thing as time. He's not doing. He's being. And I believe that when the Creator thought himself the thought "horse," this is exactly what he had in mind.

When Spartacus Jones has satisfied himself, he slows to a trot, a prancing trot, and then finally down to a walk that's about 180 proof strut. We pause to look behind us, and way, way back there, choking on our dust, we can just make out The Wind, bent-over by the side of the road, puking, swearing and gasping for breath.

And we laugh about it all the way home.

*She danced around and round to a guitar melody*
*From the fire her face was all aglow,*
*how she enchanted me*
             "Gypsy Queen"
             Santana


# CHAPTER FOURTEEN:
# GYPSY


She was a mustang.

When we first met, she was wild and unbroken, had been on her own long enough to belong to herself and to no man. Her instincts were fresh and she was rightly suspicious of any two-legged who wanted to do her a "favor."

And I was so fumblingly stunned by her beauty, that I tried hard to show her that I too longed to be free.

Perhaps, if we hadn't run out of time, we might have come to see ourselves in each other, might have learned to trust each other.

But time ran out.

She's no longer wild as she once was.

Now she knows that her fate lies in someone else's hands.

Now she must depend on another for food, for water, for fresh air, for permission to dance.

Now she knows she must accept the demands of man.

Once the world belonged to her.

Now she belongs to the world.

A world in which there is no place for freedom.

I stood with her awhile last night.

I offered her my hand and she sampled my scent.

As if she were my first lover, I explored her, going slowly, tenderly, waiting for her clear permission to continue step by step.

With weightless fingers I searched for her sweet spots, found that she enjoyed being scratched on her chest, rubbed in the hollow above her eye, stroked firmly along her neck, and I did things for her until her eyes were dreamy, her lower lip hanging softly down and relaxed.

Withdrawing from her, I settled into a corner, gazed out. Waited.

After a time, her soft muzzle nudged my hand as she memorized my scent, then brushed my ear, nickering ever so quietly.

I wondered if she could sense what a sweet privilege it is for me to be close to her.

To feel her whiskers tickle the skin of my cheek.

Her warm breath on my neck bringing on goose-bumps.

The bottomless beauty of her sin-dark eyes making my own eyes well up.

And so we stood together awhile longer, side-by-side, as if arm-in-arm.

Two resigned souls on the wrong side of a long lost battle.

She was a member of my herd, now.

I would look out for her, take care of her, and keep predators away by any means necessary.

It was both my duty and my privilege.

I learned that from Spartacus Jones.

*Just a jackknife has old Macheath, babe*
*And he keeps it, out of sight*
"Mack the Knife"
Bobby Darin


# CHAPTER FIFTEEN:
# SPARTACUS JONES AND THE RIGGING KNIFE


I hadn't routinely carried a knife on me in quite a while.
A hoof pick, yes. I've always had one. But not a knife.
I used to carry a knife on me all the time.

When I was a kid, a full colonel in the Black-Leather-Jacket
and Beatle-Boots Brigade, I carried a lovely pearl handled stiletto with
a five-inch blade. Push-button release, like the bad boys rumble with
in West Side Story. Fortunately, I never used it for anything but
cleaning my nails.

Later, I joined the Coast Guard, with visions of daring sea
rescues dancing in my head. The heroism of BM1 Bernie Webber and
his crew, who rescued 32 men from a sinking tanker during a savage
nor'easter in 1952, was already legend by the time I came along. The
Coast Guard recruiter told me that story almost before he introduced
himself. "We don't take lives," he said. "We save them." Since my
looming alternative was going to Vietnam to murder people who had
never harmed me on the orders of some asshole I didn't know, the
recruiter didn't have to say much else to get my name on the dotted
line. It didn't turn out as well as I had hoped, but at least they never
asked me to shoot anybody.
Fortunately, I was stationed on a boat for two years.

255

The first lieutenant was a warrant officer who was so salty you couldn't help getting some of it on you and I was determined to do the best job I could. That's just the way I am. I can't stand to do anything half-assed. I give it the full donkey or I don't do it at all. So I paid close attention to Mr. Hill.

He carried a rigging knife, as did most of the mates who worked on deck. It's got a marlinspike at one end, perfect for opening up wet knots, and a blade at the other end for cutting through fouled lines and knots you can't open. The blade has a rounded point so you don't stab yourself balancing on a rolling deck.

I decided to do as the Romans did — but I wanted to do it better. I found an ad for this knife in some yachting magazine. Made in Switzerland. When you really need a knife, there's a good chance you don't have both hands free to open it. The Swiss took care of that with a little built-in spring. Makes it a cinch to open with one hand. Opens up almost as easily as that old West Side Story stiletto did. Snap it open like a straight razor — but I kept it sharper than one. Because when you really need a knife, you need it to be so sharp that it will cut through the heftiest material in the wink of an eye. I honed mine to an edge that made a straight razor seem like a crowbar.

Going along with Boatswain mate culture, I carried that knife in a sheath I made out of scrap leather my first month on the boat. I braided six inches of rawhide onto the lanyard ring, so I could stick that knife deep down into the sheath, where it would never come out by accident, but I could still easily fetch it out by the tail.

Came in handy more than once.

That knife was tucked away someplace in my footlocker, somewhere between my wool long johns and my heavy socks. At least, I assumed it was. Hadn't had it out or even thought about it in a long time.

While I was busting my hump getting Chez Jack in shape, I boarded Spartacus Jones down the road at Stevie's Ark. I knew he'd get the very best care there. Outside 24/7, lots of good forage, and plenty of young fillies of both the equine and the human varieties to adore him. Only minutes away, I could easily swing by anytime I could take a coffee break; take him an apple or two. Play a little cards. Swap stories.

The first task on the farm had been to eliminate the almost brand-new horse barn.

Cleaning up the ashes and charred debris from that was a nasty chore, but it had to be done. I don't like putting horses in stalls. I spent nearly a decade in a cell that was 6 feet by 8 feet. I'm 6' even, 180 lbs. in good shape. I had enough room to pace, turn around, pace some more. Do push-ups. Practice kata. It was tight, but I could make it work.

Typical horse stall is 10' x 10'. Average horse is 8 feet long, nose to tail. Do the math.

I reached a good stopping point and decided it was horse time. Climbed into my truck and started it up.

Just as I put it in gear, I suddenly thought about that old rigging knife. It just came into my head for no particular reason.

Well, fuck it, I thought. I don't have much time and I'm not going to waste it trying to find that knife, if I even still HAVE it. But something about being knife-less nagged at me and wouldn't let go. Made me feel itchy and anxious, and unsettled. It kind of spooked me. So I got out of the truck, cursing myself, and went back for it. Felt a little silly about doing it. I hoped no one saw me. I wouldn't know how to explain it.

The knife was there.

Right where it was supposed to be. Didn't have to rummage around for it at all. I didn't feel like threading the sheath onto my belt, so I stuck it, sheath and all into my pocket. It was so bulky it looked like I was happy to see somebody.

Coming down the steep suicide hill to Stevie's Ark, I had a broad view of the place. I spotted Spartacus Jones over on the far side of his paddock, where a thick line of trees provided shade and a windbreak.

It didn't surprise me to find Spartacus Jones waiting for me on the near side of his paddock. I think he knew the sound of my truck, and knew it meant apples, on the house. But this time he was different. He was pacing back and forth along the fence in a very agitated way, tail swishing irregularly. As soon as I stepped out into the yard, he bellowed to me in his whiskey baritone, and galloped away toward the opposite side.

Halfway across the paddock he slid to a stop, turned to me and bellowed again.

What the fuck?

I ducked through the fence rails and followed him. He raced the rest of the way to the far side fence, pawing and stomping the dirt with both forefeet, and hollered at me some more.

Through the line of trees, I could see the tractor.

It didn't belong there.

Somebody was going to catch Stevie-hell for that — and hell hath no fury like Stevie protecting one of her adoptees.

Standing at the rear of the tractor was a Chestnut T-bred called Dutchess. She wasn't supposed to be there. But she was a notorious escape artist. She was wearing a halter, one of those cheap nylon web monstrosities. THAT wasn't supposed to be there either. Stevie never leaves a halter on a horse unattended.

But somebody had — somebody destined for a class A reaming out.

Dutchess had gotten that damn halter all tangled up and twisted in the tractor's mowing attachment. She was terrified, soaked with sweat, the whites of her eyes showing wide, as she pulled taut against the halter, trying to break loose.

No way to disentangle her, not with her keeping tension on the halter like that. But I whipped that knife out of my pocket, and with one quick, careful swipe, she was free. Slipped her head out of the halter and spun away, leaving the red nylon hanging there like an old used condom.

I made sure Dutchess was all right. Gave her plenty of love and comfort. She was shaken up but recovered okay.

Later, I gave Stevie a full accounting of the event, and heads rolled. One head, anyway. Spartacus Jones enjoyed a hero's celebration, which, in this case, meant lots of apples and even a few peppermint candies he had a thing for. So as the Bard says, all's well that ends well.

I can't help wondering, though, what was it that suddenly compelled me, out of the blue, to go back and get that knife?

*They say there's gold but I'm looking for thrills.*
*You can get your hands on whatever we find,*
*Because I'm only coming along for the ride.*
"The Gold It's in the..."
Roger Waters/David Jon Gilmour

# CHAPTER SIXTEEN:
# SPARTACUS JONES AND THE
# LOST CITY OF GOLD

It was a good day to be a horse.

So I played hookie, put off a few things, to spend the afternoon with Spartacus Jones. I arrived at the barn at an unusual hour, but he was right there waiting for me, like he knew I was coming.

How the hell does he DO that?

We took our time. Groomed. Shared a couple of apples. Told a few jokes. He asked me about Marlo. I ducked. He wasn't fooled. We saddled up and headed down the road with me walking beside him.

I waited for him to invite me up. I never mount either a horse or a woman without a specific invitation. When he gave me the nod, I hopped up and settled myself down easy on his back. We took on one of his favorite trails, along the streambed and up Bald Hill Road, now "seasonal" and rarely used. It has steeper parts and round-offs and dips and climbs. A good horse workout. I let him choose his own footing, his own pace.

The uniform of the day was gold.
Most of the red and browns had fallen
and lay prostrate before us
like a royal carpet spread along the path.

261

The leaves that remained were of gold.
Some newly minted gold,
still retaining the past-life memory of green.
Some were a rich, buttery gold.
A golden fire ignited by streaks of sunlight
filtering through the attending pines to dazzle the eye.
Gold that dazzles the brain with imaginings of splendor.

Others were soft, deep golden brown,
like the skin of an exotic lover.
Aztec, perhaps. Or Incan....

El Dorado, they called it. "The Golden One."
A legendary cache of jewels and golden coins.
Or an entire city made of gold.
Explorers — Gonzalo Pizarro, Phillip von Hutten
and Sir Walter Raleigh among them —
searched for it for a couple of centuries.
They searched in Mexico, in Ecuador, Peru, Bolivia,
Colombia, Venezuela, and Guyana.
They looked for it everywhere,
unable to resist the lure of easy money
and the easy life it would bring.
Some are still looking.

But maybe it's not a golden city.
Maybe it's the Holy Grail, the fountain of youth,
or Shangri-La.
Maybe it's true love.
Or happiness.
Or The Truth.
A black pearl or a white whale.
Something somewhere over the rainbow
or just at the end of one.

Maybe it's your own *personal* "holy grail,"
whatever that means for you.
Some ultimate prize important enough to you

that you spend your whole life questing after it.
Even though you know you may never find it.
Even though you know it might not even really exist.

We spoke not at all along the way. Most of the time, between us, words are either superfluous or inadequate. Half an hour later we arrived at the crudely paved road that intersected Bald Hill Road just on the far side of the crest, our turn-around point.

We came about and paused on Bald Hill
overlooking a valley strewn with autumn gold.
The subtle breeze was cool and clean.
The sun stood arms akimbo in a cloudless sky.
A distant smell of wood smoke.
He caught a mouthful of green grass,
the way some guys light a smoke,
and munched thoughtfully as we surveyed the scene.
"You want to know how to get to El Dorado, Jack?" he said.
"Sure. How?"
"Don't...You...MOVE."
He was right, of course.
He usually is.

The leg home was a long, long decline but from the crest of that hill we could see practically all the way to the end.

The golden trees that lined the road, paved in gold, were backed by a dark, anonymous throng of evergreens.

A breeze brought a handful of leaves across our path. Then another. And another. Golden blossoms strewn in homage before us by the wind.

Like a ticker-tape parade.

A dusty gust got grit into my eyes and I squeezed them shut, let them water to clean themselves out. I could feel the tiny bits of dirt, scratchy under my eyelids. I rubbed at the corner of my eye with a fingertip as Spartacus Jones snorted impatiently.

I opened my stinging eyes to a blurry world.
A different world.
We ambled almost casually along the road
and past the gates of the city.
Hundreds and hundreds of jubilant citizens, dressed mostly in gold, lined the path, pressed together like a wall on each side, gave way, opening a path before us.
Cheering.
Shouting.
Laughing.
Waving.
Their voices blended together into a roar the way individual drops of water unite to become the rush of the ocean.

We were bone weary, and still stained with sweat and grim and gore from the fight, but we collected ourselves and entered the city with dignity and humility. I felt him collect himself under me, lifting his head, squaring his shoulders. He quickened his pace under me, my hips alternately rising and falling with his steady gait, and he defied fatigue by exaggerating each beat of his hooves, stepping high and proud.

I looked into faces. The young. The old.
I knew none of these people.
I had no friends or family here.
I knew only that now, they were safe.
And they knew it, too.
Whatever it was, it was over.

A child, lifted up by a father with too few teeth in his grin.
Her tiny hand.
A blue flower.
I accepted it from her with a bow of my head,
and stuck the stem into my compadre's bridle, behind his ear.
He snorted an objection, but tolerated it.
I think, deep down, he didn't really mind at all.

We rode past the adulation to a fountain at the city center and I slipped down from his back. He drank deeply, ears twitching with each gulp, like a metronome.

I leaned over and plunged my head into the cool, crisp water, rubbed my face and stinging eyes hard.

Pulled out and let the water trickle down the back of my neck and tickle down my chest.

In my reflection, I could see that the stains on my face were now gone.

Those on my soul remained.


Spartacus Jones nudged my shoulder gently with his nose, and with that, the daydream, the vision, the fantasy evaporated.

He bent low for one more sip from the stream.

I stroked along the inside of his ear, from base to tip, the way he likes.

"So," he said, shaking out his mane.

"You still want to be a hero."

I gave a moist snort to express my utter disdain for the notion. But I think he thought I did protest too much. I think maybe I thought so, too.

"You're an incurable romantic," I retorted, not too churlishly.

He nudged me again.

Harder.

"Don't worry," he said. "I won't tell anybody."

I wasn't sure if this was his fantasy or mine.

Or maybe somebody else's.

Adam Adrian Crown

*A hundred times I told her that I loved her.*
*Each and every time my love declined.*
*You might think I might disdain repeating*
*She's always in my heart and on my mind*
                    "A Hundred and One Times"
                    Spartacus Jones




## CHAPTER SEVENTEEN: STAR


She's in no hurry.
Neither am I.

    Maybe it's because when we first met, first looked into each others' eyes, we both knew that there was something special between us and always had been, even before we met.
    There was an inexplicably comfortable familiarity that was more like recognizing an old beloved and trusted friend than it was like meeting someone new.
Whatever was going to happen was going to happen.
    It was as inevitable as sunrise.
    Knowing that, it was almost as if it had already happened and took away any uncertainty, awkwardness, or anxiety.
    Or hurry.
    We were relaxed and casual in each others' company. No airs or masks needed. We'd see through them anyway.
    We went for long walks. Mostly silent.
    When there was talking, I did it. She listened.
    But she spoke without speaking.
    A nod. An expression. A gesture.
    Only 5% of communication is verbal, anyway, according to the experts.

She would sometimes lean her head lightly against my shoulder. Sometimes brush my cheek with her soft lips and I could feel her warm breath against my neck and it gave me goose bumps right down to my soul.

After a time, a day came when it seemed right.

She gave me that invitation, knowing I would never refuse, and knowing I would not hurt her or merely use her. I rolled gently onto her, feeling the heat of her body against me in pulses like a heartbeat.

Her heartbeat.

My heartbeat.

Our heartbeat.

And her scent was the fragrance of sunshine.

I let her carry me wherever she wanted to go, moving with her, content to be part of her body and spirit. Hips swaying in a primal samba, she walked into my heart, as we rode through the cool autumn colors.

And she would remain there always.

*You ain't nothin' but a hound dog*
*Cryin' all the time*
*Well, you ain't never caught no rabbit*
*and you ain't no friend of mine*
"Hound Dog"
Elvis Presley

# CHAPTER EIGHTEEN:
# THE PIT BULLS

When I was a kid, I worked for a guy who did garbage collection, put in septic systems, sometimes graded or re-graded driveways. It was a great job. Exceptional boss. Paid well. Outside work in all kinds of weather. And I learned how to drive a truck, operate a dozer, and work a backhoe, which is a little like the claw-crane arcade game.

I bought a John Deere tractor for my place. Versatile piece of equipment, useful for approximately 3.2 gazillion jobs around a farm, from mowing pastures, to plowing snow. You can rig mine with a front loader, a snowplow, a mower, a disc harrow, a backhoe, and a toaster.

I selected a spot on my property that bordered the state forest. It wasn't an area that would get much traffic: human, equine, or otherwise. It didn't take me long to do the actual work. It was the first time I'd rigged up the backhoe and I think I spent more time trying to recall how to operate the damn thing than I did to do the actual digging. Hadn't used one of these since I was a kid. It was a little slapstick. Took me a few jerks and jolts before my hands remembered. But after that it went quickly. I made the pit eight feet deep, nine feet long and about six feet wide. That should be enough room.

You know what justice is?

269

Justice is a natural principle, like gravity. It's the principle of "for every action, there is an equal and opposite reaction." It's about karmic reciprocity. Balance. Universal equilibrium.

Justice is as ye sow, so shall ye reap. What goes around comes around. What you do unto others gets done unto you.

The law isn't justice, doesn't usually even provide justice or lead to justice. Justice is sweet to the soul as sugar on the tongue. The law is just aspartame.

Justice is "You broke it, you fix it." Restitution. Make it right again. Restore it to the way it was before you did what you did that broke it.

But some things can't be fixed.

If you kidnap someone, make them a prisoner, you can release them, but you can never give them back the time and freedom you took away from them. You cannot restore them to who and what they were before you kidnapped them. You have changed them forever.

Can't be fixed.

If you rape someone, you can't un-rape them. If you torture someone, you can't un-torture them. That pain is permanent.

Can't be fixed.

If you murder someone, you can't give them their life back. You can't give their survivors the parent, child, sibling, or friend that you took away.

Can't be fixed.

For the victims of unfixable wrong, a lawsuit is somewhere between insult and further injury. And in the end, all they get is money. But there IS no amount of money that can "compensate" a person for what they've suffered, and putting a dollar figure on it is the worst kind of trivialization. It's like saying, yes, you can kidnap, you can rape, you can torture, and you can murder, but you have to buy a license to do it. As long as you pay the fee, you're good to go.

Not everything is a commodity to be bought or sold, like so many widgets, at the current fair market price. The value of some things doesn't fluctuate like gold, today $40 dollars an ounce, tomorrow, $400 or $4 for the same ounce. One "wrongful death" suit today brings in a 5 million dollar judgment, another, 1 million. Is one life more valuable than another? Isn't each person's life just as valuable to him or her, as any other person's is to that other him or her? Me, I'd have to say yes on that one.

Say you murder my son. Then you give me a million dollars or a billion dollars. Does that fix it? Do I feel ok, now that I got the fair market price for my son's life? Hey, I can get a new car. A big-screen TV. That's fair, right?

There are some people who believe that they can have no peace as long as the malefactor who kidnapped, raped, tortured, or murdered is freely drawing painless breath. There are some people who believe that the villain must pay in kind and degree commensurate with their offense; that they should suffer precisely what they inflicted, and nothing else will balance the books, restore equilibrium. It's the equal and opposite reaction that nature craves. Some people think it's their right and their responsibility to "take the law into their own hands" rather than leaving justice up to the gamesmanship of corrupt prosecutors, indifferent judges, and brutal cops. Some people believe that establishing justice is an inescapable, uncompromisable moral imperative.

The Judge is one of those people.

So am I.


When The Judge calls, she never says, "Hello, Jack. There's someone I think you might enjoy killing. Let's get together and chat about it."

Phones are tapped. Conversations recorded. Caution is the order of the day. So we talk in code. Her elegant drawl is perfect for it.

This time she said, "Jack, I know what a dog-lover you are. I though you might like to meet my new puppy."

Only this time, it wasn't code. She actually did have a new puppy. A pit bull.

"I've re-christened him Lazarus," she said. "What do you think?"

He was café-au-lait tan with a white chest, and forlorn eyes. And he was in bad shape judging from the cast on his leg, and the sutures on his belly, rump, and neck. And the scars. Scars on his face. On his front legs. On his stifles.

"I think he's lucky you found him," I said.

A lot of people are afraid of pit bulls.

It's easy to fear what you don't understand.

To start with, pit bull isn't really a breed of dog; it's a type of dog.
Square head. Heavy, bulky body. That would include breeds like the
American Pit Bull terriers, American Staffordshire terrier, the
Staffordshire bull terrier, even the American Bulldog and Bull Terrier.

It's a fact that for generations, pit bulls were bred and trained and
bred again to be used in blood sports like bull-baiting, bear-baiting,
and cock fighting, and then later for dog-fighting.

Pit bulls are agile, strong, and there's not one drop of quit in them.
Most of the dogs used in dog-fighting here in the States are pit bulls.
Because of the reputation they have for aggression, various scumbags
employ them for guarding meth labs, chop shops, and junkyards.
Intimidation factor, see?

The funny thing is, a pit bull's temperament is no worse than most
dogs and better than many, and any normal healthy dog can be made
vicious, given the conditioning to be that way. But once people believe
something, it doesn't matter whether it's true or not. They think about
the vicious canine monsters they've heard about on TV, in the papers,
or, lord preserve us, on the Internet. Killer pit bulls swallowing
innocent babies whole. That sort of thing.

You don't hear about the pit bulls who are seeing eye dogs, search
and rescue dogs, and faithful companions. You don't hear about Lily,
the pit bull who dragged her unconscious owner off the railroad tracks
— and lost a leg when she was hit by a freight train in the process.
You don't hear about D-Boy, the pit bull who took three bullets
protecting his family from a home invasion. You don't hear about
Titan, the pit bull who saved the life of his owner's wife after she
suffered an aneurism. You don't hear about Weela, the pit bull who
braved quicksand, drop-offs, mud bogs, and swift currents to help save
32 people, 29 dogs, 3 horses, and a cat, during California floods.

No. You don't hear about those pit bulls. You only hear about the
ones said to be "naturally" mean, aggressive, and vicious.

Hell, poor dogs might as well be Muslims.

The real problem isn't the dogs.
It's the people.
Good dogs in the hands of bad people do bad things.
There's a lot of gambling on dogfights. And anytime there's
money to be made, you can bet your ass that one of the criminal
organizations out there is going to want a taste, whether it's the Italian

Cosa Nostra, the Irish mob, the Russian mafia, or the Lollypop Guild. The one criminal organization that's always involved is the police, because dog fighting is a felony in every state, and it couldn't go on without some cooperative cops getting a little piece of the action.

Just like the drug trade.

And prostitution.

Dog fighting isn't hard to spot. You don't have to be Sherlock Holmes.

You look for pit bulls on heavy chains. With padlocks.

You look for scarred up dogs. Mangled ears. Swollen faces.

You look for multiple dogs. Multiple scarred up, abused, injured, unneutered, unsocialized dogs.

You look for training tools: treadmills, jenny mills, spring poles, breaking sticks.

You look for somebody buying a LOT of vitamins, steroids, antibiotics, and vet supplies — somebody who's never gotten closer to veterinary school than swigging down a can of Red Bull.

You can also take a little investigative short cut. I asked my bookie, Nick the Mouse, about the action on dogfights.

"I don't do that kind of thing," he said.

I figured he was being square with me, because otherwise he'd have pitched it to me at some point in our long and, for him, profitable relationship. He covered ball games, whether base, basket or foot. Wagered on golf. Boxing, of course. Nothing involving animals. No horse races. No greyhounds.

"Glad to hear it," I said. Who does?"

He gave me a couple of names he'd heard. Just hearsay. Nothing solid. I'd have to solidify it, myself. A little surveillance was all it took.


I waited patiently for the effects of the drugs to wear off, passed the time by reading De Re Militari, by Flavius Vegetius Renatus. For hundreds and hundreds of years, kids played Vegetius says instead of Simon says, especially at places like West Point. My translation was slow going because part of the game was not to use a dictionary. My Latin really isn't that great. But I like puzzles. I promised myself that after I'd finished slogging through it, I'd buy a translation of it by somebody who knew a culus from a cunnus, and see if mine was anywhere in the generally accepted ballpark. I had just gotten to the part where Vegetius talks about sword fights, the principles of which also apply to knife-fights, in my opinion.

Vegetius says:

> *Praeterea non caesim sed punctim ferire discebant. Nam caesim pugnantes non solum facile uicere sed etiam derisere Romani. Caesa enim, quouis impetu ueniat, non frequenter interficit, cum et armis uitalia defendantur et ossibus; at contra puncta duas uncias adacta mortalis est; necesse est enim, ut uitalia penetret quicquid inmergitur. Deinde, dum caesa infertur, brachium dextrum latusque nudatur; puncta autem tecto corpore infertur et aduersarium sauciat, antequam uideat. Ideoque ad dimicandum hoc praecipue genere usos constat esse Romanos; dupli autem ponderis illa cratis et claua ideo dabantur, ut, cum uera et leuiora tiro arma sumpsisset, uelut grauiore pondere liberatus securior alacriorque pugnaret.*

My translation:

To cut or to thrust, that is the question.

New recruits were likewise taught not to cut but to thrust with their swords. For the Romans gave themselves hernias laughing at opponents who fought with the edge of the sword, and always found them a pushover. A cut, even a strong cut, is seldom lethal, as the soft, gooey parts of the body are protected both by the bones and armor. On the flip side, a thrust, even if it's only two inches deep is generally game over. Further, during the preparation for the cut (it don't mean a thing if it ain't got that swing) it is impossible to avoid exposing the right arm and side; (assuming there that the swordsman is right-handed) but with a thrust the attacker's body remains covered and the opponent feels the point before he ever sees it coming...

Yeah, I know it's a "loose" translation. I translate meanings, not words. Your mileage may vary.

I'd had to keep one of them sedated for a whole day while I procured the second guy. Had I screwed up the dosage? I'm not a doctor. I was starting to be a little concerned that I might have to come up with a substitute, which would be a little problematic, when the first guy finally started coming around.

"Have some water," I said. "It'll help."

"What the fuck?" he said.

It was a reasonable question. I might ask the same thing if I'd been getting a little free head in my car, and the next thing I knew I was waking up, stripped naked, in a deep, damp hole in the ground, with some other naked guy gagged and handcuffed at the other end of said hole.

"Have some water." I pointed to the canteen I'd lowered into the pit earlier. "Then help your pal." I tossed the handcuff key to him. He caught it.

He did take a drink.

"This better be a fuckin' joke, cocksucker" the Irishman said. Then he uncuffed the other naked guy and removed the hood and the gag.

"Fuck," he said again when he recognized who it was. "What the fuck is this?"

"It's a joke," I said. "A Russian and an Irishman walk into a dogfight. One says to the other, which one's your mother?"

"You are dead moather foaker, " said the Russian.

"Aren't we all?" I said.

"I get out, I kill you with my bare hands. Werry slowly."

"I appreciate your enthusiasm. If I was you, I'd be more worried about getting out of that hole than about what I was going to do if I got out. Any thoughts from you, Mr. O'Brian?"

"Fuck you, asshole. Who the fuck do you think you're fucking with, boy-o?"

"Thomas O'Brian," I said. "Pimp, crack dealer, and all-around asshole. Clancy Street Boys. You raise pit pulls for the dog fights you run. And I believe you're acquainted with your fellow asshole, Mr. Petrikova. Mr. Petrikova does the dogfights on the southwest side. Would you say you're more colleagues or competitors?"

*"Schas po ebalu poluchish, suka, blyad,"* growled Petrikov under his breath, giving me his best sanpaku glare.

"*Da?*" I said. "*Udachi, Sobaka.*"

That tapped him in the forehead like a ball-peen hammer and confused him into silence. I'm not fluent in Russian. But I think it's a good idea to be able to ask for food, water, and sex in any language, as well as to ask where the bathroom is. And of course, to tell a guy to go fuck himself.

"Here's the situation, gentlemen," I said. Only one of you has a chance of getting out of that hole alive. But I'm going to be more than fair with you. I'm going to let you decide who that's going to be. Doesn't matter to me who it is. But it's going to be the last man standing. Catch my drift?"

"You're out of your fuckin' mind," said O'Brian.

"That would explain a lot," I said.

"You want us to fight."

"Yup."

"Suppose we refuse?"

"Then I kill you both." I showed them my pistol. It made me feel like Vanna White. "If I were you, I'd get to it while I was still strong. You're not going to be getting any food or water, so you're only going to get weaker. I don't care how long this takes. I've got lots of time. You don't."

Petrikov was already calculating. Funny, I'd thought it would be O'Brian.

"We're miles from nowhere," I said. "Your cellphones are in tiny pieces at the bottom of a very deep lake. Your guys don't have a clue what's up and by the time they figure it out — if they ever do — it'll be yesterday's news. No one's riding to your rescue. You've got one chance, and one chance only, so you'd better..."

Petrikov leaped at O'Brian.

And, just like that, *alea iacta est.*

The fight was like a sadistic midget: nasty, brutish, and short. Shorter than I'd hoped, anyway. At the end of about twenty minutes it was over. They'd mauled each other in gruesome, nauseating fashion, with fists and feet, with knees and elbows, with teeth and nails. Too many injuries to catalogue, and the blood had turned the bottom of the pit to slippery sludge. The Russian was dead with one eyeball dangling against his torn cheek. The Irishman wasn't far behind. He was in a lot of pain. Funny, I'd have bet on the Russian. I guess you just never know.

"Get me out of here. I need a doctor. Ya gotta get me to a hospital."

"I don't think so," I said.

"What the fuck? You said the last fucking man standing would get out of this and I'm the last fucking man standing."

"No, I said that was your only chance to get out."

"What? For fucksake..."

"You're awfully fucked up. I don't think you're going to make it. Tell me, what do you do with dogs that get fucked up in a fight. You take them to a hospital? Spare no expense to take care of them? Or do you just let them die? Give 'em a bullet to the head if they're lucky? Well, you're not lucky."

He was panting and groaning. Not sure he really heard me, which was kind of a shame. But no plan is perfect.


It took a while.

After he was finished dying, I filled the hole back in, I hand-raked the spot, got rid of the worst of the tire tracks. Spread leaves and such around so the fresh dirt wouldn't be too obvious. No one was likely to see it, but some things you do just because that's the right way to do them, and you do them that way every time. Like you don't approach a horse suddenly, loudly and quickly from the rear — not even a horse who knows you well. If you cut corners with a horse who knows you well, one day, without thinking, you might just do it with a horse that doesn't know you so well. And then you get a mouthful of hooves.

When I was satisfied that the ground would pass casual inspection, I planted a pair of trees on the spot.

Flowering dogwood.

# PART THREE:
## Marlo

Adam Adrian Crown

*So hurry home to your mama*
*I'm sure she wonders where you are*
*Get out of here*
*Before I have the time*
*To change my mind*
*'Cause I'm afraid we'll go too far*
                    "Young Girl"
                    Gary Puckett and the Union Gap


# CHAPTER ONE:
# REGARDING MARLO


Ithaca, New York.

In the heart of the beautiful Finger Lakes.

They call them the "finger" lakes, but there are actually eleven of them, not ten, so even if you count thumbs as fingers, something's a little bit off.

Famous for waterfalls, gorges, and miles and miles of white, sandy beaches.

Ok. Two out of three ain't bad.

Several confluent elements brought my Phaeacian ship to the port of Ithaca.

I knew a guy in the joint whose wife was a hometown Ithaca girl, and he'd left me an open invitation to visit when I got out. At the time, it didn't look like I was ever going to get out, so it was a fairly easy offer to make. But life is nothing if not full of fucking surprises.

My esteemed attorney, Alice Burton, Esquire — one of those surprises I mentioned — had graduated from Cornell Law School and spoke of the Ithaca area in dreamy, nostalgic tones, describing it as a sort of Shangri-la cum Disneyworld, but with organic tofu, where it was eternally 1973. A place where a large segment of the population was comprised of former hippies — or hippies who had adopted protective camouflage for survival, wearing their tie-dyed t-shirts under their casual clothes the way Superman wears his signature leotard under his Clark Kent suit.

Most importantly, The Judge divided her time between the family ranch in Texas, and a stately colonial home in Ithaca, on Forest Home Drive. It wasn't terribly smart of me to be in the same town where The Judge was. It was a connection, if anyone ever wanted to look closely enough. Then again, I never had any intention of staying longer than necessary to satisfy my curiosity, and a couple other urges.

That's the kind of plan that makes the gods laugh out loud.

So, with no particular place to go, and no particular time I had to go there, and with money no longer being an issue, thanks to the settlement the aforementioned Ms. Burton had negotiated for me, I found myself driving south along Cayuga Lake — the longest of those fingers — on route 89 en route to the Emerald City.

Once upon a time, they made movies in Ithaca. Back in the silent film era. And the Ithaca Gun Company turned out some fine rifles and shotguns.

But that notwithstanding, Ithaca is and always has been a college town.

It's fundamentally a small town, a small rural town, with all that entails for good or ill, and it would be a place of no particular interest, except for the presence of Cornell University on one hill and Ithaca College on the other, and a few other earthly delights sprinkled in between. The population of about 30,000 more than doubles every Fall with the return of the college students who descend upon the area not unlike locusts with backpacks, and a lot of discretionary income.

While the town proper is quite the cosmopolitan little burg, with theatre, music, art and pretty maids all in a row, ten minutes from the Ithaca Commons — which is like a miniature of the Chicago Loop — you're in the sticks with the hicks, where the deer and the rednecks roam, no few of the latter just one clean sheet away from a Klan meeting.

I kid you not.

You might think that the habitat of those Ku Klux Klowns is limited to the deep south, across the Manson-Nixon line, below the Cotton Curtain, where old times are definitely not forgotten, and strange fruit hangs from the popular trees.

You'd be wrong.

Back in the 1920's, New York State boasted — if that's the right word — 40,000 Klan members. Now, that was right after DW Griffith released his putrid piece of racist propaganda, and cinematic masterpiece, "Birth of a Nation," so the Klan was enjoying a surge in popularity. If you haven't seen that film, you should. Bring an airline bag. It was the favorite flick of Democratic President Woodrow Wilson who called it "history written in lightning." The film's success proves two things. First, you can be an excellent film-maker, a master of the craft, and still be a reprehensibly ignorant sonovabitch. Second, the "solution" for racism isn't "education." Wilson had been President of Princeton University. So you can be "educated" all to hell and still be a miserable bastard. Something to keep in mind.

Latter day KKKreeps still screen that film to recruit new members.

The Klan in New York is currently fairly kkkquiet. But there are still places where you can feel it smoldering under the surface, lying in wait to a catch the right breeze to fan it into flame.

There's precious little crime in Ithaca, and violent crime is almost unknown — which makes it even more shocking when it does occur. Ithacans are too hip, too cool, too groovy. This is where the flower children sunk roots and became perennials. It's charming in a way, irritating in another.

At some National Parks, where no hunting is allowed, visitors have been feeding the animals for so long that those animals are almost domesticated — key word there being almost. I don't mean deer, rabbits, and squirrels. I mean bears. Grizzly bears. It sometimes comes to pass that a tourist encounters one of those presumably almost domesticated bears only to find that the bear is from out of town, and doesn't play that shit. It usually winds up being bad news for both the dimwit and the poor bear.

Ithacans are a little like that.

They live in a place where all the bears are cute and will eat out of your hand.

They forget that there are plenty of bears out there who would prefer to chew off your arm and wear your intestines as a hat.

So sometimes I notice folks in Ithaca doing things or saying things — not malevolently, mind you — but with a casual ignorant recklessness of word or rudeness of tone that could get you killed anywhere outside your safe little petting zoo. The average Ithacan wouldn't survive a week in my old neighborhood. The teddy bears would be having one hell of a picnic.

I'm not saying Ithacans are bad or stupid people. Some are amiable as all hell. And they really do mean well, I think. It's just that so many are so removed from the street-level reality I grew up with that it makes me feel like Valentine Michael Smith on a three-day pass from Mars.

Ithaca also has its share of "social activists."

Without any doubt, there are a lot of things to be activist about. It's like that when you live in a country run by corrupt psychopaths. But all the King's petitions and all the King's protest rallies ain't gonna lay a glove on that.

You cannot change a predator's behavior by appealing to the predator's "better nature," by whining, complaining, and begging. To begin with, predators don't have a better nature. They are what they are. You're not going to persuade one of those grizzlies to become a vegan. And when the predators in power grow weary of you trying to stuff tofu down their gullet, they'll give you an object lesson in what being a predator means. A petition makes a lousy bullet-proof vest.

Predators, whether four-legged or two-legged, respect only one thing. And you and I both know what it is. At least I certainly do and you certainly should.

So I tooled into town, found Frankie's place, met his old lady, about the sweetest young thing who ever wore Birkenstocks. Reminded me of a girl I once knew in El Paso. Deja fucking vu.

I told them I was just passing though, and really, I was. Really.

Then Frankie's wife, Issa by name, practically begged me to stay the weekend, luring me with the promise of an event called the Grassroots Festival, a sort of G-rated annual Woodstock, to be followed by a blues jam session at some club in town, and topped off with the company of a girlfriend of hers who had the morals of a lioness in heat.

Not exactly the world's hardest sell.

Turned out that there were a lot of talented musicians in Ithaca, playing all different kinds of music, which is my favorite kind. I had the pleasure of meeting some cats who played rings around my modest chops. Did an impromptu duet of "Since I Fell for You" with a hefty lady named Betsy, who could really belt it out. And Issa's girlfriend, Casey, was — as advertised, shall we say? She definitely knew her way around a bat, and never struck out.

A couple of days turned into a couple of weeks, because I agreed to sit in on an album that a local chanteuse was cutting, and then it was a couple months and you have to stay for the holidays, it's so quiet when the students are gone, with Buttermilk Falls frozen over, and, and, and — and before you could say badda-bing, badda-boom, two abara-cadabaras, an oy gevalt and a hearty Hi-yo, Silver, I was signing a 2-year lease on a studio apartment at Fairview Heights, on the seventh of seven floors, dang me. It was on the edge of Collegetown with a view of the Cornell clock tower, and the verdant valleys and amber waves of grain far to the west.

Classiest place in town. Executives. Professors. Visiting dignitaries. And me.

It was comfortable. I played music when I felt like it. I worked out when I felt like it. I played traffic cop to a steady stream of nubile transient lasses passing through my bedroom. And from time to time, I would have a chat with The Judge and undertake to remedy some intolerably egregious short-coming of the criminal justice system.

Then I got hit by lightning, right where the arrow points to the rainbow, and thereafter began spending as much time as possible in the company of horses, in hopes of getting hit again. That eventually led me to Stevie's Ark.

I first met Stevie through Jill, the "J" at "B&J Stables" where I'd been horsing around. In the beginning, I paid Jill for lessons, but I got so that I wanted to ride every day, and Jill had horses that needed to be exercised, so we kind of struck an informal deal that worked out well, all around. There were half a dozen ponies I could choose from to saddle up and take out on the trail whenever I wanted. Sometimes I'd spend a whole day in the saddle, taking out one pony, then another. It was idyllic. I didn't care so much about riding, per se; I just wanted to be around them. I was just as content to be mucking out a stall as I was to be tucking my ass into the saddle. When I wasn't riding them, I was grooming them, feeding them, watering them. Watching them. Listening to them. Horses have secrets to tell, but they whisper and you have to listen closely.

Stevie was B&J's vet. She's a voluptuous blonde cast from the same physical mold as Marilyn Monroe, but with neither the need nor inclination to hide her intelligence. Horse juju emanated from her like warmth from the sun. Wore her long blonde hair in a pony tail, of course. Quick, observant eyes. The smooth, balanced gait of an aikido master, even with that enticing swing on her back porch.

Doo-wah.

When she came up to give the ponies their required annual shots, she strongly recommended the minimum required by law, and gave the shots on different days, not all at once. That wasn't the cost-efficient way to do it, but even though it was money out of her pocket, she said it was better for the horses. That got my attention. I learned that though she was expert at conventional veterinary medicine, including surgery, she was unfettered by it, incorporating into her practice such things as Chinese herbs, chiropractic adjustments, massage, and homeopathy. You couldn't spend any time in her presence and not improve your horsemanship, just by osmosis.

I liked her the moment I met her, and that's a rare thing for me.

Turned out Stevie had a place of her own, officially called Sunny Meadow Equine Rescue, but amongst those who knew her it was referred to as "Stevie's Ark." There, with a little help from her husband and a small but dedicated crew of volunteers, she cared for a collection of rescued horses, rescued dogs, rescued cats, two rescued burros, and a few formerly wild creatures, like Archimedes the raccoon, who, after recovering from an injury, had settled in more or less permanently. Deer came and went like they owned the place. When they do Stevie's life story, it's going to be a Disney animation like Snow White, with birds singing to her, and landing on her shoulders.

With sometimes as many as four dozen horses to care for, rehabilitate, and find either foster or permanent homes for, Stevie could always use an extra hand. So at Jill's suggestion, I started volunteering at Stevie's Ark. Maybe Jill was just trying to get rid of me. Anyway, I did that for a while. Learned a lot from those ponies. Each one taught me something special, because each one *was* something special and I'll never forget any of them: Bennie and Twister, Sally and Sweet Sioux, Nobie, Tyler, Ozarb, and Impressive Kate; Canto, Jimmy-Jimmy and old blind Gus; Dearborn, True, Cisco and Zeus; Dutchess, Deguello, Buddy, Mandy and Brandy, Holly, Gracie, Danny-Boy and Apache Prince, to name a few.

And that's where I met Marlo.

She was a geeky, gawky, 10-year old, with scrawny limbs, knobby knees, and a slight overbite in a mouth one size larger than her face required. Her bronze complexion was one shade shy of swarthy and her impossibly frizzy hair was bound grudgingly into a ponytail and ever on the alert for an escape route. But behind her glasses, her dark eyes were bright and sharp, her gaze focused and direct. Her smile had the sincere innocence and innocent sincerity found only in children and fools.

She came to Stevie's Ark with a group of about a dozen or so other girls from her school, embarking on their requisite love affair with horses, and I was going to help Stevie give them the 25 cent tour, introducing them to each of the horses, telling them each horse's story, so far as we knew it, teaching the kids how to offer apple and carrot treats on a stretched-out palm. After that we'd get into some serious horse-petting disguised as grooming, and a tutorial on how to be safe around horses. It was just what it sounds like: an elaborate version of show-and-tell.

The most important thing I had to tell them was about respect. A horse isn't a puppy or a kitten. A horse is a horse and you have to respect their nature. While a horse doesn't have a mean bone in his body, he's bigger than you are, stronger than you are, faster than you are, and smarter than you are — especially when it comes to knowing what happens before what happens happens. He's a prey animal, and faced with a potential predator, he'll run first and ask questions later. But if he can't run, if you corner him, or if you threaten his family, then he'll fight, and then you'd better be wearing your hard hat, your steel-toed boots, a mouthpiece, a seat belt, a condom, and a parachute — and be sure your insurance is paid up.

While we were getting the group organized, and their teacher was taking a head count, Marlo had wandered through the barn and out toward the first paddock, currently occupied by a bay named Buddy. I remember she was wearing white. All white. It contrasted sharply with her coloring.

I went to get her, and herd her back to the group so Stevie could get started with the safety and ground rules introduction.

Buddy was a recent addition to Stevie's herd. He was one of four ponies who had suffered a combination of neglect and abuse at the hands of their owner, and had finally been seized by the County Sheriff executing a court order. They'd found the remains of two other horses in the same pasture. I won't go into details about the shape these poor ponies were in.

I can't.

Can't bear it.

When Buddy arrived, he was so weak he could barely walk, and was so starved I could almost carry him all by myself. He immediately got his hooves trimmed, his teeth floated, his abcesses treated, and his parasite infestation de-wormed away. In the month Buddy had been aboard the Ark, he had already put appreciable weight back on his emaciated frame. His body was on the road to recovery. But the emotional wounds would take much longer to heal, if they ever did. As he got his strength back, he was able to express himself, and what he expressed was a combination of distrust, fear, and anger.

All of which were feelings that I could relate to.

He took back his personal space, and refused all approaches closer than ten feet, and would withdraw, would not even come to eat until the human left the immediate area.

I understood.

Been there, myself.

Smart horse.

That's why it hit me like a stiff jab when I realized that Buddy was standing calmly at the near corner of his paddock, letting this young girl pet his nose.

I stopped where I was. I didn't want to intrude and ruin it. After a moment, she came back to the barn, and Buddy went back up to his safe place, in the middle of the paddock, where no one could sneak up on him, and turned his tail into the wind to doze in the sun.

"What's his name?" she asked.

I told her.

"Why is he so sad?"

"What's your name, honey?" I said.

"Marilyn," she said. "But I like Marlo better."


Marlo became a regular fixture at Stevie's Ark.

Spent almost as much time there as I did, myself. Hardly a day went by without her presence. It seemed she split her time between the horses and her cello. That sounds like an ideal balance to me.

That meant I spent a lot of time with her.

She was curious as a new foal, asked countless questions about countless things, and I suppose I took on the role of mentor to some degree. We had long conversations, first about horses and then about music, then on to many other things, all the varieties of cabbages and the nature of kings.

Time went by and she started to grow up, fill out, ask more sophisticated questions. I taught her what I knew about self-defense, how to fight, when to fight, and how to avoid the necessity of fighting if at all possible. Threw in a few odds and ends. I gave her a short course on the history of the blues, which begot jazz, and introduced her to classic films, putting the sin in cinema. Her curiosity was our conversational road map. Sometimes we took the interstate, and sometimes we explored those little blue roads, just for the hell of it.

I've never done anything like that with anyone else. Not before, and not since. And maybe I shouldn't have done it with Marlo, either.

But I did.

Seemed like the right thing at the time.


Sometimes, I try to remember the sequence, chapter and verse of how she and I got to where we are now, but I can't. Maybe she can. Maybe I should ask her. Mostly, I remember significant moments in our relationship. My mind skips from one to another like crossing a stream hopping from rock to rock with a steady roll.

*She takes her whiskey straight and her coffee black*
*If she ever giver her word she never takes it back*
*She's a little like me, and by now you've guessed*
*Damn, that girl's everything that I love best*
                    "Everything that I Love Best"
                    Spartacus Jones




# CHAPTER TWO:
# MARLO AND THE TROJAN HORSE


I arrived at Stevie's Ark just after the first birds started tuning up.

Marlo was already in the barn.

She'd gone on vacation someplace with her parents for almost a month. Vermont, I think. Rumor had it that she had taken some riding lessons out there. Previously, she'd hung out with the ponies at Stevie's, helped feed, groom, muck out paddocks, and so on, but hadn't been particularly inclined to ride. I don't know what changed that. Maybe the evil influence of her peers, though she didn't seem vulnerable to that the way most people are. This was the first time I'd seen her since her return.

She had a saucy thoroughbred gelding all tacked up and ready to rock. His name was named "Canto General," which means "Common Song," and most everyone had always called him "General." Me, I don't like Generals, so when he came to Stevie's, I took to greeting him, "Yo, Canto!" See, that's a pun. In Spanish, "yo canto" means " I sing." I like singing a hell of a lot more than I like Generals, and I had a feeling this pony needed to break away from his past, and start fresh. Anyway, "Yo Canto" or just "Canto," became his name.

Seeing Marlo in her little helmet and her little riding boots, and her little riding tights made me cringe all the way to my puke button. I was afraid that the forces of evil had gotten into her head, and turned her into one of those things from Invasion of the Body Snatchers. But I held on to hope.

Around 11 or 12 years old at this time, she wasn't exactly big for her age.

Canto stood 16 hands plus.

She needed an elevator to mount that pony.

She was unaware of my presence as I watched her struggle with it for a minute, her left leg stretched up so high she looked like a dog trying to scratch behind her ear, hopping around on one foot to get into position to drag herself up the side of that equine mountain. It wasn't pretty.

Good thing that horse had the patience of a hundred saints. But even saints have their limits. When Canto's tail started to get twitchy, I decided to intervene.

"Hey, Marlo," I said.

She pulled her leg out of the stirrup and quit hopping.

"Oh, hi, Jack," she said.

"Thanks," Canto snorted.

"Good to see you, kid," I said. "Whatcha up to?" That last part was rhetorical.

"Oh, just, you know." That was rhetorical, too.

I doffed my sombrero, as an idea struck me.

"You know," I said, "I've been thinking. What you need is a good hat. Maybe I'll give you this one."

I clicked the chin-strap of her velveteen helmet and lifted the brain bucket from her head, replacing it with my hat. Half her head disappeared into it. The brim all but hid her nose, and it rocked on her noggin the way the heads of those dog dolls used to do, the ones people would put in the back window of their cars. The effect was potentially side-splitting.

"Looks good on you," I said. "What do you think?"

"I think it's too big." She pushed it back on her shoulders so she could see me.

"Too big? What makes you think that? It's a great hat, you know. One hundred percent beaver. Handmade. Windproof, rainproof. Warm in winter, cool in summer. Cost you a pretty penny, that kind of hat."

"I know, " she said like she didn't want to hurt my feelings. "But it's too big."

"Too big, huh?" I said again. "How can you tell?"

She took a big breath so she could sail into an explanatory aria, but then it dawned on her. She blushed a little. She's cute when she blushes.

"I get it," she said. "I thought I just wasn't doing it right."

"Oh, I'm sure you were doing it just like they showed you." Sometimes I can hide what I think, sometimes I can't. Sometimes I don't give a fuck enough to try.

"Was there something wrong with it?"

"You're asking my opinion?" I said.

"Uh-huh."

"You're sure you want to know?"

"Yes."

So I told her. See, conventional horsemanship is basically European tradition. Handed down to us from a time when nobody gave a fuck about the horses. The belief was that horses were just here to serve human beings who had God-given dominion over the whole rest of creation, and they were more or less expendable.
I think that theory is what comes out of a horse's ass, and you have to be a horse's ass to buy into it. Beside which, "tradition" is a word that comes from Latin, meaning "too stupid to think for yourself so you just do it like you've always done, because that's the way you've always done it." Loosely translated. But I'll give you a hint: I don't think it's real smart to be hopping around on one foot when you're trying to climb up on an animal you fundamentally don't belong on, and who has a very highly developed flight response and who out-weighs you by about a thousand pounds.

She waited for my storm to spend itself, then said, "How do *you* do it?"

"Why? You want me to teach you?"

"Would you?"

"Maybe."

"Why just maybe?"

"It requires time and effort. But here's a lesson for free: never try to ride two horses at the same time."

"Wait, what?"

"You can ride *that* horse, do it the way *they* showed you, or you can ride a *different* horse and do it the way *I* show you, but you can't do both because they're opposite things. It would be a waste of everyone's time, and a pain in the ass for the horse. So you have to pick."

"I pick you," she said without hesitation. I smiled inside.

"You sure? You have to trust me."

"I trust you."

Something about the way she said that almost made me misty. She looked me dead in the eye when she said it, and it seemed to echo with all kinds of implications, like bad reverb from the 1950's.

"May it always be so," I said.

I had her untack Canto and we turned him out. He bolted into the pasture, kicking up his heels to celebrate dodging a ninety-pound bullet. Then I went to work on Marlo. I took her out to a section of fence. Split rail. I had her stand facing me, with her back to the fence and put her left foot up on a fence rail behind her. I took a place beside her, did the same thing.

"Okay, " I said. Bend your knee a little and then push up fast like this." I demonstrated what gym rats call a Bulgarian split squat, or, in this case a quarter-squat and Marlo monkey-did what the Jack monkey do.

"Push hard and fast, try to get off the ground."

She did well for her first try. We did it ten times.

"Other leg," I said, and we repeated the exercise.

"I want you to do that at least once a day — no upper limit. Got it?"

"Got it, she said.

See, the thing is, you don't step up into the stirrup with your left leg and use that to pull yourself up by pushing down against the stirrup. You spring up from your right leg. You also use your left hand, grabbing a hunk of mane to help, but it's 99% the right leg, putting as little weight in the stirrup as possible, because that's the part that's really murder on the horse's back, that sudden, uneven torque.

Personally, I prefer riding without a saddle at all, but at the time I didn't think that was the way to start with Marlo. Maybe I should have. Maybe I'd do it differently today, if I had to do it again.

Next, I had some carpentry to do.

With 2x4s and an old whiskey barrel I picked up from a guy out in Freeville who makes planters out of them, I build Marlo a practice horse. Basically, it's a saw horse with the barrel in between the legs. Not exactly high tech simulation, but adequate for our purpose. I built it to be 16 hands high, and threw a decrepit old Wade saddle on it. Then I rigged the stirrups, attaching them to the stirrup leathers with a loop of twine. The most challenging part was finding just the right weight of twine. To simulate the mane, I unbraided some manila rope and fixed the strands in place with fence staples.

In one corner of the barn, Stevie had built a low deck that stood half again higher than the standard mounting block, so she could give the horses chiropractic adjustments and massage. I set up the practice horse there. If you stood on that deck, it would be like mounting a 13-hand pony.

By the end of a week, Marlo had become the master of the Bulgarian split squat. At the barn, we did them together. I had her try a few at various depths, just for fun, but we focused on that quarter squat because form follows function and you always want to train as close as possible to the skill you're training for.

Time came to introduce Marlo to her practice horse.
"Marlo, meet Odysseus."
"Odysseus?"
"Look it up," I said.
"No, I get it. He's the one who built the Trojan horse, right?"
She was full of surprises.
"That's the guy," I said.
"You built this for me?"
"Yup."
"Then *you're* Odysseus."

I told her that my life was more oddity than odyssey, and that started the ball rolling. We riffed off of that for a while. She had a quick wit, and loved to play with words. We concluded with me agreeing with her theory that womanly beauty could be measured in millihelens — the amount of beauty it takes to launch one ship.

I set Marlo up on the deck, and double-checked to see that the stirrups were in riding position.

"Remember," I said, "Stand parallel to your horse and look where he's looking. You want to see what his ears are doing. The idea is to spring up, quickly and smoothly get your weight up over the center of your horse's back, not hanging off his side. Ready?"

"Ready."

"Okay. Mount up."

As I had anticipated, the twine holding the left stirrup in place immediately snapped under her weight, her foot slammed to the deck, and, off-balance, she bumped her nose on the skirt of saddle, which almost made her fall back on her ass. But I caught her.

"Wow," she said.

"Your mission, should you decide to accept it, is to mount so lightly that you don't break that twine."

"Seriously?" she said. "Is that even possible?"

I demonstrated it for her.

"Wow," she said again, bedazzled.

"Any science, sufficiently advanced, is indistinguishable from magic," I said. "Right leg, left hand," Push off your right leg, pull with your left hand."

"Right leg, left hand," she said.

"Right leg, left hand. I've got some work to do," I said. "Catch you later."

A couple paces into my departure, she hooked me.

"Hey, Jack?"

"Yeah?"

"How many millihelens do you think I am?"

Even at ten yards I could see the dampness in her eyes, the flush, could hear the uncertain wavering in her voice. It was a dangerous question and it took courage to ask. So it was important to her. I resisted the urge to go back and give her a long, long hug.

"I think you're a MEGAhelen, kid," I told her. Maybe it was supposed to be flippant and over the top, disperse the tension with some humor. But it was true. True on a far deeper level than either of us understood at that moment, even though I think we each felt it. She didn't grin her crooked ugly duckling grin that made her eyes disappear, the way she did when I joked with her. She locked onto my eyes and held on until the faintest smile softened her face.

"Right leg, left hand," I said, and realized that my voice was suddenly hoarse and my throat tight. "What the fuck, Jack?" I thought.

I left her on her own to practice.

*All or nothin' at all*
*Half a love never appealed to me*
*If your heart, it never could yield to me*
*Then I'd rather, rather have nothin' at all*
          "All or Nothing At All"
          Frank Sinatra


# CHAPTER THREE:
# MARLO & THE WHOLE BIT


Marlo was about thirteen or fourteen, helping me repair fences, one of the chores that never ends. The perimeter fence was bombproof, made of 6x6 posts with tight "V" mesh fencing no hoof could get caught in and a 2x8 top rail, but the interior fences, dividing up the paddocks and pastures, were all T-posts sheathed in PVC pipe sleeves and caps, and hung with electrical tape, which was powered by a solar charger.

Electrical fencing gives a horse a small shock, more a psychological than physical deterrent. It won't stop a horse who's determined to get through. The tape will stretch to a point, but then it will break. Once the electric line is down, there's nothing to keep a horse from leaning on a T-post, causing it to slant in. Tape has to be spliced, connectors replaced, posts re-set. Then too, sometimes you want to move a fence line, so you have to pull up those posts that you pounded in like they were going to be there forever. There's a lesson there somewhere.

It's not a difficult job, but there are moments when it's helpful to have a second pair of hands available. I don't rush, and there's plenty of room to chat. It was a balmy, early summer day. The air was cool, but the sun was warm and not a hint of a cloud in the sky

"You don't use a bit," Marlo said. She often asks a question like that, seemingly out of the blue, but it's usually something she's been thinking about a while.

"No, I don't."

"How come? Everybody else does."

"I'm not like everybody else," I said, stretching the kinks out of my back. "I'm not responsible for what other people do; I'm only responsible for what I do. And not everybody else uses a bit. But even if they did, I wouldn't."

"How come?"

"Same reason I don't use handcuffs on a date."

"Wait, what?

"I'll explain it when you're older. How come you're not carrying an umbrella?

"I'm...what?"

"How come you're not carrying an umbrella?"

"Um, it's not raining."

"Exactly," I said, and went back to splicing tape as if that settled the matter.

"Okay, I don't get it," she said. "Are you going to explain it when I'm older?"

I couldn't help laughing. Not at her. But because of her.

"No," I said, "I'll explain this one now. You're not carrying an umbrella because it isn't raining, so you don't need one. I don't use bits because I don't need bits. Some people think they do. They don't, but that's what they think. The truth is, the bit is probably the biggest single obstacle to being a good horseman. Hand me the hammer."

She offered me the hammer, handle first, like I'd taught her.

"But everybody else...almost everybody else uses them."

"That's true," I said. "Not everyone who owns horses loves horses. Some people love owning horses, whether they know anything about them or not, whether they know how to ride them or care for them or not. The horse is a status symbol or something. Some people love using horses. The horse is a means to an end. There are all kinds of equestrian events: jumping, dressage, barrel racing, trail riding, and endurance races, to name a few. What all these events have in common is that the horse does all the work and the human takes all the credit.

For these folks the horse is just a toy to play with, and a way to stroke the old ego by dominating others."

"They say they love horses."

"Sure. People say all kinds of shit that isn't true. For starters, you can't love horses if you don't really know horses. To love the horse is to know and accept the horse's nature, to appreciate it for what it is, on its own merits. To respect their nature. Respect. That's the first step on the road to any good relationship, don't you think?"

"Yes," she said.

"Okay. You've had plenty of time to observe horses. On their own, out in the pasture, just horsing around being horses. You've seen them walk, trot, canter. You've seen them snooze on their feet, lie down in the sun. Roll in the mud. Chase each other. Play. Argue. Eat. Drink. Turn their butts to the wind. Right?"

"Sure."

"Ever seen a horse pick up a stick, jam it way back in his mouth and run around with it like that?" I illustrated with pantomime and she laughed a little, like water giggling across the rocks in the brook.

"No," she said. "I haven't seen that."

"Uh-huh. Not likely you will, either. Having something in their mouth like that when they run is completely against their nature — against their physiological nature. They're not mouth-breathers. See those big nostrils? All the better to breath with, Red Riding Hood."

"But isn't having a rider on their back also against their nature?"

Did I mention that Marlo was smart?

"Yes, it is," I said. "Even though the Old People say that the creator sent us the horse because we were so weak, stupid and puny. We're asking the horse to do something that's NOT in its nature, NOT in its best interests. Why in hell should it do such a thing?"

"I don't know," she said.

"Me, neither. The Old People say it's a gift they give us. An act of grace. We haven't earned it, and we don't deserve it, but they give it to us, anyway. Seems to me the least we can do is show our appreciation by making it as pleasant for them as we possibly can. What do you think?"

"That sounds fair."

"I agree," I said.

I let her think about that while I finished splicing a section of tape and weaving it through the connector.

"You just got a new computer, didn't you?" I asked. I knew that she had.

"A Mac," she said.

"And a new phone?"

"Uh-huh."

"What was wrong with the old ones?"

"Nothing. These are just, like, better."

"I understand," I said. "Technology changes. People play around with things, look for ways to make it better. Those things improve over time — sometimes over a pretty short time. So most people today aren't using the same computer or telephone they used twenty years ago. Or ten years ago. Or even five years go. The technology has changed. Make sense?"

"Sure."

"Well, the bit was developed about five thousand years ago. And they remain fundamentally unchanged, even after lo these many years. Why do you suppose that is? Do you suppose ancient man stumbled upon the ideal equestrian technology, right out of the gate? The most perfect communication, and the most humane? In a moment of unparalleled epiphany, we were so enlightened, or so clever, or so lucky that we just happened to trip over utter perfection on the first try?"

"I kinda doubt it."

"You're a skeptic. Good for you. Me, too."

"Yeah, but..."

"But, what?"

"Well, you say if it isn't broke don't fix it. Bits work or people wouldn't use them. I mean, bits do work."

"Yeah? Depends on how you look at it." I held out my left arm for her. "I'll show you a trick. Grab my wrist," I said. "Grab it real tight and don't let go."

She grabbed it. She has strong hands.

"Are you ready?" I said.

"Ready for wh—?"

Before she could finish that word I twisted her hand into a wristlock, a variation of gyaku gote mae yubi I'd learned from a Shorinji Kempo teacher in the waybackwhen.

"Ow! Shit!" she said.

"Uh-huh. Hurts doesn't it?"

"What the heck?"

"If you're going to curse, honey," I said, "do it properly. If you mean 'what the fuck?' then say 'what the fuck.'"

"What the fuck?" she said. That's my girl.

"Relax," I told her. "Don't fight it. Just give in. Follow me."

She yielded as best she could, and I moved her around, leading her by the wrist. It's easy to do, once you get them into that unnatural, contorted position. You can use just the knife edge of one hand and two fingers of the other.

"That's not so bad, right? If you follow, it's awkward and uncomfortable, but not painful. Right?"

"I guess."

"Good. Now resist. I'm going to go this way, you try to go that way."

She gave it a shot. She's a brave kid and will try almost anything once. But her resistance didn't last long. About half a second.

"OW!" she said, and followed it with a little whimper that was like a spike through my heart.

"See, I said, "as long as you go where I want you to go, it's relatively painless. You try to go someplace else, you hurt yourself. I can get you to do what I want, but we're sure as hell not partners, are we? You do what I want or else."

"Could you let me go now?"

"Not yet. One more thing. Repeat after me: I carry my adornments only on my soul..."

"What??"

I put half an once of pressure on her mae yubi.

"Ow!!! Fuck!!" She proved to have a natural talent for cursing.

"I carry my adornments only on my soul..."

"Ah. I carry my adornments on my soul..."

I tweaked her finger again.

"ONLY on my soul," I corrected her. "I carry my adornments only on my soul."

"I carry my adornments only on my soul." She got it right, through gritted teeth.

"Deck'd with deeds instead of ribbons..."

"Wait, what??"

I tweaked her again.

"Deck'd with...um.. deeds not ribbons..."

I corrected her and she winced. "Deck'd with deeds INSTEAD of ribbons...Take it from the top."

"I, um, carry, um... please let me go now."

I let her go. She cradled her offended wrist in her other hand, her mouth forming a silent "Owww."

"Here," I said. "Put your hand on my shoulder."

"No way!" she said.

"C'mon. Trust me."

She very cautiously put her hand on my shoulder, ready to pull it away at any instant if I tried anything funny. I didn't. I gently stretched her wrist and massaged a pressure point. Her discomfort subsided and she allowed herself to trust me again. Cautiously.

"Better?" I said.

She nodded.

I gave her back her hand and she clenched and unclenched a fist to make sure everything still worked.

"What have you learned, Dorothy?"

"The Wizard is an asshole," she said.

"I mean besides that."

"That you know how to hurt people."

"You have no idea," I said. "But besides that? How did it feel to try to learn something while you were dealing with pain? How did you feel about me, when you were in pain? How did you feel about me afterwards? You didn't seem eager to put your hand on my shoulder. What kind of a relationship did we have?"

"Not a good one."

"How do you want your horse to feel about you?"

"Not like that, that's for sure."

"Me, neither. All bits work on the same principle as a wristlock. The horse does what you want, goes along, the pain isn't too bad. If he doesn't go along, if he resists, the pain is worse. The horse learns to avoid the pain. To fear it and avoid it. The bit does ONE thing and one thing only. It inflicts pain to coerce compliance. There are no gentle bits just as there are no gentle wrist locks. There are only bad bits and worse bits. There's no such thing as "soft hands," either. There are no hands soft enough to eliminate the pain of a bit, just as there are no hands soft enough to eliminate the pain of the wristlock."

"But people say it's for communication," she said.

"Sure. A wristlock is communication, too. It communicates who's in charge and who's going to get hurt if they don't go along with the plan."

"What about control?"

"What about it?"

"Well, people say they can't control their horse without a bit."

"Uh-huh. Ever heard of a horse running through the bit? You get a horse who's strong, defiant, independent — he might blast through the pain no matter how severe the bit is or how hard you apply it. See, if a guy ties you to a chair and pounds you in the gut to make you talk, you can get to a point where you're kind of numb and no longer feel those punches. At a time like that, you may smile and spit blood in the guy's face and tell him to go fuck himself."

Marlo's mouth dropped open and she stared at me. "Wait, what?" she said.

It was one of those moments when I realized that we were not only from different epochs, but from entirely different worlds.

"The point is," I said, brushing quickly past it, "that bits don't guarantee control. If you can't ride without a bit, you can't ride with one, either. Look, I'm not saying bits don't work. Pain and fear can be powerful motivators. So bits work. And they make it fast and easy — for the human. No real horsemanship required. But it's brutal on the horse. Most people don't really give a fuck about the horse. Most horses — like most people — will succumb. Go along to get along. There are a few who defy the pain. They resist. They rebel. Maybe even fight back. Those horses get labeled unmanageable, or aggressive, and usually wind up in the kill pens. When a horse resists, it's a problem horse. And when a woman resists being treated like chattel, she's being a castrating bitch, right? When a slave resists he's being 'uppity.' When somebody fights back to defend his home against an invading army he's a 'terrorist.' See the common thread there?"

"It's someone acting like they have a right to make somebody else do something that they don't want to do?"

I told you she was smart.

"But hey," I said, "if inflicting pain doesn't bother you, you can certainly make most every horse do what you want him to do by putting a wristlock on the sensitive part of his mouth. Just don't claim you love the horse. Don't tell me you're friends, or partners. Because you're a fucking liar. You know, once I listened for about an hour while a guy told me how much he loved his wife. Loved her. Heart and soul. This was right after he beat her to death."

Sometimes Marlo looks at me the way you look at a starving kitten, lost out in the rain. Like she wants to rescue me. Cuddle me. Make it all better. Lately, sometimes it almost seems like she can.

"Let me ask you this. I can get you to give me your money if I pull a gun on you. You give up your cash because you fear the pain and injury that a gunshot will cause. So you willingly and voluntarily choose to toss me your wallet rather than have me shoot you. So I didn't really steal your money; you gave it to me, like a donation, right?"

"Um, no."

"Of course not. That's bullshit. But that's the conventional equestrians' logic. Try to point that out and it's a lot like talking to a tumbleweed. Fact is; most people use bits just because that's what they were taught and they just accepted it without question. They do it that way because that's the way we've always done it. But there's an unspoken part of that. What they actually mean is 'That's the way I was taught because that's the way we've always done it and I'm emotionally incapable of empathizing with the horse, and intellectually incapable of critically examining the situation for myself, and reaching a rational unbiased conclusion and I think I have a right to coerce others to do my bidding because I have opposable thumbs."

"I don't want to inflict pain on a horse. Or on anyone," Marlo said, just above a whisper. Like I was hearing her confession.

"I know you don't," I said, and put a hand on her shoulder. "That's why we're having this little chat.

"So what do you do? All the horses seem to really like you. I mean, they come right over to you, and they follow you around just like a puppy. How do you do that?"

"Honey, I just try to treat them the way I would want to be treated, myself. I've had relationships in my life that were based on pain, fear, and force, and I don't care to have another one. That's a real limited way to go. But what you can accomplish with respect, trust, and affection, is unlimited. If your pony doesn't do what you ask, it's because he doesn't understand what you're asking, or he physically can't do what you're asking him to do, or he's flat out refusing to do what you're asking. So number one, be sure you're clear about what you're asking. Number two, be sure your pony is physically capable of doing what you ask, and number three, maybe he's got a damn good reason for not doing what you ask. Find out. Listen to your horse. He's smarter than you are and he's certainly better at being a horse than you are."

"But that sounds so... simple."

"It is simple, I said. "But it's not fast and it's not easy. It takes time and it takes effort. But if I can't have a relationship based on respect, trust, and affection, I'd rather have none at all. My pony isn't just my horse. He's my best friend. He's my partner — an equal partner. He's not my servant and he sure as hell isn't my slave."

We worked on the fence for about an hour or so, Marlo lost in thoughtful silence. Our conversation recalled to my mind an obscure little song I learned in Mexico. A very old song, I'm told. Hard to know if the singer is talking about a woman or a horse.

Fits either way.

Be with me
Because you see the beauty of yourself in my eyes
Feel the power of yourself in my touch
Be with me
Because we are stronger together
Than we are when we're apart
Be with me
Because I am free, and you are free, and together
We can share freedom
Be with me
Because I am not complete without you,
and you are not quite complete
Without me

Be with me
Because it's your own desire and your own choice
Or not at all.

Heading back to the barn for lunch, Marlo broke the silence.
"You know that thing you did to my wrist?"
"What about it?"
"Could you teach me how to do that?"
"Sure," I said.

*If the rain comes they run and hide their heads*
*They might as well be dead*
*If the rain comes*
"Rain"
The Beatles




# CHAPTER FOUR:
# REIN MAN


"How do you *do* that?" Marlo said.

"Do *what*?"

We were taking a pair of ponies out for a little exercise. Mine was a dun gelding named "Magic." Marlo was on a paint called, "Toka."

"It's raining. You go out, and it stops. You come back in and it starts up again. What's up with that?"

"They call that 'coincidence,' darlin'," I said.

"Uh-uh. Once is happenstance; twice is coincidence. Thrice is enemy action." She was quoting me back to myself. I really must be more careful about what I say and who I say it to. You never know when some damn fool will take your bullshit seriously.

Truth is; I have kind of a relationship with the rain beings. They look out for me a little bit. The way you might put out a saucer of milk for a stray cat. I don't know why. Goes back to when I was in the Coast Guard.

There were several factors involved.

First, this was a the height of the war against Vietnam and I had joined the USCG in large part because there was absolutely no way I was going to help murder Vietnamese people. Having a useful peacetime purpose, the Coast Guard was under the Department of Transportation, not the Department of Defense, and it was the least "military" of all the military organizations on the scene. Still, there was a certain gung-ho faction that took umbrage at my unabashed anti-war rhetoric and extra-curricular activities.

Second, I was a boom operator on a WLB class buoy tender, and there were only a couple of mates who could do that job and do it adequately. As boom operators, we often put in longer hours and had less opportunity for liberty or leave, as a result. I didn't mind that. I liked living on the ship. I had no place to go and nobody waiting when I got there.

Third, because our captain was an inveterate fuck-up who compensated for that fuckedupness with increased attention to inconsequential details — like "regulation" haircuts and shined shoes — morale was at an all-time low, AWOL's were at an all-time high and we were sailing short-handed. In addition to working the boom, there were regular watches to stand. That added up to very little sleep and a whole lot of coffee.

Fourth, our old bucket wasn't in great shape, and quite a lot of our firefighting gear was trash. Fire is the most dangerous thing on a ship. We didn't fire drill much and some of that gear never did work properly and never got repaired or replaced. Most of the crew didn't seem to know or care... but the situation made me feel, shall we say, "chronically ill at ease?"

On the night in question, we were steaming back to our homeport, South Portland, Maine, after a sweaty and sunburned week of long days, working first light to last light, and no liberty at night. This was because the Old Man took seven days to do a two-day job. He was so inept, I almost felt sorry for him. But I felt sorrier for us, the crew.

After subsisting on coffee, cigarettes, and a couple of hours of troubled sleep per night, I was run pretty ragged. I wished I had thought to secret some booze aboard.

After dinner, I dragged myself up the ladder to the flying bridge to enjoy the rush of the wind in my face, and the roar of the sea in my ears. Even on the hottest summer night, there was always a cool breeze up there when under way.

Great minds think alike. When I got there, in addition to the lookout, a couple other mates were up there. A mellow square-shaped kid named Kohlberg. A tall square-jawed lad from Texas, known as "Tex," what else? Good thing he wasn't from Louisiana. Another kid, too. Good kid, but kind of a slacker. Blonde. Goatee. Blank blue eyes. Always reminded me of the cartoon Pink Panther.

I stretched out on the deck to let the ocean rock me in the cradle.

"Fuck," I said. It was a general statement on the human condition.

"No shit," said Tex.

Kohlberg nodded at my sage wisdom.

The Pink Panther was cool.

"You want a hit?" said Kohlberg.

I wasn't sure if he had hash or hooch.

"It's good shit," said Tex.

Ah. Reefer.

Not my particular thing. But any port in a storm. All cats are grey at night. Jack be nimble jack be quick. Semper Parrot's Ass.

I took the proffered drag and returned the joint whence it had come. Then crashed back down like a marionette whose joint strings had been jointly and severally severed, to let the deep-breathing sea rock me with a steady roll.

A sampling of raindrops wept from the rolling clouds, backlit by the envious moon. They pattered soft and cool onto my face, tickling like a puppy's tongue, making me giggle — not something I'm normally inclined to do. My skin was so hot I could almost hear the raindrops sizzle.

It felt great.

Better than great.

Like tiny droplets of semen from the thunder spirits.

The yin part of me, the female aspect of me that was open and accepting, embracing and fertile, reveled in that cosmic ejaculate like a twenty-dollar porn actress on the set of a bukkake film. I wanted to drink it in, bathe in it, swim in it, and drown in it...

Hey, wait a fucking second.

311

I suddenly realized I was losing myself, dissolving, evaporating, not available in stores. I couldn't feel my body, and I was pretty sure I'd brought it with me. I was out of my control. And I hate being out of control. The abrupt realization scared the hell out of me.

"I don't feel right," I said to Kohlberg. "Medic." Our medic, HM1 Willette , a 7th Day Adventist from Idaho, whom I liked quite a lot.

Kohlberg knelt down beside me with calm unconcern. I think he put his hand on my arm.

"You're okay," he said. "Just relax. Everything's all right."

He kept saying that to me, in a low whisper, over and over like a mantra. His soft voice was rich and full with many octaves and overtones.

Because he wasn't alone.

The whole planet was reciting that reassuring mantra with him.

The earth and the sea, and the sky and the clouds, and the wind and the rain and the moon, and all the creatures that live in and on the earth and the sea and the sky. All creation, everything in existence, joined in the healing song. Mother nature was in my corner and she's one hell of a cut man. There was drumming, in synch with my heartbeat, and over the top, like a jazz soloist, I could hear my old friend Dream Chief, wailing his scratchy Lakota be-bop.

There was not a damn thing I could do about my situation.

It was beyond my puny human power.

All I could do was let go.

Trust ain't exactly my strong suit, but it's amazing what you can do when you have no choice.

Whatever was going to happen was going to happen.

It wasn't up to me.

Fuck it.

Next thing I knew, Willette and Kohlberg and other hands were helping me descend the ladder, on my way to sick bay.

But then the oddest thing happened.

I paused on the ladder, the wind pulling at my clothes, hands pulling at my clothes, gazing out at a shyly peeking moon. And I suddenly started talking as if I were the noble Lakota hero, T'shuka

Witko, known as "Crazy Horse." He was one of the guys who gave Custer what he had coming on the Greasy Grass. Don't get me wrong. I knew I wasn't Crazy Horse. I had no idea why I was saying this shit. The words were coming out of my mouth, but I wasn't saying them. Indeed, I was thinking, "what the fuck am I saying," even while I was saying it.

I seemed to take the medic for a relative. I called him "cousin." I knew he was going to bayonette me in the back, because I'd seen it in a thousand dreams. "It always ends the same," I told him. "But I forgive you." And I hugged him.

Well, I don't know who was more freaked out, me or the rest of the crew.

When I got down to sickbay, I wouldn't let go of that Medic. It was like I could only feel my own material existence by touching someone else. I kept rambling and rapping and wide-eyed contingents of the crew assembled at my feet to hear Buddha's wisdom. I have no idea what I said, and I had no control over it, but I know I didn't shut up.

When we made landfall, they had a welcome wagon waiting, and whisked me off to the nearest hospital. A couple of the mates tagged along. Kohlberg. The Medic. The diagnosis was "exhaustion." I believe I slept through two days and nights, and they hung on to me for another day, during which I spent my time eating everything in sight. I caught up to my ship in Southwest Harbor, and that was that.

Except.

I've spent much time reflecting on this experience.

Since that time, the rain beings have looked out for me.

Maybe they adopted me.

For a time, I kept a sort of diary, noting the times when it would not rain when I needed it not to rain, and then rain when I needed it to rain. According to my calculations, it's a statistical mind-fucker.

I didn't tell Marlo about all of this. Maybe I will some time. But I just said, "Sometimes the spirits take care of you."

She looked at me like she was measuring me for a tin foil hat. Can't say I blame her.

313

Adam Adrian Crown

*And when I get that feeling*
*I want sexual healing*
*Sexual healing, oh baby*
*Makes me feel so fine*
"Sexual Healing"
Marvin Gaye

# CHAPTER FIVE:
## SEXUS PLEXUS VEXUS

I've had good sex and hood sex,
meet sex, greet sex and sweet sex.
I've had flirty sex and dirty sex, and coming in at 4:30 sex.
I've had happy hour sex, flower power sex, hot shower sex,
and up in the clock tower sex.

I've had single sex, double sex, trouble sex and bubbles sex,
whore sex, shore sex, floor sex, store sex,
and up against the door sex.
I've had anal sex and banal sex;
casual sex and causal sex;
break-up sex, make-up sex,
shake-up sex and fake sex.
I've had great sex and hate sex, jealous sex and zealous sex,
revenge sex and stonehenge sex; binge sex,
unhinged sex, grin sex and living in sin sex.

I've had sex for breakfast, sex for lunch,
sex for dinner, sex for brunch;
sweaty Saturday night tequila sex;
lazy, drowsy Sunday morning sunshine sex;
I've had beach sex, bleacher sex,
student sex and teacher sex;

Adam Adrian Crown

sex in the kitchen, sex in the hall,
sex before I took a great fall.

I've had upside-down sex,
turned around sex, and way downtown sex;
sex at twilight, sex at dawn,
sex with the sun and sex with the moon;
sex like a fork and sex like spoons;
I've had doggy sex and soggy sex,
pounding sex and hounding sex,
flaunting sex, haunting sex, taunting sex and daunting sex.

I've had sex on a mountain, sex on the grass,
sex on my mind and sex on my ass.
I've had sex like the fury of a winter storm,
sex in the bathroom of the girls' dorm;
sex at a bash, sex on hash, sex for cash and sex totally trashed.

I've had sex at a rally, sex in the alley,
sex with Venus and with Long, Tall Sally;
sex in the surf, sex on the turf,
sex in a tux and sex in the buff,
and sex on a whim, and sex on a bluff;
sex when I was starving, sex when I was stuffed.

I've had smart sex and darts sex,
tangled limbs and parts sex;
poker sex and joker sex,
straight sex, flush sex, two pair sex ,
full house sex and sex with four of a kind.

I've had sex with the top down,
sex at a flop down.
Sex to Sinatra, sex in Sumatra, sex on a merry-go-round.
Sex on a grab, sex in a cab, sex with the lost and profound.

I've had sex on the sea, sex in the air,
sex on a balcony, sex on the stair,

316

sex that was brutal, sex at the Faire,
sex with panache in the Devil's own lair.
I've had sex that was weak, sex that was strong,
sex that was right, left, center, and wrong.
I've had sex that was gentle, sex that was rough,
sex that involved all kinds of stuff;
sex that was hot, sex that was cool,
sex like a knave, sex like a fool,
swing and a miss sex, sex like a grand slam hit
sex slow as molasses and sex lickety-split.

I've had sex that was secret, sex that was news,
and sex as a cure for the summertime blues;
sex that was false, sex that was true,
sex way too early, and long over-due.
I've had swinging sex and winging sex,
stinging sex and singing sex,
sex in a hurry, sex in a huff,
and every kind of sex but "enough."

*What's your name?*
*Who's your daddy?*
*Is he rich like me?*
*Has he taken, any time*
*To show you what you need to live?*
               "Time of the Season"
               The Zombies


# CHAPTER SIX:
## SEXUS VEXUS PLEXUS


Marlo and I talked about sex quite a lot. And love, too. And where the midnight twain to Georgia met on that one. She was an intelligent kid, and therefore curious. It was a case of curiosity thrilled the cat.

When I was a kid, there weren't many adults I could count on for a straight answer about anything, least of all about sex. And all the answers I did get were wrong. In fact, I can only think of one adult in my ill-spent youth who was square with me, my beautiful teacher and friend, Camile, bless her heart. We had some wonderfully frank conversations in the short time I knew her. I loved her for that. Still do.

From the beginning of our long, meandering relationship, I guess Marlo and I established that she could ask me about most anything and I'd give her a straight answer if I could, and if I couldn't, then I'd decline to answer her question at all. Not sure how we established that, but it seemed to be so.

Even so, sex is a tricky topic.

Your parents should be the ones to fill you in on that, but it seems like they almost never are, or don't do a very good job of it. Sex education in school is all about avoiding — avoiding pregnancy, avoiding disease, avoiding social condemnation, avoiding the wrath of god. They leave out the part where an orgasm is the best you'll ever feel, how it's natural and healthy and just plain fun. I guess some administrator thinks if they don't talk about the pleasure of sex, how wonderful it feels to be the vehicle of another's pleasure, the kids won't show any interest in it. They don't tell you that just about the highest compliment you can get is being someone else's reason to masturbate.

When first the course of our discussion veered too close to the rocky shoals of romance or vivid anatomical detail, I avoided entering those waters with her, declining to answer by teasingly saying, "Hang on to that question and I'll explain it when you're older." It became a kind of running joke between us, a dirty joke, and just as we got to the salacious punch line, I'd say, "I'll tell you when you're older."

But then she got older.

And it got trickier.

Because I always keep my word.

One day, we were having one of our endless conversations with the world's longest good-byes, hitting tangents like Ricky Henderson stealing bases. It started out, as always, talking about horses, but we ended up with her asking me about love and sex. Mostly sex.

"So," she said, How many different sexual partners have you had?"

"Two," I said.

She arched a skeptical eyebrow. She's adorable when she does that. It's like her cri du fer.

"Wait, *two*? That doesn't makes sense. You've talked about more that."

"Oh. Sorry, " I said, deadpan. "I thought you meant how many since I saw you yesterday."

Stopped her in her tracks, that did.

I was teasing her. That was a slight exaggeration.

But only slight.

I must have hit puberty when I was about eight years old, and it hit back with a hook-uppercut combination that knocked my inhibitions and most of my other interests to the canvas for the full count.

I'd had that thing with my older sister, and that was a quantum leap forward in my sexuality, but it didn't start there. Maybe there was a time when I wasn't sexually conscious, but if there was, I don't remember it. For as far back as my memory goes, I've always been aware of the incredible capacity of a pound of flesh to provide incomparable pleasure, if you pound it right. Faced with an opportunity to have an orgasm, I've always had a lot of trouble coming up with reasons why not.

In the brutal, abusive torture chamber that was my childhood, masturbation was my sole tiding of comfort and joy, and I indulged whenever I got the chance. In the roaring traffic's boom, in the silence of my lonely room, I masturbated night and day. Virtually every female I saw took a turn fueling my fantasies. The little girls at school. The teachers. Strangers on the street. Movie stars. Mothers and grandmothers. Fantasy Females of every age and description suited the action to the word and the word to the action, from solo scenes to orgies with a cast of thousands. Sometimes boys or men showed up, too, mostly in cameos, but some had speaking parts, and others did the more challenging stunts. More about that later.

These days, I'm a firm believer in regular exercise. The principle of specific adaptations to imposed demands, says if you don't use it, you lose it, and I've continued exercising my penis regularly, rarely missing a day, even when I had plenty of workout partners available to train with. Sure, there was that time I got the shit kicked out of me so bad I could barely take a breath without a stabbing pain in my ribs, and it hurt too much to tense up any muscle anywhere for any reason, even that one. But there haven't been too many times like that, knock on morning wood.

It's a lead pipe cinch that if you haven't explored your own capacity for pleasure, you're sure not going to be much help to anybody else wanting to explore theirs. And besides, some lovers like to watch you get yourself off. Why would anyone say no to that?

But masturbation aside, I guess I've had my share of sex. Some would say *more* than my share.

I like sex.

Like it a lot.

Yeah, Maybe I like it too much.

From time to time, it's gotten me into hot water, and not just in the Jacuzzi. I've had all kinds of sex and I like all kinds of sex. After my sister started me off with that hands-on tutorial, I was always on the lookout for my favorite kind of sex: more.

I've never been too particular about what kind of "more," and I'm not much for carefully coloring inside the lines, either. There are heterosexuals, homosexuals, and bisexuals. I'm more of a tri-sexual — if it's sexual, I'll try it. Male, female, animal, vegetable, or mineral. I can become aroused by the come-hither exhibitionism of a full moon, or a breeze licking my skin on a hot day. "Pansexual" might be the right word, though that sounds a bit like I have a thing for pixies or boys who never grow up. That last one would be kind of narcissistic, wouldn't it?

The occasional quid pro cock notwithstanding, women have always been my favorite flavor, and I guess I've been with a few — I honesty don't know how many. I didn't cut notches into my bedpost. Or keep a diary. Maybe I should have. Never crossed my mind. Carpe diem, which means don't look a gift fish in the mouth.

I had plenty of motive and reliable means, and fate soon provided me with ample opportunity. I made Casanova look like that shy, fat geeky kid standing all alone over in the corner at the junior high school dance.

See, I was a musician for a long time, and it was right at the dawning of the age of Beatlemania and even small-fish, local rock stars were treated like, well, rock stars. I still play once in a while. Started as a young teenager in blaring rock & roll bands, did some dirty blues, then made the folk scene as solo singer/songwriter, purveyor of soft songs and tales of power. Traveled around the country quite a lot doing the wandering troubadour bit. Mostly one-nighters, I played so many gigs in so many towns — a lot of them small towns — from sea to shining sea; I became familiar with dozens of blue roads to Nowheresville. You have to appreciate the position that put me in, sex-wise.

To start with, I was the mysterious stranger in town. The ladies couldn't help but be curious. That's just natural. They say curiosity kills cats, but in this case, it drew pussy in my direction. What can actually kill the cat is the ladies' laddies getting jealous. Stick and move, daddy-o. Hit and run. Get out before the angry townsfolk carrying torches and pitchforks can find out where you parked your car. Poof! There he is: gone.

Besides being a novelty, I was carrying around a lot of anger and a lot of pain from my own past, plus substantial seething outrage over the rank social injustice that pervaded every fibre of our culture at that time — and still does. From racial inequality, to the Vietnam War; from the subjugation of women to the exploitation of men. I was no adherent to convention, respecter of rules, follower of laws, obey-er of orders, or kisser of asses. Frankly, my dear, I didn't give a damn. The only code I cared about was my own. A very simple code, that. It included lofty, if ill-defined and poorly expressed, concepts like freedom and truth and justice and honor and love. I may not have understood my code very well, but I would rather have died than violate it. To my audience, I was as anti an anti-hero as ever sulked across the silver screen or coffee house stage. A renegade cocktail: one part Elvis as Danny Fisher in King Creole, and one part Bogey as Rick Blaine in Casa Blanca, with a twist of James Dean angst in Rebel Without a Cause, and two Brando olives; as Terry Malloy in On the Waterfront and as Johnny Strabler in The Wild One. That's a heady brew. First stirred, then shaken. My character was the wounded, dangerous, brooding bad boy that women like to think they can heal with a little tenderness. Sexual healing, brother Marvin called it. It's a rare lady who can resist a fixer-upper challenge. Who was I to refuse them the chance to pull it off?

I don't mean to be flippant about that rebel thing. I wasn't pretending or acting out a part. I was dead serious about it. It's only now, looking back on it that I can understand why I was the way I was — and why I still am. All the things I valued most at seventeen, I still value today, maybe even more so. And all the things that pissed me off when I was seventeen still piss me off — maybe even more so. If the day ever comes when that's no longer true, just shoot me.

I naturally sang about what I was passionate about: the aforementioned love and freedom and justice, etc. — or the lack of it. Wrote quite a few of my own songs, too. A couple of them weren't too bad. What women saw onstage was a veritable symbol of both freedom and rebellion. Add into the mix that I don't look quite white. Suspiciously dark, in fact. Folks might guess Italian or Greek. Possibly Spanish — if they didn't notice the fringed buckskin medicine bag that hung from my belt. Indian. Native American. Heathen Savage. What's the politically correct term these days? I hope you know by now that I'm just kidding.

Anyway, I wonder how many young girls had sex with me in order to piss off their fathers, spite their mothers and stick it to The Man. They wanted to screw the system and I was content to be the system's proxy.

But it's not the cards you're dealt that matter; it's how you play them. The Big Dealer in the Sky tossed me a shitty hand, but I played it as best I could, keeping my lone ace and drawing four cards. I picked up another ace and a pair of one eyed Jacks. My first ace was the ability to endure shitty cards and not fold, but play them out. Sometimes "nothing" can be a real cool hand, according to Saint Lucas.

My second ace was that I could croon a ballad as well as anyone, and better than most, and I knew how to make eye contact with my audience in a way that made each woman there feel like I was singing specifically to her, for her, about her, killing her softly with my songs. See, in part of my heart, that was true.

The pair of one-eyed Jacks? They're the Jacks of hearts and spades. Hearts, symbolizing love, and spades symbolizing war. Those jacks are one-eyed, because they're only showing one side of themselves. In love and in war, you keep part of yourself hidden. Secret. At least, you do if you're smart. A secret is a secret, says the fortune cookie, when only two people know it — and one of them is dead. In the spirit of full disclosure, in some circles, one-eyed jack is also slang for penis. Make of that what you will.

"If you can't be with the one you love," quoth the sage, "love the one you're with." That sounded like damn good advice and I took it to heart, hearth, and hard-on. With little provocation, I could fall passionately in love with a woman, like she was the only woman in the world, a woman of breath-taking beauty, like she was Venus de Milo, Helen of Troy, and Marilyn Monroe, all rolled into one. As B.B. King said, it didn't matter to me if she was 6 feet tall and 110lbs soaking wet, or 5 feet 5inches, any way you want to measure her. Big or small, short or tall, Black or White, day or night, young or old, shy or bold, made no difference to me. All she had to be was present.

Well, not quite all.

You know what makes a woman desirable?

Desire.

It's hard not to be turned on by a woman who wants you so bad she aches. I know that feeling, myself. That longing for someone that starts way down deep in your gut. Can't eat, can't sleep, can't even breathe. It's a sweet thing to be somebody else's reason to masturbate. Compliments don't get much better than that. So if a woman turned up turned on, I couldn't turn her down.

Whatever flaws or faults she might have, I had the daintiness of eye to see only the beauty. I wasn't pretending about that part, either. It wasn't so much that I was in love with the lady of the moment, but that I was in love with the feeling of being in love, which everyone knows, is falling for make-believe. I could fall ardently in love and be out again faster than Wu's Dry Cleaning could turn around a shirt. I was so addicted to it I made Dobie Gillis look like a monk, and I don't mean Thelonious. Closer to felonious. Close, but not over the line.

If you don't have a strong moral compass, the power to seduce can be dangerously seductive. I confess that sometimes I set out to bed a particular woman specifically because she showed no interest — or even antagonism to the prospect. Fucking someone who already loves you is no challenge. Fucking someone who starts out strongly disliking you, that's something else again. Didn't do that but a couple of times. It requires concentration and that burns a tremendous amount of energy. As a rule the take just isn't worth the effort of the score.

When I say I "loved" each one, I don't mean I wanted to ride off into the sunset with her, white-picket-fence it with 2.3 children, happily ever after. I mean that I was living in the moment with her, focused on the now of being with her, body, mind and spirit. Now is a good place to be, no matter which Jack you are at the moment.

There are Zen masters who stretch a bow, wield a sword, or arrange flowers to be in the now. There are people who chant mantras to be in the now.

My method was slightly different.

Or maybe all that's nothing but esoteric-sounding, self-serving bullshit.

Maybe all those women were just expensive and complex masturbation aids.

You figure out what the truth is on that, give me a call.

Anyway.

325

A lot of women had sex with me not because of who I was, but because of what I was. I was a dark, dangerous adventure — and I'd be leaving soon. I was practically the perfect one-night stand. They didn't really want me. Hell, they didn't know me. They wanted the character they saw on stage, the role, the symbol. That's right, my fine feminist-feathered friends, they saw me as nothing but a sexual object.

You should be so lucky.

I'm not much at crunching numbers. Being conservative, I'd guess that, on average, I was with a different lover every weekend, weekend in and weak end out.

For around 10 or 12 years. Do the math. Now there were, no doubt, a few brief dry spells, when I wasn't with anyone. There were a few times I was with the same person for longer than a weekend, too. There were also many times when I was with more than one lady in the course of a week — or even in the course of a day. But I'm ball parking here. Which reminds me, once I met this girl at the Fenway Park. She was a hot dog vender and had the buns for it, too. Nothing sauer about her kraut. Make a great blues song.

Thing is, of all the wonderful, beautiful girls and women I ever deeply loved — or just fucked — most of them, I just don't remember. Names? Not a chance. Faces? Not really. Looks like I'll probably be wearing a clown suit in hell. Most of them disappear into the blender of my memory to become ingredients in an unpalatable sludge of eyes, lips, breasts, cunts, whey protein, and desiccated liver.

But there are a few, a happy few, a band of sisters I shall never forget. Maybe not whole relationships, or even entire episodes of relationships. But in moments. Like snapshots.

I told Marlo about some of them.
I might as well tell you.

*All these places had their moments*
*With lovers and friends, I still can recall*
*Some are dead, and some are living*
*In my life, I've loved them all.*
"In My Life"
The Beatles


# CHAPTER SEVEN:
# LOVERS AND FRIENDS


I've played a lot of gigs, but very few of them stand out in memory. Sang the same songs at so many of them, there's not much to distinguish them, unless something really sweet happened, like a real good crowd, or something really fucked up went down, like showing up to find out it's basically a Ku Klux Kocksucker rally — I shit you not.

The same is pretty true of the women I've known, too. Some made my cock hard. Some made my life hard. The in-between gets kind of lost. And some memories only come out when I'm really drunk, in a kind of state-bound consciousness.

But there are a few, a happy few, a band of sisters whose memory I relish, pickled or not. I'm not likely to ever forget them as long as I have a cock in my trousers and a single functioning synapse left in my brain. I may only remember them as moments, like single frames of a film isolated for a detailed study of mise-en-scene, but they're spliced into my highlight reel permanently.

The feline Leni, blonde and sumptuous as a fledgling Bridget Bardot.

The ascerbic Adlue.

The Mountainous Mabel.

Jeannie with the light brown hair who worked in a barbershop, and devilishly arched one brow as she asked, "Shall I blow you dry?"

G-L-O-R-I-A, Gloria, who made me feel all right.

And Cindy, oh, Cindy who had a bee-hive hairdo with real bees. Looked like a cotton-candy helmet. Pale pink lipstick that nearly glowed in the dark. She was a great kisser, but she let me down. I remember her because she was the only one who ever actually said to me, "I'm not that kind of girl."

Strike three! Next batter.

Suzanne who had a place down by the river where she fed me tea and oranges, and serenaded me with Judy Collins songs.

Sweet Caroline, an angel in church, but a demon in the back seat, touching me touching her.

Brandy, who was a fine girl, and I might have loved her if I hadn't been so in love with the sea at the time.

Mustang Sally, who drove a yellow '66 Mustang convertible. She loved to ride. And ride. And ride.

Yeah, there's a few.


**FLASHBACK**

I had this gig once at the Farland Hotel. It was a charming little marina/hotel and cocktail lounge that had been a sprawling family mansion in a previous life. Situated right on the lake, it was a favorite of a wealthier, older crowd who wanted to get away from the city but still have room service.

Skipper's Lounge is where I played, named after the owner, a dashing player named Skip Farland who always had a martini in one hand, some nubile chick in the other and a shit-eating grin on his face. He didn't really run a hotel. He was the host of a party, a summer-long soiree that ran from happy hour on Friday through Sunday brunch, which coincidentally, is when I played.

As a single-o, I did a variety of mellow tunes borrowed from the folk scene, some blues, a couple jazz standards, and a big bunch of bossa nova, which I loved. I also did some of my own material, most of which was still crap. You have to write a thousand songs before you write anything that's worth a fuck, and I was only on number 750.

On some occasions, especially Saturday nights, or holiday weekends like the Fourth of July, I brought in some additional personnel. The stage was in the corner of the bar and was about the size of a large postage stamp. It was luxurious for one, ample for two, crowded for three, and utterly impossible for four. On the Fourth of July Saturday night, we crammed in five. Don't know how I did that. Must have used a lot of Vaseline.

The first person I added was always Catherine "Cat" Finley. She was a classical flautist during the day, but at night her demons came out to play, and she did things with the flute that her teachers would disavow. Besides that, she sang great, and our voices complimented each other well, which sometimes doesn't work out when two singers get together who are both accustomed to being the soloist and star of the show. I was in a weight class somewhere between Elvis and Old Blue Eyes, and she grooved along, part Esther Phillip and part Wanda de Sah.

The next sideman I added was a bass player named Ricky something. Not sure I ever knew his last name. But for a young guy who looked like an extra from a biker movie, he had a real feel for Brazilian jazz. There was no way to get an acoustic upright up onto that stage, but an electric bass fit fine, since he leaned back against the corner of the bar — and on that 5-man Saturday, he perched his butt up on the unusable section of it.

The fourth member of our merry band was percussionist Gilberto Sanchez. As you've probably guessed, there was no room for a set of tubs up there. But Gil brought in a high hat and select lineup of congas, bongos, and unidentified artifacts with which he worked some sweet magic.

On the Fourth of July I brought in Sweet Alice Kent on electric piano. She was possibly the flakiest chick I ever met, but could play the hell out of the ivories and could sing harmony too.

The pay wasn't great, but the crowds were appreciative, keeping the tip jar filled with green, and the amenities were exceptional. Drinks were always on the house, and Skip also threw in dinner for me on Saturday night, Sunday brunch, and the use of a small room that wasn't ready for prime time. Nothing wrong with that room, though. Leave the windows open, you got the breeze from the lake, carrying the lullaby of the waves. I would crash there Saturday night, get up Sunday morning, go for a run on the beach, a short swim, and then do the brunch gig. AND I got paid. It cut damn close to being a thief's paradise.

One end of the bar bordered part of the stage ahead and on the right. The opposite side had huge windows all along the wall, right up to the lounge entrance.

Directly across from the bar was a row of cozy booths, and beyond them up on a dais, a second row, against the wall. On the other side of the wall was the dining room. One booth, on the end of the row that was up on the dais, faced almost directly toward me, center stage.

Which is how I came to meet Tinker Belle.

She was a regular, though she didn't look like a boater by a long shot. She was about thirty, not much over 5 feet tall, had a broad mouth, dimples in her cheeks, a button nose, and hazel eyes that were set at a somewhat Asian angle. Her hair was dark honey-blonde and done in a pixie cut that was only slightly too long to meet Marine Corps standards. She favored billowy off-the-shoulder peasant blouses and mini-skirts that were so mini they were practically just belts. Never had so mini done so little for so much.

She was always alone. Never a boyfriend or a girlfriend for company. Didn't need it. A loner. But not lonely. Like me. That's the first thing I noticed.

The second thing I noticed was that she listened when I played. Listened closely. She especially liked tunes by Jobim and by Sergio Mendes. Her eyes would get dreamy, almost closed, and she'd keep the rhythm with little bobs, and tilts of her head, like she was dancing from the neck up, as she took long, languid drags of her cigarette, letting the smoke find its own way out. For most people, I was just background music, but she was attentive during my sets, and never failed to applaud after a tune. That helped me a lot. It sparked other people to applaud, see, and that gave everyone the impression that I was a lot better than I really was. Stimulated green condensation in the tip jar.

I noticed, too, that she never left during a set, but only after I finished it. One night, after a set, I went to the bar, but as Ed the Bartender threw the lime twist into my rum and coke, he told me "This one's on the lady."

I looked in her spot for her, but she had already gone.

It got so that I looked forward to her coming in, which she did every Friday night and most Saturday nights as well. I often sang in her direction the songs I knew she liked most. I couldn't help but wonder what her scene was, and I started writing stories about her in my head. Then I started writing myself into those stories. They were not stories for children.

One night, on a whim, I sent a drink to her. She drank brandy Manhattans. She raised the drink to me and nodded a "thank you." It was quiet that night of quiet stars. The storm had kept people in, was my guess. Starting my last set to an almost empty house, I found myself playing more or less a private serenade to My Lady of the Brandy Manhattans.

I was finishing up a soft bossa called "Like a Lover," when I noticed her subtly open her legs wide under the table. Not as wide as a church door, but enough to shake my spear. Her miniskirt didn't give her much covering fire in the first place, and when she parted her legs like that, it hiked up substantially and ran entirely out of ammunition. She had a thick, healthy bush around her cunt.

Just the kind that sets my lower brain stirring.

Lately, women shaving away their pubic hair is all the rage, but personally, I don't care for the fashion. Maybe it's because they shave the heads of prisoners and military recruits, as a guard against head lice and a cure for individuality. I find the association anti-erotic. Plus to me, it seems silly for any woman past her teens to affect the pubic appearance of a 6-year old. I guess either I don't have a thing for 6-year-old girls, or I really do and I'm deeply in denial. It's one thing to HAVE no pubic hair, but it's quite another to shave it, or wax it off, opting for that raw plucked chicken look. But at that time, virtually no woman depilated her pubis, and it's definitely one of the things about my ill-spent youth that I miss most.

That, and freedom.

Or at least, the hope of freedom.

Chivalrous lad that I was, I pretended, at first, not to notice her crotch on parade, assuming it to be a pleasant accident. But her wearing nothing under that miniskirt — which, I suppose, technically, made it a kilt — had to be intentional. She pretended not to notice me pretending not to notice.

I transitioned seamlessly into "The Look of Love," which had been a monster hit for Sergio Mendes and had become something of a standard. It made her smile. Her smile made me smile. And that's how wars get started.

Ending my set to the soft applause of Ed and My Lady of the Parted Thighs, I hand-signaled to her to ask if she'd like another drink and she nodded "yes." So I got us one of hers and one of mine and ascended the tower.

"Brandy Manhattan?" I said.

She nodded. "Thanks."

I gestured to the bench beside her.

"May I?"

"Please," she said.

I settled in, close but not presumptuously close. She smelled of cinnamon and clove and musky sweat. If I could bottle that scent, my fortune would be made.

"I like the way you sing," she said.

"Thanks," I said. "I like the way you listen."

"You're finished for tonight?"

"Uh-huh."

"It doesn't feel that late. It's the full moon."

"Oh? Et tu Brute?"

She nodded. "Sometimes I can't sleep at all until it starts to wane."

"How do you like to spend those extra hours?" I couldn't help asking.

"Would you rather I tell you," she said, "or show you?"

It was an easy choice.

I stood up, grabbed both our glasses with one hand, and offered her my other. She took it, slid across the booth to slightly unsteady feet and leaned on my shoulder a moment.

"Mmmm. You smell good," she whispered into my cheek and kissed the lobe of my libido.

I set our glasses down on the bar on our way out.

"G'night, Ed," I said.

"Hey, g'night, folks. Sorry we didn't have much of a crowd tonight, but you sounded great. I always enjoy it."

"Thanks, Ed. That's sweet to hear. Glad you dug it, brother."

We shook hands briefly, each stretching over the bar.

That night I was glad I had that room to crash in. Neither of us was in either the mood or the condition to drive anywhere. She was strong, and fucked me hard, like she was trying to pound me to death, but I'm tougher than I look. Which was fortunate for me because I later found out she had already committed one murder that night. Maybe I'll tell you about that sometime.

Tinker Belle had a hobby: photography. Sort of. Had a great camera. Leica 35mm SLR. Pro quality. But she didn't want to use it as much as she wanted me to use it.
She like being photographed.
Specifically, she liked being photographed in crowded public places giving me a subtle — or not so subtle — beaver flash. Teeth and all. To facilitate modeling, she wore a lot of very short dresses, and never any underwear. I must have taken a hundred shots of her during our whirlwind pas a deux. From the front, from the back, bending over, spreading out, standing up, sitting down, boogie all around, disco lady. She hid behind a deadpan expression and her Foster Grant Wayfarers, believing she was invisible if you couldn't see her eyes.
She flashed me at dinner in the Palmer House restaurant. Union Station at rush hour. Outside the State-Lake Theatre. Leaning against that massive Picasso outside Civic Center. At the top of the Sears Tower. The bar at the Six East Club at happy hour. During the third race at Arlington Park. At her friend's wedding. Sometimes, innocent bystanders got castored in the crossfire, suddenly aware of what she was doing, even catching a glimpse of her industrious little rodent for themselves. She didn't care. In fact, it added to her fun. Once, in the lobby of the Sheraton-Blackstone, a distinguished old-money couple got out of the elevator and passed us, just as she was opening up wider than the Dan Ryan expressway. The matron pretended not to see, but her expression screamed volumes about being scandalized. Behind her, so unseen by her, the gentleman smiled pleasantly and gave Tink a gallant tip of his hat.
When we got together privately later, she'd recall the best moments of the day. "Did you see the look on Madame Richbitch? I thought she was going to have a stroke. But Mr. Rich was okay. I think

333

he wanted to give me a stroke…" And so on, during which time she fucked me with the insatiable ferocity of a lioness in heat.

It was fun for a while, but I had to move on.


## VIKING

Her name was Hildegaard, which became "Hilly," in common usage. She was an outsider, like me. For one thing, she was taller than most of the boys, including me, and stronger too. Her long, straight hair was so blonde it was almost white. Her eyes were blue and deep like the water of the coast of Iceland. Quiet and demure, she always seemed to have them averted, peering up only long enough to peak at the goings-on around her. She was a voracious reader, and I saw her in the library all the time, so we started smiling at each other.

One day in late November, I caught her eye and wandered over to the 100's where teen angels rarely tread. She followed me, and somewhere between metaphysics and epistemology, she leaned in close, to within a tongue's reach of my ear and whispered, "What are you looking for?"

There was the faintest hint of Scandinavian accent in her voice, like salt on an ocean breeze. Subtle.

"I just found it," I said and reached past her so close I was just about hugging her.

Oh, yes, I was wickedly suave, I thought.

She didn't move. She smelled like vanilla and juniper.

I plucked some book off the shelf. No idea what it was. Flipped a few pages, pretending to care whether or not they were blank.

"When do you have lunch?" she asked.

I told her. We had different lunch periods. But I was confident that my English teacher and friend, Mrs. Roper, would write me a pass so I could switch, and in fact, she did.

After lunch, I walked Hilde to her next class, which meant I was late for mine. Didn't care. I'd gotten an invitation to come to her house to "study," the teen-age equivalent of getting together for "coffee."

But that's when things changed.

I met her parents.

Mother was a matronly woman who had plenty of calories in reserve in case of famine. Red cheeks and a crooked, up-turned nose. Teeth a little crooked.

Hilde's dad was a frost giant, with the same whitish hair and arctic eyes, barrel-chested and with the arms of a blacksmith. His accent was heavy as a deadlift and his tongue struggled with the tangled fishnet of English. He frequently resorted to Finnish and let Hilde translate. The perfect host, he invited me to partake of refreshments and introduced me to a drink called "Akvavit," a Scandinavian word meaning "kerosene." After searing my esophagus with a shot-glass-sized serving, he invited me to "sauna." I had no idea what that was but I was about to find out.

He had built his house around the sauna, as many people back home in Finland did. Through Hilde, he assured me that the only thing a sauna couldn't cure was death.

In short order, I found myself sitting on a wooden bench along with Dad, Mom, and Hilde, all clothed in bare skin and somehow it felt like the most natural thing in the world. I'd never been naked with the parents of a girl I wanted to fuck, and in retrospect, I'd expect it to be awkward. But I was in Rome and naked seemed to be the uniform of the day. Who was I to quibble?

Hilde had tiny breasts, but huge puffy nipples, and, like her mother, shaved neither legs nor underarms. Indeed, she had a coat of fine blonde hairs, including a patch on her lower back, just above the cleavage of her heart-shape ass. She was aware that other girls shave legs and armpits, and I suspect had been rebuffed on that account by some potential love interest.

"Does that turn you off?" she had once asked.

When she asked me that, she was cradling my cock in her warm palm, gently stroking back and forth.

"Apparently not," I told her.

Fascinating as she was, what I remember most was her dad telling about the Vikings.

Most heroes face overwhelming odds and triumph. That's what makes them heroes. But not so, Vikings, according to Hilde's father, and he looked like he ought to know.

The Aesir, the gods, are the good guys. An evil god named Loki is chained up in the underworld for having engineered the death of

Baldour, the favorite of the gods. The Aesir know that sooner or later, Loki is going to escape his chains, and he'll gather his crew together for one final, ultimate battle of Good versus Evil. Ragnarok, they call it. And the Aesir know that when this final apocalyptic battle comes, they're going to lose.

But they're going to fight, anyway.

They'll spend the intervening eternity drinking, and feasting, and wenching, so when the call comes, they're ready to ragnarok-and-roll like the wild bunch.

It was a lesson I took to heart. Maybe it just put lyrics to a tune I already knew.

Behold, the power of "fuck it."


## BELLADONNA

Belladonna is a kissing cousin to the tomato. Also known as "deadly nightshade." The leaves and berries are extremely toxic, resulting in delirium, hallucinations, and death. The name is derived from the Italian "bella donna," meaning, "beautiful woman" — something *else* that can be extremely toxic resulting in delirium, hallucinations, and death.

Sigmund Fraud theorized that young women go through a stage in their psychosexual development in which they suddenly realize that they don't have a penis, and that lack leads to feelings of inferiority, and defensive, compensatory, and covetive behavior. I assume this stage comes before women discover that with a vagina, they can get as many penises as they want. Siggy called it "penis envy. That's *penisneid*, in Deutchland.

That theory always sounded a tad bullshitfraughten to me. I figured it might have been product of all that cocaine. But that was before I met Donna. I guess I might owe *Herr Doktor* an *entschuldigung*. If somebody had been publishing Penis Envy Magazine, Donna would have been der centerfoldenchik.

Maybe I should have seen it coming, but it's very difficult to see anything clearly when you're coming. But I'm getting ahead of myself.

336

I suppose you could argue that Donna should have been a man. She had lovely, very feminine features — small turned-up nose, hazel eyes, shoulder-length brown hair, and a wide mouth flanked by lips that were full, and puffy, the ways lips get when they've been doing a lot of serious kissing. Or et cetera. With her bright smile she could have launched a few ships. But that was prima facie.

On closer inspection you found she had shoulders so broad that she'd have to go through your average barn door turned sideways, and a back to match — the kind you see only on swimmers, galley slaves, and hooded cobras. All that breadth squeezed down into a tiny waist, and narrow hips. Not a "V" shaped body, more of a 'Y" shape. Almost an "X" shape because she had thick, powerful thighs. Her quads were more like quints. While the average man is a lot stronger than the average woman, Donna was proof that a strong woman could kick the shit out of the average man, and give the above-average man a run for his money, too.

Donna was so strong, in fact, that she had tried to hide it as a kid. As soon as she figured out that girls weren't supposed to beat the boys at every sport, game, and physical activity, she withdrew and adopted make-up and girlie stuff as protective coloration. But she was aggressive by nature. It was torment for her to play the modest, submissive role foisted upon the female sex like that muzzle they put on Hannibal Lechter. It was only in the gym that she could let herself be herself. No one was watching and the people who were watching didn't care.

Me, I like strength. I like it in myself, so I'm attracted to it in others. Thus was the course of events here predictable, since Donna turned out to be dictable. There was a lot of yang in her, considering what a lovely yin she had, and for a while the yang that she had a yin for was mine.

I first met her while working out at Tony's 3rd Street Gym. It was an old school gym. Not one fucking Nautilus machine, even though nautilus was all the rage at the time. Tony's was filled with high school and college athletes, cops and ex-cons. Nobody went there to "tone" anything. There were no mirrors. There was no music. Just racks and bars and tons of iron plates. They lifted weights to get stronger. When they wanted to do "cardio," they lifted weights *faster*.

Tony had what he called "the list" of people he considered serious. Others paid dues, too, but they were just visiting. To get on that list, you had to have a combined total — squat, bench press, and dead lift — of 1000 pounds if you were a man, 500 pounds if you were a woman. My fucked-up shoulder meant no bench-press heavier than 200 for me, but I could squat 425 and dead lift 375, so I found myself on the list. But most guys there were lifting a lot more than that. A WHOLE lot more. Guys doing four TIMES my sissy little bench press. Two or three times my candy-ass squat. And double my dead lift. Yeah. You could go in that place and take a couple of deep breaths and leave 5% stronger.

There were only three women on the list, and Donna was one of them. I'd tell you what she was lifting at a bodyweight of only 140, but you probably wouldn't believe me, and if you did believe me, you'd probably have to run away and join the circus or some other religious order.

It was a dark, stormy leg day, and as I was wobbling to the locker room after my workout, she intercepted me.

"You always train alone," she said. It was an observation, not a question. It didn't require an answer. I might have grunted an affirmation. I train alone because I like training alone. Other people aren't crazy enough and they tend to just get in the way.

"Me, too," she said. "Maybe we could try training together sometime." For a gym rat, that's the equivalent of "getting together for coffee," or "come up and see my etchings." Euphemism Sweet Euphemism. But we did actually train together. We first met on a Pushday.

"This is what I usually like to do," she said and detailed her training plan for me. It was completely nuts. All kinds of negatives, drop sets, forced reps, and other extreme and painful shit. Only a lunatic would love it.

"Sounds good," I said.

And it was.

Afterwards, I persuaded her to indulge in one of my favorite vices: Asti Cinzano and egg rolls. We took it back to her place.

Sex with a strong woman is a sweet thing. She can give as good as she gets. It's like the Kama Sutra meets Greco-Roman wrestling.

I once came by an antique Colt cavalry revolver, the type with a 7½" barrel, vintage circa 1875, which I sold to a collector. He took it into his hands like a sacred relic, fondled it lovingly. His eyes gleamed with a mixture of joy, wonder, and jealousy as he examined it in every detail.

That's the way Donna handled my cock. Like she'd struck gold. Found the Holy Grail. Discovered the Beatles lost recordings. It was that penis envy thing, see?

I didn't mind.

She had meaty labia, my favorite kind, and it was easy to get completely lost in going down on her, cunnilingus being probably my favorite pass-time anyway. She wasn't shy about showing her enthusiasm. She grabbed my head with both hands, ground her cunt hard against my face, and cheered me on with hoarsely whispered instructions: "right there," faster," "harder," "deeper," "just like that," and my personal favorite, "don't stop." She was aggressive about it the way those skanky guys are who abusively slam their cocks into women's mouths in raunchy throat-fuck porn. But I didn't find it abusive. Not one little bit.

When it came time to mount up, we tried on positions the way some people shop for a new hat. I don't have a particular favorite, myself. But then I don't much wear hats, either, though I do have one.

Turns out she had a favorite, though. It goes like this: You start out in missionary, then roll over so she's on top. Then you pull your knees up toward your chest, so she's kind of kneeling/squatting between your legs, supporting herself on your bent legs, and you lay back while she does the fucking. Not a lot of body contact. It's all genital all the time, and she can hammer that nail to her heart's content just as hard as she's able. I realized right away why this was her favorite: the illusion that it was *her* cock and she was slamming that meat into *me*, and not the other way around. It was that penis envy thing again. And again, I didn't mind.

When she was on a roll, she liked to talk dirty, playing the part of what I think she thought a man would think and say, or think and not say.

"You like that, don't you," she'd say slamming "her" cock in hard.

"I do," I'd say.

"That's because you're my bitch, aren't you?
"I am."
"You're my cunt."
"I'm your cunt. Baby."
It was call and response like singing old time blues or gospel, and it pushed all her best buttons. Never doubt the power of aural sex.

In every position we passed through, she seemed to always find a way to get a fingertip into my ass, which suggested to me that it was another thing she liked, and it turned out I could always help my Amazonian Sisyphus get her boulder over the crest of the hill by probing into her ass at the right moment.

Not to sound like a prude, but anal sex has never been my particular scene, not even in the joint. It doesn't disgust me or anything, but I can take it or leave it.

When I was a kid, when "good" girls kept their thighs glued together, the Catholic chicks from St. Mary Me's School were famous for anal sex, because it allowed them to remain vaginal virgins. Anal sex was the final stop on the Around-the-World Tour, and my teen mentor, The Cicero Kid, advised me, "Ya find a chick who loves it in the ass, fuckin' KEEP her." Words to live by.

I've known about half a dozen women who specifically asked for anal penetration, and, what the hell, if I'm playing to a good audience, I'll take a request once in a while.

So it didn't exactly shock me when Donna asked me to fuck her ass.

It didn't even really surprise me when she asked me whether had I ever fucked another guy? Or would I? Or how about if I called her by a man's name and fucked her like she was a man. We settled on the vaguely androgynous name "Bobby." At least it wasn't Proud Mary.

Donna liked anal penetration deep and over toward the rough side of town. I'd reach around to work her clit, or she would do it herself, which was tactically a better choice. Judging from her gasping, groaning, trembling, and howling, I'd say she maybe got off better that way than anything else. For me, well, I'm flexible. Nothing gets me off better than my partner getting off. So all's well that ends well.

Anal stuff gradually became the bead-and-butter of our playbook. Not always a full court press, but a dependable pick and roll. Donna asked me if I had ever let another guy fuck me. I know she wanted me to say yes, and tell her all about it. I hated to disappoint her. She followed up by asking if I thought I *might* ever let a guy fuck me.

Well, hell. I'd already done lots of things I never thought I would do. The right situation, the right circumstances, anybody's capable of anything. Maybe I'd just never been drunk enough. So I said "maybe."

But she wanted to know more. She wanted to know WHO I'd let fuck me. What kind of guy? Name names. Inquiring minds want to know.

"Hell, I don't know," I said. "Sean Connery? Johnny Depp?" I didn't exactly have a list prepared.

"How about Elvis?" she said. Long live The King.

"Maybe."

"Steve McQueen?"

"I don't know. Maybe."

"Steve Reeves?"

"Maybe."

"Hugh Grant?"

Hmmmm...

She seemed to like that scenario.

"I'd love to watch you take it in the ass," she said.

"Well, if any of those guys call me, I'll let you know."

She laughed.

She had another plan.


It was a full moon night.

We ate, drank, and made merry and then drank some more.

She rolled off the damp sheets and said, "I've got something I want to give you," padded across the carpet and disappeared.

Something to give me.

A gift?

Was it Christmas? My birthday? Elvis' Comeback Anniversary?

When she returned, she was wearing an old flannel work shirt, blue and black plaid and about ten sizes to big for her, the tails reaching down to her knees. Sleeves rolled up. Her cock was peeking out from between the...

Wait a second.

It was a visual non sequitur.

It took my booze-beleaguered brain a beat or two to make sense of it.

Her cock was the rubber, or latex, or silicone variety. It was flesh-colored, if your flesh is that color, of modest dimensions, with a slightly mushrooming head, and affixed to her crotch by means of a black nylon harness.

"Turn over," she said. She could barely speak.

I turned over.

She caught my hipbones like handles and pulled me back onto my knees so I was ass-up, head-down. She laid her palms on my glutes, spreading them, and set to work seducing my anus with finger and tongue. Oh, she gave some attention to my cock and testicles, too, but that was almost gratuitous. (Operant term "almost.") But this was all about my ass and her fantasy. Did I mention that penis envy thing?

Tongue led to finger, one finger led to two fingers, deep led to deeper. She was in no hurry, and I was in no condition to resist, even if I'd had a mind to, which, to be honest, I didn't. Desire is contagious. It spreads like fire, doubling itself about every thirty seconds on a good day. She was all-aflame and it kindled something in me, too. Maybe it was my homoerotic side. Maybe it was the appeal of giving up the burden of command for a moment. Maybe it was something else I don't understand, or, if I do, can't or won't admit.

After long and lavish licking, probing, massaging and lubricating inside and out, Donna started rubbing the length of her cock back and forth along the cleavage of my ass.

"Do you think you're drunk enough?" she said with a chuckle.

I guess I was.

It's not an easy thing to describe, because it's not like anything else. I didn't find it painful, not exactly. But then I have a love-hate relationship with pain so maybe I'm not the one to ask about that. The stretched feeling is unique. I understand that some people compare it to having a huge bowel movement, but that comparison doesn't work for me. There's some prostate bumping involved, and that's a pretty good feeling. They say the prostate is the male g-spot, assuming there's actually a female g-spot. But I think, more than anything else, it's your partner getting off that really does it for me. And Donna went through the roof with this. So I did, too.

I think, if you're a man who likes to fuck women in the ass, you might benefit from the experience of being the fuckee instead of the fucker just once. It requires a lot of trust, something that isn't my strong suit. It requires relaxing and letting go, too. Donna went so slowly, taking it in the tiniest increments, one step forward, one step back. Two steps forward, one step back. Advance a little, retreat a little. Advance a little more. Slow and easy.

Yeah.

That's exactly the way I do with a pony.

Little by little.

Build trust.

You don't force it.

You don't take it all in one big leap.

Respect comes first.

Then trust.

Then affection.

Once you have respect, trust and affection, anything is possible.

So how come Belladonna and St. Jack didn't live happily ever after?

Toward the end of our run together, we got into an argument. A fight, really. I can't remember what it was about. But it got heated. And loud. And animated. And she hauled off and slapped my face. Now, from this woman, that was not your average bitch-slap. Donna was capable of knocking down a guy with forty pounds on her. This was more like getting clocked with a 2 by 4. I'm not ashamed to say she rocked me a moment, and I saw a few sparklers in my head celebrating the Emperor's birthday. Sure, part of it was that she had sucker-punched me. I didn't expect it and the punch that lays you down isn't the hardest punch; it's the punch you're not ready for.

Reflex took over.

I slapped her right back.

I was raised to believe that a man never hits a woman, and I'm old school enough to still believe that. My response wasn't a decision. It was pure instinct, and it happened without me.

I'm strong, too. And I can hit hard. You can ask a few guys I've hit — if they ever get up.

The slap was harder than I hope I'd intended. Hard enough to knock her back against the wall. She hung there a moment, looking like she might slide down to sit on the floor. Eyes squeezed shut. Face twisted into a grimace. Blood showing at the corner of her lips. A soft moan started in her throat.

"Are you ok?" I said.

Without answering, she reached down for her crotch and reached out to me with the other. "C'mere," she said. She ground herself against my thigh and was soon shuddering out an orgasm.

At that point, I said to myself, "Jack, my boy, this girl is too crazy, even for you, and this scene is headed nowhere you want to go. We're getting the fuck out of here."

But by then she had a hand in my pants, digging for my cock, and my cock was already digging her. The little head may not have veto power over the big head, but it's one hell of a negotiator.

Yes. We were getting the fuck out of here. But did we have to be in a *hurry?*

Both heads agreed that morning would be soon enough.

Probably lucky for me they didn't go back on the deal.


## THE LADIES AMEN

When Stede and I went down to El Paso, refugees from the brutality of the Windy City winter, and the corrupt proclivities of the Chicago Police, we took along a third wastrel by the name of Jarrod. Skinny, red-haired Irishman from Bahston, Mass., with a crooked nose, and a wicked laugh, like a leprechaun on a steroid-ecstasy mix. He fancied himself quite suave and deboner, a ladies' man, but was, in fact, slightly less subtle than a 20-pound maul.

We blew our limited funds on a fashionable and upscale apartment on Sun Bowl Drive. We went for the three bedroom model because we humbly anticipated needing our privacy: it was raiding distance from the university. It came furnished. Right down to a coffee-maker and a oil painting of a majestic prairie sunrise in a faux golden frame hung over the sofa.

Stede and I, dope dealer and musician respectively, were both night owls but Jarrod had been working construction and was used to rising early.

Too early.

We'd brought a small record player with us, but only a few platters, and Jarrod's favorite was by brother Marvin Gaye. "Can I Get a Witness," was on the B side, but Jarrod never played that. After hitting the rack at 2 or 3 AM, we'd be hearin' it through the grapevine at 0530 and at decibel levels that even rock guitarists would complain about. It became a daily ritual.

An irritating ritual.

Irritating and annoying.

Irritating, annoying, and infuriating.

Irritating, annoying, infuriating and…

Camels' backs aren't indestructible.

One night we'd gotten in extra late, or Jarrod had gotten up extra early. By the time Marvin found out that his honey was lettin' him go, Stede and I were  simultaneously opening our respective bedroom doors, like demented figurines on the Devil's Swiss clock. Somehow, we were not surprised to see each other across the hallway. Grated-on minds think alike.

Without a word, we did a sharp left and right face, and marched down the hall in perfect step. My scout leader would have been proud.

Jarrod was in the living room, rockin' and a-boppin' and a-flopping his incredibly pink cock to all points of the compass, apparently unaware that music has a regular, predictable beat. Beneath his battering of freckles, his skin was milky white, and I wondered how he could possibly get laid.

Pausing for a moment, Stede and I watched Jarrod's scrawny pale ass twitching randomly, oblivious to Marvin's straight-ahead 4/4 rhythm. Then we approached the hi-fi from opposite sides, a classic encirclement of the flanks. In this case, Jarrod's. When he saw us, his a-boppin' petered out like a music box losing steam.

Stede daintily lifted the needle from the record.

With both hands, I carefully lifted the record from the turntable, pinkies out.

I proffered it to Stede.

"Would you care to...?" said I.

"The pleasure should be yours," Stede said.

"No, no. I *couldn't*. After *you*, Stanley."

"Oh, no. After *you*, Ollie.

"Wishbone?" I said.

"An excellent idea."

We grasped opposite edges of the disc and each put a finger through the hole in the middle.

"On three?" I said.

"Please."

"Delighted. Make a wish. One...two..."

On "three" we snapped the grapevine in half.

We put our halves back down on the turn-table, and saluted each other with a single, precise, satisfied nod. Thereupon, we executed a right and left face and marched back down the hallway whence we had come.

"Good night, Stanley."

"Good night, Ollie."

Jarrod remained, throughout, uncharacteristically speechless.

But wait — there's more.

Across the cactus-festooned parking lot from us, there lived a group of incredibly beautiful young women, mini-skirted, go-go booted, fashionably coiffed and painted, with apparently well-lubricated moving parts. I wonder what you call that. A group of beautiful women.

A herd? No, that's horses.

A colony? No. Ants.

A swarm, like bees? There must be an answer.

A flock? Only if they were from Liverpool.

A clouder? Too overcast.

A troop? Only if they were mounted.

A harem? Too patriarchal.

An army? Too jingoistic.

A bed? Too obvious.

School? Too prissy and fishy.
A murder? Gang? Mob? Too Chicago.
A Horde? Or Whorde? Too misogynistic.
A drove? A brood? Clattering? Band? Cackle?
Nothing seems to quite fit.
Let's call it a "mascara." That sounds a lot like "massacre."
Perfect.

These lovelies would all come out every day at around 9am en route to place or places unknown, and we watched them with out little noses pressed up against the window glass like starving street urchins from David Copperfield, only we were looking out instead of looking in. They would return in the afternoon, and then there would be a second show when they went out for the evening.

Speculation ran wild as a 3-month old colt.
Models? Stewardesses? Hookers? High-end jewelry store clerks? Hostesses? Receptionists? There weren't that many jobs a girl would get that dolled-up for. Doctor, lawyer and Indian Chief were definitely off the list.
Since we were just about flat broke, we weren't likely to get much closer to them than those nose marks on our picture window.
It then came to pass that we took notice of a jarring phenomenon: sometimes one of these girls would take out the garbage. Could it be that these perfect goddesses somehow generated garbage? Unbelievable as it seemed, early one morning we witnessed it for ourselves. One of these creatures emerged and walked to the brick-walled trash house carrying what could only be a bag of garbage. She had it when she went into the trash house, and she didn't have it when she came out, so what else could it be?

Thus began the Great Garbage Lottery in which the three of us libidinous lotharios vied for the privilege of taking out the garbage, perchance to strike up a conversation with something well over on the feminine side of the scale.
Trouble was, we didn't *have* any garbage.
Because we didn't buy anything.
Because we didn't have any money.

I'd hunted around for some solo gigs, but this was country music country, and I, fresh from Chi-town, still considered country and western music to be the evil of two lessers. My nasal repertoire was real thin, and there were only so many gigs you could get with two Hank Williams songs (Your Cheatin' Heart, and So Lonesome I Could Cry).

Stede got a job at a pizza place, and through his good offices I got a job there, too. As soon as we were competent pizza wranglers, we volunteered for the late late shift, which no one else seemed to like. We loved it.

Gave us a chance to make an extra pizza or two for ourselves which we would chow down on after closing — we sneaked Jarrod in, too, of course. All for one and one for all, daddy-o. The three muttsketeers.

But that didn't still generate much garbage.

The solution was to bring a bag of garbage home with us from the pizzeria, so we could arrange for at least one of us to bump into one of those girls. With luck, repeatedly.

Rather than fight over it, we drew lots, cut cards, flipped coins.

The girls were all as lovely close-up as they were from across the way. Perfume that smelled like sex on a stick. Eyelashes you could hide under in the rain. Smiles so dazzling you couldn't look at them directly or be turned to stone. Full lips made for whispering and licking and brushing against ear lobes. And figures that were several decimal places past perfect, built to last and designed to samba all over your febrile brain. Next to the prospect of being with any one of them for even an hour, Heaven, itself, seemed like a flophouse on van Buren street shrouded in the stink of puke and piss, with cum-stained sheets, and hot and cold running roaches.

And the girls were friendly, too. Even spoke Earthling with us.

I suspect that they all had starring roles in Stede's and Jarrod's one-fisted fantasies. I know they were getting top billing in mine.

Around about Christmas time, Jarrod was the big winner in Garbage Fraud Roulette, and returned from the see chore, grinning and strutting like a fighting cock with ears. He had been invited, he informed us, to a party at the girls' place, high atop Mount Olympus.

Of course, it had never occurred to the selfish prick to get his

348

alleged pals invited, too.

In any case, Stede had another thing to do, at the church, where he was hoping to bang the minister's daughter, and me, I was reading, The Spy Who Came in From the Cold, so I was too busy to be interested in any kind of untoward frivolity of the flesh, you see. No, not me.

Jarrod anticipated the occasion all day long by continually preening: nudging us with his elbow, winking, wiggling his eyebrows, smoothing back his hair, and shooting his cuffs, prompting me to be alert for suitably heavy blunt objects with which to part his hair and I carefully weighed the probable costs and benefits of strangling him with his own tongue.

That evening, Jarrod dressed in his finest — actually a combination of Stede's finest and my own finest, borrowed for the occasion — having marinated himself in Old Spice, and, ever the optimist, armed himself a handful of condoms, and he long, tall sallied forth, leaving John le Carre and me all alone, stretched out on the sofa, to hold down the fort.


Leamus had just seen Liz shot, and decided to come in from the cold by climbing off the wall on the east side, committing suicide-by-commie-cop. His choice angered and saddened and touched me. I wondered what I would have done.

It was at that moment that Jarrod burst through the door.

He was panting like he'd just sprinted a hundred yards carrying a fat lady singing on his back, and it took him a minute to catch his breath. He was so disheveled I thought maybe he'd been hit by a twister instead of playing it. His tie (actually *my* tie for he had spilled rum on it) was askew, his shirt (actually Stede's shirt) was unbuttoned, his fly had flown and a bit of boxer was sticking out. Hair mussed, cheeks flushed and lipstick-smudged — and traces of a hickey blossoming on his neck.

His features were twisted into an expression of unspeakable horror, green eyes wide as pie plates.

"What the fuck?" I inquired.

"Those ladies..." he said between pants and without zipping up his. "...amen."

For a just a fraction of a moment, before factoring in his heavy Westie accent, I was off balance, and nothing made sense. I thought, "What is he, fucking *praying*?"

He wasn't.

"Those chicks," he said. "Those chicks ah guys, I'm tellin' ya."

Sometimes, I think there *is* a God.

But he's half Woodie Allen and half Charles Manson.

Amen.

I laughed so loud that even today, hikers on the sunny hills around El Paso still report hearing the echo.

When Jarrod's sputtering subsided, I got all the delightful details.

Yes, these gorgeous girls were not all-female, they were all female impersonators, doing a drag queen act at a very popular but off-the-radar local club.

In EL PASO? Whoda thunkit?

Seems at least one of them wanted to have her way with Jarrod.

"Really?" I said. "I didn't know drag queens did charity work."

"Fuck you."

"You really should consider it a *compliment*..."

"*Fuck* you."

"Man, I didn't know you were such a prude."

"FUCK *YOU*!"

He stumbled to his room like a beaten fighter trying to make it to his corner. Slammed the door behind him so hard that the prairie sunrise became a sunset.

A few minutes later, I heard someone coming up the steel steps to our door. There was a tentative knock. Like an undecided mouse.

It was one of the ladies. A delicious blonde, stacked with all the cards in her favor.

"Hi," I said.

"Hi," she said, wringing her hands. "I'm Gabrielle. Is your friend all right? I mean, he freaked out. Like, *all* the way out."

"He'll get over it."

"I'm so sorry. I mean, we thought he *knew*, you know?"

"Gabrielle," I said, "you're an absolute eye-scorcher. It's hard to see anything past that."

She smiled. A broad smile.

"I'm Jack," I told her and offered my hand.

She laid her fingers lightly on my hand, like she was royalty.

"Pleased to meet you, Jack."

What the hell. I bowed down and kissed her hand.

"Jack," she said, "would *you* like to come over?"

"Sweet of you to invite me. I'm not a big party-guy," I told her.
"Rain-check? Maybe coffee?"

"Sure. You know where I live."

For the next few days Stede and I showed Jarrod our sympathy
and support by continually preening: nudging him with our elbows,
winking, wiggling our eyebrows, smoothing back our hair, and
shooting our cuffs. We relented only when he had completely
exhausted his supply of "fuck you's."


I cashed that rain-check a couple days later.

Gabrielle was a bright, funny, gentle and sensuous person with
no inhibitions I could detect. We got along well. *Very* well. But that's
another story.

I don't mind people who color outside the lines. I kind of like
them.

Me, I don't do that.

I *move* the damn lines.

*Then* I color outside of them.



# ROCKVILLE

Her name was Claudette, but everyone called her "Crawdad."

She didn't like that nickname, but had become resigned to it. She
was 13 or 14 years old and looked it: greasy blonde hair, scrawny
body, all arms and legs. Her chest had not even heard the wild rumor
about breasts. She wasn't homeless, but didn't spend much time at
home, preferred the street, and I could relate to that. She seemed to
have few changes of clothes, and did not often get a chance to clean
up. She favored khaki cut-off shorts, and tank tops. Canvas Keds like
all the cheerleaders wore, but no longer white. A black leather
motorcycle jacket that was a couple sizes too large for her. The kind

with all the zippers and buckles. She wore a peace medal pinned to the collar.

This was Rockville, Illinois. Short hop to the birthplace of Ulysses S. Grant, speaking of dubious claims to fame.

I was doing an undercover job for the Barrens Detective agency in a local factory, where most everybody in town worked. As part of my cover, I hung out at a basement coffeehouse co-op called "The Boiling Point." Fifty different kinds of coffee and tea, and a small stage. It was always open mic night, except Saturday night. That's when the paid performers came in. It was hardcore folk. The revolution might not be televised, but these guys were playing all the songs on the soundtrack. I fit right in and became a regular.

I also occasionally jammed with some guys doing a James Brown repertoire. But they didn't have a horn section. If you're going to do Soul Brother Number One without that funky horn section, you'd better be able to walk on water. This singer was no slouch, but was still only wading ankle deep. It was fun though. I dig funk.

Claudette was a permanent fixture at the Boiling Point. She took a liking to me, a liking that bordered on stalking, and slipped across the border when nobody was watching. She'd be waiting for me outside the hovel where I rented a room the size of a bathtub, a week at a time, and walk me to work. Sometimes she'd bring me a coffee from the Dunkin' Donuts. Sometimes I'd buy her breakfast. I wasn't sure how many other meals she was getting. She'd be waiting for me after my shift, too. She tagged along everywhere I went, except to the john, always smiling, chatty, happy just to be along for the ride. It was a lot like having a real good dog.

I don't mean that as a put-down.

I love dogs.

As far as my investigation went, I had to either get rid of her or find a way to work her into the scene, a way that wouldn't fuck it up, and that would also keep her safe. I didn't have the heart to get rid of her. So I started thinking up errands for her to run at critical times, and she ways only too happy to do them. Bop down to the store for smokes. Take some clothes to the laundromat. Things like that. I bought her a new pair of jeans. Hip-huggers cut so low only her clitoris held them up. Bell-bottoms the envy of every sailor.

She acted like those jeans had saved her life.

I wondered if they had.

The house rules at Fleabag Rooming House included no female company with the door closed or after 9PM. Most of the guys there were ex-cons. It served as a sort of unofficial halfway house. That's why I'd chosen it. By happy coincidence it also provided a buffer between little Claudette and my baser instincts.

One morning she met me after work (I had taken an 11pm-7am shift for investigative purposes) and she seemed particularly giggly and upbeat, like Gigit on reefer. She tugged at my hand with both of hers.

"Take a walk with me, " she said. "Pleeeese?"

How could I refuse?

She led me to a neighborhood of raised ranch homes, all cookie cutter identical. Little boxes. The kind that spring up faster than mushrooms. Made of tickey-tacky, too. Some were set off by the proverbial white picket fences. As we passed through a gate, she held up a set of keys, jingling them like out-of-tune bells.

"Is this your house?" I asked her.

"Shhh. It's a surprise."

I hate surprises.

In a jiffy, we were inside. The place was silent. Nobody home.

"Whose house is this?"

"Belongs to a friend," she said. "They're in Peoria. Won't be back until tomorrow."

"What are we doing here?"

"Well, we can't use your place. And I don't have a place."

Without further preliminaries, she launched herself against me, wrapping her arms tightly around my neck, and preceded to devour my face. She wasn't a polished kisser, but she was nothing if not enthusiastic. She kissed hard. Checked all the fillings in my molars with her tongue.

Enthusiasm can be contagious if you're not careful, and I wasn't yet savvy enough to be all that careful.

I disengaged from her gently, as if just to catch my breath.

"This is a surprise, all right," I said.

"Really? You didn't know I like you?"

"I like you, too, Claudette." I never called her "Crawdad." "But you're too young, honey." That was technically bullshit. I may have

353

had I.D. that said I was a lot older, but in reality, I wasn't that much older than she was. Not enough for it to be a felony. But I was a lot older as far as she knew, as far as anyone knew, and as far as I was going to say. I was playing a character. I didn't understand that you are what you pretend to be. See, I hadn't read Kurt Vonnegut yet.

"No I'm not," she said. "I know how to do it. I'm not stupid. I'm not a virgin."

I believed her, but wondered how that had come to be.

She slipped out of her bell-bottoms faster than a bos'un's mate abandoning ship. She didn't wear anything under them.

"I know how to do lots of stuff," she said trying to close the sail. "Want me to show you?"

She smiled the devil's smile, confident that she already knew the answer.

Which she did.

She did, in fact, know how to do lots of stuff, and I let her show me everything she knew how to do. Then I let her show me again.

And again.

You know how quicksand feels?

I do.

It was a one-time thing. It had to be, for all kinds of reasons.

I choreographed things to make sure, but let her believe that it was all circumstances beyond my control, let her believe that I really wanted to be with her again, wanted it as much as she did.

She bought that.

I sold it well because it was partly true.

The day came that the investigation was over, and it was time for me to split. Barrens already had another job lined up for me. Denver.

"You leaving," she said.

"Yes."

"Are you coming back?"-

"No."

"Are you leaving because of me?"

"Claudette," I said, "if I ever did come back, it would only be because of you."

I don't know why I said that. It's possible that I meant it.

She hugged me.

We kissed.

Not a tonsillectomy, just a kiss.

I gave her a going-away present, a gold I.D. bracelet with her name on it. All the rage at that time.

"I should have one with your name on it," she said. "And you should keep this one."

"No," I said. "This is for you. To always remind you who you are. To remind you that you decide who you are, and nobody else does."

It didn't say "Crawdad."

It said "Claudette."


## CANADIAN HOSPITALITY

Shortly after I got out of the service, while I was hanging around Portland, Maine looking to catch a breeze, I carpooled with some guys from the dojo to go to a tournament up in Fredericton, New Brunswick. We packed the four of us, plus gymbags, plus sleeping bags, plus a month's supply of munchies, plus a big bad bagful of bo's, jo's, sai's, tonfa, and nunchaku, into my VW bug, and drove all night. Do-dah, do-dah.

The route took us fairly close to the end of the earth. We could have seen it from the road, but for the pitch blackness broken only by the limited sight of our headlights. It should only have taken us five or six hours, but I had failed to take into account pea-soup fog that shrouded our route, and badly misestimated our travel time. By the time we got to the border, dawn wasn't far away, and we were no longer running on just fumes, but on the memory of fumes.

The crossing included a gas station and a greasy spoon, and a guard shack the size and shape of a single-seater outhouse. We weren't hungry but the greasy spoon was open. We were out of gas, but the gas station was closed. And the gods laughed.

I couldn't help reflecting that I'd have been wise to make this crossing several years earlier, rather than opting for a stretch in the Coast Guard. Oh, well. Live and learn.

The crossing also included a couple of Mounties. One came over to examine my driver's license, the other poked the beam of his flashlight around inside the bug. He didn't miss that huge duffle bag.

"What's in the bag, eh?" Flashlight said.

Before I could answer, Kenny, riding shotgun, replied. Had I known he was a fucking moron I'd have lashed him to the roof.

"Weapons," Kenny said.

I don't recommend this answer at a border crossing. Any border crossing.

"NOT weapons," I stepped on the Kenny's line hoping the audience hadn't heard it.

But they had.

"Weapons, eh?"

"No, sir. NOT weapons. Karate stuff. Not WEAPONS weapons. You can look if you want." I twisted around to face the back seat crew. "Open the fuckin' bag," I said.

Then I tried to smooth-talk the first gendarme.

"We're heading up to U of F for a tournament. That is IF we can find a place to get gas. We're dry as a James Bond martini. You wouldn't happen to know a place that's open, would you?"

He pointed to a parking space between the greasy spoon and the guard shack.

"Pull over there, please, Sir."

He didn't hand me back my license.

Fuck.

My Mountie conferred with Flashlight, and Flashlight went into the greasy spoon while his partner stood there like he was idly waiting for a bus, apparently oblivious to us. In a couple of minutes, Flashlight returned, trailed by a guy in coveralls and a hunting cap, stuffing the last of something into his mouth. It made his cheeks puff out like a squirrel doing Dizzy Gillespie. He went to the gas station, unlocked the door, went inside, turned on the lights. And the pumps.

Then My Mountie handed me back my license.

"He said he don't mind opening a little early for ya. What school are you from?"

I told him.

"Shoto-kan, myself," he said. "Know your way around town?"

"Never been here before."

He then proceeded to give me directions that were a whole hell of a lot better than the ones we had. I thanked him, we filled up the tank, and headed for the University. That may have been about the most hospitable welcome I've ever gotten.

356

Certainly my best experience involving a cop.

The karate club at the university was hosting the event, and they were considerate hosts. They had even arranged for us to crash with some of their club members.

The first day of the two-day event was kata. The first round began at 0830. We'd pulled into town about 0730. Some of us had caught some winks on the drive up, but some of us were too macho to let anyone else take a turn at the helm, and hadn't gotten any sleep at all. And it showed. My kata performance looked like the Scarecrow from the Wizard of Oz with epilepsy and on acid. Didn't make it past the first round. On the up side, that meant I could catch up on my z's.

I had just bowed out and was leaving the floor, when I happened to catch the eye of a girl in the stands. Not a whole lot of spectators, but there were a few. Most people didn't understand kata; they only liked to watch the kickee-punchee portion of the program. She wasn't exactly a tiny little thing. Six feet tall for sure, and on the voluptuous side of the scale, wide of hip and full of breast. She had a sallow complexion, brown, somewhat stringy hair and a somewhat compressed face, as if someone had put her head and chin in a vise and squeezed them toward each other. She also had the brightest, twinkling brown eyes imaginable, and a perpetual half-smile, like one of a set of parentheses around her mouth. It was a wry smile, a dirty smile, the way you smile at a stripper, and it made me want to strip for her.

"Leaving?" she said. Easy, like we were already old pals. Her English was thick with French accent.

"I'm done. Going to lie down before I hurt myself. Tomorrow's another day."

"I thought you did ok," she said.

"You have a charitable streak in you."

She stood close to me. Closer than necessary. Closer than casual. Our eyes held hands.

"Where're you going to do your lying down?"

"Excellent question. I don't really have a place."

"No? I have a place."

And just like that we threw in together.

She promised me a nap. She promised me a drink, and she promised me a meal. And she promised to get me to the church on time. She promised to be excellent company.

"I'm here with some friends," I told her. "Let me just fill them in?"

"OK," she said.

The only one of the group I could spot was Kenny the fucking moron. I explained to him that I had arranged alternative accommodations for myself for the night, and that I'd connect up with them again tomorrow. I limited myself to monosyllables for his edification. Kenny noticed the young amazon waiting by the door, watching.

"Are you staying with her?

"Yes."

"Are you going to fuck her?"

"If the wind blows southerly."

"Huh?"

"Probably."

"She's not very pretty," he said.

I told you he was a fucking moron.

"No, I said. "No, she's not very 'pretty.' Who are you sleeping with tonight?"

As it turned out, she was a sweet and sassy lover, joyful and uninhibited, and a pleasure to spend time with. Because of her size, I think she intimidated many males, and I suspect she didn't get anywhere near the amount of play she deserved. She was generous with her apartment, with her food, and with her body. I tried to be a grateful guest.

And she did get me to the church on time.

I won my kumite division the next day.

The trophy was a small shield-shaped plaque.

Before I set out for home with my crew, I slipped it into her purse when she wasn't looking.

I'm not keen on trophies.


## THICK AS THEBES

His name was Jim.

Not James.

Not Jimmy.

He was the kind of student that can make you believe you're a good teacher.

He was always the first one to show up for class, and was always the last one to leave. Like Marlo, he always had questions, good, insightful questions, and he listened to the answers, too, when I had them. You could tell he'd think about it because next class he'd have a follow-up question generated from his reflections on that previous week's exchange.

When I learned that Jim played the clarinet in his school's marching band, but hadn't yet discovered Sidney Bechet, I gave him a Chris Barber album. Had "Petite Fleur" on it. It struck him like lightning. After that, a lot of our after-class conversations were as much about music as about mayhem.

Jim's mom, a chattery Earth-mother named Claudia, taught math at the school, and she'd been the one who'd asked me to teach self-defense to a mixed group of teens. She was a friend of Dr. Stevie by five degrees of separation, so that's probably how she'd heard of me. Or it could have been Kevin Bacon.

Despite being a single mom, Claudia had home-schooled Jim until he was ready for high school, and like so many other home-schooled kids, he left his conventionally-taught fellow students way back there in his dust. He was 14 or 15, but a grade ahead of where he was supposed to be, and could easy have been two grades ahead. Academically, I could envision him collecting degrees like stray cats collect ticks.

His rosy cheeks were whisker-free, but there was a hint of blond fuzz sprawled out along his upper lip, like a "coming soon on this site" sign for a mustache. He had large brown eyes, sharp and bright and encaged by gold wire-framed glasses, perched above a small straight nose. His heart-shaped face was surrounded by a halo of honey-blonde baby-fine hair that fell in casual waves to his shoulders. His was a happy mouth, quick to smile, quick to laugh, and when he did, a cohort of dimples guarded the flanks. Solomon could have written a song about him. He was long-legged and narrow, perfect for cross-country running, at which he excelled.

Contemplative and conscientious, Jim was now on the road to becoming a pretty good man.

I began to notice a couple of things.

First, I noticed his body language. He liked to stand close to me when we talked, closer than the "normal" distance in the States. Mediterranean distance. He had started out farther away but had gradually worked his way inside my space. The increments were tiny, advancing and retreating, then advancing a little closer — just like I might do with a new pony. It was a subtle thing. He also began to touch me. Put his hand briefly on my arm. Then retreat. Not too much pressure, or for too long. Didn't want to spook me.

The other thing I noticed was his gaze.

Eye contact is a specific personal acknowledgment of another. Most people find it uncomfortable, avoid it, and can't maintain it for long. Extended, sustained direct eye contact almost always means one of two things: somebody's going to bleed or somebody's going to breed. I'd only experienced this with women who wanted to fuck me and men who wanted to fuck me up. Boxers often do this stare-down thing while the ref is reading them their rights. Dominance. Predators do a similar thing, not eye to eye with each other so much, but extreme focus on their prey.

I didn't get the feeling that Jim wanted to kill me.

It threw me off a little bit. Thought it was my imagination, at first. Laughed at myself for making a big deal out of nothing. I should have known better. Never second-guess your gut.

I had some homoerotic hijinks in my ill-spent youth, but that was pure sex play. Like two guys drag racing, taking their cars out on a long stretch of open country road, just to see what they can do. I never had romantic feelings about these playmates, though. Never saw myself riding off into the sunset to live happily ever after with another man.

But then, I haven't had romantic feelings about very many women, either. At least, not since I was a teenage piñata.

My man-to-man encounters after that had been in the context of heterosexual sex. For example, if two guys are fucking the same woman at the same time, a little incidental contact between the lads is bound to happen, and it's best just to roll with it. Sometimes, in those conditions, three bodies become an indistinguishable sexual mass, and what part belongs to whom can get to be a toss-up. It's all friendly and pleasant, and you take it in stride.

But it wasn't love; unless you define that word so broadly it becomes meaningless.

Maybe that's the trouble.

The word "love" has been used by so many people to describe so many different things that the word has become meaningless, and can now mean just about any damn thing the speaker wants it to mean.

Like the word "terrorist."

I love music. I love my horse. I love my country. I love hard physical work. I love my lover. I love Chinese food. I love autumn. I love the sea. Each of these feelings is quite different from the others. How can one word possibly fit to describe them all?

They say the esquimaux have forty-seven words for "snow," distinguishing between many varieties, whether wetter or dryer, heavy or light and so on.

Defining different things with the same word, or the same thing with two different words is piss-poor communication. That's how wars get started, and that's how they convince the suckers to fight in them.

The ancient Greeks were smarter. They had at least seven different words for different kinds of love.

Storge is the love between parent and child.

Philautia, was love for one's self. Not narcissism, but self-esteem. Not arrogance, but self-respect.

Pragma describes a deep-understanding, long-lasting love, like the love between a long-married couple. I'd used this to describe the love between me and my horse, too.

Agape is the fundamental empathy and compassion you have for everyone. I love humanity. It's just people I can't stand.

Philia is the love between close friends, brothers, comrades. Those with whom you have survived the field of battle. Those friends to whom you give your loyalty, for whom you would sacrifice yourself, and with whom you share your most private secrets and most profound emotions. I'd use this one with my horse, too.

Ludus is playful love. It covers affection between young children, the flirting and teasing of a new relationship, but it also includes joking around with friends. I'd say jamming with other musicians falls into this category. And so is just hanging out with my horse, snoozing in the sun. Or just standing together in the rain with our backs to the wind.

Eros is sexual passion, even sexual obsession. The French would call it "l'amour fou," "crazy love." Mad, wild, lusty, out-of-control, in-spite-of-your-self, unreasonable, irrational, totally smitten, carried away, moth-to-the-candle-flame, can't-eat-can't-sleep, can't-think-about-anything-else, gotta-have-it, can't-get-enough-of-it love. Everybody's favorite kind.

I suppose I think of the ancient Greeks because history was Jim's favorite subject.

I'm not sure what kind of "love" cocktail I experienced with him. Eros, certainly. Ludus, very likely. A shot of storge, perhaps. Probably some Philautia. And a twist of lime. Which is to say, I have to admit my affection for him was to some degree emotional as well as mechanical.

I liked that kid.

When the weather warmed up, lots of the kids started wearing shorts, Jim among them. One afternoon, he came extra early to class, wearing track shorts. Made of nylon that was so clingy you could tell what religion he was. Split up the side for maximum range of motion without interference from your clothes. Almost like running naked, he said.

I like to run naked. I wondered if he did, too.

Jim wanted to point out to me the best features of his new running apparel.

"These are really comfortable," he said. "You should try a pair."

"You think so?"

"Totally. They're split up the side so they won't chafe. See?"

He showed me.

"Plus," he said, "you don't have to wear a supporter. I hate supporters, don't you? These have a built-in brief."

He showed me that, too.

"Hey, come on," I said, throwing up my hands to ward off evil. "What are you trying to do, seduce me?"

Dammit.

Why the hell did I say *that*? It was supposed to be a joke. He was supposed to laugh it off. Maybe, deep down, I was protesting too much and we both knew it. He didn't laugh it off. He gave me a hint of a smile, just enough to put his dimples on yellow alert. Eyes on mine like he was going to eat them.

"Do you think I could?" he said.

Other kids started arriving for class.

Saved by the bell.

But this wasn't the last round.

I suppose it was inevitable.

He biked out to my place. Apologized for dropping in uninvited. Gave me that "just in the neighborhood" line that's always baloney.

"Could I talk to you?" he said.

"Sure. What about?"

"The Sacred Band of Thebes. Do you know about them?"

I'd read Plutarch and Polyaneus in prison.

"A little," I said. I had a feeling where this was going. I should have said, "I like you lad, and I value you as a student, but this is extremely inappropriate and I have to draw a line here somewhere."

I didn't say that.

I said, "Would you like to come in?"

"Thanks," he said. "I would."

I had only whiskey, coffee, or mineral water to drink, and I wasn't about to offer him whiskey. He followed me to the kitchen and I cracked a bottle of Gerolsteiner, poured it into ice-filled highball glasses.

We perched on barstools at opposite sides of the island.

He dug out a book on Ancient Greece, an Osprey Elite book, with loads of illustrations.

"So everybody knows about the Spartans," he said. "Kind of the ultimate warrior society. Even the women were bad asses. Thermopylae, right?"

"Right."

"So guess who was bad ass enough to kick the Spartans' bad asses at the battle of Leuctra?"

"Surprise me."

"The Sacred Band of Thebes." He said it with pride, as if he were a veteran of the encounter. Here's where subtext really counts.

See, the sacred band of Thebes, organized by either Gorgidas or Epaminodas in the 4th Century BC, was an elite regiment of handpicked soldiers consisting of 150 pairs of male lovers. At Leuctra, the sacred band defeated the Spartans even though outnumbered 10,000 to 6,000. They became the Special Forces of the

Theban Army; invincible right up to the moment they were annihilated by Philip and the Macedonians at Chaeronea in 338 BC. Philip and the Macedonians went on to form a do-wop group and had big hit with "At the Hoplite."

"Each man was selected strictly on his prowess regardless of social class," said Jim. One of the partners was an older man, the other was younger."

He was correct. The older of the pair was known as the *erastês*, or "lover," and a younger man was called the *erômenos* ("beloved.) The outfit picked up the "sacred" tag from their exchange of devotional vows at the shrine of Iolaus. According to Plutarch, anyway. I wasn't there.

"One book says that the older warrior was like a mentor to the younger one. Kind of the way you've been with me."

"Well," I said, trying to wiggle free, "if I've taught you anything of value, I'm glad."

"Could I give you a hug?" he said.

A hug.

What could be more innocent than a li'l ol' hug.

"Sure," I said.

Just like there are all kinds of love, there are all kinds of hugs, too.

There's a quick squeeze-and release hug.

There's the Franco-Italian handshake hug, just long enough to kiss both cheeks.

There's the macho-American clinch hug accompanied by two or three pats on the back and not lasting more than three or four seconds.

There's the grapple, which is when the clinch goes longer than four seconds and you have to make up for that by throwing in some twisting or shaking like you're about to break into some spontaneous Greco-Roman sumo.

Five seconds with no backslapping or wrestling, and you're moving into embrace territory.

Ten seconds or longer or with any degree of nestling, stroking, or fondling and you'd better be dancing, or else you're not hugging, you're holding, cuddling, or snuggling.

Our hug was not a squeeze, a handshake, a clinch, or an embrace.

And we weren't dancing.

We took it to the sofa. I sat at one end, and he sat at the other, like we'd fucked up our places in a canoe. He asked me if I'd ever kissed another guy, this and that, and I was honest with him because I don't like liars and don't want to be one. He told me he'd been thinking about me for a long time, and so on. And he asked if he could kiss me. I told him he could.

I'd never kissed another man, not seriously, not on the mouth, not with romantic intent. It's one thing to suck another man's cock, it's quite another to kiss another man on the lips. You have to draw the line someplace.

He went about it with great care, not too fast, not too slow, soft but firm, with the perfect amount of tongue. A Goldilocks kiss. It was just right. It was a first kiss and it had all the breathless anticipation, feverish rush, and heart throbbing thrill appertaining thereunto.

That was the straw that broke the camel's zipper.

We kissed some more.

A lot more.

Caressed.

Explored.

Slowly. With hands. With lips and tongues.

It was a sensuous seven-course feast and we made it last all afternoon, savoring each bite, enjoying each course to the fullest. I think we both knew that there would be no coming back for seconds.

In my previous man-to-man engagements, ejaculation was the checkered flag, and it was wham, bam, thank ya, Sam, pants quickly back on and we return you now to your regularly scheduled heterosexual program. I had never before lain entwined in a lingering embrace afterward, enjoying the closeness, the simple pleasure of feeling the warmth of his body against me, the rise and fall of his breathing, the beat of his heart. He was a beautiful child, inside as well as outside.

Then time did what it does best: it ran out.

We grudgingly got dressed, in quiet contentment. I watched him tuck himself into his jeans, suddenly aware that, like me, he wore nothing under them.

"Thank you for this," he said, softly breaking the silence. "Thank you for today."

"I'm glad you came," I said. I didn't mean it as a double entendre, but it made him smile. A full dimple salute.

"Me, too. I had to. My dad just took this new job and we're moving to Oregon, like immediately. I don't know when I'll ever see you again and I didn't want to leave without..."

I understood that. He was smarter than I was. I had left too many times without...

When I was seeing him out, he turned back one last time.

"I don't want to say good-bye," he almost whispered. "I want to say I love you."

"You don't have to say either one," I told him, and offered him my hand. "Take good care of yourself, Jim. Maybe I'll see you sometime. You never know."

He smiled and took my hand, and held it tightly like he was trying to memorize my fingerprints.

And that was it.

As it turns out, I never did see him again.
But you can't un-ring the bell.
Wouldn't want to.

## BARN CHORES

When I was a young teenager, I got some part-time work for a lady who had the horse farm next to the horse farm that belonged to the parents of my current squeeze. She had half a dozen horses and a couple of dogs. A few barn cats, too. I did some barn work for her — mucking out stalls, repairing fences, stacking hay bales. She couldn't pay much, but I also got to hang out there as much as I wanted, and I spent a lot of thinking time there with the horses.

Roberta, by name. Tequila drinker. Brown shoulder-length hair, kind of hacked off at the bottom. Might've cut it herself. Hazel eyes. On the chubby side. High cheekbones. Button nose. Like a little panda bear. Strong. Hard worker and exceptionally adept with horses. Did her own hoof trimming and such.

One time, I came over at an unusual hour. She had one of the stallions out, and I thought she was cleaning his sheath. I didn't want to sneak up behind her, startle that pony, and I was just about to call out "hello" to her, when I realized she wasn't cleaning his sheath. She was loving up his cock, kissing, licking, pressing it against her face and so on.

I was momentarily dumbfounded, I guess. I stood stock-still and watched. It was clear she was sucking on him, stroking him. It's not like I'd never heard of such a thing, but I'd never seen it personally before.

I watched awhile longer. Then I cleared my throat.

She bolted up and spun around, tried to act like she hadn't been caught at anything.

A giant question mark hung suspended in the air between us like the scent from a spritz of mane-detangler. Neither of us knew what to say or how in hell to say it.

"How's Chico doing?" I asked her. Chico was the horse. A paint stud.

"OK." she said.

"Anything I can help you with?"

"No, that's ok. Thanks."

"You sure? I don't mind giving you a hand. So you can finish what you were working on."

I think we stared at each other some more while she tried to figure out if I knew what I was talking about.

Finally she said, "You want to hold him for me?"

That really wasn't necessary. He ground-tied like a champ.

"Sure," I said, and took the end of the lead rope. The loop of it still lay on the ground. It was a long lead. Fifteen-footer. Gave me plenty of slack so I could move around, get the best vantage point from which to take notes as she got down on her knees and sucked that pony off. I have to say, I enjoyed watching her work on that huge penis. Like she couldn't get enough of it. Like she'd die unless she got some of that pony's semen for herself. She made hungry little noises, and then gagged a little when he ejaculated. She spit it out, coughed a little. But horses shoot quite a bit of semen and some of it overflowed her mouth, ran down her chin and onto the front of her ragged coveralls.

She wiped off her face and chest with a rag she had tucked into her back pocket.

When she stood up she was red-faced, eyes watery. I couldn't prove whether she'd had an orgasm, too, but the circumstantial evidence was compelling.

"Thanks for your help," she said. Searching my eyes for sign.

"Any time," I told her.

"Let me know if there's anything I can do for you."

Turns out, there was.


## AD INFINITUM AD GYMNASIUM

I met Rachel when I was playing at a campus coffeehouse known as "The Tammany Club," a hangout for artsy types and pissed-off radicals. She invited me back to her apartment, invited me to stay the night, and that night turned into several weeks — a long relationship for me at that time. She had wavy red-blonde hair that looked well arranged even when wind-blown, and when she smiled, she showed lots of gums, like a shark.

Rachel is memorable for two reasons.

First, she was a terrific musician. Viola. Piano.

She was up early every morning and spent an hour playing scales. The repetition almost turned me into an axe murderer. At that time, I wasn't much of a musician, even though I'd been playing music professionally for a long time. For me it was about eliciting an emotional response in the audience — and preferably a sexual response. That and free booze and easy cash.

But for Rachel, it was about the music, itself. To get lost in it, play it perfectly. The music was the alpha and the omega and all points in between. I asked her if she didn't get bored playing scales, she replied that playing scales was making music just as much as performing it for an audience was making music. And she put a period on it by playing a harmonic minor scale that brought tears to my eyes.

In that moment, she taught me what an asshole I had been about it, and the realization brought me up short.

It was like getting hammered with a Zen koan.

It changed me.

The other reason I remember Rachel is that she was both athletic and uninhibited. She had been a champion gymnast in high school, but, unable to serve two masters, had given it up to dedicate herself to music. She still kept in shape, though.

We got up late on Saturday morning. No classes. I was doing some yoga because I was feeling too lazy for a more yang workout and because I always needed extra focus on stretching because I hate it. Flexibility doesn't come easily for me.

I was laid out on her Persian rug — intricate golden designs on a deep red background — heels over head in what's known as the Hala-asana, or "plow" pose because you have to be plowed to do it.

Rachel came out of the bathroom, toweling her hair, came over and sat on the floor beside me.

"A yogi?" she asked.

"More like Yogi Berra," I said. "And a Berra of bad tidings at that."

She studied my position like she was judging fine art.

"Have you ever thought about sucking your own cock?"

"I beg your pardon?"

"Come on, you've never thought about it?"

I let myself down easy and arched my back to stretch. This was not a plow-friendly topic.

"I've thought about," I said.

"Have you ever tried it?"

What does one say?

"I've tried it," I said. " A couple of times."

"And...?"

"I'm not flexible enough. Or my cock's not long enough. Or both."

"Too bad," she said. "I'd like to see that."

"If I ever manage it, you'll be the first one I call."

"I hope so."

But she wasn't quite finished with me just yet.

"Have you ever tasted you own cum?"

"Yes, "I said. "Last night. On your lips."

She grinned. Gums. Like Jaws.

"No, I mean just on your own. Like you could do plow or a shoulder stand and masturbate. Let it come down on your face. In your mouth. Have you ever done that?"

"No, I haven't."

"I'd like to see that."

I'm so easy.

In a twinkling, with her enthusiastic assistance, I was shoulder standing with my feet up on the wall, stroking away for her. I discovered that, like blood and smoke, semen burns when it gets in your eyes.

She lay next to me, head propped up on one elbow. She dipped a fingertip in semen and licked it off. Then did the same again and offered it to me to lick. It reminded me of something my sister had done when we were kids. Getting the whipped cream off the beaters of mother's electric hand-mixer.

I licked it from her finger, and then, like a puppy, she licked the rest off my face.

"I like you," she said. "You're crazy."

Uh-huh. Pot. Kettle. Black.

"Still, too bad you can't reach to suck it, yourself" she said. "But, if you want, I'll suck it for you."

You can probably guess what my answer was.

For a former ace gymnast like herself, it was no challenging feat to lock hers behind her neck — or even lower, behind her arms — a posture that classics scholars would refer to as "the Viennese oyster." I can see where that would give them something to waltz about.

Rachel got into this position as effortlessly as most people would sit back in an Easy-Boy recliner. I believe it was her favorite.

"I can see better this way," she said. "I like to watch you."

I gave her ample opportunity to indulge in her voyeuristic predelicktions. I even arranged a mirror for her convenience.

"I love the way that looks," she said. "Don't you?"

"Yes."

"I could watch that...sliding in...and out... indefinitely," she said, showing gums. "Like a meditation mantra."

I've known a few women who would bend over backwards to please you, but Rachel was the only one I knew who ever did it literally. She could backbend low enough to reach my cock with her mouth, and could continue into a handstand that brought her thighs up to rest on my shoulders. When it came to soixante-neuf, she was a real stand-up girl.

She performed her crowning achievement on what turned out to be our last night together, and it was a stunning thing, indeed. If you were walking your dog, and Fido suddenly started hovering like a hummingbird, that would not be a tenth as unexpected as what she did.

When you're fucking a lady from behind, with her bending over, the soft slap of your bodies meeting in a soothing, seething rhythm, about the last thing you expect is to feel your lover's tongue brush your scrotum.

But my Lady of the Play-dough Skeleton could bend forward so far that she was capable of sneaking up on herself. To feel her breath on my thighs while I was pounding against her ass like the ocean waves against the rocks in San Sebastian, to feel her kissing, nibbling, and sucking where it was impossible for her to be, was enough to make me doubt the laws of anatomy entirely, and double-check the laws of physics. It was truly the most remarkable thing, so remarkable, I wasn't certain it had happened, except in my demented imagination. Even the Romanian judge gave her a 9.5.

I had to ask her to do that again.

She was happy to oblige.

My imagination compelled me to ask her whether she was able to lick her own cunt.

"I've tried," she said. "I wish I could. But I don't think it's possible."

"Too bad," I said. "I'd pay to see that. But, if you want, I'll lick it for you."

You can probably guess what her answer was.

## THE SIZZLING SCISSOR SISTERS: GOSH-IT'S-WANDA AND RODEO LOLA

It wasn't the only time I ever sat in as part of a trio. Though I tend to prefer duets, I've done some trios, a few quartets, and a couple of big bands.

I was playing a gig in Kenosha, Wisconsin. Coffee house scene, just off campus. Part of a string of one-nighters.

Two young women staked out a stage-side table and camped out there all night. They were a good audience. We inevitably exchanged glances and smiles, and I sang a couple of tunes in their direction.

I thought they might be sisters. Not that they looked alike. In fact, they were more like opposites — one a bronzed-skinned medium blonde, the other darker-haired with a milky complexion — Surfer Girl and Snow White — but they seemed to have a conspiratorial telepathic energy between them usually found only in twins, sometimes siblings, or, more rarely, between friends so close that they might as well be.

I forget their names. Mandy and Candy? Brandy and Andy? Jekyll and Hyde? Hyde and Seek? Doesn't matter.

They both wore blue jeans, heavily embroidered and ragged at the knees. Leather sandals. Many bracelets on wrist and ankle, brass, beaded, and braided. Surfer girl wore a white tank top, Snow White, a gauzy short-cropped peasant blouse. Bras were anathema. Rather standard hippy drag.

They both seemed amenable to some extracurricular hanky-panky, and by the time I was closing my last set with a rousing rendition of Bob Dylan's Blowin' in the Wind, I was considering which of these ladies I was going to get my lariat on, and calculating just how I'd cut her out from the rest of her herd. But I needn't have bothered. When I stepped down from the stage, they bustled over to me, lavishing smiles upon me like roses. They jointly invited me to come back to their place and have some brownies, and I jointly accepted.

Their pad was only a short jaunt away, and we strolled there with them flanking me, the three of us arm-in-arm, like we were dancing our way to see the wizard. It had been a warm day, but now there was a light breeze out of the southwest. Zillions of stars shimmered brightly in the moonless sky and I noted that we traveled due north, just like my anticipating compass.

Once in the door of their flat, Surf set sandalwood incense a-burning as automatically as most folks turn on the lights, and I have to say to this day, that scent remains one of my favorites, right after

Horse-sweat and Hay. In a trice, Snowie put the needle to wax and Peter Walker's Rainy Day Raga floated lazily into the room like hookah smoke. Jeremy Steig on flute. Badass flute.

Georgia O'Keefe prints graced their walls, and beanbag chairs dotted the living room like toadstools popping up from the Persian rugs. Lava lamps of red and blue — do they still make those? Bookshelves constructed of bricks and boards held scores of texts, heavy both in form and content. The classics were all there: Aristotle, Plato, Socrates, and Kurt Vonnegut. Shakespeare, complete works. Maya Angelou's Caged Bird. Atwood's Edible Woman. Sexual Politics. Custer Died for Your Sins. Very interesting assortment. You can tell a lot about a person from the books they read.

Through a beaded curtain, I could see an enormous waterbed in an adjacent room. Had to be king-size. Maybe kinger. Turned out to be heated, too. I love waterbeds. I miss them.

By "brownies," Surf and Snow were referring to the Alice B. Toklas variety, loaded up with prime grade A organic hash. They'd made a batch big enough to get Caesar's entire 9th Legion stoned and lost forever in the woods of Britain. Served it up with mead so sweet it made your momma's teeth ache.

Despite their superficial ivy league hippiness, S & S fancied themselves a quantum leap ahead of hippies — free-spirited neo-pagans, awakened, enlightened and evolved, which meant that they strove to be in touch with Man's true nature, and as a result had no qualms at all about taking pleasure wherever they could find it, and I was happy to help them look around.

While we munched brownies that were frosted with thick, rich milk chocolate, and sipped honey wine, the looks and caresses they exchanged suggested to me that Surfer and Snowie were both really a lot more into each other than either of them was into me. Not that they ignored me. But it seems I was to be nothing more than a dildo they were going to share. Just a sex object.

Basically, I'm fine with that.

Before you could say polymathicpsychopathicexpialidocious ten times fast, we were naked and making 18 knots of ourselves on that waterbed.

Surfer's yang warrior body was trim and taut, with orange-sized breasts, and narrow hips, and her vagina resembled a sharp slit in a fine golden forest. Snowie was all yin, the earth-mother with pendulous blue-veined breasts, wide baby-maker hips. Her vaginal lips pouted out freely, like they were blowing a kiss. Coarse dark hair sprouted on her legs, and crotch and belly, in contrast to the fine, delicate flax of her partner. Shaving was another anathema to them, oppressive artificial beauty ritual that it was. Full bush was the fashion, then. I like women with body hair. I like the scent of it, the way it feels against my face. I'm not a fan of the pre-pubescent plucked chicken look that's currently a la mode.

With the aid of some coconut oil, we explored each other thoroughly and systematically, like Stanley searching for Livingstone, slipping and sliding away into our most intimate crevices with fingers and tongues. A single deft roll put Surfer in position to go one-on-one with Snowie, lickety-split. But she surfed farther down the bed, and instead interspliced legs with her, Siamese twins joined at the clitoris. I leaned in close to enjoy the lovely sight of swollen labia, rubbing together, back and forth, hither and yon and Tyler, too, like two heavily-bearded lumberjacks French kissing. My cock smiled. Maybe it laughed. Fingers reached out to stroke me, assuring me I hadn't been forgotten in the shuffle.

We circled after each other disdainful of Cyrano's contempts, and set upon each other like famished wolves.

The heat we generated melted us into a swirling whirlpool of yin-yang-yin, clockwise and counter-clockwise like canis major chasing his tail something sirius. We counted our blessings — 328,509 to be exact — and then I stretched out on my back like an indolent comet while Surfer cowgirled at a leisurely hand-gallop and Snowie saddled up for a mustache ride. Or maybe it was Snowie who cowgirled and Surfer... Well, it didn't matter. They were interchangeable and they interchanged a lot.

Through it all, while riding me, they shared many hugs, nipple-licks and deep kisses, whispering sweet nothings to each other that I couldn't quite make out. This went on for several thousand years that went by at the speed of light. A traffic light. On the North side.

A short distance away, I sat in a director's chair, like Otto Preminger, dressed in jodhpurs and riding boots with a megaphone in my lap. Leaning in to myself, I put the megaphone right up to my ear. "Now in zis scene, you are becomink vun vit de universe, yes? Und you just schtopped in to zee vat condition your condition vas in."

Semen flowed out of me like I was a chubby cherub pissing into the fountain in Brussels, scores of sperm cavalry in a long column-of-4's singing, "There's a yellow rose in Texas…" Women cheered, strong men cried, and multi-colored banners undulated on the breeze.

On the far side of the moon, my mystical mentor, Old Dream Chief, danced to the jingle of the rainbow, singing some scratchy pornographic Lakota be-bop to celebrate such an excellent copulation, while his moonlight-pale pony pranced sparks on verdant grass and the dish ran away with the spoon.


## THE GHOSTS OF KISSES PAST

Do you remember that first kiss?
I do.
Cautious, uncertain, hungry.
Poised on the brink of discovery. It's exciting. Like turning over the last card, the one that will determine whether you fill that straight flush or go bust.
It's a little like being born.
And a little like dying.
Her face drawing close to mine, I can smell sunshine on her skin. Sunshine and Ivory soap. She pulls an errant strand of hair away from the corner of her mouth to clear the way. Her feverish eyes, half closed. She cocks her head and parts her lips slightly. I feel her warm breath against my cheek, the scent of cinnamon and clove. My heart pounds in my chest like a lion trying to claw his way out of his cage. My face feels hot and flushed, my ears swept with fuzzy fire.
I can't breathe.
I can't think.
I don't care.
My lips find hers, soft and moist, and they caress, scarcely moving. Then I feel the tip of her tongue searching for mine. We press together. She wraps her arms around my neck. I pull her close,

crushing her budding breasts against my chest. Closer. Tighter. I want to feel all of her against all of me. I want to kiss her with my whole body. And more.

That shit can make you crazy.

The smart monkey says that I've been trying to re-live that first kiss all my life. Each new love has that first-kiss moment, and as soon as that kiss happens, it's a *fait accompli*. The discovery is over. The mystery is gone. The excitement dissipates. On to the next true love. Over and over, I keep making the same mistake, tearing my heart out time after time. I keep looking for something I'm never going to find.

But once, I thought I found it.

Let me tell you about Diana.

I need a running start.

I was a high school freshman and not long for that world. Coming off a string of crushes on young girls, each of whom had broken my little heart in quick succession, hitting me like a jab-cross-hook-uppercut combination. I was staggering around, trying to cover up and weather the round on my feet.

As always, I took refuge in making music. Licking my wounds with licks. That's why the blues was invented. Should have called it the black and blues, because it's always what you want to play when you've taken a real beating.

I was playing rhythm guitar and singing the lead vocals in a glorified garage band called The Wastrels. Our leadoff tune was "I'm Not Like Everybody Else," by the Kinks. Should have had the lyrics tattooed on my chest. It was my personal anthem as well as the perfect expression of teenage angst.

We'd played a gig on Saturday night. Junior High dance in a neighboring burg. We played passionately, if not expertly, and as the lead singer, it was up to me to lay waste the emotions of the females in the audience. We had seen the dawning of the Age of Beatlemania, and it was *a la mode* for young girls to go into a feeding frenzy at the first indication of an up-tempo backbeat. The pay wasn't great, but the fringe benefits were out of sight. Pussy fell upon us like manna from heaven. My buddies and me were getting real well known; the bad girls knew us and wouldn't leave us alone. Waste not want not, daddy-o.

So I'd stayed around and played around much too long after the gig, making out in the back seat of Ritchie the Drummer's '57 Chevy — it had more bondo on it than original body. We'd picked up these two little chickadees. His was named Renee. I remember her name because he later complained that she'd left him with a case of blue balls that was nearly fatal, and it became a running joke with us. Wrote a song about it called "Bluebells." People thought it was about being in love with a girl named Renee who liked flowers. It wasn't.

I don't remember the name of the girl I was with. Not sure I ever knew it. Didn't matter. She went to second base right out of the dugout. If you're going to play second, your job is to cover the middle, and you need good hands, ready to make a double play. She handled the position like Bill Mazeroski. Knew exactly what to do with a bat and balls.

Me, I was rounding third, and ready to steal home, and getting all set to slide in safe, when Ritchie's Renee decided she had to walk away and get her tight little ass home before daddy awoke at daybreak, or she'd have to face the sun rising on a brutish umpire. I guess you could say that the game was called on account of Renee.

Around noon, Stede knocks on my door. I'd seen him around school a little. From a distance. He was a senior; I was a freshman and the marks of the twain never meet.

He didn't introduce himself.

"Hey," he said. Like we knew each other. Like we were pals.

"Yeah. Hey."

He stood there dumbly with his hands shoved deeply into his jeans pockets, looking anywhere but at my face. It was an uncomfortable elevator pause, and I was about to ask him what the fuck, when he spit it out like warm, rancid piss.

"Look," he said, "I want to go see my girlfriend and her fuckin' sister says if I don't bring *you*, then I can't come."

"What the *fuck*?" I said.

"That's what *I* said," he said.

So there were these two sisters. Greta and I forget the other one's name. Maybe Janice. Janet. Janine. Something like that. Let's call her "Jan." Though the sisters were four years apart in age, they looked very much alike. You had to look close or you could easily confuse them.

Sure, Greta was little shorter and more on the voluptuous side. Janice — if that was her name — was taller and what poets call willowy. Jan had a few more freckles.

But both had very straight corn-blonde hair all the way down to their asses. Both had iceberg blue eyes. Both had broad mouths full of dental triumph. And both were completely spoiled little bitches. They were so self-consumed they made Scarlet O'Hara look like Mother Teresa. You could say they were like identical twats.

"So. Can you fuckin' come, man?" Stede said.

I should have said, "no."

But I was an untutored youth so I said, "Sure. Why the fuck not?"

I got dressed and off we went. The rest, as they say, is hysteria.

Stede was a senior and was seeing Jan, who was a freshman. Greta was a senior and apparently had designs on me, a lowly freshman. It was an odd social cross-match, see? Violated the high school norm of strict segregation by graduating class. It was cool for Stede to be banging a younger girl, but me going with a senior chick would really piss a lot of people off. Male people, anyway. Male people who presumably thought I was encroaching on their natural and moral right to get into her pants themselves. Need I say, "Fuck 'em?"

For the female people, it was a little different.

They giggled and cooed about me they way they would have done had Greta taken in a stray puppy. A stray puppy that could sing and play guitar. Most of her friends — she was a *very* popular girl — were content to watch the puppy play fetch, maybe sneak in a quick scratch behind the ear. But some of her crowd clearly wanted the puppy for their own. Greta chased them off and herded me around like she had the blood of a blue healer in her own family tree.

Greta's gang became regulars at all the Wastrel gigs, but when I wasn't actually on stage, she hung on my arm like she'd lost a leg to mortar fire, and that put a bright red neon "No Vacancy" sign on my crotch. Yeah, this love affair was doomed. You can't roller skate in a buffalo herd.

Stede and I spent the ensuing spring and summer more or less wound around the little fingers of these two girls.

They lived on a small horse farm. Both girls competed in western riding events, mostly barrel-racing. The foyer of their house was festooned with all kinds of ribbons, mostly blue, and photos of the girls, mostly sitting ahorse. Apparently, they could ride before they could toddle. Their old man had some kind of a square job — welder, maybe — that fed the bulldog.

We were there all the time. Helped with barn chores. Stayed for dinner. Day and night, night and day, we were the ones.

This would be the summer I learned what "haying" was: like workin' on the chain gang, only itchier. There's nothing like tossing a few hundred hay bales around to give you a good workout. But hay particles made their way under your clothes and into your throat despite the bandana tied across your face bandito-style. Hooh! Ah! Cough! Wheeze! That's the sound of the men workin' on the hay gang.

I would also learn to sit back in the saddle unless you want your monster mashed.

Their dad, sometimes called "Red," sported a handlebar mustache waxed to a fine pair of curls. Mom was a sullen brunette, who didn't care much for the constant horny dallyings, such that the girls were going around "all hot and bothered" all the time. But the old man would say "They're *teenagers*. What do you expect? Hell, remember when we used to?" He never got to finish that line because mama-san would smack him on the arm, but it always shut her up. Too bad. I would have liked to hear the rest of that story.

I didn't have wheels, so Stede did the driving. He had a station wagon. A '52 Ford. They called it a "woody wagon" because it still had some real wood trim on it. With its spacious seats that you could practically stretch out on full length, I'll bet you can figure out why *we* called it a "woody wagon."

Went to drive-in theatres a lot, but I couldn't tell you a single film we saw. Didn't go there to watch movies. It was a heavy-petting double-header and it often went into extra innings. Part of that double-date scene is that there's a certain amount of voyeurism/exhibitionism inherent to the plot.

Sometimes it's just that you don't care if somebody sees you. You have other priorities. But other times, part of the fun is that somebody sees you, might be watching you. Or maybe you get to watch someone else, too. Clearly, Stede didn't care who saw what. But just as clearly, those two girls enjoyed watching each other. I can recall Janice — if that was her name — giving Stede a cowgirl dry hump in the front seat, looking back at me with my fingertip in Greta's cunt up to my wrist, and smiling at me as she leaned over so she could see my handiwork better.

That sort of thing can throw gasoline on your fire, if you're in the right mood. Seems I was always in the right mood.

Over the summer, these ladies bludgeoned our emotions with a sexual carrot-and-stick. Or maybe it was rock-paper-scissors. I don't know if Stede and Jan were doing any actual fucking, but Greta and I seemed to have stalled at the scandaglio stage. She had a boyfriend in the Army and apparently felt that, while everything else was acceptable, actually fucking would be disloyal. Don't ask me how she arrived at that conclusion. There's no logic to it.

"Wise Chinese say hand-job better than no job at all," Stede told me, and I suppose he had a point. To a point. She did a decent job of jerking me off, and I got to know her cunt well enough that I could hit her high F sharp, chorus after chorus.

But our petting began to feel petty. Routinized.

I figured there was a reason they call it foreplay.

Nothing wrong with foreplay, mind you, but at that time I was interested in getting to five. I had to do my more advanced mathematical calculations independently.

When the inevitable double break-up came at summer's end, it was almost a relief.

Almost.

Stede and I both took it kind of hard, though.

The best part of the whole ordeal was that Stede and I got to know each other. We were both from dirt-poor families, both interested in karate, both permanently pissed-off at the world. He didn't play, but he dug the music I dug. We made a good team for a while. Butch and Sundance, but without the laughs.

Which brings me to Diana.

Diana wasn't my first real girlfriend in the world. But she was the first girl I ever went around it with.

I had a bad case of the sighing, abandoned puppy-dog blues from the Greta break-up. Don't ask me why. She just wasted my precious time. But don't think twice, that's all right. Jesus, how had I gotten myself so emotionally invested in that chick? If I'm going to be honest, I guess I have to admit that it was the way she hooked me with unbridled adulation for my music. In my world, I could have cured fucking cancer and I still would have been a "juvenile delinquent" in the eyes of all the "good" people. Playing music wasn't a redeeming activity. It was an additional offense. So when Greta greeted me with those adoring eyes, I was a sucker for it. She was devoted to her puppy — until she found out she'd have to feed it and take it out for walks. Anyway, I fell for it. Hook, line, and concrete overcoat. No excuses. I'll plead temporary inanity and throw myself on the Mercy of the court.

As the autumn leaves started to fall, I spent a lot of time at the Wolf Lake Plaza shopping center — back before they called them malls — wandering aimlessly past shop windows, like Scrooge's wage-slave, Bob Catshit, daydreaming of a nice, big hunk of coal. I was floating past Woolworth's rattling my chains and moaning, when I realized some waitress inside was pacing me, trying to flag me down.

Not very subtle of her.

And not very subtle was just what I needed.

She was dusky, not quite swarthy, but you could see Swarthyville from where she was standing. She could have had a mustache with very little difficulty, and I think she was self-conscious about that. Kept her lip attended to. Had a hard time keeping up with the coarse stubble on her legs. She boasted a dark, dense tangle of pubic hair, trailing faintly up to her belly button in front, and well into the crevice of her buttocks behind, something which cruel fashion did not require her to butcher. A few wild hairs sprouted around her nipples, too, but she rode herd on those.

Her long, brown hair she ironed to make as straight as possible, a la Cher, of Sonny and Cher fame. Bangs like a filly's forelock that fell into her eyes — eyes very large, very soft, very deep brown. You find a pony with eyes like that, you buy it.

Diana affected one of those fisherman caps that the Beatles made popular, and wore her jeans so tight that she was the envy of every camel at the Sahara.

I don't know if I loved dark, hirsute women before Diana left her fingerprints on my soul, but I did swear her fair and think her bright, and now that's how I roll.

Still, there was only one Diana.

Our first date, we went to a movie. Never saw a frame of it. Soon as the lights went down, so did she. We spent a lot of time together after that, but it was never enough. When we weren't together, we were talking on the phone. Now, my family was too broke to have a phone, but there was a pay phone at the bar next door and no one ever used it. So I adopted it like a lost cat. When things were bad at home — and things were always bad at home — sometimes I'd get to that phone and call her, and she was always there. Sometimes we'd talk. Sometimes I'd just listen to her breathe. It was proof of life — *mine*.

According to my romantic mentor, The Cicero Kid, to "go around the world" with a girl was to fuck her "hand, tits, mouth, cunt and ass." More or less in that order. Diana was the first female — maybe the only female — I ever met whose sexual appetite was as voracious and varied as my own. She was always in the mood, and game for anything.

I've never met a woman who could jack me off as well as I could do it myself, but, to be fair, I have direct evidence of just what I need, and all they have is hearsay. Plus I've had a lot of practice. Nevertheless, Diana cut pretty close to the bone. To call it a hand job would be like calling Jaws a fish. She had the *leisure de main* of a powerhouse prestidigitator. She could shuffle the dick overhand, Hindu, or riffle style, and Charlier cut to a one-eyed Jack with one hand while simultaneously executing ball-handling worthy of Marques Haynes with the other.

And she took her time. She delighted in bringing me right to the brink — then slowing down, backing off, making it stay, ahhh, just a little bit longer. When I finally ejaculated, she would give me this smug succubus stare as she licked my semen from her fingers.

Tasted like victory.

To be fair, I have to concede that I enjoyed torturing her with kindness, too. I love the taste of a woman's cunt, and Diana's mound was indescribably delicious. Salty and fresh, with the scent of the primal sea. I would have been content to nestle my face against her soft, purple-rimmed lips until the end of the world. She put deep scratches in my shoulders when she climaxed, and I loved the way they stung in the shower.

"Holy fuck," she said, after the first time I gave her cunt a few laps around the track. "I thought guys didn't like to do that."

I didn't know what to say. So I quoted a song.

"I'm not like everybody else," I said.

I didn't realize at the time how prophetic that was. No way I could foresee how often I'd find myself repeating those words.

It was Diana's idea to try anal sex, but she didn't exactly have to twist my arm. She suggested it like she thought we should try out that new Chinese restaurant that opened up in town: Wang Ho's. Yeah, I could go someplace with that.

We didn't know what the hell we were doing. A little saliva wasn't enough lubrication, plus I probably went too fast, impatient to be inside her. She lurched away from me like I'd hit her ass with a branding iron, and curled up in a ball, squeezing her eyes shut. I was so green, for a moment I wasn't sure whether she was experiencing rapture or rupture. It wasn't rapture. I felt terrible about it and apologized all over the place. Started to get up. She pulled me back to her. "It's all right," she said. "Don't say you're sorry. Just fuck me."

What else could I do?

I owed her one.

The next time, she brought out a big jar of Vaseline.

There was no quit in that girl.

It was Christmas time.

A white one.

Cold, but not too cold, as long as you weren't out in it for long.

A Norman Rockwell Christmas, with evergreens dutifully tricked out, snowmen waving their oak twig arms, tiny multi-colored lights strung up in unlikely places, and a church group of wholesome lunatics pompously chirping out carols on the corner of Sacrilege and Saccharin.

It was a funny old town. Norman Rockwell on the surface, George Lincoln Rockwell underneath.

Diana and I met by the Wolf Lake Theatre to exchange gifts.

She handed me a small box wrapped with candy-cane festooned paper and tied with a red ribbon. Inside was a pair of her panties. White cotton. Bikini style. The crotch was stiff with dried juices from close encounters of the digital kind, and rich with her scent.

"Merry Christmas," she said. "Now when you're thinking of me, you can think of me thinking of you."

"Fuck, I said. "All I got for you was a necklace."

I handed her the culpatory evidence.

On a petite golden chain, a medallion, shaped like a heart. Only, you know, hearts aren't really shaped like that. That heart shape more closely resembles labia minora, or, upside-down, the shape of a woman's ass. I'd had the medallion engraved. It said, *"plus qu'hier, moins que demain."* That's French for "bullshit."

"I love it," she said. "But I bet that's not *all* you've got for me. Let's go for a walk."

She took my hand and led me off on a stroll through the woods along the shore of Wolf Lake, frozen solid now. The moon was full, and reflecting off the snow made it almost seem like daytime. There was no one else around. Who but a couple of horny teenagers would be out and about on a night like that? We settled on a spot that we figured was far enough away from the beaten path to be safe from any prying eyes, just in case.

She leaned back against one of those old birch trees, and I leaned in. I remember our noses were a little runny with the cold, and our kisses tasted salty. It didn't take long for her to have her jeans down, and my jeans down, trying to find an angle that would get my cock into her while at the same time exposing the least amount of skin to the sharp bite of the winter air.

Didn't work very well.

She had to pull her jeans all the way down, around her boots and lean way, way back. I sort of stepped into the space between her legs, and between her jeans and her cunt. With me supporting her, she was able to spread her knees, reach down and guide my cock to where it belonged. That was the easy part. She was always wet as a Mississippi swamp.

It was so damn cold. My ass and legs were freezing and I'm sure hers were, too. But that just made her cunt feel that much warmer. The contrast was stunning.

My ears were numb, my fingers were dick-stiff, and Jack Frost was taking big bites at my nose, but my cock was on fire with the heat of Diana's body. It was cold enough that I wanted to finish in a hurry, but it was so good to be inside her I wanted to make it last, and I sure as hell didn't want to stop before she came at least once.

Once I felt her going over the edge, I let myself go, too, and every spurt felt like a 180 proof shot of heaven on earth.

If there's anything sweeter than that, it is unknown to humankind.

Thing is, as soon as that wave subsided, we realized we were no longer fucking — we were fucking *freezing*. We hurried to bundle up again. But our clothes as well as our limbs had gotten into quite a tangle, and it was no easy chore to figure out what belonged to whom. We managed to do it, though, and without falling down half-naked in the snow. Afterward, we went someplace to get something hot to drink. We were both shivering like nervous newlyweds by the time we got there. The coffee maker turned out to be on the fritz so we had to drink hot chocolate.

I hate chocolate.

But in this case I made an exception.

It took a lot of hot chocolate, and sharing a small mountain of French fries, but eventually we thawed out enough to even open our coats and relax, sprawl out a bit.

We survived it ok, though.

And didn't even wear a helmet.

I guess I really had it bad for Diana and as we all know, that ain't good.

Had she not proven to be almost fatally perfidious, I might have stayed with that girl indefinitely.

But she did, so I didn't.

Last time I saw her, she was on the arm of a big, dumb St. Bernard whose mummy and daddy had just bought him a brand new fire engine red Corvette for graduation.

No way true love or a poor boy like me could compete with that.

And *that*, boys and girls, is what you call a narrow escape.

Lucky me.

But here's the thing.

One afternoon, while we were still going strong, in love forever, Diana brought over her new Polaroid Swinger camera, along with a truckload of film. We shot a couple zillion rolls of each other in a variety of obscene poses. We made a game of it. Took turns. Played each other's requests. See who could top whom on the lewdness scale. It was a close match. Might've been a tie.

One shot in particular, I took by complete accident, while it was my turn to think up a pose for her and I couldn't think of one. She was waiting for Mr. de Mille to do her close-up now, stretched languidly out on the bed, propped up on one elbow. She bent one knee up; the other had fallen to open her crotch to view and display that wonderfully dense bush that flourished there. Just a hint of labia peeking through. Her head was turned to the side, and she gazed sleepily out the window, and a distant, dreamy expression floated on the surface of her face like a lost butterfly.

I snapped that picture just at that moment. Didn't mean to. But I did.

I don't know what ever happened to that photo. I kept it in my wallet for a long time after I found out how short a time "forever" can be. I mean, I kept it for years. Sandwiched between a pair of one-eyed Jacks. Something about that captured moment, brought a stillness to my turbulent spirit. Stillness and solace. I clung to that photo until it got so decrepit you could hardly make it out. Of all the shots I took of her, even the most pornographic ones, that's the one I wish I still had.

For times like this.

## SAX AND VIOLINS

Lacey played tenor sax. Doubled on flute. To hear her honk on that horn, you'd have guessed she was a middle-aged Black smack artist from Chicago. But Lacey was a slender White waif from the North shore suburbs, with honey blonde hair, sleepy blue eyes, and a crooked mouth. When she smiled, her mouth took over her whole face, eyes reduced to crinkles. She could wail on that tenor like she was possessed by a wandering Tibetan demon stranded in Chi-town with a case of the blues. That would be an off-track Tibetan.

Spielberg's creature feature "Jurassic Park" was hot at that time. Featured a badass tyrannosaurus rex, lovingly referred to as a t-rex, for short. I told Lacey she was such a monster on that horn that she should be classified as a tyrannosaurus sax. T-sax, for short.
"How about a little T- SEX?" she said.
"Jurassic Park," I said.
"What?"
"Just park jur ass right here, darlin.'"
We kept company for a month or two. She liked what I wrote. I liked how she played what I wrote. One thing led to another. Played some gigs together. Mike, a friend of hers, on upright bass. Teddy G on percussion. Hand-drums. Congas, bongos, timbales, tortillas and whatnot. Had a fun time unwinding afterwards. See, when you play music with somebody, when you're in that groove together, it's just like sex. It's intimate. Connected. Intimately connected. In the now and wow.
Lacey was a serious musician, not like me, and inevitably, she got an offer to go out to the coast. Fame. Fortune. Hot and cold running pool boys. There was no question about whether she should go. Made me the obligatory offer to tag along. "Home is where your horses are," I said. "But if you feel like it, come back and see me now and again."
She promised she would.
I knew she wouldn't.
But it was cool.
You're ever out west, L.A., Frisco; keep an eye out for the Lacey Clark Quintet. Do yourself a favor and have a listen.
Tell her I sent you.
She'll get a kick out of that.

## TWO INTO ONE GOES FIVE TIMES

After Lacey split I had a bad relapse of my recurring blues. Teddy G. and his lady, Heather, made it their mission to look after me, cheer me up. One night, they had me over for dinner, and afterward we lounged around drinking champagne, smoking reefer, and listening to some classics: Miles, Mingus and Monk. Plus a little Dizzy. And a bit of Wes.

Teddy's an imposing figure, milk chocolate, impish smirk ever-present. Unless he's drumming, then he's someplace else where smirks dare not tread. I loved this guy.

Heather was lean and blonde with playful hazel eyes, and large breasts that looked out of place on her narrow frame. I liked her quite a lot, too.

We were all about as relaxed as we could get, I think. Teddy and Heather started dancing together, bumping and grinding and snickering suggestively. I might have taken that as my cue to split, but I was too drunk and too high to be operating any complex machines, including my legs.

In short order Teddy was sitting in the leather easy chair, and Heather was straddling his lap, her back to him, posting slowly and deeply. The look on her face made me smile. She rode him for a long while, moaning softly as she went. She noticed me watching and I noticed her noticing, and next thing I knew, I was there kissing her, and sliding my cock into her right alongside Teddy's. She was no bible-thumper, but she started talking to God soon after that.

We played that string out, and then lay sprawled out on the living room carpet, in a largely liquid state. Heather was the first to attempt locomotion. It failed. She lay there in a puddle, and started laughing. "Holy FUCK, you guys," she said. She was religious after all.


## AUNT EDITH

To start with, she wasn't really my aunt. For some reason, we were told to call her that. Don't ask me why.

One reason I remember her visit so clearly is because no one ever came to visit us. We virtually never had company. We were isolated. Alienated. Like the feral cats who lurked in the nearby woods.

She was of my mother's generation, but she wasn't stuck in it like an old truck in Mississippi mud. Traces remained, of course, but time hadn't gone on without her. She had wavy medium blonde hair that she wore in a tight bun when traveling, but let loose to shoulder length when relaxing. She wore a full palette of make-up, but made it seem invisible, even though her lips bore the blood red hue of her regiment.

She arrived wearing large pearl earrings and a single strand necklace to match, a mannish white shirt, with the collar turned up, and a skirt that clung to every curve and sway of her hips the way a bronc rider holds on to the saddle. They used to refer to that full-breasted, wide-hipped figure as "voluptuous," which means, "giving pleasure to the senses."

Yeah, daddy-o.

With her bright smile, throaty laugh, and cooing voice, she was like a movie star, in the same league as Audrey Hepburn, going lightly, and Marilyn Monroe (who I'd recently seen in "The Misfits") and Sophia Loren (who I would soon fall in love with after seeing her in "El Cid"), and she was positively the most glamorous woman I had ever seen in person so far.

So far.

That was about an inch.

I think I must have been about ten years old the summer she came to visit.

"My, my," she said when we were introduced. "Your mom told me you were handsome as the devil. I see she was telling the truth."

My situation was such that my heart soaked up those words faster than spilled water gets sucked up by the Sahara sand. I fell in love with her immediately.

I don't recall how long she stayed. A few days, I think. While she was there, my dad was on his best behavior. It bewildered me. He was pretending to be someone else, like he wanted to impress her. And so was my mother. There were no be-littlings or be-ratings or beatings in her presence. Another reason I would miss the hell out of her after she had gone.

Most of the occasion is lost in the blur of memory. I remember her being nice to me. Singing along with me to the records we owned — Bing Crosby, Elvis, Nat King Cole. She had a voice as glamorous as her appearance.

At night, I slept on the living room couch while the adults talked and played cards in the kitchen long into the night. I have no idea what they talked about, but it was a pleasant white noise in the background. Like the sound of the wheels on the tracks, clacking over the intersections, on a long train ride.

Edith slept, when she finally turned in, on a rollaway bed, folded open in her honor. She slept in a blue pajama top and white panties, which struck me funny because I slept in blue pajama bottoms and a white t-shirt. Something symbolic there, I'm sure.

Between the light of the moon blazing in through the windows like a search beacon, and the small lamp always left on in the kitchen, there was enough light to see her fairly well. She had tossed and turned a while, and then had curled up with her back to me, her fleshy ass straining against the inadequate cotton fabric of her panties, the sheerness of the fabric making the contours painfully clear. The waistband pulled low, exposing the valley mouth of her buttocks cleavage. And in the crotch, a few stray pubic hairs had left the reservation.

It was more than I could bear.

My gaze fixed on her ass, I dug out my cock and went quietly to work, quietly so as not to wake her.

But not quietly enough.

All at once, she rolled over to face me, and propped her head up on one elbow, catching me with a handful of cock and no ready explanation, and too wrapped up in what I was doing to quickly cover my tracks.

"Can't sleep, hon?" she cooed.

While I wasn't paying attention, someone had tied a taut-line hitch in my tongue, and I nearly choked on it trying to find a suave reply.

"Me, neither," she said, like she was revealing her deepest secret. "Would you like to cuddle up with me? It might help."

She didn't have to ask me twice.

I got there as fast as I could get there. I stubbed my little toe on the corner of the coffee table, real hard, too. I clenched my teeth and pretended I hadn't. In short order, I was spooned up with her lying behind me, wrapping me in her arms, her breasts cushioning my back. The heat of her swept through me, her scent nearly made me swoon, and my cock ached so hard I could barely breathe. It was at one time

390

the most enjoyable place I'd ever been — and the most tortuous. I must have been tense as a 2x4 because after a while she cooed softly into my ear, "You're still not sleepy, huh? Try to relax."

It was at that point that her hand fell absently across the front of my pajama's where my cock was acting like a water witch's dousing rod approaching the Pacific Ocean. A fold of fabric unfolded, and my cock to poked its head out from the fly to take a quick look around. I had no idea how to get my cock back inside my pants and be subtle at the same time.

Turned out I didn't have to worry about it.

Edith's fingers brushed against my cock, and for a moment, I thought she was going to tuck me back in.

I was wrong.

Instead, she petted, caressed, stroked, pulled, squeezed, massaged, tugged, and put the whole rest of the thesaurus into play until she felt me tremble with that delicious ripple of pleasure, from toes to nose, turning my bones to lime jello. As my breathing slowed down to normal, she kissed me on top of my head.

"Go to sleep now, hon," she said.

Never slept so well in my life.


## BLOWIN' IN THE WIND

We were taking a break after mending a fence. Not quite feeding time. A light, cool breeze briefly brushed away the summer heat, and I searched a moment for the answer but found none. I tossed the tools in the back of the gator. We climbed aboard, but she didn't start the engine up right away.

"How come you never got married, Jack?" Like an ace off the bottom of the deck. "Didn't you ever find anyone you liked enough?"

"I never found anyone I DISliked enough." I told her I felt about marriage about the same way I felt about bits. I finished it with a chorus of "Don't Fence Me in."

"Ever even come close?" she asked.

"One time," I said. "When I was young and foolish." I didn't mention that I was now old and foolish.

"When?"

"Long story."

"It isn't feeding time yet."

It was getting to the point where I had no sense when it came to Marlo. Couldn't refuse her anything. So I went ahead and told her about it.

I had decided to go straight.

As in "be a regular citizen."

A square.

A mark.

A sucker.

Never trust any decision you make while under the influence of perfume.

But I hadn't learned that yet.

She was a classy filly. Her name was Mary. She wasn't the most beautiful girl I'd ever met, or the sexiest, or the most anything. But there was something about her. When we danced it was, for her, the dance of the matador, only she was facing the bull alone and naked and unarmed. For me, it was tiptoeing along a high wire stretched across the Grand Canyon during a thunderstorm with gale force winds.

But there was something about her.

Her smile, maybe. It was easy and playful and sincere and she used it a lot, used it whenever she looked at me. The way you might smile at a puppy or a sunrise or a rainbow.

Maybe it was the way she looked not at me but into me, her eyes the blue of unpolluted sky, looking directly into mine. That look, combined with that impish smile, gave me the feeling that she knew me better than anyone else knew me, better than I knew myself, and she had secrets to share.

She was a hometown girl and not at all the type to go gallivanting around with an itinerant musician cum hustler just one thin blonde hair this side of the law. She was all white picket fences, apple pie and PTA. She'd been born in this town, had grown up there. She would get married, raise a family there, and be buried there, and be content.

She was America according to Ozzie and Harriet and Frank Capra. She said her prayers at night and pledged allegiance to the flag — or maybe it was the other way around. She was a hick, a rube. Gullible, trusting, naïve, brainwashed.

But there was something about her. Something that made me want to be with her, and although I was the diametrical opposite of everything she was, everything she thought, everything she believed in, she wanted to be with me, too.

It didn't make any sense at all on paper, but that was the scene.

And I temporarily lost my mind.

See, being an outlaw is hard.

Always swimming against the current. Running against the wind.

When you know what's wrong, and you know what's right, your whole life is just one long fight. Always out-numbered, always out-gunned. Sooner or later —and usually sooner — you go down alone, bloody and without having changed a damn thing. Them that's got shall still get, the rest will still lose and the only thing new in the news is your very short obituary on that back page, near the help wanted ads.

It's so much easier to stop fighting, to give in, give up, go along and get along. Like one of those pod people from Invasion of the Body Snatchers.

Get with the program, son, and you get to have nice things. A nice house. A nice car. Nice friends. A nice family. You can have the nicest goddam cell on the whole goddam block. An outlaw understands that having those things, needing those things, loving those things — that's what they use to keep you in line. You don't own them; they own you. Make any waves, any waves at all, and they'll take it all away from you so fast it'll make your head spin. The motherfuckers giveth and the motherfuckers taketh away.

All you have to do to be a square is let go. Let go of every ugly thing you know about the world, all the lying, cheating, brutality and injustice, from war-profiteering to starving children, from environmental pollution to political corruption. Let it all go. Pretend it doesn't exist, that it's not your problem; that God or Jesus or the President or some other white man will take care of it.

Mary's voluptuous flesh sang to me like the Sirens, and her lips were made of the lotus. They made me forget who I was.

So I decided to stick around this little town where everybody called each other by their first names, where everybody knew whose check was good and whose husband wasn't. I could still do music on the side. Part-time. Pull out the guitar on special occasions to entertain the townsfolk. Christmas. Fourth of July. In a pond this small, I'd be a Moby Dick.

Found a square barbershop. The kind with the candy-striped pole on one side of the door and an American flag on the other. Got myself a square haircut from a bald barber. That should have told me something, but it didn't.

I drove along Main Street to the other side of town where there was a menswear store. It was the place where all the kids bought their suits for high school graduation, rented their tuxes for the prom.

It was about a one and a half mile stretch. Just for fun I counted flags that peppered the route. There were 47. That's a flag every 168 feet. There was a flag flying from every vertical structure, from power pole to lamppost, plus the dedicated flagpoles at the post office, and the town hall, and the school. Flags, flags everywhere, but not a drop of freedom to spare. Squint a little and it's easy to see swastikas flapping in the breeze instead of the stars and stripes. The more flags you see, the less freedom you have. That's a mathematical formula you want to remember.

I ran the red, white, and blue gauntlet to Kettinger's Polyester Palace. Not a natural fiber in the whole store. I selected some square clothes for my disguise: button-down shirt, navy blazer, khaki slacks. Striped tie.

I found a square job at the little shopping mall on the outskirts of Squaresville, The Squaresville Plaza. A place called Shoe World. A chain store — how's that for foreshadowing?

The manager, a square named Tim, had been a football star the year the local high school had won some kind of championship. Caught the winning pass, ran the winning touchdown, something like that. There was a trophy, and a team photo, and a decrepit newspaper clipping recounting the event on permanent display near the cash register. If you looked close you could spot Tim in the picture, thicker on top, thinner around the middle. That clipping was his obituary. There was no life after football. Just a shoe store.

He told me he was glad to have me on the team. He spoke in a dialect made up of 90% sports slogans, sayings and metaphors. Giving CPR to a skeleton.

I started the next day. "Suit up and we'll get you in the game tomorrow," he said.

I got up early

Broke my fast with black coffee, scrambled eggs, and cold pizza, left over from the previous night. Then I suited up.

I scarcely recognized myself in the mirror. I could write a book: "Square Like Me."

Didn't know whether to laugh, puke, or cut my throat.

About an hour after Tim gave me the lay of the land, I sold somebody's grandma a pair of sensible shoes. About the only perk in shoe sales is looking up a lady's dress. Wasn't even tempted. Old Tim gave me a slap on the back. "Way to get on the scoreboard," he said.

When I met up with Mary, she made a point to tell me how sharp I looked. Several times. She was proud of me. This was the start of great things. Yada-yada-yada. We did our usual heavy petting and deep kissing, and dry humping — nothing you could actually call sex. She was saving herself, of course. I walked her home, and when I got back to my place, I masturbated until my shoulder felt like it would fall off.

This went on for a week.

On Friday Tim gave me my check like it was the Heisman Trophy. I opened the envelope on my coffee break. After this tax and that tax, paying my fair share to keep the poor children of the military-industrial complex from starving, I was left with just about what I would spend on a decent dinner in The Windy City, including the tip. Are you fucking kidding me?

That night, after making out with Mary, walking her home and doing my arm exercises, I slugged down several servings of Jack Daniels and hit the rack. I was so dazed and confused you'd have thought I had lead in my zephlin.

Dream Chief came to rescue me.

He arrived with his pony beside him, and singing in that high, scratchy voice, like Lakota bebop. I was kind of glad to see him. Not sure he was so glad to see me.

"Go where the arrow points to the rainbow," he said and stretched out a fringed arm to point the way, like the Ghost of Christmas-Yet-to-Come. I had a creepy feeling that I didn't want to see what he was pointing at, but I couldn't help myself. I had to look.

Here's what I saw:

Me.

It was a different Me. A future version of Me I almost didn't recognize. I was there in that fucking shoe store, 50 pounds heavier and sporting the world's most inept comb-over. I was standing near the cash register, but the football trophy was gone, and in its place hung my beat-up guitar. The team photo had disappeared, and my current publicity headshot hung there instead. There was a news clipping recounting my "toe tapping" performance at the town fair.

I watched Me stare wistfully out the window, as a funky I-IV blues vamp came up in the background, and then I listened to Me sing the tune to Myself.

The lyrics went like this:

When I was a young boy, a sultry, scented breeze
Brought me wild imaginings of wanton ecstasies
I could have become a scholar of the mysteries therein
Tutored by the voices in the wind.

And this was followed by a reflective refrain:
I guess I could have listened
I guess I could have listened
I guess I could have listened to the wind.

A brass section came in to build up to the second verse:
Pushing stock and punching clocks, I'm theirs from 9 to 5
I over-spend on the long weekends and I'm just barely alive
I never took the chance to be what I'm sure I could have been
My "yes, sirs" get me nowhere and my hair is getting thin
And all I ever wanted was to be like Errol Flynn
I guess I should have listened to the wind.

There following again the poignant refrain:
I guess I should have listened
I guess I should have listened
I guess I should have listened to the wind

For the last verse, I watched Me singing directly to Me. It was like a mirror reflected in a mirror, reflected in a mirror, reflected in a mirror:

Some night when you're all alone, a sultry, scented breeze
May bring you wild imaginings of wanton ecstasies
Don't throw away your chance, you fool. To waste it is a sin.
Dare to learn the secrets of the mysteries therein
Take big bites of Life, my friend, or else, to your chagrin
You'll wish that you had listened to the wind

And there came the concluding cautionary refrain that lingered on
with a repeat, and fade out:
You'll wish that you had listened
You'll wish that you had listened
You'll wish that you had listened to the wind.

As the song faded out, the scene faded to black and I turned to
Dream Chief for some solace or explanation.

"Go where the arrow points to the rainbow," was all he said.

But his pony nudged me with his nose, as if to emphasize the
point. Nudged me roughly, too, as if to say, "Get your ass moving,
Dummy."

I awoke in a panic, having fallen out of bed. It was 3AM. I tried to
pull myself together, but I couldn't pull hard enough.

"Spirit," I said out loud to no one there, not even the chair, "are
these the shadows of the things that will be, or are they shadows of
things that may be, only? Men's courses will fucking foreshadow
certain ends, to which, if persevered in, they must lead, but if the damn
courses be departed from, the ends will change. Say it is thus with
what you show me! Don't be a fuckin' drag."

The next day was Saturday. Mary's parents had invited me to
lunch. I arrived early carrying a large cardboard box. I exchanged
pleasantries with her mom, who was scurrying around the kitchen like
a little brown mouse, and I swapped grunts with her dad who was
ensconced in his favorite chair reading Field and Stream. He gave the
box a quizzical glance, but didn't ask. "Kids, these days," his
expression seemed to say.

"Can we talk for a minute?" I whispered to Mary under parental
hearing range. "Outside?'

We stepped out on to the porch. The air was warm, but the wind had picked up, and the trees were swaying, wind chimes tinkling. Storm coming.

"I'm glad you came for lunch, today," Mary said. "Don't mind my dad. He's impressed that you got a real job."

"Yeah. About that," I said. "Actually, I didn't come for lunch. I came to say good-bye."

"Good-bye? Don't be silly. What do you mean, good-bye?"

"I mean if I stay here, it'll kill me. Slowly. And painfully. And I'll end up hating you for doing it to me, and hating myself for letting you. And you'll end up hating me too. Look, I dig you, Sugar. But this just isn't my scene. So I'm going to split."

"When?"

"I'm already gone." I handed her the box.

"What's this?"

"You can dispose of the remains any way you like."

She opened the box and pulled out that polyester blazer. The button-down shirt, and khaki pants were in there, too. And the striped tie.

She looked sad a moment, eyes misty, chin quivering. But she was a strong girl. Maybe that's one of the things I liked about her. She took one deep, deep breath and let it out in a long sigh.

"I guess I should have known, really. I tried to make you into a hobbyhorse. But you're a mustang, aren't you?"

"I guess I am."

At that moment a cocky gust blew up, came whistling through the corner rose bushes.

"Listen to that wind," Mary said.

"That's my plan."

"What?"

I kissed her on the cheek, and shoved off.

Sometimes I wonder what she did with those clothes.

Scarecrow, maybe.


**MABEL'S TABLE**

Mabel was the proprietress and chef bottle-washer of the Parkway Diner, just off 47th and South Parkway. She was elegantly proper in public, addressing me as "Mr. Lucky," when other ears might hear. She was of that generation that commonly called folks by "Miss" or "Mr." and then their first name. Miss Sharon. Mr. Leroy. In private I was "Sweet Thing." I've been called lots worse things.

She was a mountainous beauty. A mountain of the finest milk chocolate. She nevertheless waltzed her callipygian figure around her restaurant with the effortless grace of an Olympic figure skater. She had bouffant hair like Diana Ross, and very clever hands.

Appropriate to her profession, Mabel also possessed a sophisticated palate, able to distinguish the most subtle variations in flavor and texture. She had developed her gustatory sense the way a blind man might develop his hearing. She did not so much experience the world as she tasted it. It was no accident that hers was the most legendary greasy spoon on the South Side.

Our high times together were always at her home, where she delighted in showing off her culinary skills for me, making fanciful hors d'oeuvres, feeding them to me with her own delicate fingers. She served me homemade whipped cream which I licked from her mammoth breasts, and I sampled other delicious sauces from delectable parts of her.

Some people might say, "Give me some sugar," meaning "Give me a little kiss," but when Mabel said it, she wasn't the least bit interested in my lips. We had breakfast together the morning after the first night we spent together. A foot-high stack of French toast, made with cinnamon and nutmeg and a touch of ginger, dressed with butter and honey, and a jigger of maple syrup.

"Give me some sugar, Sweet Thing," she said as she finished pouring out cups of steaming java. At first I wasn't sure whether she wanted me to kiss her or pass the sugar.

Turned out to be neither.

She reached into my boxers, pulled out my cock, and started stroking with a smooth easy rhythm, so she wouldn't get lumps in her gravy. If the Dairy Association ever holds a milking contest, she'd be a cinch for a gold medal. With her expertise, and my bad attitude, it took her so little time to jack me off, that breakfast didn't even get cold. She held up her coffee cup and caught my ejaculate therein. Stirred it with a spoon. Took a sip. Smiled.

I hurled myself body and soul into the French Toast, until I was so stuffed I was on the verge of blowing up, throwing up, or passing out. She took my piggery as a high compliment.

"I love to watch a man eat," she said.

And she wasn't kidding.

But the thing she most liked to watch me eat was her. That was okay by me.

Not that we didn't fuck. We did. I'm sure we did. But our intimate explorations were more gastronomical than anatomical. Her vagina was a gustatory delight, and I was happy to be her gourmand, and I was always in the mood for a snack. I could almost hear Tammy Wynette crooning, "Stand by, Gourmand."

By trial and trial, we found that the most commodious approach was for her to lie back on her bed with me kneeling on the floor with a pillow under my knees. I was surprised at first, by how flexible she was, how wide she could spread her legs. Her protuberant belly was like a sot, hanging over, and threatened to get in the way, about which I could do nothing, since my hands were occupied parting her ample thighs like a pornographic Moses. She didn't mind reaching down, cradling her belly in her arms and pulling it up. It struck me that, for such a big woman, her vulva was very small and round, with perfectly symmetrical lips that mimicked the small round mouth of her face. No better match of artist and medium has ever been made. She loved to be eaten, and I love to eat.

Remembering Mabel now, I can't help contrasting her with another black woman I knew a few years later. Adlue, by name. Not that these were the only two black women I'd ever known. In the musical, political, and criminal circles I ran in, I met a lot of black people, so it's no surprise that I might have had a disproportionate number of black friends and lovers. But, as I think I mentioned, very few of those women proved memorable, regardless of race, color, or religion, unless she had two heads, or the immoral equivalent thereof.

Adlue and Mabel were as opposite as you could imagine. One Reubenesque, with extra Thousand Island dressing, the other as lean and spare as a decathlete. One was a huge woman with tiny labia; the other was a small woman with huge labia. Mabel was softer than her garlic and parsley whipped potatoes; Adlue was harder than the crust on a 3-day old bagel. Mabel came from a place where she down-played her blackness as if she hoped white folks wouldn't notice until after she'd gotten away clean, a big woman who tried to make herself small; Adlue put her blackness right in your face, not necessarily always looking for a fight, but always ready for one. She was a sleek cat who appeared four sizes larger when her fur puffed up with righteous indignation. Mabel was all "we shall over-come." Adlue was 100% "Stick it to the Man." Mabel catered to my self-indulgent side, nurturing my hedonistic inclinations. Adlue slapped the living shit out of my self-indulgent side and forced me take a hard look at the gap between what I thought I believed, and what I thought I was doing about it. If I had to pick, I choose Adlue for a wife, and Mabel as a girlfriend. I never had to pick. Nobody's that lucky.

Fiery Adlue, the mighty Afrodite, rode me like a Valkyrie on acid, pounding my poor loins into chittlin's. Her ascerbic political pillow talk was so radical she made Angela Davis seem like a "house negro." In the totally exhausted, highly suggestive post-coital haze, into which she bludgeoned me, she persuaded me, with cold compelling logic to believe in possibilities that were demonstrably absurd, which in turn led me to do things that were patently ridiculous — and nearly fatal.

I miss her.

I guess I miss them both.

*When Spring rain comes in the Autumn,*
*When lemons taste like honeydew,*
*When snowflakes fall in the Summer,*
*I'll stop loving you.*

"When Snowflakes Fall In the Summer"<br>The Everly Brothers

# CHAPTER EIGHT:
## FINGERPRINTS AND SNOWFLAKES

No two fingerprints are identical.

No matter how many similarities they may have, there are differences.

No two snowflakes are identical.

No matter how many similarities they may have, there are differences.

No two women are identical, either.

No matter how many similarities they may have, there are differences.

The myriad variations in vaginal-labial size and shape, texture and color, scent and taste seem to be, if not mathematically infinite, close enough to infinite to keep my curiosity peaked for the foreseeable future.

As my old running buddy Stede once told me, "The trouble with you, my friend, is that you want to taste too many kinds of pie." Easy for him to say. He was born to be wildly monogamous. But that ain't me, Babe. No, no, no, it ain't me, Babe.

One time I sat in on a session with an old Chicago blues man known as Pop Miller, aka, Backdoor Miller. His signature song was "(I'm your) Backdoor Man." It's a song about servicing married women and slipping out the backdoor just as hubby was coming in the front door. Either that, or it was about anal sex. Either one could fit, and certain musicologists like to argue about it. That moanin' 12-bar solo on the end that fades out? That's me having a grand old time in B flat.

During a break, Miller opined to me that there was just ONE perfect song a man was wanting to write, or ONE perfect solo he was wanting to play, and he spent his whole life chasing it. Found a little piece now and then, here and there. Just enough to make him keep him looking.

"What happens when you find it?" I asked.

"Don't know, son," he said. "Nobody ever done that."

Yeah. It's a metaphor. Maybe a metafive.

It was late.

Late enough that Marlo might as well crash on my couch. She'd done that a few times before.

"So," I said. "Aren't you glad you asked?"

"I don't know," she said. "I think I am. How do you feel about it now, looking back on it? Do you wish you'd done it differently? Wait; let me put that another way. Would you make the same choices today? I mean, if you knew then, what you know now?"

We had recently watched some classic Errol Flynn swashbucklers together. She liked them. I decided to quote something my spiritual godfather says in "The Adventures of Don Juan." I knew she'd recognize it.

"An artist may paint a thousand canvasses before achieving one work of art, would you deny a lover the same practice?"

"There's a little bit of Don Juan in every man," Marlo said, quote for quote. "And since you are Don Juan there must be more of it in you."

"Bravo," I said. "And like Don Juan, I believe in practice."

She curled up and fell almost immediately to sleep.

I covered her with a wool blanket. It was a saddle blanket, the kind the cavalry used to fold into a multi-layered pad to use under the McClellan saddle.

I watched her sleep. Listened to her snoring almost imperceptibly, like a mouse. I treated myself to a few impure thoughts before heading to my own bed.

404

I suppose that, like Don Juan, I've always been searching for an imaginary woman, endowed with all the virtues, clothed in perfection, and, though I seek her relentlessly, deep down I know that she only exists in my mind. Issa once suggested that I was supposed to be twins, but my twin died in the womb. I've been looking for her ever since.

So I used to be like Don Juan.

Now I'm more like Don Quixote.

I just hope I don't turn out to be most like Don Knotts.

Adam Adrian Crown

*She loves you, yeah, yeah, yeah*
*She loves you, yeah, yeah, yeah*
*With a love like that*
*You know you should be glad*
            "She Loves You"
            The Beatles


# CHAPTER NINE:
# MARLO'S PROMISE


Horses are blessed with keen senses.

They have the largest eyes of any land mammal, and can see almost 360 degrees around them. Monocular vision on the sides, binocular vision down their nose. They have acute long vision and are excellent at detecting movement. Up closer, they see detail as well or better than humans. Colors are more muted for them. They see blue well, green and yellow less well, red not at all. Their night vision is superior — although they can't adjust rapidly from light to dark, which is why a horse will often hesitate when going from bright sunlight into a dark barn.

A horse can hear in two directions at once, and catch sounds that humans miss. The ultrasonic squeak of a bat. The footfalls of a cat on soft grass. They can hear each other nearly three miles away. And they can distinguish between similar sounds, for example a particular truck engine. Which explains why my pony is always waiting at the paddock gate for me by the time I finish coming down that long road that ends at the barn. Horses are highly sensitive to volume and tone of voice. And they like music — preferably soft, melodious, and cheerful non-vocal music — although my pony does seem to like it when I sing to him.

Horses have a highly developed sense of smell, and a sense of touch so keen and precise that they can feel a gnat light on their rump.

But of all the horses senses, the one that impresses me most is their extremely acute "sixth sense," ESP or psychic perception, or whatever you want to call it. Whatever it is, it's been researched quite a bit and well documented. It includes not only a homing instinct, but also an uncanny ability to sense danger, and to read the moods and intentions of others. As you can well imagine, that's something that would come in real handy for a prey animal.

Marlo was getting ready to head off for college. New England Conservatory of Music. I'd known this girl since she was about 10 years old, and I suppose I'd become something of a mentor to her. We had many a long, long talk over those years, about all manner of things. From soup to nuts. From cabbages to kings.

She was quite something. Honest and direct. Adventurous. Not afraid of hard work. And she had a sweet way with horses — even with horses who have been so abused that they won't let any other human get close to them.

I liked this girl. Liked her a lot. If the cards fell the right way, she could turn out to be one hell of a human being. When she was a child, it wasn't hard for me to imagine her my daughter-in-spirit. As she got older, started becoming a woman, I thought of her in a lot of different ways, not always fatherly.

It was late July. We were having a run of almost two weeks with no day below 85 degrees, and not a drop of rain. Stevie was keeping her horses sheltered during the day, turning them out at night, which is why Marlo and I — having become Stevie's top volunteers, and with Stevie pulling a long shift at the Vet School, and husband Roger off doing a concert someplace out of town — were sitting by the pond watching the sun go down onto a bed of cream and purple clouds. She started talking philosophy and I knew she had something on her mind, but she was talking all around it. By the time she zeroed in on it, we were watching for shooting stars to streak across the moonless sky, listening to the soothing mantra of horses munching hay, enjoying the freshened breeze, skipping across the pond to run its fingers through her dark locks.

"Have you ever fallen in love?" Nearly like a whisper in church.

"No," I said. "But I think I've stepped in it once or twice."

She reached over and gave my arm a light, playful backhand remonstrance. Didn't have to reach far. We were sitting side by side in a couple of those adjustable incline/decline lawn chairs. I had mine set on full metal lazy.

"I'm serious," she said.

"You think I'm not?"

"You must have known some women you liked."

"One or two."

"But you never got married?"

"I'm philosophically opposed to torture," I said, which was mostly true.

Another backhand.

"C'mon. Be serious with me."

Darlin', I thought, I don't dare.

"I'm serious as a heart attack," I said.

I took a fifth of tequila out of my jacket pocket, cracked it open, and offered it to her. Strictly speaking, that was against the law, but strictly speaking, I didn't give a damn. I had already taught her about how to drink without being a fool about it — something I had to learn the hard way, myself. She took a sip and handed it back.

"Did you ever come close?

"Once."

"Did you dislike her that much?" She listens, and never forgets a thing.

"I guess I liked the way she made me feel," I said.

"How did she make you feel?"

Not a simple question. I took a long pull of hooch to lubricate my thoughts. A shooting star crossed the sky to the north. Somewhere out near the state forest, coyotes were tuning up, singing the coyote blues.

"Normal," I said. "She made me feel normal."

She took the bottle from my hand, and had another dainty sip.

"Normal kind of sucks, doesn't it?"

"Yeah, kind of."

Something splashed in the pond and we fell silent a moment, listening hard. It was shopping time for coons and foxes. Good fishing for them in that pond.

"So what happened with her?" she asked softly so as not to scare the fish.

"No battle plan survives the first contact with the enemy," I said.

"There's more to the story, isn't there?"

"There always is, darlin.'"

"Will you tell me sometime?"

"Sometime."

"Bullshit," cried an owl nearby. Or was it "Whoo-oo?" Hard to tell.

That tequila didn't last long enough.

We took a stroll around the edge of the pond, accompanied by the peepers' do-wop choir.

"How do you know when you're really in love?"

"You're asking the wrong guy," I said.

"No, I'm not."

I looked out to where I'd last seen the sun, the way you might look over to your friend, to give them the "come rescue me" signal at a party. No sign of the cavalry.

"You know what phantom limb syndrome is?"

"Wait. Yes. That's when you, like cut something off, but you have pain in the...OK. What is it?"

"You were on the right track," I said. "Don't give up so easy. It's when people feel pain in an arm or a leg that's been amputated. It's gone, but they feel pain in it. You could say it hurts because it's not there. I think that's a reasonably good analogy for love. Something hurts because it's missing. Then you meet somebody who supplies that missing part and it stops hurting. And you do the same for them. And that's love. At least, that's what the fortune cookie said."

She nodded as if she understood what I was talking about. Cool. Then you can explain it to me.

"I get that," she said. "It hurts because it's missing. Totally. Could I kiss you?"

WHAT???

"Now why would you want to—"

She didn't let me finish it.

Her lips were warm and soft on my lips, and she nuzzled them softly against my mouth for a millisecond that lasted a thousand years. Heat swept through me all the way down to my boots and back up again, until I thought my brain would flashover. I told myself it was the tequila.

It wasn't.

After a moment, she backed off enough to look up at me. She tugged on my shirt like she had done when she was much, much younger.

"Kiss me back," she said.

Part of me wanted to decline, push her away, run away as hard and as fast as I could and embrace sanity.

Turned out it wasn't a very big part of me.

I kissed her back.

If you could bottle that combination of sweet and hot, you'd make a fortune on Buffalo wings.

I remember once trying my hand at surfing, getting wiped out, and swimming like hell for the surface only to reach up and grab a handful of sand because I'd become disoriented and didn't know which way was up.

This was similar.

I had no idea which way was up, and I was running out of breath and afraid I was going to grab a handful of sand. I grabbed her instead, and held on tight as we kissed a rapidly deepening kiss, and I felt her powerful arms clutching me close, her hand (fingering hand, not bowing hand) on the back of my head pulling me deeper into the kiss, like she was Ms. American Mantis and she was getting religious, with our tongues flashing like the swords in an old Errol Flynn movie, engage-press-disengage, tac-au-tac, and her body pressed up against me so hard, so close, that I could begin to believe all our missing parts got found, because it stopped hurting.

"I guess you kept your word," she said softly, as she lay with her head on my chest.

"I always keep my word," I said. "What are we talking about?"

She propped herself up on one elbow, caught a lock of her hair and laid it across her upper lip. Dropping her voice a couple of octaves, and furrowing her brow, she said, "I'll explain that to you when you're older, darlin.'" Followed by a mischievous raccoon chuckle.

"Is that supposed to be me?" I said. "Mustache needs some work."

She lay back down and snuggled more closely against my side, and I pulled her even closer. I could feel her heart beating against my ribs. It was chilly enough to discourage insects, but not chilly enough for us to be in a hurry to re-arrange our clothes.

The moon was just creeping up, and it was enormous and deep gold, and its face was perfectly reflected in the still water of the pond. Not far away, horses were munching hay, and there was a vague fragrance of apples.

"It doesn't get any better than this," I said. Not sure whether that was to her or to myself.

It was sweet, the way it can only be when you finally get to do something after a long period of anticipation and fantasy. Sometimes the fantasy to turns out to be better than the reality. Not this time. This time, the reality beat fantasy by several weight classes.

It was also, I thought, the best and most final of our customary long good-byes. Our intimate little interlude was certainly a one-time thing. Her curiosity was satisfied now, and no repetition was needed. Like the time she saw me put Tabasco sauce on my eggs and wanted to try it, herself. Though this time, the immediate aftermath was not quite as comical.

Tomorrow, she'd be on her way to the New England Conservatory of Music, where I had no doubt she would excel. Then probably on to Julliard. Then, who knows? She had the chops. Chops with wings. She was going places. Places where I wasn't going.

There would be lots of fine, talented, clean-cut lads in those places who would be more than happy to occupy her time. Gradually, the late summer consummation of our offbeat relationship would become a cherished memory, frozen in time, like a dragonfly in amber. Maybe I'd get a dragonfly tattoo. Didn't have any tattoos. Never needed one.

"I'd better get going," she said. "Still have some last-minute packing to do."

"I imagine you better had."

We got lazily to our feet, buttoning, tucking, and zipping."

"Wait," she said, and knelt down to nuzzle my stomach. I almost expected to hear her nicker. "Okay," she sighed, getting back up.

I pulled a stray leaf from her hair and set it free.

"I feel like I want to say something," she said.

Sometimes words are either inadequate or superfluous. This was one of those times. I told her so.

"I get that," she said. "But sometimes words belong to a thing. Like the way you say 'ouch' when you step on a sharp stone. Or 'wow' when you're so overwhelmed, you can't think of any other word. So I have to say it. I love you."

"Ouch," I said.

"Ouch?"

"I'll explain it when you're older, darlin.'"

She'd picked up my hat, and caressed the shape of it before handing it to me.

"For what it's worth," I said, "I love you, too, kid. Always have. Always will."

She looked up at me, studying my face in the near darkness.

"Wow," she said.

Adam Adrian Crown

*You must remember this*
*A kiss is just a kiss, a sigh is just a sigh.*
*The fundamental things apply*
*As time goes by...*
        "As Time Goes By"
        Doolie Wilson


# CHAPTER TEN:
# CASABLANCA


Maybe Marlo and I were living proof that opposites attract.

We came from opposite ends of society, she closer to the top, and me just about at the bottom. She was an educated musician who could transform wild squiggles on paper into breath-taking melody; I played what I heard in my head and could only decipher written music given a great deal of time and a crow bar. She was hardly broken in, I'm closer to broken down. She's just getting warmed up; I'm just about burned out.

But somehow, when we were together, we balanced out at some indeterminate age, and it seemed to work as long as we stayed right there at the intersection of Shangri-La and Never-Neverland. Southwest corner. Across from Billy Blue's Coffee Shop. In a wondrous land of imagination called The Twilight Zone.

Marlo and I were spending every possible moment together, and it felt right, the rightest thing I've ever felt — felt about another human, anyway. In a lot of ways, we'd gone as deeply inside each other as it was possible to go. Sometimes The Judge would call, and then I'd have to be gone for a day or a week, and we never discussed those absences. Marlo never asked where I went or what I did while I was away. When I returned, we'd pick up where we'd left off as if there weren't a gap there at all. But I knew part of her wondered what the hell I was up to and wanted to ask me about it, and part of me — not the smart part — wanted to tell her.

She liked me, possibly even loved me, but there was a substantial slice of me that she didn't know anything about, couldn't begin to imagine, and therefore couldn't love or even like. The part of me I kept hidden from her. One-eyed Jack.

Maybe I wanted to protect her. What she didn't know couldn't hurt her. Except it *was* hurting her. It was leading her to have unrealistic expectations about our relationship, which in turn was leading her to make some very bad choices about her life. Specifically, she was considering taking a ho-hum teaching job, instead of stepping out and dazzling the ears of the world with her performances. No way I could let her do that.

Maybe I was more concerned about protecting myself. What she didn't know couldn't hurt her, but it couldn't hurt me, either. Loose lips sinks ships, daddy-o. What she didn't know she couldn't accidentally mention. There's no statute of limitations on murder.

I didn't care to entertain the other possibility: that if she knew the truth of me, the whole truth, and nothing but the truth, she would be reviled by it, so reviled by it that she would bounce her exceptionally little ass right over to the gendarmes and give the hue and cry in my direction. It was a possibility. What if I weren't the only one hiding something? There might be a part of herself that she was hiding from me, too.

And whether she blew the whistle or not, there would always remain the possibility that she might. She would have something on me she could use at any time. And sweet love affairs that end up turning bitter as a peach pit are a dime a dozen. Did I want to put myself at the mercy of a young girl's inconstancy?

A secret is a secret when only two people know it, and one of them is dead.

And yet...

Suppose she knew it all? Every bloody bit of it. If she still wanted to stick around, that would be really something, wouldn't it?

Was the impossible prize worth the incredible risk — to both of us?

I got an idea.

416

I'd write it all down.

I'd leave out certain specific details, change some others around, but let the essential truth remain intact. You can be truthful without being factual. Writers have done that since Cervantes donned his coyote. I could do it, too. I could then present it to her to read without telling her whether it was fact or fiction. See how she takes it, how she reacts.

Then I can either reveal that's it's autobiographical, or tell her it's a work of fiction, a novel I've been working on.

That way, I can take it step-by-step, see what happens.

I can protect her, and I can protect me.

Have my Kate and Edith, too.

So that's what I did.

"Any other questions?" I said.

Marlo peered forlornly into the empty beef and broccoli carton.

"So it *is* true. *All* of it?"

"Let's suppose for the moment that it is," I said. "What then?"

She scooted over to me, wrapped her legs around my waist to sit Indian-style on my lap, put her arms around me, and rested her forehead on my shoulder.

"I don't care," she said. "I don't care where you came from or where you've been, or how many women you've fucked, or what other things you've done. I don't care who you've been. I love who you are now."

When she spoke those sweet, tender words expressing such unconditional love, I knew, at last, that we were finished. Over. Doomsville, daddy-o.

I took her face in my hands and looked her hard in the eye.

"Darlin,' " I said. "That IS who I am now."

"I've never seen that in you," she said, unconsciously shaking her head to underscore her disbelief. "I've never seen anything *like* that. Not even a glimmer of it. But I've seen you with horses. The way you treat them. Especially the way you are with horses that have been hurt or abused. You're totally the kindest, gentlest person on Earth."

"Are there Japanese people in Tokyo?

She looked at me as if I'd begun speaking in tongues.

"Um, what?" she said.

"Are there Japanese people in Tokyo?"

"What are you talking about?"

"Answer the question, kid. Are there Japanese people in Tokyo?"

"I'm going to go with 'yes?'"

"How do you know? Have you *seen* them?"

She drew back from me, studying my face like she'd never seen it before. I suspect she hadn't.

"Wait a minute," she said. "Oh, my God, are you trying to tell me...is this our *Casablanca* moment?"

During the course of our relationship I had undertaken the task of tutoring her, not only in the wicked ways of the world, the social graces, and the jazz greats, but also the classic films. The Battleship Potemkin. Citizen Kane. Gone With the Wind. To Kill a Mockingbird. High Noon. The Grapes of Wrath. We had long discussions about Sergei Eisenstein, DW Griffith, and John Ford; Kuleshov, Kurasawa and Kubrick. Hitchcock and Tarentino. Moe, Larry and Curly.

I think we watched Casablanca about a hundred times. Double Indemnity was a close second, but Casablanca was number one.

"I guess it is, Kid," I said. "It's Casablanca. And you're getting your lovely little ass on that plane."

"Why can't I be Louis instead of Ilsa?"

"You don't have the mustache for it."

"I could grow one."

"It would look good on you, too," I said. "But it wouldn't be the same. Look. You've got things to do, places to go, asses to kick. You've got incredible talent and you haven't even peeked at your peak. Now's not the time for you to retire from the fire and take a teaching job in nowheresville the better to hang out with little old me."

"You don't want to be with me?"

"Don't ask foolish questions," I said. "Being your cowboy is about the sweetest thing I've ever known. That's not the point. The point is, you've got to go out there and take your best shot. And I want you to do it. See how far you can run with it. It's your time and your prime. Don't piss it away hanging out with a has-been never-was like yours truly."

"You're not a has-been or a never-was, and I wouldn't be pissing anything away. I love being with you. I love being with the horses. I love it more than anything."

"Don't bullshit me, honey chil'. I've seen you play. Most importantly, don't bullshit yourself. Much as I enjoy you wrapping your thighs around me, you were clearly meant to wrap them around that cello. Nobody rocks on it the way you do. Nobody. You're going someplace and that's the pony that's going to take you there. So stick a feather in your cap and call it macaroni."

"You're just saying this to make me go."

"Yeah. But I'm also saying it because it's true. Deep inside, we both know you don't belong here with me. If your plane leaves and you and your axe aren't on board, you'll regret it. Maybe not today, maybe not tomorrow, but soon, and for the rest of your life. I wouldn't do that to you, darlin.' And I wouldn't do it to me, either. It's more weight than I can carry."

"But I love you, Jack," she said. "What about that?"

"I love you, too, kid. That's forever. What we've had together, we'll always have. Nobody and nothing can ever take that away from us. But whatever this thing is between us, it doesn't have a happily-ever-after ending to it. That wouldn't be believable in fiction OR in reality. Timing is everything, honey."

"What makes you think it will end badly?"

"Because all relationships end badly. Sooner or later. House rules."

We talked more.

A lot more.

We talked until were talked-out and then kept talking. There were tears and hugs, and coffee, and a few other things. But in the end, there was only one way this could go and I think we both knew it. But, as always, neither one of us wanted to be the first to say good-bye.

"Can I still...see you?"

"Now and then," I said, "As time goes by."

"Can we still be... close?"

"We'll always be close."

"That's not what I mean."

"I know."

I chucked her under the chin. There are limits to my capacity for nobility and I didn't know how long I could hold out before the little head Clarence Darrowed the resolve out of the big head.

"I would really miss that," she said.

"Me, too." That part was honest, at least.

En finale, I poured us each a finger of White Horse, and we drank a toast to our new understanding, which was…what the fuck was it exactly?

We agreed she would not bail out on her performance career. She could always take a teaching job in another decade or two, if she still wanted to. After she'd made her bones. And we agreed she would not put all her eggs in Jack's basket. She should shop around. Try on lots of shoes. One of them could turn out to be a glass slipper. You never know.

On the other hand, we also agreed that our renegade relationship had certain unique and kind of beautiful elements to it that we both valued and wanted to keep. Our friendship. The horses. Music. The sex.

So what changed?

Her expectations, I guess. And mine, too, to be honest. Our thing was what it was, and it was best to let it be what it was without trying to turn it into something else.

And what it was, most of all was over.

We'd had a good run, but done is done.

Every horse is a good horse. But not every horse is a good riding horse. And not every good riding horse is a good riding horse for you. Some horses were never meant to be saddled. Not by you. Not by me. Not by anybody. They're too wild, too smart, too headstrong, too free. The relationship between Marlo and me was like one of those unbreakable mustangs. Don't try to ride it. You're not getting anywhere near it with a saddle and bridle. It's going to stay where it is as long as the grass is green and the water's clean, and then it's going to go on its way, leave you standing there alone with dust on your face and the memory of its beauty seared into your heart.

"Here's looking at you, kid," I said, raising my glass. The bonus bogus Bogart.

So I guess, of all our long good-byes, this was our longest long good-bye of all. With luck, it would take months. Maybe years. Possibly forever. Maybe it wasn't even a real good-bye. Just au revoir. Yeah, I was already having second thoughts. Emotionally hedging my bets, see?

But, hell, anything can happen.

Life is full of fucking surprises.

I saw her to the door.

She balked and spun around.

Her voice cracked as she said, "Do I get a good-bye kiss?"

"One for my baby," I said.

"And one more for the road."

We made it a good one.

After she left, her scent remained behind. Our juices had mingled, and dried into soft crustiness on my pubic hair, and the thought of showering, washing it away, almost made me cry.

But I showered, anyway.

*There's no more to say*
*You're not coming back*
*You just closed the door*
*Leaving me alone now*
> "Pra Dizer Adeus (To Say Good-bye)"
> Sarah Vaughan

# CODA:
## Some Kind of Blues

I went to see my doctor and told him I'd been feeling so damn bad. I described in rich detail every little symptom I thought I might've had. He lit another cigarette, shook his head and looked real sad.

He said, "Has your baby left you, or have you read the news? Uh-huh. I see. Were you born under a bad sign, and now have nothing left to lose? Uh-huh. I see. If you've checked those boxes on the form, I'm afraid you might have some kind of blues."

I said, "Uh-huh. I see."

He said, "I recommend you abstain from all l'amour. Or you could take an ocean cruise."

I said, "Uh-huh. I see."

"You might try to modify or amplify your current intake of booze."

I said, "Uh-huh. I see."

"We can palliate, but there's no cure. Not if you've got some kind of blues."

I had the blues, all right.
The Marlo Blues.

And I had it bad.

Not exactly my first dance with that particular devil.

You could say I've had the blues since the day I was born under a bad sign. Once you've had it, it's always with you. In your blood. It may lie dormant for periods of time, but it's still there, lurking around behind the dark side of your heart, and it doesn't take much to trigger a full-blown recurrence. I guess the blues is a little like emotional herpes.

My blues has always been bitter. Equal parts of pain, despair, and defiance.

But the Marlo Blues was different.

Like schoolin' has the three r's — readin', 'ritin' and 'rithmetic — the blues has the three l's — love, loss and longing — and all three were apparent this time, too.

But there was something else.

Despite the chasm that separated our ages, Marlo and I had always been simpatico on some fundamental level. We'd had a good thing, and even at the end it was still good.

Hell, *I* was the one who decided we should cool it, and she took no small amount of steadfast convincing. Our parting was characterized more by reluctance than rancor. There was a sweetness to it, bittersweet, the poets call that. Like a cup of strong, two-day-old, re-heated espresso with a shot of amaretto in it.

There are two ways to beat the blues — and neither one works.

You can purge your heart of the old love by immersing yourself in a new love.

Or you can keep yourself crazy busy and try not to think about it until you stop thinking about it.

I tried a little of each.

There were enough people I could call on for some remedial sex. Women — and a couple of men — I hadn't seen much of lately, preoccupied as I had been with She Whose Blues Afflicted Me. Any of them would be good company and great exercise, but none of them was the volcano I could throw myself into, erupting with the glowing-hot passion I needed to cauterize my wound.

Nevertheless, I gave it my best shot.

424

Jointly and severally. Until I was sore from my eyeballs down. "Strike one," the umpire said.

There's a million and one chores to do on a horse farm and I did them all, dawn to dusk, whether they needed to be done or not. Thing is, I'd created a horse haven that closely simulated my ponies' natural environment, and the closer I got to that, the less work it took. I wound up having to invent shit to do.

I polished brass that didn't need polishing, oiled leather that didn't need oiling, turned over the compost though it didn't need turning, picked manure out of the grass, cleaned windows, split and stacked firewood enough for the next decade, assuming a solar minimum. I alphabetized by albums, and then re-arranged them in chronological order; decided I didn't like that, and put them back alphabetically. Did the same with DVDs. And food in the fridge. I considered whether to name my forks and spoons.

Spartacus Jones and company received more brushings and combings and hoof-groomings than a rich girl's show pony.

One grey morning when the sun refused to get out of bed, I took a grooming box out to give Spartacus Jones yet another beauty treatment.

When I approached he swung his head toward me and gave his tail a deliberate swish. "Just what do you think you're doing with that brush?" he said.

"Thought I'd give you a quick spruce-up."

"Again?"

"You're covered with mud."

"Yes, I know. It took me all morning to get it just right."

"You're a mess, Pal."

"Well, there goes my modeling career."

"How about just hand grooming? No brush."

"Give me a break, will you, Jack?"

"Just mane and tail? No conditioner?"

"Look, I like you. And I'd hate to have to see how silly you'd look with that brush up your ass. Know what I mean?"

"Got, it" I said.

He snorted and shook his shaggy head.

425

"Still, thinking about that girl, huh?"

"Who me?"

"No, Bugs Bunny."

"I'm doing all right."

"Uh-huh, I see. Okay, go ahead if it'll make you feel better. But just hands. No brush."

"Thanks, I said.

I made a point of massaging his withers. He likes that.

When I couldn't invent any more unnecessary chores, I bopped down to Stevie's Ark to help out there. The problem is that no matter how hard you run, your problem is right there with you at the finish line, chuckling at your expense when you finally arrive bent and spent. It's like a dog trying to run away from his own tail.

"Strike two," the umpire said.

It dawned on me that there was actually a third option to work it or jerk it: let it bleed.

So I put on my hard hat and my steel-toed-shoes, snugged up my seat belt, and steered head-on into the blue tsunami.

Figuring I'd get by with a little help from my friends, I dug out the saddest songs I had in my collection, threw them on the turntable, fired up my guitar and played along. Sang along, too. It was a mournful and maudlin exercise in self-indulgence. Pathetic. I'm glad you weren't there to see it.

Plus, these tunes didn't quite fit.

They were plenty bitter, but not enough sweet.

I felt like I was playing an all-Bach set at Billy Bob Joe's Down Home Country Bar-B-Q: wrong material for the gig.

When you need bittersweet, you need bossa nova.

I set my electric guitar aside, and dug out my classical guitar, instead. I kicked off the festivities with *the* definitive Bossa Nova tune.

Had to.

The way red, white, and blue Nazis feel compelled to precede every possible sporting event, picnic, spelling bee, and outdoor urination with the national anthem, I couldn't very well launch the good ship bossa nova without the song that was the Hal-le-loofa Chorus, Star-Spangled Banner and Jingle Bells of Brazilian jazz, all rolled into one.

The Girl from Ipanema, natch.

Inspired by Heloisa Enelda Menezes Paes Pinto — later known as Helo Pinheira, but everyone knew her as Nancy — tall and tan and young and lovely.

Dedicated to my girl, Marlo, tall and tan and young and lovely.

Sung by my girl Astrud Gilberto, tall and tan and young and lovely, and featured vocalist on the soundtrack of my amorous childhood fantasies.

Funny thing, she wasn't supposed to sing it.

According to the funny papers, sax man Stan Getz was set to record the tune with Joao Gilberto singing it in Portugese. Somebody got the bright idea to record a version in English. They tapped lyricist Norman Gimbel to do the honors and he whipped up a story as wistful and melancholy as it is arch-typical. Thing is, Joao's English was the pits. But his wife, Astrud, spoke it well enough. So, even though she'd never sung professionally before, Getz asked her to sit in.

BOOM.

Girl from Ipanema became a breakout tune. Gold record, a Grammy, and a silver star. Crossed all genre barriers to become an international hit, and one of the most recorded songs of all time. It would be easier to make a list of artists who *haven't* covered it than to list all those who have. It made bossa nova a popular thing for people who hadn't been jazz aficionados, and launched the singing career of the aforementioned Mrs. Gilberto

How's that one grab you, Mr, Ripley?

I had the tune on a couple of different albums, but put on the .45 platter.

Her dreamy voice took me back to long ago. Pre-Marlo. To sultry summer nights and long champagne kisses, to slow dancing at 3AM, out on the balcony to catch the lake breeze. Far below the city streets, festooned with all manner of twinkling lights. The dampness under my tux. The warmth of her seeping into me through the fabric of her gown, sheer and delicate as a dragonfly wing. We swayed, scarcely moving, her breath against my cheek, a dance we would dance forever, knowing that forever would fade away at sunrise.

Suddenly swept up in it I let the record track and re-track about half a dozen times, delighting in her soft, breathy, unpretentious delivery that captured the essence of innocence lost.

Only then did I realize how much I had missed her. I let her take me to Manha de Carnaval and she left me remembering the shadow of her smile.

Misery loves company, but it absolutely thrives on accompaniment. Marlo had often been my muse, and now I was mused and infused, so I put it to use.

Must have written a dozen songs a day over the next couple of weeks. Well, maybe not a dozen. But five or six, anyway. Lots of bossa nova, of course. Some standard blues. Some minor blues. Some ii-V-I songs. Some that defy categorization.

I'll tell you what writing music feels like to me.

Imagine you saddle up some pony, and for some reason it spooks. Goes absolutely nuts. Takes off at a dead gallop and runs around a cross-country obstacle course, flying over fences, downed trees, splashing across streams, zigzagging through tight clumps of trees. Somehow, hanging on for dear life, you remain in the saddle, even though it defies all the known laws of physics. Nearby, there are some folks watching you as you are completely caught up in the chaos.

"Wow," they say. "That Jack sure can ride."

See, I'm not riding the music; the music is taking me for one.

I'm not the one in control.

It's more like catching fish.

The fish are already out there.

Every once in a while, I just hook one of them.

In the middle of all that jazz, there came a kind of slow blues bolero.

The bolero has a rhythm that suggests a long slow amble on horseback. The chords were straight and square, major and minor, but the melody was Chet Baker on flugelhorn.

Part of the lyric went like this:

> After all that's past
> Will you leave at last?
> Never to return
> Never tomorrow.
> Or will you pretend
> Nothing's at an end
> Never let your eyes meet
> My eyes again.

I sang this one for Spartacus Jones, out in his paddock under a full moon. He listened to the verses, nodding to the beat, and nickered along in the chorus. We sounded pretty good together. Maybe we should start a band. He can be the front man.

So did all that purge me of the Marlo Blues?
Yeah, right.
Ten thousand times a day I wanted to call her.
Tell her I had changed my mind. Fuck it. Come back, stay with me. Be my love and let me be your love. Nobody will ever love you the way I do, baby, and I've never loved anyone the way I love you. Yes, I included in my imaginary dialogue all the worst possible amorous clichés. That's one of the signature symptoms of the disease.

One morning, my phone rang, and for some reason, I thought it might be Marlo. I hoped it was her, was sure it must be her, please let it be her. My heart did a cartwheel and I pounced on the phone like a starving barn cat on a plump, juicy mouse.
But it wasn't Marlo.
It was The Judge.

## Acknowledgements

Thanks for reading this book. I hope you enjoyed it.

Thanks to the people who read parts or all of this work while it was just a baby: Linda Wyatt, Richard P. Alvarez, Kim Strauss, and Hanita Blair. Thanks to Leah Cook for helping me with my Latin Loopy-Loo, and for those who tutored me in Russian cursing, you know who you are. Special thanks to Kathy Crown for her inestimable support, both moral and immoral.

Thanks to Richard Turylo for the beautiful cover art, and to Marza Wilks, a wonderful musician and long-time friend, who allowed me to base part of the cover art on an image of her.

Thanks to Leanne Dillon, to Pam Watros, and to The Horse Nation.

Thanks to Benny, Twister, Blackjack, Shyla, Canto, Jimmy, Leo, Miracle, Stormy, Cisco, Musky, Impressive Kate, Captain America, Gus, Star Dancer, Apache Prince, Brigit, Mandy and Brandy, to Kelsey the Arabian, and to many ponies more.

Mitakuye oyasin.

AAC Dec 2020

# Musical Notes

| | |
|---|---|
| "I'm Not Like Everybody Else" | Ray Davies |
| "Bad to the Bone" | George Thorogood |
| "Young Girl" | Jerry Fuller |
| "Old Stewball" | Traditional: author unknown |
| "On the Road Again" | Willie Nelson |
| "Shipbuilding" | Elvis Costello |
| "The Boxer" | Paul Simon |
| "Keepin' the Faith" | Billy Joel |
| "Mamas Don't Let Your Babies Grow Up to Be Cowboys" | |
| | Willie Nelson |
| "The Jolly Cowboy" | John Avery Lomax, collector |
| "The Windmills of Your Mind" | Michel Legrand/ |
| | Allan & Marilyn Bergman |
| "Sympathy for the Devil" | Mick Jagger/Keith Richards |
| "Don't Fence Me In" | Cole Porter/Robert Fletcher |
| "Superstition" | Stevie Wonder |
| "There's Something About A Soldier…" | |
| | Noel Gay |
| "Bang Bang (My Baby Shot Me Down)" | |
| | Sonny Bono |
| "Sweet Caroline" | Neil Diamond |
| "Thirty Years of Tears" | John Hiatt |
| "The Street Corner Hustler's Blues" | Lou Rawls |
| "Ghost Riders in the Sky" | Stan Jones |
| "Splish Splash I Was Takin' a Bath" | Bobby Darin/Murray Kaufman |
| "She Loves You" | John Lennon/Paul McCartney |
| "Downtown" | Tony Hatch |
| "You've Lost that Lovin' Feeling" | Phil Spector/Barry Mann/ |
| | Cynthia Weil |
| "World Without Love" | Paul McCartney |
| "Come On Over To My House" | Julia Lee |
| "Pepito" | Art Truscott/Carmen Taylor |
| "Patricia" | Perez Prado/Bob Marcus |

| | |
|---|---|
| "Itsy Bitsy Polka Dot…" | Paul Vance/Lee Pockriss |
| "Take Me Out To The Ball Game" | Jack Norworth/Albert Von Tilzer |
| "I'll Be Your Mirror" | Lou Reed |
| "Lightning Strikes" | Lou Christie/Twyla Herbert |
| "Respect" | Otis Redding |
| "The Wayward Wind" | Herbert Newman/ |
| | Stanley R. Lebowsky |
| "Gypsy Queen" | Gabor Szabo |
| "Mack the Knife" | Bertolt Brecht/Kurt Weill |
| "The Gold It's in The…" | Roger Waters/David John Gilmore |
| "A Hundred and One Times" | Spartacus Jones |
| "Hound Dog" | Jerry Lieber/Mike Stroller |
| "Everything That I Love Best" | |
| | Spartacus Jones |
| "All or Nothing At All" | Arthur Altman |
| | with lyrics by Jack Lawrence |
| "Rain" | John Lennon/Paul McCartney |
| "Sexual Healing" | Marvin Gaye/Odell Brown |
| "Time of the Season" | Rod Argent |
| "Love the one you're with…" | |
| | Stephan Stills |
| "In My Life" | John Lennon/Paul McCartney |
| "Can I Get a Witness" | Brian Holland/ Lamont Dozier/ |
| | Eddie Holland |
| "Grapevine" | Norman Whitfield and Barrett Strong |
| "Blowin' In the Wind" | Bob Dylan |
| "When Snowflakes Fall in the Summer" | |
| | Barry Mann/Cynthia Weil |
| "She Loves You" | John Lennon/Paul McCartney |
| "As Time Goes By" | Herman Hupfeld |
| "Pra Dizer Adeus…" | Lani Hall/Edu Lobo/Torquato Neto |
| "Girl From Ipanema" | Norman Gimbel / Antonio Carlos Jobim/ |
| | Vinicius De Moraes |

Made in the USA
Middletown, DE
15 January 2021